PRAISE FOR RICH BULLOCK

"A first-rate thriller that grabs you in Chapter One and doesn't let go."

JAMES SCOTT BELL

"His small lake town felt real to me. There was a history. There were people I knew. I believed they were real and I wanted to see how things would work out for them."

SALLY A.

"It takes me three days to read the last chapter because I simply just don't want it to end."

ROGER CROSS

"I'm a sucker for both romance novels and murder mysteries so Perilous Cove is a perfect balance between the two."

ERIN B.

DESPERATION FALLS

RICH BULLOCK

REDDING, CALIFORNIA

Book cover design by Robert Henslin

Published by RichWords Press
V 5/11/24

DEDICATION

Mom was one of a kind: strong, talented, independent—and she did it all when being a single mother was frowned upon. She could drive nails, paint walls, and match lemon meringue pies with the best. You might just find a small part of her in Lena and Bibs.

Mom loved reading a good story, and I think she would have liked this one.

Thanks, Mom.

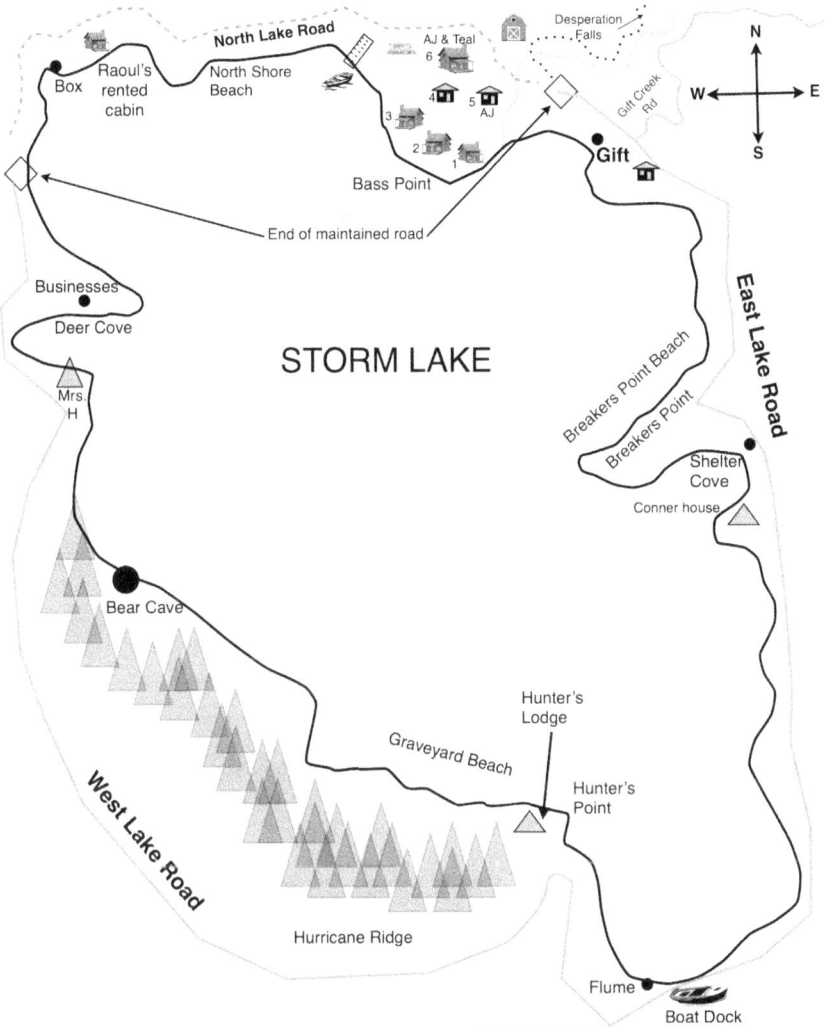

North Lake Road

Box

Raoul's rented cabin

North Shore Beach

AJ & Teal
6

AJ

Desperation Falls

N
W — E
S

4

5 AJ

3

Gift Creek Rd

2

1

Gift

Bass Point

End of maintained road

Businesses

Deer Cove

STORM LAKE

East Lake Road

Mrs. H

Breakers Point Beach

Breakers Point

Shelter Cove

Conner house

Bear Cave

Hunter's Lodge

Graveyard Beach

Hunter's Point

West Lake Road

Hurricane Ridge

Flume

Boat Dock

To Perilous Cove - 15 miles

DESPERATION FALLS

PROLOGUE

"You'd better step away from that laptop, buster, or I'm gonna have to get my new gun."

Lena McKinley's husband, Bobby Blaylock, had grabbed their MacBook computer the moment he'd come home from the office. It wasn't like he didn't spend enough time on his work laptop he carried everywhere.

Bobby raised his hands. "Don't shoot." He flashed her his movie-star grin, not a bad imitation for someone not in "the industry." He might be a Los Angeles assistant district attorney, but he had star qualities in Lena's eyes.

"I promise I won't be long, babe." Bobby's head dipped in concentration as his fingers flew and clicked. "I just have to copy some files on the office server."

Lena blew wayward hairs out of her eyes as she placed the bread and salad on the dining room table. She'd been slaving in the kitchen all afternoon, trying not to ruin their special dinner. No easy task, that. As a carpenter and general contractor, she could handle a down-to-the-studs remodel easier than preparing a perfectly timed dinner.

She recognized Bobby's laser intensity as he slipped back into work mode. Clearly, breaking his focus tonight would take some extra effort.

Lena walked behind the couch and snaked her arms around his neck. Bobby half closed the laptop screen, hiding his work. Something big and secret. Whatever it was, it deepened his worry lines when he didn't notice her watching him. He turned into her kiss, his lips soft and warm against hers.

"You taste like pasta sauce," he said, licking his lips as she broke the kiss. He reached an arm around her head and pulled her down until they met again.

"Okay, Mr. Hotshot Attorney," Lena mumbled against his mouth. "I'm giving you a two-minute warning. I busted my butt on this anniversary dinner. So if you're not done with work, I'll have to arrest you."

Bobby trailed kisses along her jaw toward her ear. "Are you going to use handcuffs?"

He reached the sensitive spot on her neck and Lena's knees went weak. She would have chucked the whole dinner idea right then if she hadn't heard a splat and sizzle from the other room. Lena put a hand on his chest.

"If I don't get back to the kitchen, the pasta will boil over and *you'll* be cleaning the stove."

Bobby raised an eyebrow, then released her. "Later then."

It was a promise Lena would hold him to.

"I'll be done soon," Bobby called as she hurried toward the kitchen.

Of all the guys who'd gone gaga over her cable TV persona—including a few memorable nut cases who gave her the creeps—he was the one who had wrangled an introduction by calling in every favor he could with the show's production people. Lena kidded with her friends that he'd had to fix a thousand parking tickets to win her hand. It was probably true. But *she* was the lucky one.

For their first date, he'd come to her door not just with flowers, but also with a super cool Leatherman Multi-Tool with belt sheath. She almost wore it on the date.

So most of the time Lena didn't mind that he was tenacious in his work and passionate about his cases. She understood. She was as bad when it came to tools. Just not tonight.

Lena drained the pasta in a colander, filling the kitchen with white steam. He'd wanted to take her out for their six-month celebration, but with their hectic schedules they already spent too much time in restaurants. Tonight she wanted him all to herself.

Plus, she had a special gift for him. The flat box on the dining table contained her renewed contract—never a sure thing in L.A.—and she'd had the studio officially change her last name to Blaylock. From now on, it would read that way on the show credits, and allow Bobby to boast all over again to his colleagues that he'd married the sexy carpenter from the *Nail It!* TV show. She grinned. He'd love it.

Just as she loved the new Paslode Framing Nailer he'd given her this morning. The nail gun, fuel cartridges, and manual sat on the other end of the dining table. She'd read every word, and her fingers itched to try the gun out on some scrap two-by-fours in the garage. But that would have to wait.

Lena clicked on the stereo and Andrea Bocelli serenaded them as she filled two oven-warmed bowls with spaghetti. She ladled on homemade meat sauce, courtesy of their short, round neighbor, Mrs. Lagano—Mamma L to everyone—whose Italian was still better than her English. Lena hand-grated fresh Parmesan over the top and added sprigs of parsley exactly as she'd practiced with Mamma L. Lena breathed in the melting cheese and sauce, amazed at how much better it smelled than her normal can-based recipe.

Lena sighed. Bobby had said she was "cooking challenged," right after the first time she'd presented him with scrambled eggs.

But hey, she was a TV star—even if it was only a cable home improvement show—and stars *never* cooked. It was like a Hollywood rule or something. She picked up the bowls and left the kitchen, snapping off the light switch with her elbow on the way out.

"Okay, counselor, step away from the computer," she said, using her best command voice and holding the bowls aloft. "Unless you want to do hard time with hot noodles."

"All done." Bobby closed the laptop and rose from the sofa.

Lena was lowering the dishes to the dining table when firecrackers sounded on the street out front. Searing stings slammed into her wrist, shoulder, and leg. She collapsed as the light fixture over the table flashed and sparked like a neon sign above a seedy motel. The bowls of food shattered and landed a foot from where her face hit the new Berber. The white fibers hungrily soaked in the red sauce. She blinked at Bobby towering above her, his body jerking like a macabre marionette, then toppling. Shards of glass, wood, and fabric rained like airborne confetti.

The popping ceased, and tires screeched outside their shattered living room window.

"Bobby!" She had to get to him. Her left wrist wouldn't work, and something wet kept running into her right eye, but her right leg was fine. The laptop lay between them, its silver surface dotted with bright red. Lena army-crawled over it until she was side by side with her husband, like they had been in bed this morning before rushing off to their busy days.

With her good hand, she gently pushed his long hair off his face.

"Bobby?" His eyes were open. That was good, wasn't it?

Their color was what first attracted her—brown, with beautiful gold flecks that came alive in the sun, and especially when he looked at her.

But Bobby's eyes weren't looking at her now. And all the gold had vanished.

1

This was her one chance to escape. God help her if she failed.

But Teal Kinshaw hadn't seen any sign of the deity in this stinking basement.

Grit crunched under her bare foot and she froze mid-step, not daring even a shallow breath until her lungs burned hot and lack of oxygen blackened the edges of her vision. Even then she allowed only the barest trickle of air past her dry tongue, just enough to quiet her throbbing heart.

The man hadn't stirred from his slumber in the blue velour recliner, the only chair in the room. She'd never learned his true name, but mentally called him Fred, after Freddy Krueger in the *Nightmare on Elm Street* slasher movies. Fred didn't have the razor-armed glove of the fictional character, but one thing she knew about this man: he'd kill her sooner or later. Sooner would be a kindness. His chest rose and fell evenly. The three cutouts in the ski mask screamed *Serial Killer!* It always covered his face and gave away little. The only thing she'd ever noticed was a tiny white scar on his upper lip.

Don't move, Fred.

He didn't. She dared another few inches, searching the dark concrete this time before lowering her foot.

A single fluorescent shop light fixture cast stark shadows, its long cord extending to a wall-mounted receptacle. She shuddered at the flowing electricity, and touched her right wrist where Fred always attached the first conducting strap. He took perverse pleasure in explaining the process as he bound her:

"You see, you need a positive and a ground. You always need a good ground..." and how increasing the voltage boosted the current flow, how the salty sweat pouring from her glands was a good thing and improved conductivity.

Fred snorted in his sleep, and she crouched low while he coughed and then finally settled into a restless slumber. Her left leg cramped as she rose—a symptom that had begun after the third shock treatment. She ventured two steps forward, carefully skirting two crumpled beer cans behind the recliner.

Twenty more feet down the narrow room, then up seven plank stairs and through the door at the top. Easy.

Are you locked, Mr. Door? A hundred times she'd asked, staring at it between the bars of her cage. But like always, the door kept its secret.

Another step.

Should she try for a weapon? Strike Fred unconscious? A rough workbench held a 27" television, a VCR and tapes, rags, dozens of dusty canning jars, and stacks of newspapers. A college-sized refrigerator underneath contained his beer and a few bottles of water he doled out to her if she obeyed. A mismatched washer and dryer huddled under layers of grime so thick she marveled how clothes could be cleaned by machines so filthy. She'd never seen him use them. Nothing in the dim light looked substantial enough to bash in a man's head. Worse case she'd wake him and increase his anger—if that were possible.

One tiny crust of pizza lay on the floor beside the chair, missed from tonight's dinner—or last night's. She held her breath and leaned closer to Fred's arm where it flopped over the chair arm. Heat radiated from the hairy skin to her cheek, and she kept her eyes on his masked profile. She snatched the baked dough and popped it in her mouth, not dwelling on what might have crawled on it—or might still be crawling on it. Any bugs were no doubt cleaner than his fingers and puffy lips.

Too stale to bite without a crunch, she let the hard scrap soak up sparse moisture from her tongue. The pizza box lay askew atop magazines on the table in front of his chair. Her mouth watered at the thought of a slice covered in pepperoni, cheese, and other toppings. But the cardboard lid was closed and she didn't dare try to open it for the noise it might make. She'd take another dry crust off the floor, but there were none to be had. Besides, she had to keep moving.

The threadbare La-Z-Boy fell behind, as did the snores. But this was even worse—hearing the snorts but never knowing if he faked sleep while watching, that twisted grin showing gleaming white teeth as he called out, *"Where you going, girl?"* He'd fooled her before.

She drew even with The Table—the place he carried out all his "games."

"We're going to play a game on The Table today, little girl. Are you ready?" He always asked—as if she had a choice.

Sweat and blood permeated the platform's rough surface—not all hers— and rust-stained ropes hung from large iron rings along the sides and ends. How many others had felt the hand-hewn boards at their backs, or had their faces pressed against its pungent cracks and fissures? She may not be The Table's last occupant, but it may very well be the last thing she saw if her escape failed.

Under The Table, nearly hidden behind one of the four-by-four legs, a bit of color shone against the blackened concrete. With shaking fingers, Teal reached for the object, stretching half under the low frame until she could touch it. Its soft threads were cool from its time on the floor. It was the only thing in this room that belonged to her, and she took that as a sign. She wrapped the bracelet tight in her hand and continued her agonizingly slow journey.

Two more steps.

And then, somehow, she'd reached the stairs. She nearly gasped in relief, suddenly aware she'd always assumed failure, expected the man would awake from his slumber, kick forward in the recliner, and snag her wrist before she could…

She shook her head, slowing her breathing. *Concentrate.* Dizziness washed over her, and she yearned to sit on the old steps and rest. But there'd be no rest if she were caught. She pinched her forearm until the blood welled and pain cleared her brain, then she examined the incline before her.

Cut from the same thick boards as The Table, they appeared too sturdy to squeak, but she knew differently. For weeks, every time Fred descended the stairs, she'd peered through her cage, memorized where he'd placed each booted foot, and listened for which areas were silent or spoke distinctly.

With great care, she set her right foot on the first tread and walked her toes forward for a firm footing. She'd never had the advantage of seeing him ascend—being unconscious and thrown back into her cage after each of his games limited one's observation skills. She leaned forward and put weight on her foot. No squeak.

Now, left tread edge, then right, then two lefts, another right, and two more lefts. Seven steps—practiced repeatedly in her mind like a tennis pro visualizing his game—and she finally stood at the top, her hand on the doorknob. A twist and the door opened noiselessly. *Unlocked.*

Teetering on the upper step, she fought for balance. The doorknob slipped from her fingers and slid away. Before she could stop it, the heavy door bumped against the wall, and a sleepy "huh?" sounded from behind her.

Noise no longer mattered. She jumped through the doorway. Speed was everything now.

She sprinted down a narrow hall. The barest of images registered: two closed doors, an open one framing a bathroom vanity gray with grime, a cockeyed painting of some bucolic vineyard hillside, a lone bloody handprint smeared at knee level—not hers. After so long on the cold concrete, the carpeting—dirty as it was—felt heavenly against her feet, and she had the insane desire to pause and wriggle her toes in the soft threads.

At the end of the hallway she spied a slab door painted gaudy salmon so it stood like a beacon. Dents covered its surface as if a hundred shoes had kicked it. But where did it lead?

Behind her, boots thumped across the basement floor.

Please lead outside.

She wrenched the door open.

***

"Admit it, Blaylock," Lena mumbled to herself, "you're in love." She shivered in delight as rain dripped off the back of her ball cap and ran rivulets inside her shirt. She hadn't felt like this since…well, since Bobby.

Even the gathering December twilight couldn't dampen her soaring spirits. Before her was the future. She just wished Bobby were here to share it. Absently, she rubbed the scar on her wrist where one of the bullets had passed through. They said she'd been lucky.

"I take it you like what you've seen so far?" Roger Trollen's voice came from behind, obsequious and hopeful as the wind dislodged fat droplets off the shielding oak leaves above.

Lena dropped her wrist. Maybe her luck was changing.

Yes, she more than *liked* what she saw. *Perfect* came to mind, but she didn't want to tip her hand. Realtor Roger could suffer a while longer. He was clearly doing his best, playing his assigned role even in the face of rapidly deteriorating weather. Lena strode from beneath the branches and headed for the stairs of the third cabin along the lakeshore. They'd already seen the two other waterfront cabins, and two more up the hill—all part of an old resort compound on the shore of Storm Lake. Buying the whole property would be a massive bite out of her finances.

"It's almost dark. I don't think there's much to see in there," Roger called, then followed her from the tree's meager protection from the heavy downpour. "It's just like the others."

Lena stepped over one of the streamlets rounding the side of the cabin. The mini-river rushed downhill toward the lake, carrying leaves and twigs in an ever-widening flow. She covered a smile as the realtor hopped over the deepening ditch, only to land in a hole on the other side. Water sloshed over the tops of his leather loafers as he scurried out onto higher—though no less muddy—ground. He shook first one foot, then the other, but his dance did little to dislodge the sticky clumps of black adobe for which California's central coast was famous.

Lena shook her head. Who wore loafers out here? Her ten-inch work boots repelled the water and crud as she mounted the steps to the porch. Without waiting for the realtor, she twisted the doorknob and hip-bumped the stuck door. Lena added the door to her mental list of repairs.

Roger was correct that the layout was generally the same as the other cabins. A small living room to the right consisted of scarred hardwood flooring, walls that might have once been beige, and a potbelly woodstove with its door hanging by one hinge. Black soot spread across the ceiling above the stove, and the windows were framed with red-checked scraps that might have once been curtains. Straight ahead, a hallway led to the back of the house, but with the light failing and no electricity to the property, she couldn't make out details. The bathroom was undoubtedly as much a disaster as the others.

Lena switched on the tiny penlight she kept attached to her key ring. It was good for finding the keyhole in the dark, but not much else. She played the light around the dining area to the left of the door. A square card table sat forlornly, listing on a bent leg. A single folding chair lay on a pile of rubble under the front window…a window that would have another fantastic view of Storm Lake on a sunny day. *Cha-ching!* More rental dollars.

Lena shone the light into the galley kitchen's open refrigerator. Dirty, but no mold. If it worked, that was one less appliance she'd have to buy.

"I hate to rush you, Ms. Blaylock, but with this rain, the creek crossing will be getting deeper. We don't—"

Lena held up a hand in acknowledgement as she pirouetted, surveying the serviceable countertops, cupboards, filthy gas stove, and single sink beneath a six-paned window. She could work with it all. The rain thrummed against the roof, and she pointed the light at the ceiling. Too dark to look for leaks, but she was certain there were some. She couldn't wait to get started.

"All right, Roger, I've seen enough. It really is quite a mess." Lena gave her best dramatic sigh, one she'd learned from her mother, and was gratified as Roger's hopeful countenance sagged a little. "Let's head back to your office and discuss this...opportunity." She shook her head in disappointment, hoping it wasn't over the top. Sometimes her television training came in pretty handy.

With his own sigh—of relief, probably—Roger nearly sprinted out of the cabin and pranced his way through mud and water back to his gold Lexus. Most realtors showing their own listing would be excited about not having to split the commission on a sale, but Roger was clearly a fair-weather agent. *Probably too many episodes of Selling New York.* Lena ducked into the passenger seat. Mud covered the floor mats. He'd probably have to get the car detailed after this trip. Perfect.

The sedan slid sideways on the dirt road, and Roger let out a little squeak before he got it corrected. Lena couldn't wait to get her Jeep Wrangler up here and throw it into four-wheel drive.

She was counting on today's rain and mud to work in her favor, especially if they tracked said mud onto the white carpet in Roger's immaculate office in Mission Peak. If he resisted her lowball offer, she'd suggest another visit tomorrow, the last day of her visit, when the heaviest rain was predicted. One thing her dad had taught her about real estate: never reject a first offer too quickly; you might not get another. Lena hoped Realtor Roger knew that maxim.

Wet blowing leaves splattered the Lexus's windshield as Roger squinted at the dark, constantly searching for the road. Lena smiled with each pothole, each stretch of pooling water that caused the car to hydroplane just enough to cause Roger to slow. The weather was a gift from God, and right now she could use a little good fortune.

Please, God.

Please, God!

She had to get away.

Thick, misty fog had swirled around her the moment she left the house.

Little light came from the sky, and Teal couldn't tell if it was sunrise or sunset. If the former, she'd be in trouble.

Within minutes, each ragged breath seared her throat as she hurdled basketball-size rocks and dodged menacing trees. She winced and hopped as something sharp speared her bare foot, but she clamped her teeth against the pain and used it for speed. She cast a fleeting search over her shoulder, raking the billowing gray for a ski-masked face. And his voice. Fred.

She couldn't hear him over the drumming of her heart, but she knew he was back there. He'd never let her go, not after marking her. If he caught her... That shuddering possibility, the memory of what he'd done to her body, propelled her forward into what she recognized as the deepening night.

A sapling branch slapped her face and sent her spinning to the ground. She rolled to a stop and sat up, wiping the stinging tears away with the back of her hand. Every bone ached as she pushed to her feet and turned in a circle. Which way had she come? Which way had she been going? A wrong choice would be deadly.

In the murky light, she located the offending low-hanging branch and saw the scattered leaves where she'd sprawled. Her body begged to lie down and rest. Instead, she shoved past a prickly bush and hurled down a slope as fast as she dared.

2

Lena jogged the short distance from the realtor office to her Jeep parked at the curb. Wind and rain lashed the trees lining the sidewalks, hurling leaves and branches through the glow of yellow streetlights. The air had turned frigid while she'd been inside, and every wet drop felt like it was on the verge of turning to hail.

Squinting against the deluge, she unlocked the door and threw herself inside. Rain drummed on the canvas top, and she turned on the interior light to check for leaks. The top was a few years old, but everything looked good.

She started the engine and turned the heat and fan on high to dry things out. But instead of driving away, she relaxed into the seat and grinned. It was late and she was exhausted, but the property was hers! Yes, it had cost more than she wanted to spend, but the storm had arrived with predicted ferocity, and Realtor Roger had come down substantially in price when she pushed for another visit to the cabins. In the end, they'd both gotten a decent deal.

Now came the hard part. Not the roofing, plumbing, and rebuilding—those things were doable for her. It was waiting for escrow to close that killed her. Six more weeks. She was ready to break out her tools tonight!

Lena shifted into first gear and checked her mirror, waiting for a lonely pair of headlights to pass before pulling out. Most people were smart enough to be home safe by now.

Teal had no idea how long she'd been running, walking, then mostly stumbling. Even as she willed her emaciated body faster, her legs rebelled. They'd become disobedient stumps, too heavy to move except in small, shuffling steps. She was almost thankful when complete darkness blocked her way as effectively as the trees she collided with.

Heavy drizzle ran into her eyes, and she wiped it away. She managed another few feet before her extended left hand jammed into a mass of unyielding wet rock. Patting the surface, she felt her way along what could be a huge boulder or a mountain. It certainly felt as *solid* as a mountain. She tested the ground with her toes, afraid she might step off a cliff as she inched ahead. Abruptly, the rock wall curved away to her left, and she followed it another dozen steps before sagging against it, wishing its strength and resolve could become her own.

The desperate energy she'd commanded leaked away, and shivers rippled her soaked skin. Cold air snaked around her bare legs, and the sprinkles that had been falling from above now turned into solid rain. When the muscle of her left thigh cramped, she leaned forward and stretched against the pain, breathing through her mouth as silently as possible. She spit out bits of bark and leaves from the many bushes she'd plowed through.

In an odd way, the sensations—even painful ones—were a comfort, a taste of the normal world beyond the cage. For too long the shivers she'd known were due to the hands of another.

Stay tough—like the stone.

Once her heartbeat and breathing calmed, she listened to the night. There was only the shushing rain. No swish of cars. No crickets or night birds.

No pounding boots.

She sighed and leaned back against the rock and cradled her wrists across her body, wincing as water stung the flesh still raw from her bindings.

The darkness gave no indication how far she'd come, or where she was, but the air was redolent with grasses and sage. That meant California's golden hills. Probably. This still could be a hundred miles from where he'd snatched her. One thing she'd learned in Mr. Long's geography class: California was *big*.

So now what? She couldn't remain here or she'd die of exposure in a few hours. She searched the sky for a helpful moon. There was none. Nor were there any stars. Maybe later—if the storm clouds passed.

Her stomach issued a grumbling protest about its emptiness. Why couldn't she have stumbled into a shopping center with Mickey D's friendly golden arches?

Something cracked off to her right and her heart bolted like a spooked rabbit, roaring in her ears so loud it masked everything else. She panted shallow breaths, willing the rebellious organ to calm down.

Leaves rustled—too big for a deer. The sound stopped...started... stopped.

Fred.

Despair strangled her courage, and she cursed herself for not finding a sturdy branch for a weapon while the light had remained. She shrank against the rock and began inching sideways, away from the sound. If this *was* a boulder, she could put it between them, she'd have—

A hand snaked from behind and clamped over her mouth, and an arm harder than steel pinned her arms and torso. Before she could kick, a leg locked around hers, trapping her nude body against cold, coarse cloth. She twisted and screamed into the hot palm, but it was nothing more than muffled frustration.

So close. She'd been *so close!*

She writhed and growled, but her life was over now. He'd never let her go, and never allow her another chance to escape. She'd blown it.

Oh, God, oh, God. Please, please, please!

Warm lips pressed against her right ear, just as he'd done when he had her on The Table playing his games. Her lungs sucked the wet air even faster, if that was possible. He always told her what he was about to do. It gave him pleasure, he said, knowing she anticipated their *"coming adventure"* as much as he did.

Her whole body shuddered against his. Above her pounding blood, she could barely hear his tickling whisper.

"Shhh. If you want to live, don't...make...a sound."

3

Lena woke to the sounds of a savage coastal storm pounding the Perilous Cove Inn where she'd splurged on a room. She left the luxurious raised bed and toasty comforter, and hurried to the ocean view windows. Black clouds barreled onshore, hurling rain at the front of the inn.

Although it was nearly dawn, there was no sun. Probably wouldn't be today. Bits of hail clattered on the glass—tiny diamonds determined to score the panes. She backed away as the glass bowed inward under pressure from a particularly violent blast.

A smile curved her mouth. If she hadn't closed the deal on the property last night, this would have been a perfect day for another look at the cabins with Realtor Roger. She almost laughed picturing the expression on his face. But she *had* closed the deal. The property was hers!

Arms wide, Lena twirled away from the window like a schoolgirl, then stopped, realizing the room was freezing. It had been hot when she'd climbed into bed last night, so she'd turned down the thermostat and cracked one of the low, crank-out windows on the side of the bay to get some ocean breeze. Now icy air billowed the sheers and curled around her ankles. Lena hurried to close it, hoping the carpet below the window was merely damp, not soaked. Then she flicked the wall switch for the raised gas fireplace, dragged the floral comforter off the king-sized bed, and settled onto the small chaise near the fireplace to watch the storm and wait for the room to warm.

Of course, she could have simply turned up the thermostat, but there was something mystical about sitting in the near dark lit by primordial flames while watching a fierce storm. Okay, it was a gas fireplace, but still…

She snuggled deeper into the warm covering, leaning her head back on the rest. The inn's breakfast menu promised Eggs Benedict, fresh berries with locally produced yogurt, more of those olallieberry muffins that were to die for, fresh squeezed OJ, and hand churned butter.

"I'm gonna gain ten pounds before noon," Lena moaned to the storm. No wonder people usually booked B&Bs for only two night stays. A third breakfast would kill them off. Lena nearly laughed when her stomach rumbled.

More ice pelted the glass, and she angled her face toward the fire, glad to be indoors. Maybe she'd call the desk and ask for a late checkout.

———

Teal woke, thrashing against the material restraining her, but it fell away easily as she sat up. Not the ropes he used to tie her on The Table, but only a scratchy blanket that had been wrapped around her, head to foot.

Weak light filtered in through pine trees outside, barely enough to reveal the few feet of cave in which she lay. Rain swept past the opening in sheets, and steady streams ran from rocks above the opening. Deeper in the cave, a hissing one-burner backpacking stove spewed blue flame under a small saucepan. A pack on a frame leaned against one wall, and a sleeping bag stretched out beside it. The top of the bag was partially unzipped. And empty.

Her blanket slipped farther, and frigid air stole her body heat. A second blanket padded the ground beneath her. She pulled the top one tight again, burrowing into the warmth. Scratchy or not, it beat freezing.

A soft scraping snapped her head around in time to see a hand fumbling about the edge of the cave mouth before latching onto a convenient rock. A shiver shook her body as she recalled that hand when it covered her mouth, but it had kept her from screaming when Fred passed by less than twenty feet away.

The hand was joined by its opposite twin, and then a camouflage ski mask crowned with a poncho rose into view. The mask was similar to Fred's, with cutouts for eyes, nose, and mouth. Teal sat still as a mouse, shuddering inside as the rest of the man's body crawled into the cave on hands and knees, blocking most of the meager light.

Her savior from last night.

"Ahh. I see you're awake," he said quietly, water sheeting off the plastic poncho. Without awaiting her response, he made his way past her feet, peeling off the rain protection as he went. A small lantern switched on and chased the shadows from the rounded back wall of the cave. He dipped his finger in the open pan, then jerked it back and put it in his mouth. "Water's hot. I have hot chocolate, oatmeal, or coffee. Your choice."

Teal's stomach growled louder than his voice, and he chuckled.

"Or you can have all three if you like. We'll start with oatmeal." He pulled off his ski mask, and Teal got her first look at him. Blond hair stuck up in crazy directions, and he had a tiny soul patch of beard below his lower lip. He looked…extraordinarily normal. Boyish. Not like a serial killer. Of course, she wasn't an expert on killers. She'd only met one.

Fred.

This guy wore some kind of heavy camouflage pants and jacket, as well as camo boots. Even the poncho was camo. He'd be hard to spot in the forest. Were these the clothes she'd been trapped against last night?

"I figured I'd be back before you woke. Nature's call, you know." Camo Guy grinned at her, then dug in his pack and came up with two envelopes of instant oatmeal.

Teal's mouth immediately began watering, and she was tempted to snatch the packages and inhale the dry contents. Before she could do so, he dumped them into the water and stirred the mixture with a spoon. Cinnamon and peaches filled the low cave, and Teal thought she'd pass out before he scraped the whole pot into a metal cup, stuck the spoon in it, and brought it to her. The meager light from the cave mouth lit his eyes a startling blue.

"Careful, it's hot," he said.

She accepted the cup, but kept her eyes on him until he retreated to the stove. The oatmeal's aroma made her dizzy. It had been so long. She dipped the spoon in the thickening mixture, blew once, and sucked the spoon clean.

"Oh!" Tears filled her eyes, and she sucked in cold air around the scalding bite.

"Here." Camo Guy thrust a canteen into her hands.

She swirled the cold water around her mouth, then swallowed it with the oatmeal. Using her tongue, she explored the roof of her mouth. Tender, but not too bad. She took another swig of the cooling liquid. She'd had worse.

Much worse.

"Told you it was hot."

She nodded, and handed the water back to him. He used it to refill the saucepan, then he sat back against the wall while the next batch heated. Teal took a smaller, second bite, blowing on the spoon thoroughly before testing it with the tip of her tongue. Her body continued to growl, but she forced herself to eat slowly. Her stomach was probably the size of a walnut after all these months.

"So, before I ask what you were doing running naked as a sprite through the mountains in winter from a bad guy, what's your name?" he asked, resting his chin on his palm.

It was lighter outside now, and he turned off the lantern—probably to conserve the batteries. His lips were curled into a slight smile. Could he be trusted? She'd been on her own for some time, and it had worked out pretty well—up until Fred had grabbed her and she'd woken in his stinking basement cage. How did she know this guy wasn't worse than Fred? Well for one, at least this guy fed her. And she needed help to get farther away from here.

"My name is Teal," she said around another bite. "Like the color." The oatmeal was cooling in the thin metal cup, and it went down like the sweetest dessert. She wondered if he had more in the pack.

"Teal," he said, mulling it over and nodding. "I like it."

"What's yours?" she asked, as she dragged the spoon around the inside of the container and captured every tiny bit of breakfast. Camo Guy rubbed his soul patch for a minute, as if considering whether, or what, to tell her. He looked mid to late twenties, but acted younger. How many secrets could someone that age have? Teal grunted. Like she was one to talk about secrets.

Camo Guy's blue eyes were on her, a big grin on his face.

"What?" she asked, putting down the empty cup.

"You're a lot of fun to watch. It's like your face puts on a whole stage play in sixty seconds."

Good to know. She'd better not go on the pro poker circuit. She'd never been much good at lying, either, if the number of times she'd been caught at it was any indication.

"So...your name?" She wasn't letting him off the hook.

"You may call me Delta." His voice deepened. "As in Delta Force."

She raised a brow. What was he, twelve? Playing army commando in his backyard? Maybe "Camo Guy" wasn't so bad. A lot better than Delta Force. Sheesh.

"Now," he said, getting to his knees and moving to his pack, "let's see if I can find enough clothing from my limited wardrobe to keep you from being naked."

———

Camo Guy politely turned his back while Teal pulled on the stretchy long underwear pants and top he'd dug out of his pack. The pants weren't too bad when she rolled up the legs ten inches, but the long-sleeve top, made to fit like a second skin on her cave mate, hung like a tent. No amount of elastic could make up for it being too big for her bony body. She tucked the leftovers into the waist of the pants and rolled up the sleeves. He helped her pull the sweatshirt—camouflage, of course—over her raw wrists. It hung to her knees. Finally, he handed her a pair of heavy wool socks, which she eased over her battered and bloody feet. In this case, the large size was a blessing.

"Sorry, but the only shoes I have are my boots. I wasn't expecting… guests."

She needed to ask him about what he'd said concerning her running from a "bad guy," but for just a little while she wanted to pretend she was safe. It had been so long since she'd been able to relax. Being unconscious didn't count.

It felt so good to have clothes on. The only thing better would be a steaming bathtub, brimming with strawberry-scented bubbles. That had been her dream as long as she could remember, and she vowed that before she was twenty years old, she'd treat herself to a spa day, with cucumber slices on her eyes, mud bath, and all.

But for now she still felt like a Popsicle, and tugged the blanket around her.

"I'll make you some hot chocolate," Camo Guy said, turning to the camp stove.

Teal watched his hunched form for a few minutes, until her eyelids became too heavy to hold up. Then she listened to the sounds of him pouring water and adjusting the flame. He'd held her immobile in the dark last night while Fred passed by. Everything after that was sort of a blur. Probably a good thing. She remembered stumbling along beside him for what seemed like an hour or two, his arm supporting her, tight around her waist. Then, when she'd slid over the edge into total exhaustion, he'd carried her.

She didn't remember climbing up into the cave that was obviously above the ground, nor him wrapping her up in the blankets. She *did* remember that she'd been naked.

"Teal."

Cracking her eyes open, she saw Camo Guy set a cup of steaming hot chocolate by her head.

"I've got to leave for a while. My cell phone battery died, so I have to hike out to my truck, then go into town to get help from the sheriff's Search and Rescue."

"No!" Teal said, struggling to sit up as her heart raced. The fear of being alone again was overpowering, but even worse was having cops involved. She'd be back in foster care before the day was over, stuck again in some house with five other kids, and adults who were in it for the state money.

"It's way too far for you to walk without better equipment. And I can't carry you that far. It's our only option."

"Don't tell anyone else. Just get me some clothes and shoes. I can walk." She grabbed his jacket and pulled him close. "Promise."

"Teal..." He looked down at her wrists. "Teal, when I wrapped you in the blankets...I saw the cuts. Some are still bleeding. You...need help."

"*Promise me!*"

He sighed, and ran a hand through his hair. "Okay." But he didn't sound as if he liked it, or particularly sincere.

She jerked him again.

"Okay, okay," he said, palms out. "Easy."

This time she believed him. Maybe. She released her grip and fell back onto the blanket, panting.

"But it's gonna take a while. By the time I walk out, get the stuff, and come back, I'll be gone for at least several hours. It'll be dark—maybe even tomorrow morning. You'll be okay here. We're a long way from where that guy was. If you get hungry, there are protein bars in my pack. Okay?" Camo Guy gently tucked the covers around her.

"'Kay," she sighed, burying her nose under the blanket's edge. The clouds had thickened, turning day into virtual night, and the chill wind swirling into the cave carried the scent of soggy air. He'd be hiking in the rain. "No cops," she reinforced, and was rewarded with a grudging nod.

"If you get cold, crawl into my sleeping bag. Now, what sizes do you wear?"

Teal mumbled the answers, though she'd lost so much weight everything would probably swim on her. She wriggled deeper into the wool. The chocolate smelled good, but the roof of her mouth was still tender from the oatmeal. It could cool a couple of minutes. Her eyes closed again while she listened to him making preparations. Then the scrape of his boots registered as he went over the edge of the cave mouth.

"Delta," she said, stopping him before his head disappeared.

"Yeah?"

"What's the date today?" She wasn't sure why it was important, but she'd been lost in a fog of fear and pain for so long…

Camo Guy checked his watch dial. "December 10th. Worried about getting your Christmas shopping done? I'm partial to wool socks." He gave her a lopsided grin.

"I'll add them to my list." Teal snuggled down again, wincing as one of the wounds on her back cracked open. She hoped it didn't bleed on Camo Guy's shirt. Now that her tummy was full, her brain went fuzzy with exhaustion and release from the constant fear she'd lived under. "Hurry back."

He winked, then he sank out of sight into the wet, early afternoon.

When Teal woke sometime later, the sun had disappeared. Rain sizzled through the trees outside the cave, splatting on the ground cover. Teal wondered how Camo Guy was doing, but he seemed well prepared for just about everything. She didn't think a little rain would stop him.

4

Teal checked the pack again to make sure she hadn't missed a power bar or package of oatmeal—even a stick of gum. But every zippered compartment was empty. After two days in the cave by herself, she had eaten every scrap of food, then watched the flame die on the little stove as the propane ran out while heating the last of the water. By the time the light began to fail in the late afternoon yesterday, she'd been positive—Camo Guy wasn't coming back.

Now it had to be close to noon on day three. December 13th. She hoped today wasn't Friday.

But she had no choice, really. It was leave today, or let someone find her bones in this cave—if a bear didn't drag her body off somewhere and eat it. She glanced at the cave mouth, half expecting a furry black head to come over the edge. Water dripped from the rocks above the entrance. It had stormed for two days, but the rain had stopped an hour or so ago and the sky seemed marginally brighter.

"You can do this," she pep-talked herself as she pulled on a second pair of socks and layers of shirts from Camo Guy's pack. There were no shoes or gloves, or even a hat, but she found a scarf. She pulled the sweatshirt over her head, then knotted the scarf around her neck.

The packframe was far too large for her skinny body, so she pushed it aside. But she did find a couple of bungee cords, and used them to tie up one of the blankets in a roll and secure it around her shoulder. She wrapped herself in the other blanket and limped to the cave edge.

It was only about seven or eight feet to the leaf-covered ground. It looked soft. *Yeah, right.* She tossed the blankets down.

Using her cut-up feet to navigate the protruding rocks was no fun, but she made it to the forest floor. She wished she'd watched which direction Camo Guy went when he deserted her, but wishes hadn't done her much good so far. Spotting a few scuff marks leading away along the rock edge, she set out.

Within fifteen minutes, her socks had soaked through. Then the rain started again, fat drops splatting the ground like mini meteors. Soon her outer blanket grew so heavy she couldn't carry it, and she had no choice but to let its sopping mess slough to the ground. Standing under the partial shelter of a tree, she shifted the remaining blanket roll around to her front and tucked it under the sweatshirt. If she was going to survive, the blanket had to remain dry. It wasn't cold enough for snow right now, but it could easily freeze tonight.

Beginning again was almost more than her feet could bear, but eventually they became numbed by the deepening cold. She kept her head down, watching the path grow more prominent as it joined with first one, then a second trail. The bright spot in the sky overhead told her it was about noon. It provided no sense of her direction, but then she really didn't *have* a direction in mind. Her only goal was to find someplace safe. Somewhere she could call her own.

That's all she'd ever wanted, ever since her mom was taken away and Teal had been thrust into the foster care system. It didn't seem like too much to ask.

Rain dripped from her hair and soaked the top shirt, then the next, and the one below that. The long underwear pants sagged with water, flopping against her legs as she trudged along. At every gap in the trees, she looked for a house or cabin. Wherever she was, this wasn't near civilization. Finally, she grew too weary to look, or even care. It became all about putting one foot in front of the other.

Some of the foster homes hadn't been bad. But about the time she got settled at a new school and made a friend, a lady in an official car would show up, pack her few clothes, and take her to a new home. Her *why* questions were never answered. It was as if no one wanted a nine, then ten, then eleven, twelve, thirteen year old. At least, that's what it felt like. Right now, even one of the bad homes sounded good.

Teal hadn't noticed when the rain stopped, but she was acutely aware of when the wind began. It funneled up the twisting trail, scattering leaves and slamming into her exposed face and saturated clothing. Her teeth began chattering almost immediately, and she stepped behind some bushes to escape the direct blast. Removing the bungee, she unrolled the remaining blanket. It was already mostly soaked through, but she draped the heavy cloth over her head and clinched it closed in front.

The wind tore at the flaps when she stepped out from behind the shrubs, and she dipped her head. There was no way she could go back, away from the wind. She'd never find the cave again. Her only hope was forward. The path under her feet had widened even more, evidence that there had to be a trailhead somewhere with a parking lot and cars. People. She leaned into the gale.

Teal's resolve faltered a half hour later when rain joined the wind, smacking her with ice-cold bullets that stung her skin. She shivered so violently that she wobbled from one side of the trail to the other. Had anyone ever broken teeth from chattering?

She put one foot in front of the other, knowing that survival depended on her alone. Darkness gradually stole the murky light. But nightfall didn't diminish the wind...only made it colder. She longed for the relative warmth of the cave, the scratchy blankets, the comforting hiss of the little stove.

Her face hitting the ground shocked Teal awake. Using a dirty hand, she swiped away the worst of the mud, leaves, and blood. Her whole body shivered, and she gritted her teeth and tensed her muscles in an effort to stop it. She rolled on her stomach and worked her knees under her, then rose on her elbows, but that was as much as she could do. She crawled forward.

Trees thrashed above her, whipping the air into a chaos of sound, and pummeling her body with falling debris. The blanket caught on something and slid down her back as she lurched forward another foot.

Using numb fingers, she tried to pull it back over her, but the wind wrenched the meager covering from her grasp and sent it flying into the dark, exposing her to even more cold. She curled into a fetal position and surrendered to the shaking. Just a minute and she'd try again.

Please, God. I don't want to die out here.

Teal thought of the relative warmth of the cave, of Camo Guy's promised return. She prayed he'd come along and find her on this path. It had to be the same one, didn't it? But her mother had promised to come back, too.

All Teal wanted was someplace to belong, where she fit in. Someplace *hers*. Was that too much to ask?

Please.

A fuzzy numbness suffused her body. Although aware of her shaking limbs, she no longer felt as cold. She'd read about hypothermia, how it lulled people into sleep…a frozen slumber that killed them. She had to get moving, make it to the trailhead. Still, she burrowed into a foot-thick layer of leaves that had drifted against the path's edge, hoping their slight protection might be enough until the wind died down. Teal slitted her eyes open enough to make out the whipping branches against the nearly black sky. Eight or more hours before dawn. From the months of imprisonment in the basement, her body was accustomed to cold. Maybe she could hold out. Just a few hours.

If not, this forest path would be her last resting place. When the weather warmed, someone would find her, leaves plastered to her body and stuck in her hair.

Teal wished she could sleep in a soft bed one more time. These leaves weren't bad, but her skin was so cold she couldn't feel their softness. If only she hadn't been captured by Fred. If Camo Guy had come back. If her mom hadn't…

Her eyes closed of their own accord, blocking out the *if*s. She used the last of her strength to burrow deeper in the drift of leaves. The wind scoured her unprotected face with pebbles, leaves, and twigs, but it no longer bothered her as much. If this was the end, at least it wouldn't be on The Table, Fred grinning as he tightened the bindings and inserted a new blade in his razor knife.

Teal closed her eyes against Fred, too. She had escaped. Maybe he'd never know where she'd gone and, for the rest of his life, he'd be looking over his shoulder. That would have to be enough.

Light flashed, and Teal waited for the following thunder. Instead, more light lit the bushes around her. A pair of boots thumped by inches from her face. Then another set of boots walked past, splashing muddy water into her face. Teal closed her eyes against the grit.

She called out, but her teeth were chattering and she couldn't form the words. The roaring wind drowned out her pathetic mewing.

Peeling her left hand free where it was clinched against her, she thrust it into the path. She swung it back and forth, finding nothing but air. Had they all passed by?

Then her hand struck something. Cloth. She forced her fingers to clinch around the stiff material and held on. She was rewarded with a scream, bright light, and cursing as the leg jerked away.

"Hey. Hey, guys! Over here!"

The ground beneath Teal's cheek vibrated with footfalls. Swinging light beams caught her eyes, then illuminated arms, legs, boots...all covered in camouflage. Was she the only one who hadn't gotten the fashion memo?

"Teal." Warm fingers trailed fire on her cheeks as they brushed away mud. "We're here. You're safe now."

Camo Guy. The lights in her eyes made it impossible to see him, but she recognized his voice. He'd come back after all. Someone turned on a bright lantern, and his face swam into view.

"I'm so sorry, Teal. My truck got stuck in the mud." He lifted her shoulders off the ground. "Why didn't you wait? I said I'd come back."

She tried to reach for him, to make a sound, but her body refused to obey orders.

"Teal?"

Other voices asked questions her frozen lips couldn't answer. Black rifle barrels swung through the beams. Dimly, she thought about being afraid, but it seemed too much work. Besides, Camo Guy was here to protect her.

There was a moment of vertigo as she was lifted, and hands wrapped her in something silvery that cut the wind's mindless cruelty, but did little to alleviate the cold. Then they wrapped her in a blanket, her arms tight against her body like a mummy ready for burial. One of the men wrestled a ski cap over her wet hair.

Aware only of lights, jostling movement, and the sapping cold, one snippet of conversation drilled through to her brain:

"...let the sheriff know."

Camo Guy had betrayed her to the authorities, and they'd soon have her back in foster care. Dreams of a place all her own would have to wait. She wouldn't be "home" for Christmas, not the special place she sought, but at least she wouldn't be dead.

He'd saved her life—twice. Dimly, she wondered if wool socks came in camouflage, and how many pairs it would take to repay her debt.

He lay in the brush not fifteen feet off the trail, and watched through his night vision goggles as the trio of men helped the girl. He'd spotted her, almost reached her, but then he'd seen the approaching hikers' lights. This was bad. He'd been so close.

And why wasn't she dead? She *should* be dead. Three days he'd been searching through these mountains behind his house, and not a sign of her. He'd had to call in sick. If only he'd had his goggles the night she escaped. How could she have survived?

One of the men lifted her shoulders and brushed off leaves.

"I'm so sorry, Teal. My truck got stuck in the mud. Why didn't you wait? I said I'd come back."

So, she'd had help. The fact she hadn't eluded him on her own made the sting a little less severe. But if Reynaldo found out… Well, he wouldn't. This was the last one. It had to be. That Mexican already had too much on him. He couldn't find out about this girl.

The rescue party began hiking down the trail with their burden shared between them, and he watched their progress until they disappeared around an outcropping of rock. He knew which trailhead they were headed for—the only place vehicles could be in this area.

He rose to his feet. There was a shorter route, up and across the ridge. Too hard for the men with their burden, but he could beat them there. Maybe find out which one had stopped his entertainment.

He ached to get her back on his table and continue his work.

5

Five weeks later

The third week of January, Lena drove through the tiny Storm Lake village of
Shelter Cove. The Jeep's wipers chattered on the drying windshield, and she
switched them off. According to the weather forecasters, this storm was the
last in a nearly two-week series during the unusually wet winter. The light
spritzes today hadn't amounted to much, and she was trusting luck that the
creek crossing would be passable.

Besides, she'd already twiddled her thumbs for six weeks waiting for the
blasted escrow to close. She wasn't waiting another second, even if she had
to wade onto her new property.

She wound through the houses and cabins of the tiny enclave of Gift.
According to the road sign, it was named for its pure spring water that the
first settlers had described as "a gift from God." Lena didn't see the famed
spring, but the houses soon fell behind, and she reached the *End of County
Maintained Road* sign where the pavement ended. The Jeep's tires dropped
into a splattered field of muddy potholes.

Lena engaged the four-wheel drive—not because she needed it yet, but
just because she could. "Now the fun begins." She patted the dash of the
nearly two-decade old Wrangler. "Don't let me down, baby. This is what you
were created for."

Despite the ominous warning sign, the road wasn't in bad shape, and the oversized knobby tires rolled effortlessly through the shallow puddles. She checked the rearview mirror, ensuring the utility trailer was behaving. A big blue tarp covered all her worldly possessions. After Bobby died, Lena had taken the bare essentials out of their destroyed home—mostly her clothes and tools—then called an estate sale company. Mama L hugged her and shed loud tears, but for Lena, living there after that terrible night had been impossible.

Trees arched high over the narrowing road, creating a tunnel of greenery that extended a hundred feet or more, before opening as the path widened and sloped steeply downward toward the edge of the creek. Lena braked to a stop. Fifteen or twenty feet of fast-moving water separated her from her new property—and home. She climbed out and walked to the edge. Question was, how deep? Erosion marks on the far bank indicated the water had been flowing maybe a couple of feet higher during the worst of the storms, making it impassible then.

Overhead, the clouds broke apart as they moved east, and shafts of sunlight shot through the openings, highlighting the banks, rocks, and water. Spring was still weeks away, but Lena could almost smell the freshness of renewed life emerging from the mat of moldy leaves that covered the area. It wouldn't be long before a green haze of new buds wrapped the deciduous trees. Time to get started on her new life.

If she could get there.

She dislodged a potato-sized rock and heaved it toward the center of the crossing. It splashed and immediately clunked against the bottom rocks. Not deep. Maybe eighteen to twenty inches. She tugged her bottom lip between her teeth. No problem for the Jeep, but pulling the trailer through was the bigger challenge. She could unhitch the trailer and try the crossing with the Jeep alone. That would be the wise approach. But she needed everything on the trailer. And what was life without a little risk?

With a wry grin, Lena climbed back in, shifted into four-wheel-drive low range, and drove off the edge into the stream. Once level, she kept pressure on the gas pedal, proceeding steadily across the rumbling stream bed. The rocks rolled and clunked under the tires. When the Jeep's rear slewed sideways, Lena wrestled the steering wheel and gave the engine more gas to maintain a straight track. A few feet from the far bank, Lena's breath caught as the front wheels dropped into a deep hole. Water surged over the submerged bumper and through the radiator. The engine fan sliced into the incoming flow like an outboard motor, and blasted water out the edges of the hood and over the windshield.

"Whoa!" Lena yelled, struggling to see through the drenched glass as she mashed the gas pedal down and held on.

The front tires, then the rear, bounced onto the other bank as she kept her right foot solidly on the floor. Rocks clattered under the fenders as all four tires sprayed brown geysers into the air. She flicked her eyes to the rearview mirror to make sure she hadn't lost the trailer, but she didn't slow the growling Jeep until it climbed onto the level road.

Lena laughed and pounded the steering wheel. "Now, *that's* what I'm talking about!"

She ran the wipers a few passes to clear the muddy water off the glass. Brown grit littered the hood, and the trailer's tarp was no longer blue. She'd have to dig out the hose and wash it off before she unpacked. And the crossing required a complete rebuild before any guests could pull their boats across.

Lena looked around at the trees and rocks. It was the same terrain as the other side of the creek, but this was *her property*! Well, the road was technically the county's right of way, but it cut an easement through her land.

Less than two minutes later she veered left at the Y off the main road and topped a small hill. A couple hundred yards later, she braked to a stop in front of her new home. Roofing shingles littered the yard in ominous greeting.

"Good thing the rain quit," she muttered, as she mounted the porch steps and turned to face the lake. Because of all the oaks and a few pines, the view wasn't the best from this vantage point, but she could see sunlight sparkling across the water. The view would be even less when the trees filled in during spring, but that's one of the reasons she'd picked this cabin for her own.

The cabin's door scraped the floor when she opened it. She flipped the light switch inside, and the ceiling fixture in the living room lit up, revealing a floor littered with dirt, leaves, and things that could be dead critters. She blew out a breath and started a mental list.

Broom, dustpan, shop vacuum, a Windex spray bottle with a gallon refill, a dozen rolls of paper towels. All things she had under the tarp. She sighed at the enormity of just making this place habitable for tonight, let alone turning it into a home.

An hour later, she sprinkled the third application of scouring powder across the kitchen counter. "I should have bought a pressure washer," she said, as she scrubbed at the gray-black grime. "And a leaf blower."

As soon as she had the sink and counters sparkling, she unpacked her coffee maker and got a pot going. She was going to need it tonight. While the appliance was happily dripping, she hung the wall calendar she'd gotten from Realtor Roger. January's picture was of snow-covered mountains with Roger's smiling face in the bottom right corner, but Lena wasn't putting it up for decoration. Taking a black Sharpie from her pocket, she drew a large X through January 20th. Today. Roughly four and a half months until Memorial Day weekend when she planned to rent out the three cabins by the lake.

She blew out a breath. They had to be completely refurbished first. Of the five cabins on the property, this one was in the best shape. That was scary. The three nearest the water would appeal more to the renters. She hoped the X-ed squares on the calendar didn't overtake Memorial Day before she got the work done.

The calendar also reminded her it had been over a year since that November night when everything changed. The cops still hadn't put anyone in jail. And although she'd talked with them a couple of times, it didn't seem like much was happening anymore. She made a mental note to call Bobby's old coworker, Chet Marquette, and ask if he knew anything.

Lena shrugged off the momentary gloom. She had to get moving if she wanted to sleep before dawn. By 2:30 a.m., Lena had dusted for cobwebs ceiling to floor in every room, swept out all the disgusting dirt, used her shop vacuum in every corner, drunk a full pot of coffee, cleaned the bathroom and bedroom, and chased all the spiders off the screened back porch.

Adrenaline and caffeine eventually ran out, and it was all she could do to take a shower, the first in her new place, and that was particularly satisfying. She inflated her air mattress on the wood floor of the single bedroom, and slid inside her sleeping bag with a groan. Finally lying still, the quiet of the night settled in around her, and she closed her eyes to crickets singing a happy chorus outside.

Thankfulness washed over her. She had running water and electricity. Before her, with a little hard work, was a chance for a new beginning. A new life.

There was no way it could be worse than the last one.

6

Four months later - May

Lena tucked her hands in her jean pockets and watched Merle Ferris back the mid-century Caterpillar tractor off the tilted flatbed trailer and spin it in place until it faced the road. His blue chambray work shirt threatened to pop buttons if he ate one more cheeseburger from the grill in Deer Cove, and his splotched jeans—held up by taxed red suspenders—stank of hydraulic oil. The scars on his poor work boots spoke their life-sentence to hard labor, and they were all the recommendation Lena had needed when she hired him to construct her creek crossing.

But she hadn't counted on how irritatingly methodical the man could be. She still had a hundred small things to do to get the cabins ready for her first renters this weekend.

"Come on, Merle, get a move on, will ya?" she muttered, as he took time to slap dust from his cap, then carefully align it on his frizzy gray hair so the emblazoned yellow CAT faced proudly ahead.

This creek crossing was the last major obstacle that prevented her from earning some income. She'd tried to get it done right after the rains had petered out at the end of March, but it had been delayed for weeks by the county's convoluted permit process. It seemed everyone from the Sierra Club to the Girl Scouts had a say on whether she would be allowed to build a crossing to access her own property. A couple of environmentalists had even filed a protest, arguing the crossing shouldn't be rebuilt, and that the property be left to revert to nature. Easy for them to say; they hadn't sunk all their money into the project like she had. But she'd finally walked out of the county office with the permit in hand.

Merle engaged the drive, rolled forward, and scooped up road base from a large pile that had been delivered earlier. Then he eased the Cat D2 down the creek bank where the three, sixteen-foot long corrugated steel culvert pipes lay partially embedded in freshly cured concrete. Water from the streambed ran about two inches deep through each of the pipes, and it was Merle's job today to make this into a drivable road for the first time in years. He spread the gravel across the three pipes, filling the gaps and packing it down. Soon, the roadbed began taking shape.

Lena perched on a lichen-covered log and watched while the old man wrestled the old iron. They made a good pair. The steel tracks punched hundreds of inch-deep cuts in the dusty earth, only to obliterate them on the next pass, and pungent white smoke from the thrumming diesel filled the clearing, banishing all thoughts of peace, solitude, and fresh air. She wiped dusty sweat from her brow. May was nearly over, and the early summer heat had arrived last week, depositing a carpet of yellow pollen on her Jeep hood every morning. The oaks and sycamores filled the air with sweet aromas, and the single, gnarled apple tree by the barn had lost its pink blossoms and now sported promising little buds. She'd never made an apple pie, but had high hopes for the opportunity.

Lena loved it all, and wished for the hundredth time Bobby could be here with her. In their brief courtship and marriage, they had dreamed about someday getting away from the rat race and buying a place at a lake. And here she was, making it happen. Except now it was her dream alone.

She shook her head again at the nightmare of that night. The gnawing inside had relinquished a little, but was still raw enough she wished the diesel smoke could mask those memories without clouding Bobby, too.

Merle hopped off the tractor and trotted over to Lena. He had sufficiently buried the three pipes, but there was still gravel in the pile.

"Wanna give it a try, AJ?" he shouted, hooking a thumb at the machine. "Couple more scoops, then smooth out the roadway. Easy work." He winked at her.

Everyone she'd met at the lake knew her as AJ, from the initials of her first and middle names, Alena Jewel. So far that minor adjustment had kept probing questions away, as well as the nosey media.

Lena grinned at Merle and followed him to the yellow beast. She loved machinery, and counted as one of her greatest experiences driving a decrepit John Deere hayride tractor for three seasons at a pumpkin patch farm. But she'd never had an opportunity to drive a tracklayer.

The smell of hot oil from the engine cowling backwashed over Lena as she swung onto a canvas-covered seat held together with a yard or two of duct tape. She wrapped her fingers around the vibrating levers. It reminded her of the time she'd ridden in the cab of a steam locomotive in northern California as a little girl. Belching fire and smoke, the engine had seemed like a creature alive, something to be cajoled down the track rather than driven. This old Cat was the same way.

Merle gave instruction on the control levers and transmission, then stood on the rear hitch so he could watch over her shoulder. She shifted the tractor into low and pulled back the engaging lever. The machine bucked forward a few feet and plowed the bucket into the remaining rock pile. She raised the bucket, reversed direction, and soon had the treads clanking toward the new bridge. Merle showed her how to dump and spread the gravel, then he hopped off as she whirled around for the final loads.

Two successful trips later, Lena hated to see only one more load of gravel remained. She lowered the bucket and drove into the pile, but she misjudged the bucket depth and scooped up several inches of dirt beneath the gravel. Not wanting to waste the last of the rock, there wasn't anything else to do but go ahead and dump it on the crossing. The soil would wash out of the rock at the first fall rain, so it wouldn't be a problem.

She raised the bucket as she backed up, and started to turn in place when she noticed Merle running toward her, waving and making a cutting gesture across his neck. He was red-faced and puffing like he couldn't get his breath, though he'd only run thirty feet. Alarmed, Lena killed the engine and it clattered to a stop.

"What's the matter?" Lena jumped off the tractor into the dust cloud, afraid the man might be having some kind of attack. Or maybe she'd broken something on the Caterpillar.

"It's...it's..." Merle panted, pointing back and forth between the tractor bucket and the hole she'd left in the earth. He bent over and put his other hand on his knee, wheezing and coughing.

"What?" Lena said, coming around to the front of the Cat so she could see what he was trying to tell her. A sickly sweet odor met her, leaching onto every dust particle swirling in the hot air, and snaking its way into her lungs. She gagged and covered her face with her hand.

From the dirt at the bottom of the bucket dangled a half-rotted human arm.

Teal dragged herself over the crest of the ridge and slid into the protective shade of a manzanita bush on the other side. She automatically checked the path behind her, then shook her head. "Don't be paranoid."

The bush's smooth, red bark had the beauty of burnished leather. Although the sparse leaves provided only partial shelter from the relentless noon sun, it was better than the baking heat, and she'd take it.

She almost wished for the rainy weather of a couple of months ago. At least it had been cool. Now, at the end of May, summer had arrived early. She rubbed sweat from her face. Yes, cool would be good.

What she *wasn't* wishing for was the cold of winter, like December when she almost died from hypothermia. *Should* have. If Camo Guy and the others hadn't found her…

These hadn't been the best months of her life.

Teal laughed out loud at her own understatement.

A wedge of weathered granite stuck up high enough to serve as a backrest, and Teal leaned against its hot surface while she surveyed the rugged hills from her high vantage point. Huge oaks dotted the slopes below, casting deep pools of shade. She longed to stretch out beneath one of them, feel its cool darkness. This western side of the mountain looked like easier going. Downhill at least.

It was about time, too. On the gas station map two days ago, the terrain hadn't appeared so difficult. Once again, she regretted landing in Paso Robles. That's what she got for falling asleep while catching a ride. She'd planned to head up the coast, not inland. Oh, well. Live and learn…with the emphasis on *live*.

After two patrolling sheriff's cars forced her into the brush to avoid detection, she'd quit hiking on the main route to the coast and struck out overland. That kept her away from "helpful" authorities. She liked being on her own and intended to keep it that way.

Teal pulled out her water bottle and drained half, swirling the tepid liquid in her mouth before swallowing. Only a few ounces remained, and she saved it for later. She'd have to find a stream, a house, or at least a livestock watering trough. Surely someone lived in these hills, though she hadn't seen so much as a rabbit today.

"Mountain lions probably killed all the rabbits," she muttered, searching the surrounding rock outcroppings for pointy cat ears. A hawk's screech tore the air overhead, and she located the bird against the bright sky. That was the only sound besides the endless whine of insects. They seemed to be everywhere—and nowhere. Still, the solitude filled her with peace. The world could do with more nature and fewer people.

She wondered if Camo Guy had ever hiked these hills. They were a long way from L.A. He'd disappeared right after they reached the hospital, and she hadn't gotten a chance to thank him. Her first purchase after she'd gotten a little money had been a pair of camouflage wool socks. They were safely sealed in a plastic bag in her backpack. She knew she'd see him again.

"Ouch!" Teal jerked her left arm close. The cuff of her shirt had slid up, and a shaft of sunlight had practically sizzled against the white puckered scars encircling her wrist. She removed the leather-banded watch she wore to hide the hideous marks and put it in her backpack—no people to fool around here—then tugged the shirt material down against her woven wristband she'd bought for a nickel at a thrift store over a year ago. She'd liked the color and the name, so she'd adopted both. *Teal*. It sounded bold, confident. It was a minor miracle she'd saved it from beneath The Table during her escape. Its rich teal threads—thoroughly laundered after Fred— were soft enough not to chafe.

Teal checked her wrist again. The scars, though healed, were still a little tender and susceptible to sunburn. The doctor had said to use a special anti-scarring lotion and sunblock, but she'd never had anything to use except regular hand lotion, and not even that now. A soak in a cool stream sounded good. Maybe there was one hidden somewhere in the trees below.

It was still a long way to the coast where she planned to catch a ride up Highway 1 to Big Sur. She'd heard some of the old hippies from the 60s and 70s still lived their lives any way they pleased. Sounded good, a place where she might fit.

Teal wiped her brow with the shirt's cuff and got to her feet. She wouldn't get there by sitting on her rear.

7

Lena followed Sheriff Derrek Cabot's four-by-four south on East Lake Road into Shelter Cove. Although she'd assured him she was fine, her knuckles were white against the Jeep's steering wheel. She uncurled her fingers and flexed each hand.

She'd left the area before the investigating team began digging up the remainder of the body, and driven her Jeep a hundred yards down the road to wait for the sheriff. There was no way she could watch that.

It was now after four o'clock. The county coroner had driven by a few minutes ago with the exhumed body, including the left arm she'd torn off with the tractor bucket. A shudder raced through Lena. Too late to block that image. It would haunt her for a long time.

As she drove behind the sheriff, she turned the heater up another notch, even though the day was toasty warm.

The sheriff's car turned into the Shelter Cove General Store lot, and Lena followed and parked beside him. Cabot climbed out and waited for her. Lena blew out a breath and elbowed open the door. Her muscles were stiff, whether from driving the tractor or from tension she didn't know, but she'd be sore tomorrow. She rolled her neck to work out the kinks. The screen door screeched as the sheriff pulled it open. He indicated she should precede him inside.

The only store on this side of the lake, it was your typical all-purpose establishment for a lake community, stocking everything from firewood to lettuce, fish bait to sewing kits. One aisle was dedicated to camping supplies, another to fishing, complete with a forest of poles arching overhead. All of the merchandise sported a layer of dust, its thickness evidence of how long the item had been on the shelves. Lena wound her way behind the sheriff toward one of three small clear pine tables along the right-hand wall.

"Have a seat, Mrs. Blaylock. I'll get us some coffee. Regular okay?"

Lena nodded. Normally she took some creamer and sugar, but it seemed too much work to give him those instructions. She needed the caffeine and warmth. It wasn't cold in the store, but her body refused to believe that. Shock, she guessed, and hugged her arms as she waited for the sheriff's return.

Like a mini-mart, the food counter had hotdogs sizzling on stainless rollers, a drink machine, a refrigerated case with prepared sandwiches and salads, and two large coffee dispensers. Her stomach roiled as she imagined her throat and lungs coated with dust particles suffused with the sickening sweetness of death and decay. She barely resisted the urge to blow her nose yet again. Perhaps the stench could be washed away if she showered until the hot water ran out.

While the sheriff filled two disposable cups, Lena let her body mold to the chair. It wasn't particularly comfortable, but the new surroundings siphoned off a portion of the tension she'd held for a few hours. She rested her chin on her palm and stared out the side window. Tall pines swayed in the light breeze, and a kid's swing dangled from long, white ropes, the seat moving back and forth, abandoned for the moment, but ready for fun at the touch of a child's hand.

"We have to grab fun when we find it, babe. Never know what will come next."

That had been eighteen months ago, before they were married, kayaking in Mission Bay, San Diego. Bobby had been right. Everything had been going so well then.

Same as today. Only a few hours ago she'd been excited to finish the creek crossing and ready her cabins for rental. And she'd gotten to drive the tracklayer to boot.

But then the fun had stopped. The fun always stopped.

"Here you go, Mrs. Blaylock," Sheriff Cabot said. He placed the cups on the table and slid onto the chair opposite.

"Thank you." Lena wrapped her hands around the hot drink, absorbing its warmth, its life. She took a sip of the scalding liquid, and her stomach growled.

"Are you hungry?" The sheriff's brows arched and he hooked a thumb toward the food counter. "I can get you a sandwich or…"

She shook her head. "Eating wouldn't be a good idea right now." Her breakfast this morning had consisted of a piece of toast and a banana. Too excited about Merle coming, she hadn't bothered with lunch. Right this moment she was very glad her stomach was empty.

"I understand. Something like this can be unsettling." Cabot sipped his coffee and paused, his gaze shifting toward a family of four—mom, dad, son, daughter—gathering armfuls of supplies.

The girl, no more than seven and twig skinny, wore pink flip-flops with rhinestone straps. Her blonde ponytail swished out the back of a pink ball cap that proclaimed *Cowabunga!*

A normal family activity—on such an abnormal day.

Then the lawman turned to Lena. "Here's what we know so far. The coroner said the body is male, Caucasian, probably mid-twenties to thirties, thin."

The image of the wristwatch-clad arm surged into Lena's mind, unbidden, unwanted. The remaining skin on the arm had been dark, stained by the earth and death. If she'd seen his face, would she have known he was white? She suppressed another shudder and nearly dropped her cup.

"Been dead about three weeks…maybe more," the sheriff went on to say, as if this were everyday conversation over a cup. Perhaps for him it was. "They'll have to do more tests back at the lab to pin it down. Shaggy blond hair. Have you seen anyone like that around since you moved in, Mrs. Blaylock?"

So young…only a few years past high school. How could someone with his whole life before him have it cut so short and in such a horrible way? Same as Bobby.

"I don't recall anyone like that." She concentrated on keeping her hand steady. "But I haven't met a lot of people yet."

Derek Cabot lifted his cup and sipped the steaming brew, his dark eyes hooded under his bushy black brows. They reminded her of an eagle, missing nothing. She, a juicy rabbit.

"I got a report on the radio that you had some trouble a while back." His nonchalance contrasted his gaze.

"Yes," she said, and felt guilty for demoting Bobby's death to *some trouble*. Of course the sheriff would have checked her background. Now he'd probably want the whole story in all its gruesome detail. She'd have to relive the panic of those desperate minutes again, as she already did most nights.

"Do you suppose that has any connection with the body today?" he asked.

His question surprised her. After leaving the TV show—which she'd done immediately—and selling the house, she'd spent ten months on the road, with extended stays in Pocatello, Idaho, and Wichita, Kansas, working some construction jobs after her wrist healed. She'd kept a very low profile, only calling a few friends to assure them she was okay. They were mad she wouldn't tell them where she was, but the cops still hadn't caught whoever murdered Bobby.

The detectives speculated that he, as an assistant district attorney, was the killer's target—probably revenge because of a past case. Two of Bobby's friends told her he'd been working on a big drug case. No one seemed to know details. But also, before the attack, Lena's studio security had detained two different men who had been stalking her. It sounded ridiculous that *she* might have been the target, but she wasn't taking chances.

"The reason I ask, Mrs. Blaylock," the sheriff continued, leaning toward her and speaking in a low voice, "is that this is a particularly unusual situation."

Lena opened her mouth to ask what the *usual* discovery of a dead body was like, but couldn't find the words.

"I'm sorry to be so gruesome, but you see, the man's legs were missing. We looked all around, but there was no sign of them at the scene." He sat back and took a sip of his coffee, watching her reaction.

The bizarre thought that he hoped she knew where they were zipped through her mind. The few sips of coffee she'd had bubbled in her stomach, threatening. She pushed the cup as far to the side as the table allowed. Finding half a body was much worse than finding a whole one. It meant someone had... Lena stopped that thought, focusing on the pine tabletop.

The sheriff hesitated, as if determining how much to tell her. "This probably isn't someone local."

"Oh," Lena said, his meaning finally dawning. A report of someone missing in this small community, even in the whole county, would immediately be compared to the body. Two non-locals. One was dead, and Lena, with a history of *some trouble*, was the other mystery card in the sheriff's deck.

Of course, not everyone who disappeared met with foul play. Nor, as she well knew, did they necessarily desire to be found.

And certainly no one anywhere around had found the man's legs. Law enforcement would have circulated that information far and wide.

Sheriff Cabot suddenly leveled his flat-brimmed campaign hat on his head. "Well, I'm sorry you had to find this young man today, especially considering the circumstances."

Were the "circumstances" the mutilated body, or the fact Lena had ripped off the arm with a tractor? She didn't even want to contemplate which was the more grisly.

The sheriff slid a white business card across the tabletop and tapped it twice with a blunt fingernail. "I want you to call me if you think of anything. Even small details can make a difference."

Small details were the last things she wanted to remember, but she accepted the card and nodded as he scooted back his chair and stood.

"I'll let you know as soon as we have an identification of the body. Maybe that will tell us how John Doe ended up by your creek crossing."

"Sheriff," Lena stood as well, choosing her next words. "I hope you know how important it is for me to remain—"

"Hidden?" Sheriff Derek Cabot wasn't smiling, obviously miffed she hadn't stopped by his office her first day here and given him her life history. After a moment, his face softened. "The story right now, Mrs. Blaylock, is that Merle Ferris discovered the body—which he did, since he saw it first—while repairing the crossing at the end of the county road."

"Does he…does Merle know my background?"

Cabot shook his head. "Only that you're keeping a low profile for personal reasons. Which, I assume, is entirely true." His raised brow made it a question.

Lena nodded.

He adjusted his perfectly straight hat. "Merle's a good man. He'll keep to himself."

Some of the tension seeped from Lena's shoulders. "Thank you, Sheriff. I do appreciate it."

Cabot turned to leave, then stopped and stared at the ceiling. "I've heard tell Merle's partial to brownies. The gooey kind, not the cakes. No nuts." This time he did smile—a little. Then he paid for the two coffees and left.

Lena sank back into the chair, her mind reeling between brownies and bodies. The location of the body was an important distinction. It had been buried on the south side of the crossing on county land, not on her property, which began on the north side of the creek.

Thank God for small favors.

Lena covered her face. She was thanking God that a young man hadn't been buried on her property. He'd once been special to someone—a mom, a dad. Perhaps someone's lover. Whether a criminal or an innocent, he was now gone and never to return. She knew that loss. She'd moved over two hundred miles to escape the emptiness.

After a minute, she got up and dumped out the acidic coffee. Her body craved salt. Something to settle her stomach.

She lifted a silent hand to Thomas, the quiet, skinny kid with bad skin who manned the counter most days. He returned the wave, eyes following her as she turned toward the refrigerated doors in the back. Some deep-seated domestic gene—probably from her mother—sent her shopping for a dinner she didn't want.

After perusing the frozen food section and dismissing lasagna, fried chicken, and pizza, she grabbed a package of cured ham lunchmeat and some pepperjack cheese, then snagged a loaf of whole wheat bread, a bag of Fritos, and a six-pack of Diet Pepsi.

Not much of a dinner, but at least the whole wheat had a token health component. The Fritos fulfilled the salt need, and reminded her of hot summer days when nothing tasted better than a ham sandwich slathered with yellow mustard and crushed corn chips. A little weird, maybe.

She drew a breath as she realized she'd have to pass the creek crossing on her way home. Juggling the items in her arms, she grabbed a brownie mix and a package of chocolate covered donuts, then headed for the checkout. The donuts would be her reward for making it back to safety—if there was such a place.

Only the barest glow on the western horizon told Teal she was still heading the right direction, and she stumbled regularly on the rocky trail. The spreading oaks had provided welcome shade during the day, but now they shielded most of the stars, and the moon had yet to make an appearance.

A low-hanging branch poked her face, and she brushed it aside. It was far too dark to hike now, and she should have set up camp twenty minutes ago. But what choice did she have? Water was a priority, and she hadn't found so much as a muddy puddle all afternoon. She shivered as a cold wind skittered oak leaves up the path, and crickets chirped happily.

Teal shifted her backpack straps onto slightly less raw areas, but lost her balance. Her toe caught an exposed rock at the side of the trail, and she pitched headlong onto the dirt.

"Ow." She rolled onto her back and sat up, cradling her throbbing left arm. While she unbuttoned the cuff and rolled up the soft flannel, she surveyed her surroundings. Shadowy trees against a cobalt sky, and a darker line where the dirt path cut through grass. That was it. In a few minutes, she'd be hiking in total darkness.

Teal carefully folded the soft shirt material past her elbow. Luckily, the person she'd borrowed it from—okay, she'd stolen it—had been quite a bit bigger, so the sleeve was loose. She dug her iPod, Springsteen, out of her backpack and used its display light to inspect her skin. Blood seeped from two small abrasions. "*Hurts worse than it looks,*" her grandmother used to say. True enough. The cuts would heal—she was more concerned about the shirt since she didn't have another one with long sleeves. She sighed in relief as the music player's light didn't reveal any rips.

"Well, that's *one* thing that went right today, Springsteen." Of course, it would have been better if she hadn't taken the tumble in the first place. The player's light blinked off, and darkness closed in, more intense than thirty seconds ago.

She transferred the iPod to her left hand, slung the pack over her right shoulder, and got to her feet. Hiking with two fingers pressed against the wounds on her left elbow was awkward, but it would stop the bleeding and keep blood off her shirt. Not for the first time, she wished for a real flashlight, but by pressing the iPod's Click Wheel at regular intervals, it lit the path for a few feet. It was enough to keep her from running into trees and tripping over more rocks. Or worse, losing the trail altogether.

She didn't want to think about how long Springsteen's little battery would last without recharging. It had showed a full charge when she found it and a pair of ear buds stuffed in the shirt's pocket. Honestly, she meant to take only the shirt from where it was draped over the back of one of the stained plastic chairs at the bus station, but when she got far enough away from the building to slip it on, she found the pocket wasn't empty. Returning the device certainly wasn't an option—not unless she wanted to be introduced to a nice policeman. Plus, she needed the shirt. She felt bad for the guy who'd lost his music player, but what could she do? So she had inserted the tiny speakers in her ears and turned it on. The first song was The Boss wailing about being born to run. The song of her life. Right then, she'd named the iPod Springsteen.

After a few minutes of the strobe-effect hiking, Teal stopped. A distant shushing floated on the night air. Water? Immediately, her mouth turned drier—if possible. Her plastic bottle had run out shortly after her rest at the summit, and she'd sweated gallons picking her way through brush and boulders. Even though the temperature had dropped with the sun, it worried her that she had *stopped* sweating. Her head felt like a balloon bobbing at the end of a string tenuously attached to her neck.

She plowed ahead, willing the sound to get louder, frantic when it didn't. The western horizon was as dark as the other three now, but direction was no longer important. Water was all that mattered. She prayed the little light in her hand would hold out.

The path, nothing more than a deer trail for the last hour, became more defined. Others had traveled this way, pushing the stones aside and trampling the weeds. The track curved right, then dropped steeply downward as the water sounds grew. Teal released her elbow and held onto saplings as she descended. Moisture infused the dry mountain air, and the soil turned from dust to slick mud. She slipped from tree to tree as the splashing sounds increased. Too much for a creek.

A waterfall.

She couldn't tell if she was descending into a ravine or a parking lot, but she put her faith in the well-worn trail until it finally leveled off. The waterfall had become a modest, but consistent, roar. She wished she could see the source of the fragrant mist swirling in the iPod's glow, but the tiny light only penetrated a few feet before being swallowed up. She shone it at the ground and found beach ball-sized boulders on one side of the path. The falls lay that direction, and she set off, hopping from mound to mound.

The smell of moss and wet rocks drew her across the rock field until she spotted a small pool about a foot in diameter. Inky water flowed through the area, clear of debris. Teal balanced on two of the smooth stones and retrieved the empty Aquafina bottle from her pack.

The plastic crackled as she submerged it in the cold water. Before it was half full, she pulled it out and drank. Heaven—with a slightly fishy flavor. She wasn't complaining. It was cold, with a pure, sweet taste that the original contents of the store-bought bottle could only poorly mimic.

After another long drink, Teal did a final fill of the bottle before tottering back to the path. There, she scrounged the last granola bar from the side pocket of the pack, broke the bar in half, and carefully rewrapped the remaining part for tomorrow. She munched, chewing each nibble twenty times to squeeze out every calorie: 240 from a full bar, 120 from a half.

Now, with her tummy a little fuller with water and food, weariness dragged at her eyes. Her pack yielded a baby blanket, barely three-foot square and made of soft cotton, which she wrapped tightly around herself. Then, using the pack as a pillow, she lay down on the leaves beside the trail. With luck, she wouldn't be eaten by a cougar.

8

Lena started at dawn on Wednesday. It was the last push before her first renters arrived around noon Friday, and she couldn't wait for the big day. Neither could her bank account.

After the initial clean up of Cabin 5 for her own use, Lena's priority had been finishing the three nearest the lake in time for the summer rental season. They were already booked solid most of the summer, and their cash flow would power all the other projects.

By seven thirty, she had disconnected the rusted-out water heater in Cabin 4 and tilt-walked it out into the living area. She still had work to do on the first three cabins, but she wanted a clean slate on this one when she began serious work on it in a few days. The summer rental season didn't last long. The faster she made Cabin 4 habitable—and therefore, rentable—the faster she could build a financial pad for winter.

The final building, Cabin 6, hadn't been part of her original group. It was actually a tiny two-bedroom house she'd spotted while driving through Shelter Cove. It had been slated for demolition to make way for a bigger home. After some negotiation, she'd convinced the owner to sell it to her for a dollar and avoid the teardown cost. The timing had been terrible, what with all the other work she had to do, but fantastic deals like that didn't come along often. A house-moving company was far cheaper than building anything new. The distance had been minimal but, due to the seller's new house project, the move had to happen before she could rebuild the creek crossing. The moving company constructed a temporary stream crossing of railroad ties for their big truck, and now Cabin 6 sat on a new concrete pier foundation, uphill from the other five, awaiting complete renovation.

Lena plugged in her shop vacuum and sucked up a decade or two of dust in the tiny closet where the water heater had been, along with dead earwigs and some impressive dunes of termite granules. She pulled the folded spreadsheet checklist from her jeans pocket, smoothed it open, and drew lines through several items, then added *Call exterminator* to the bottom of the paper.

"It's only money." A sigh escaped her lips.

Over the next hours, she hoed, raked, painted porch railings, and amassed a teetering load of junk on the small trailer attached to the Jeep. Her stomach growled, reminding her she'd had only coffee for breakfast, but she ignored the hollowness.

She drove the Jeep and trailer up behind the barn to dump the load. After sweeping out the last of the debris, she slammed the trailer gate and wiped her brow with her shirtsleeve. The junk pile had grown impressively in the last three weeks, and she'd have to start making trips to the county landfill soon. But for now the stuff was out of sight from renters.

Lena pulled the empty trailer around to the front of the barn and unhitched it from the Jeep. Then she headed toward the lakeshore. Her compound of six cabins was located on Bass Point, one of the best fishing spots on the lake, and Desperation Falls was only a quarter-mile hike up the trail from her creek crossing. If she could ever get around to it, she could market the falls as another attraction for renters.

Skirting the towering oaks that rose over the compound, she walked down to Cabin 3, the farthest north along the shore. It sported a new roof of dark green shingles, thanks to handyman Colby Hartgrave. Lena checked her watch and saw it was past noon. Where had the day gone?

"And where did *you* go, Colby?" she wondered to the trees. He'd promised to arrive by eleven today. Either the fish were biting somewhere, or he was nursing last night's hangover from too many rounds at The Fish Hook, the locals' hangout bar across the lake in Deer Cove. One thing about Colby, you could count on not counting on him.

Lena stared around the dusty compound. He was supposed to bring a truck with a dozen wine barrel halves to use as planters to add some color to the endless dark green and tan of the area. Colby did good work when he showed up. More importantly, he was cheap, often doing small jobs for a home cooked dinner and half a pie. Lena wasn't much of a cook, but Colby liked store-bought desserts just fine.

A rumble drew her attention, and a large flatbed truck came over the hill, billowing dust behind and above in a sunlit halo. It squealed to a stop in the center of the compound, and Colby hopped out. Lena kicked herself for thinking badly of the man.

"Hey, boss." He grinned and hooked a thumb toward the back of the truck. "Got what we needed. Come take a look." Just under six feet tall, Colby couldn't weigh more than a hundred and fifty pounds, and had a half-starved vibe about him. Only the bony protrusions of his hips prevented his jeans from pooling around his ankles. But he had a wiry strength, and could work circles around others his age, which had to be somewhere north of forty.

Lena followed him around the back of the flatbed. Her heart sank when she counted at least twenty half barrels stacked on and around a giant mountain of planting soil. Several flats of various flowers and small shrubs ringed the mound.

"Colby, I can't afford all—"

"Don't worry about it, AJ. I got a steal on this stuff."

She hoped not literally. Although Colby *did* have a reputation, she'd never known him to be anything but honest with her. He rolled the half barrels to the end of the truck bed, and Lena manhandled them to the ground. They reeked of fermented wine and oak, and must have come straight from a nearby winery.

Colby didn't mention yesterday's news of the man's body and Lena sent up a thankful prayer. She couldn't bear to rehash it all again. She was glad to have Colby around today. Living past the end of the road all by herself got a little creepy, especially at night.

"I'll have these spread out and planted in a couple of hours, don't you worry," Colby enthused. He'd taken a particular ownership in her project, and she wished she could afford him for more work.

For the next half hour, Lena helped him bore drain holes in the bottoms of the barrels. Then they hand-trucked the barrels around the property, placing pairs at the bottom of the cabin steps or at the corners of the buildings. The remaining barrels bookended the simple benches she had built under four majestic oaks. She left him to the planting and headed to her cabin for something to eat.

She fixed a sandwich and sat on her porch to eat, but guilt wouldn't let her relax with Colby wheelbarrowing loads of topsoil around the property.

Besides, the food tasted like sand. Better than last night's dinner, though, which had threatened to come back up a few times. Pushing that memory aside, she fixed Colby a sandwich, then headed for Cabin 3.

Ten minutes later, Lena swore as the pipe wrench slipped again and she banged her knuckles. She wriggled farther into the cabinet below the kitchen sink, contorting her bruised back as she reset the wrench. Stinky plumbing was her least favorite job. Although it had seemed fine when she'd turned on the water a few weeks ago, the old metal p-trap had rusted through at the bottom and now dripped. The hot water she'd run through it when cleaning had probably washed out some grease plugging the holes.

The fitting gave way, and the pipes literally fell apart in her hands, but not before splattering her face with reeking gunk.

She scooted out and wiped black, stringy stuff off her face. The parts list was growing longer by the hour, but it wasn't nearly as bad as many she'd carried through the front door of Brodie's Hardware in Perilous Cove on an almost daily basis these last few months. Old man Brodie practically danced a jig whenever he spotted Lena drive into his parking lot.

"Probably bought his new bass boat by now on what I've paid him," she muttered as she walked to her Jeep. Brodie was an avid fisherman. He'd be motoring to her dock any day now. He'd better bring her some fish.

"What was that?" Colby asked, from where he was shoveling planting mix into a wheelbarrow.

"Nothing," she sang over her shoulder and swung into the Wrangler. "Heading to the hardware store."

She turned the ever-present ignition key and cranked the motor to life before she'd fully settled in the seat. Twenty-five minutes round trip to Perilous Cove, then another fifteen to find everything in the store that hadn't been inventoried since the Eisenhower administration. Add another half hour if Stan Billows was working, which he always seemed to be. The man could talk for days, and felt it his place to instruct Lena on how to do a "man's job" fixing whatever project she had, then offering to come up and do it for her. He always said she could pay him in—wink, wink—barter.

"As if." Lena swung the Jeep around and sprayed gravel as she gunned it over the hill toward the new crossing. One more innuendo from Mr. Stan Billows and she'd use a pipe wrench on his parts. She smiled at that pleasant thought, and shook out her hair in the buffeting wind.

Teal woke to the most beautiful sight ever. She'd been shivering in her thin blanket with her head tucked inside her cotton hoodie, pretending to be warm and cozy during the pre-dawn chill. Then the sun rose over the eastern hill, and light rays danced off the tumble of water that plunged down sheer rocks for fifty feet or more before landing in a swimming pool-sized grotto. A zillion ferns sprouted from the rocks at the edges of the drop, the tips of their fronds batted playfully by the falling droplets. Hummingbirds flitted to and fro, hovering momentarily at flowers that covered the damp earth on the sides of the pool, before darting away at bullet speeds. Bees staggered between plants, so drunk with pollen they could barely fly, and dragonflies investigated every flower and rock. One even buzzed Teal's face before deeming her unimportant.

At first she couldn't move. To think she'd been sleeping all night within a stone's throw of this incredible beauty. It reminded her of a Disney movie she'd seen once—Snow White, maybe?—where singing birds tied the ribbon around the girl's waist or hair. It seemed like a long time ago. A shiver shook her, but not from the night's cold. It *was* a long time ago. A lifetime.

A few minutes later, she was standing barefoot in knee-deep shallows with her jeans rolled up. The center of the pool disappeared into unknown, greenish-black depths, and the cool water soothed her raw toes and heels. It would be agony to put her shoes on again for today's hike. Goose bumps ran up her arms and down her spine, but she removed her shirt and quickly washed, scrubbing off the previous days' sweat. She'd never take a hot shower for granted again—not that she'd had that many since walking away from the last foster home many weeks ago.

The parents hadn't been too bad. Teal even liked the psychologist they'd taken her to a couple of times to help with her "traumatic event." One of the other kids at the house was kind of grossed out when she first saw Teal's scars, but that was nothing compared to the school's gym teacher at the start of Teal's third week in the new school.

Disregarding the note Teal had on file, the woman insisted Teal dress in a T-shirt and shorts that day like the other girls, then shower with them. When the last period bell rang and Teal walked into the hall, at least fifty kids turned and stared at her, the new freak.

The next morning, every kid in front of the school stood watching her walk across the lawn toward the entrance. Teal had turned around, packed her things at the house while the parents were at work, and hitched a ride out of town with a sympathetic college girl driving a rusty VW. Unfortunately, while Teal napped, the girl had turned north on the 101 which ran inland at that point instead of going up the coast route like Teal expected.

As Teal squeegeed water off with the edge of her hand, a sun-dappled grassy clearing not far from where she'd slept caught her eye. She hobbled over, spread out the blanket, and pulled a small sketch pad and colored pencils from her backpack. She'd found the art supplies at a church rummage sale for seventy-five cents, part of the money she'd collected panhandling at a Walmart parking lot exit until the regular resident showed up and ran her off. It was just as well. If a cop had come by and realized how young she was, she'd have been back in foster care before dinner.

Beginning at the center of the paper, Teal drew the waterfall as it curled over a wide rock lip before free-falling smooth as a sheet of plastic wrap to the pool. The last of the granola bar disappeared in an instant, but she pushed hunger aside as she added the ferns, trees, and the shallows of the boulder field she'd discovered last night.

Hypnotizing light danced across the paper as the sun rose higher and filtered through the leaves overhead, warming her body after the cold night and bath. She finally gave into her drooping eyelids and stretched out on the blanket, listening to the buzzing insects as the heated air released the flowers' scent. Sleeping when warm was the best.

9

Lena dusted off her jeans and headed up the three plank stairs to the rental cabin's porch. The space was just large enough for the two rustic rocking chairs she'd found at a yard sale, and they were a luxury she wished she had for her own porch. She sank into one and set it moving. The westerly view across Storm Lake spread out before her like an oil painting, framed by pines and oaks. A pair of ducks made a running takeoff, dripping water as they headed north. She loved the hypnotic rhythm of wavelets lapping against the rocky shore a mere one hundred feet away.

Man, she was tired, but it felt good. She was working for herself, and tomorrow—Friday of Memorial Day weekend—was her first payday.

Her property. She still pinched herself once in a while.

It had been a busy morning. Colby had come and gone, delivering the last bed frames and mattresses for the three rental cabins. The propane kitchen stove in Cabin 3 had required partial disassembly to clean properly. She'd picked years of dried food from the burner orifices, and cursed the slobs who'd used it over the decades—exactly why she'd instituted a cleaning fee in her contracts. Then she'd scrubbed the kitchens and bathrooms in the first three cabins a final time until the surfaces shone.

The main floors still had to be mopped, but they were almost ready for occupancy. She'd made her deadline.

Lena closed her eyes for a minute, listening to the distant sounds of birds, chittering squirrels, and outboard motors. She had work to do, but it was heaven to relax for a few minutes. She propped her feet on the porch rail and got the rocker going again. The curved wood bumped over the rough porch boards in a steady rhythm, and the heat of the May day massaged sweet fragrance from the oaks. Bottle that and she could make millions.

"This how you prepare for paying customers, AJ?"

Startled from her impromptu nap, Lena cracked an eye, then sighed. A cowboy, complete with straw hat, stood on the bottom step silhouetted by the sun.

"Roarke. You're interrupting my well-earned siesta." She closed her eyes and kicked the chair into motion again. The slight vertigo reminded her of swinging at a playground while tilting her head back as far as she could. It felt daring when she was a little girl, and comforting now. She didn't want this man to intrude when she was lapsing into happy nostalgia.

The step boards creaked and the other rocker began rolling back and forth with a clunkity-clunk, clunkity-clunk on the boards. She kept her eyes closed and concentrated on her own motion.

"New creek crossing looks good. Told you Merle would do a fine job."

It wasn't a question, so she felt no need to respond. Anyway, Roarke talked enough for the both of them.

"The word's out about Merle finding the body."

That wasn't a question either.

"Came to invite you to dinner."

Another non-question, but this one demanded a response. Cracking an eye, she took in his profile. She'd met him one night a couple of months ago when she was getting takeout at The Crab Shack in Deer Cove. He'd introduced her to a few of the other locals while she waited for her order, then convinced her to stay and eat with him. She learned Roarke Hamilton was single and thirty-two, two years her junior. She didn't date younger men. Or older ones, for that matter. And after finding a dead body, who felt like going on a date?

Lena opened her mouth to tell him what to do with his invitation, but his next words stopped her.

"Gran wants you to come over tomorrow night."

Lena's eyes were drawn to the far shore. His grandmother, Olivia Hamilton, lived almost directly across the lake in a beautiful Craftsman style home built many years ago by her deceased husband, John. Roarke had told her all about it. Lena had only seen it from the road, but it looked like the kind of home where people raised families and grew old—sturdy, comfortable, and safe. Lena appreciated safe.

"Tomorrow's not good. Can we do it next week?" she asked rolling her head on the chair back so she could see him.

"She wants you to meet some people, and they're coming tomorrow night."

She might be able to refuse Roarke with his too-good looks, but Mrs. H, as everyone called her, had been super nice to Lena when she'd first arrived. They'd met at the grocery store in Deer Cove, and another time when young Quin Conner brought Mrs. H over in his motorboat to check out Lena's new dock. A one-woman welcoming committee for the community, the old lady had brought Tupperware containers of fried chicken, potato salad, and raspberry truffle. It fed Lena for three days. She wondered if Mrs. H would have more of the truffle at the dinner.

But tomorrow was Friday, with renters arriving at noon. Everything had to be ready. The curtain rod in the bedroom of Cabin 3 threatened to fall any second, glazing putty still stained a number of new window panes, and she had a pile of old roofing materials behind this cabin to clean up. Still had those floors to mop, too. All that had to be done today or tomorrow morning. When Friday night arrived, Lena planned on collapsing into bed at dark. She opened her mouth to decline, but Roarke lowered the killing blow.

"Plus, she has a favor to ask of you."

Rats. She rolled her head back in his direction. The corner of his mouth turned up in a lopsided smile, way too sweet to actually be so.

She tried not to grumble. "Time?"

"Five thirty." All innocent eyes and smile.

That was two-thirds through her eighteen-hour workday, but at least it was early enough she wouldn't fall asleep and face-plant into her dinner plate.

She'd have to make sure her guests were settled in and had everything they needed, shower, then leave time to drive all the way around the lower part of the lake and up the other side. She wished the road around the north end had remained open; that route would be a lot shorter, but storms years ago had washed out several sections. The county planners deemed it too expensive to keep open for the few who would use it. That was why she'd had to repair her own creek crossing—it was past the end of the maintained road. A few weeks ago she'd driven her Jeep north until she came across a section with three-foot deep ruts. She didn't dare go farther without bumper-mounted winches and someone who knew how to use them.

Roarke's chair rocked rapidly as he rose.

Lena squinted at him in the glare. "Tell your grandmother I'll be there by six thirty—that's about the best I can do."

Roarke tipped his straw hat at her, descended the stairs and strode across the yard. She tilted her head for a better view of how the jeans hugged his tight rear. Tall and lean, the man certainly had confidence. He pivoted and caught her looking. A grin deepened his dimples as he cocked his hand in a facsimile of a pistol and fired at her, complete with blowing smoke off his upturned index finger. He touched the brim of his hat again before continuing to his truck.

Disgusted with herself, Lena pushed out of the chair. She had work to do. No time for wannabe cowboys. He'd probably never been on a horse.

As she watched his truck drive away, she kicked herself for not having him help her move the old water heater out of Cabin 4.

"What you get for being distracted, girl."

Teal rolled on her back and stretched, arms above her head, twisting one way, then the other. The sun had reached its zenith and graced the grassy ground with yellow blotches. The second night at the falls had given her muscles a needed rest, and her rehydrated body thanked her. She sighed, knowing that, as beautiful as this was, she couldn't stay. Her stomach was concaved against her spine like a deflated volleyball. Or maybe more like a squashed walnut. She'd seen a special on TV about starvation once, and it said people who were starving lost their sense of hunger. It wasn't long after that they died. She wasn't quite there yet, but couldn't afford another day on a water diet or she'd be a headline in a local newspaper: *Girl's Skeleton Found in Mountains.*

She stood and tightened the belt of her jeans to its last notch, but they still hung loose on her hipbones. She had to find some food. For the next half-hour she searched the overgrown waterhole area again, but ultimately concluded edible berries must not like the moisture. Or maybe bears ate them all.

Time to move on.

Gingerly, she pulled on her tennis shoes and laced them. She stuffed her few belongings in the pack and took a last look at her waterfall. If life was fair she could build a little cabin right at the water's edge, just big enough for her, and live happily ever after. Maybe she'd adopt a dog for company. Two strays.

With a sigh, she turned away from the beautiful sight, and headed down what was obviously a maintained trail. That meant the falls were a popular destination. And *that* meant people, cars, and food.

Prepared for a full day of hiking, a mere fifteen minutes later Teal emerged from a group of scrub oak that gave way to a small clearing where the trail split. The main trail, which had paralleled the stream, angled left and led across a skinny, rickety-looking footbridge of mismatched planks and a single railing along the downstream side. The path on the right leg of the Y headed away from the stream. It was less defined, and grass sprouted in the packed earth. A redwood signpost marked the trail with an arrow pointing the direction she'd come from. *Desperation Falls 0.25 mi.* It gave no indication what lay the other direction.

The waterfall was so beautiful, Teal wondered why the ominous name. *Butterfly Falls* made more sense. Except, she *had* been desperate. The water had saved her life.

She debated whether to cross the bridge. If there was a parking area, it must be deserted. There were no people on the trail she'd come down. She pivoted toward the less traveled path and spotted a rustic barn through the trees. And there appeared to be cabins a bit farther.

Food, or at least the possibility. Her stomach growled and she patted it. "Just a little longer." Decision made, she turned away from the bridge.

Teal passed the barn and headed toward the cabins. That's where the food would be. The closest one, uphill from the others, sat on a fresh concrete block foundation, the ground circling it scraped and bare. The siding was made of rough shingles, many of which were hanging crookedly by one nail or missing entirely. Only the frame of one window remained, and two others had missing panes. It looked like a teardown to Teal. Surely no one lived in it.

While circling the structure, she noticed sun sparkling through the oaks off distant water. The Pacific Ocean? The uphill breeze carried none of the salty scents she expected. The air was bone dry, and smelled of oak and sage. No, this had to be a lake. She didn't remember one from the map, but maybe this was a community where she could score something to eat.

On that hope, Teal's stomach rumbled to life, bringing a wave of dizziness so strong it forced her to lean against the splintered shingles and catch her breath. She sipped some more water, waiting for the lightheadedness to pass. It did, but the liquid didn't satisfy her body's need.

"If I was a contestant on Biggest Loser, I could so win right now."

Teal steadied herself with one hand against the crumbling siding as she walked to the cabin's doorless rear entry. No stairs, but a rock the size of a basketball had been positioned in their place. She balanced on it and stepped onto the enclosed porch. Except for dirt and dust, the area was empty. A flimsy paneled door with a window in the top half lay directly ahead, leading to the main part of the cabin. Teal placed one finger against the glass, and the door swung open. The silence of disuse greeted her, and she crept down the narrow hall on creaking boards.

The first door on the right appeared to be a bedroom, cozy enough for a twin bed and dresser, but that was about all. The room's window opened onto the back porch. Across the hall was another, larger bedroom, and a couple steps farther down the hall revealed a bathroom—or what had once been one. Nothing remained except holes in the floor. Waist-high, yellow tile paneling ran around each wall, notched where a wall-mounted sink had once been. Bits of the yellow surface had chipped off, and brown fiberboard showed through. Everything had water stains and smelled rotten. Teal backed out.

The hall opened into the main area at the front of the building, where Teal could envision a small living room. The room was bare, except for a dusty brick hearth where a woodstove would normally sit. Blue sky shone through the round hole above the hearth. A tiny kitchen with a few cabinets occupied the right side, with enough room for a dining table with a view out the front window. The lake sparkled through the streaked glass.

Someone was probably going to fix up the old place, but there weren't tools and materials around like they were working on it now. Maybe she could sneak a night or two in the bedroom near the back door while she scouted the surrounding area. The covered front porch had four new stairs leading down to a graveled yard, so anyone coming to the cabin would likely enter that way, giving her time to hop out the back and hide in the trees.

Teal exited the way she'd come in, and then walked toward the three buildings closer to the lake, staying in the afternoon shadows and peeking around corners as she moved from cabin to cabin. No one was around, but an old Jeep sat by one of the cabins, keys dangling from the ignition switch. Large barrels of newly planted flowers showed that someone cared for the place.

She was almost to the stairs of one cabin near the lake when a booted foot shoved a rolling mop bucket out the open door, slopping water on the plank front porch. Teal scampered around the corner of the building, heart hammering as she listened to the water drip through the cracks of the porch and splatter in the dust below.

Don't get caught. Not again.

A small rivulet of soapy water made a snaking path from under the porch, the ground so dry the water seemed to pass over without wetting it.

A woman backed into view. She had blonde hair secured in a high ponytail, dangling silver and turquoise earrings against tanned skin, and wore jeans and a plaid work shirt with long sleeves rolled up. Sweat streamed down her face. Teal watched as the woman mopped her way out the opening, and then closed the door. Without even stopping to catch her breath, she hoisted the bucket and nearly ran for the cabin next door.

"She must be getting paid by the job," Teal muttered to herself, as she watched the woman climb the other cabin's steps and carry the bucket inside. Teal relaxed against the side of the building while she gathered some strength, then hurried back up the hill to hide and watch from the seclusion of a low-hanging tree.

After a couple of hours, the blonde woman used the hood of the Jeep as a desk as she scratched notes on a legal pad. Then she climbed in and drove away.

It was a little after four o'clock, but the sun was still high. Teal left her concealment and peered in the windows of each cabin while keeping an eye out for anyone else who might surprise her. The three buildings closest to the water had curtains, furniture, and beds with sheets and blankets folded neatly in their centers. Carved signs by the front doors showed them to be Cabin 1, Cabin 2, and Cabin 3, and she realized they must be rentals. That's why the woman was cleaning them. The first cabin where Teal had seen the woman had two twin beds. What Teal wouldn't give for a night on one of those soft mattresses on painted metal frames.

She explored another structure labeled Cabin 4 that had a round water heater standing in the middle of the bare living room. Two of the wooden windows had been removed from their frames and leaned against the inside wall, and paint cans and roller trays were stacked on the kitchen counter. It definitely had a ways to go before it was ready for use, but clearly someone was working on it.

Cabin 5 was much more interesting. Unlike the others, it appeared someone lived in it. However, with its mismatched curtains, it wasn't quite as put together as the three cabins closest to the lake—like this one got the leftovers. Teal wasn't sure the chair on the porch would support even her skinny behind.

Through the window, Teal saw a coffeemaker and toaster next to a dish rack, and the small stove had a chipped yellow teakettle on one burner. Near the front corner window, a round table with two chairs was covered with a white tablecloth. A napkin holder and salt and pepper shakers stood next to a single placemat. Teal wondered if the woman lived in this one by herself. Or maybe someone else lived here. She would have to keep a close lookout.

A twisting cramp wrapped around her stomach, and sweat popped out on her forehead as she doubled over panting. She needed food. Now.

She staggered to the rear of the cabin and had her hand on the porch's screen door when she heard the growl of an engine and crunching gravel. The red Jeep came into view, bouncing on the bumpy road as the woman wheeled it directly toward Teal.

She crouched on the single back stair and hugged the wall as the car angled toward the front of the cabin and skidded to a halt out of view. Teal scampered up the hill toward the barn and slipped around the corner. The back of the Jeep was in view, and a second later the woman opened the rear door and lifted out a grocery bag. She slammed the door and disappeared toward the front of the cabin. Even from this distance, Teal heard the woman stamping her feet—probably to get the dust off. The screen door opened with a screech, and closed with a bang.

Teal sank against the old barn while she imagined the woman pulling fresh fruit, salad fixings, onions, and hamburger from the grocery sack. She'd chop the onion before sautéing it in butter, then crumble in the meat along with some taco seasoning. In no time, she'd be sitting down at her table with the single place setting, enjoying taco salad, complete with sour cream, chunky salsa, and salty tortilla chips.

Tears stung Teal's eyes as she clutched her stomach and backed along the side of the barn, away from the cabin. She'd spend the night at the falls again.

Food would have to wait.

10

Lena started at sunrise Friday, sweeping the porches, raking the yards, watering the flower barrels, and checking her computer database one more time. At eleven thirty, she scrubbed the worst of the sweat and dirt off her face and arms, combed her hair, then nearly went stir crazy while waiting for the first renters.

She couldn't believe this day had finally arrived. Months of planning and hard work. And today was payday. None too soon, either, after balancing her last bank statement. She wasn't broke—yet—but man, the money sure flowed out in a hurry.

The noise of a car filtered through the screen door and Lena jumped to her feet. She reached for the door handle, then held herself back long enough for the vehicle to stop and the dust settle. "Don't appear too anxious." She practiced an easy smile in the mirror by the door before pushing open the screen and stepping outside.

The driver door of a Ford Explorer towing a boat and trailer swung open, and a middle-age man climbed out. He stretched with his hands on the small of his back, and looked toward the lake.

"Hello," Lena called as she descended the steps and went around the front of the Ford. "I'm AJ Blaylock."

"Ned Arnold," the man said, stepping forward with a smile to shake hands. "This is a great spot you have here."

"Thanks."

"I've been coming up to the lake for years, but this is the first time with my son."

Lena followed Ned's gaze through the bug-splattered windshield where a young-teen boy sat hunched over something.

"Brandon. Turn off that Nintendo and come out here."

With exaggerated reluctance, the black-haired youth shouldered the door open and climbed out, electronic game clutched firmly in his hand.

"Hi, Brandon," Lena said, holding out her hand. "I'm AJ." The boy shook her hand with a shockingly limp effort. For a second, Lena was afraid she'd hurt him, but he seemed not to notice.

"Do you have high-speed Internet here?" he asked.

"Brandon—" his father began.

"Nope," Lena jumped in. "Even my dialup is iffy."

"Cell service?"

"Depends on the carrier," Lena answered.

"Verizon?" the boy asked hopefully.

Lena shook her head. "Sorry."

"We're not here to play games and surf the Internet, Brandon," the father interjected.

It was obvious this outing wasn't the son's idea. Lena wondered why it had taken so many years for the father to bring his son on a fishing trip. Then again, her own father hadn't exactly been the nurturing type. Lena gave herself a mental shake and gestured downhill.

"Come on. Let me show you to your cabin." They were booked in the middle cabin, number two, and she led them that direction. "There's a parking area up past Cabin 3 where the boat ramp is. I can help if you need a hand with your launch."

Lena led the way up Cabin 2's steps and inside. She showed them the kitchen and cooking gear, the heater controls, then handed over the key and asked if they had any questions.

"Do you have a barbecue grill?" Ned asked, then chuckled. "Just in case we catch something and want to cook it up."

Lena blanched. How could she have forgotten the barbecue? It had been on her list when she went to Brodie's Hardware last week, but they'd been out of any of the models she'd wanted. Colby had even leveled a spot for it, laid down pavers, and stacked firewood.

She apologized to the Arnolds, promising the grill for Saturday. A car horn tooted. The next guests had arrived.

As Lena hurried up the hill, her cell phone rang and she answered it, hoping it was another booking.

"Hello, Lena?" the booming voice said. "It's Chet Marquette. I—" Voices sounded in the background, and the call grew muffled, as if Chet were holding the microphone against his shirt.

"Chet? Can you hear me?" Lena asked, stopping in the shade of one of the oaks. Someone's loud voice came through, but she couldn't make out what they were saying. Suddenly, the line became clear.

"Lena? I'll have to call you back. Something's come up, and these idiots can't go to the crapper without me holding their hands. Talk to you later."

"Chet, what's..." But the line was dead.

Chet was Bobby's old coworker in the district attorney's office. He had a few years of both age and experience on Bobby, and the two men had worked together on several cases while Bobby learned the ropes. They'd had a bit of a falling out after Bobby became the office golden boy, informally tagged as next in line by the retiring DA. Now Chet was up for that top spot.

She hadn't heard from him since before Thanksgiving, and wondered if he had news about Bobby's case—his murder. Had they arrested someone?

The car horn tooted again, and Lena tucked the phone in her pocket. She had to get these new arrivals and the final renters settled, then clean up and head for Mrs. Hamilton's.

And find a barbecue grill by tomorrow. She hoped Chet would call back soon.

"Hello, AJ," Olivia Hamilton said, as she opened the door. She drew Lena inside. "I'm so glad you could come. I know it's a busy time for you." Mrs. H wore a khaki pantsuit with a wide brown belt around her matronly waist. A pith helmet would have set her in the middle of Africa, ready for a safari. From her ears dangled shoulder dusters made of red feathers that matched the red high-top sneakers poking from under the pant cuffs. Lena had to smile. The woman was one of a kind.

Mrs. H closed the door and led Lena into the great room while inquiring how the new renters were settling in. She seemed to know all about Lena's operation, though they'd only met a couple of times.

The home was a rectangle, with the long wall opposite the front door facing a shallow slope and east across the lake where Lena's property lay. It was dark now, the glass reflecting the warm, woody interior of the house, but sunrise would be magnificent when watched from the bulky brown leather sofa situated to make the best of the view. Area rugs splashed color across dark hardwood floors, while table and floor lamps cast pools of inviting light. It was a place you could snuggle down with a good book by candlelight and watch a storm over the lake.

Voices to her left drew Lena's attention, and Mrs. H touched her arm. "Come into the kitchen. I want you to meet everyone."

Lena took a deep breath. One-on-one was okay, but groups—well, it had been a while since she'd last been in a social setting. Not since Bobby's funeral.

She rubbed her palms against her dark gray camouflage fatigues, self-conscious about her outfit. She'd found a blob of mud on her only black jeans when she'd pulled them out of the dresser, and there hadn't been time to wash them. The yellow-green sleeveless top set off her bronzed skin, so she looked decent from the waist up. Maybe if she stayed behind a counter or sat down.

Besides, people around the lake never dressed up. That suited Lena. Although she'd been supportive of Bobby's career and accompanied him to business and social gatherings in Los Angeles, she had never felt comfortable in that pretentious world where everyone was "on."

She let out a breath as they stepped into the kitchen.

"Everyone, I'd like you to meet AJ Blaylock," Mrs. H said, stepping to the side and urging Lena forward.

Lena fought the urge to duck her head and run for the nearest exit. She'd spent months in strategic disappearance mode, and here she was, revealed to a room of strangers. She forced her head up and concentrated on Mrs. H.

"You know Quin, of course," Mrs. H said, and Lena followed the woman's eyes. Quin Conner was perched on a barstool, stuffing a corn chip and huge glob of salsa into his mouth. Lena had to smile as he nearly choked trying to swallow and say hello at the same time. He was about seventeen and looked like he'd recently passed that gangly growing phase boys went through. His skin was more deeply tanned than hers, and his shoulders showed the beginnings of a muscular frame.

Mrs. H pointed to a man and woman. "And these are his parents, Ben and Rayne Conner."

Lena stepped forward and extended her hand, hoping her palm wouldn't betray her nervousness.

"It's good to meet you, AJ." Ben Conner had trimmed blond hair, crinkly blue eyes, and a handshake that spoke of manual labor. He wore jeans and a chambray work shirt. He was tall, over six feet, and handsome.

But it was his wife, Rayne, who captured Lena's attention. Her auburn hair with red and black highlights hung past her shoulders in a glorious, softly curled cascade. This mass of color contrasted with porcelain skin and striking, cool green eyes. She was nearly as tall as her husband, and imbued her dark jeans and T-shirt with a sophistication that few others could have achieved. Rayne exuded confidence and grace in the simple way she extended her hand. Three wavy lines of a tattoo covered the inside of her right wrist, and the strength of her grip surprised Lena.

"Rayne is a musician and singer," Mrs. H said. "You'll hear her later this summer, after she and Ben return from Europe and her tour. Quite the star over there, you know."

Since Lena *didn't* know, she raised her eyebrow in question, and was rewarded with a bit of embarrassment on Rayne's part as Mrs. H gushed.

"Just some follow-up dates with my old band," Rayne Conner dismissed. "It's good to meet you, AJ." Quin grinned openly at Rayne, clearly proud of his mother's career. Lena looked back and forth between the boy and woman. They looked nothing alike. Quin looked nothing like Ben Conner, either. Interesting.

The back door from what Lena assumed was the garage banged open, and they all turned as a young woman strode in holding a grocery sack. "Steaks and veggies for the grill. Got it going yet, Ben?"

"That's *Uncle* Ben to you, young lady," Ben growled, but the corners of his mouth quirked. "And yes, the grill's hot. Thought the fire'd go out before you got back."

The young woman shot him a look as she deposited the bag on the counter, then turned and spotted Lena. "Hi. You must be AJ. I'm Amanda Conner," she said in a deep alto that reminded Lena of late night radio DJs, the ones you imagined sitting in a glass room high over the city, alone in their dimly lit world of microphones and music players, imparting provocative wisdom between mellow tunes. "But you can call me Mandy, because we're going to be great friends."

That was kind of different, but Lena found herself smiling back at the black-haired beauty who matched Rayne and Ben for height. Even without the "uncle" comment, the resemblance was evident in the broad mouth and wide-set eyes. Lena, even at her respectable five-seven, felt like a shrimp next to this clan.

A sliding door in the great room slammed shut. A gust of cool air spilled through the kitchen door, followed by Roarke Hamilton smelling of wood smoke as he rubbed his hands together.

"Getting cold out there." He spotted Lena. "Well, it's my favorite woman. Hi, AJ," he said and, before she could backpedal, enveloped her in a smoky embrace that lasted a couple beats too long. It was broken by someone clearing her throat. Roarke stepped back.

Mandy stood with arms crossed, brows together, and foot tapping the plank floor. "I thought *I* was your favorite woman, Roarke Hamilton." Mandy's glare could have boiled ice—after freezing it in the first place.

Roarke didn't miss a beat and spread his arms out wide at Mandy. "Babe," he grinned at the girl and stepped forward to hug her as well. "No, you're my *special* woman." Fast as a striking rattler, Mandy cocked her right arm and punched him in the stomach. He doubled over with a groan and slipped to the floor.

Lena's mouth fell open. She didn't know whether to help Roarke, who seemed in genuine pain, or stand shoulder-to-shoulder with Mandy against the cad. She was leaning toward the latter when Mrs. H took her arm.

"Stop it, you two," Mrs. H said, addressing Mandy and the downed Roarke. "You're like children. AJ doesn't know you're playing around."

"Who's playing?" Mandy arched a brow. She toed Roarke, then grinned and offered him a hand. He took it, and she yanked him to his feet. She stepped close to him, hands still gripped between them. "*Next time I won't pull my punch,*" she whispered just loud enough for Roarke, Lena, and Mrs. H to hear.

Roarke massaged his stomach with his left hand. "You pulled it? Dang, girl," he squeezed her bicep. "You been working out?"

Mandy playfully shoved him away and winked at Lena. Then to Roarke: "Come on, weakling, let's get these steaks on the fire." Roarke grabbed the packages of meat. Mandy unhooked a long barbecue fork from the end of a cabinet and threatened to poke him in the rear to get him moving toward the outside deck.

Lena looked around to see what the others made of the pair's antics. Ben and Rayne paid no attention to the two, lost in their own world of whispered conversation, and Quin shoveled in another load of salsa. Lena smiled weakly at Mrs. H. This was clearly unlike the L.A. crowds she and Bobby used to hang with, where business cards were more prevalent than cocktail napkins.

Lena's nervousness had evaporated while watching Mandy and Roarke spar, and she took a deep breath, rolling her shoulders. Then she stopped breathing altogether as a man stepped forward from where he'd been hidden from view on the other side of the refrigerator. He had close-cut brown hair, hard eyes that took her in with a head-to-foot sweep, and a face that looked like someone had taken the flat of a shovel to it—more than once. This was a man who'd lived a hard life. Or still did.

Mrs. H smiled between Lena and the new man. "AJ Blaylock, I'd like you to meet Alex Stone."

The instant Lena's eyes met Alex Stone's, she thought, *cop*.

Or at least law enforcement of some kind. Former military if the cut of his hair and muscular arms were any indication. Maybe it was the firm set of his jaw, but his presence unnerved her.

Bobby had made several friends in the police and sheriff's department. They were good people. Oh, maybe a few were adrenaline junkies, but most were careful in their jobs, making sure they and their partners got home safely each night. The ones that *wanted* to go home, that is. Lena shook off her childhood, and focused on the man before her.

Everything about Alex Stone warned of danger, from the way his biceps threatened the fabric of his black T-shirt, to his trim waist that was probably used to carrying a weapon concealed under a jacket. Based on his battered face, he was obviously a fighter, choosing confrontation over negotiation.

Still, there was something compelling about his dark eyes, the way they scanned her features from hair to chin, then lingered on her mouth. If there had been a sketch artist handy, Lena had no doubt Alex Stone could have given a perfect description of her. She reminded herself to breathe.

Lena knew before she accepted his outstretched hand it was a bad idea. She should have backed two steps out of the kitchen and fled to her Jeep. However, doing that and maintaining any semblance of decorum seemed remote, and she didn't want to hurt Mrs. H's feelings.

Still, it might have been the safer choice as Stone's hand wrapped around hers. It felt like a bricklayer's might, toughened by years of working with... well, stone. Hands told a lot about a person. They could be soft, hard, sweaty, sullied by white-collar crime, trembling, or rough.

Stone's were strong enough to kill.

It was a disconcerting thought to have when meeting someone for the first time, especially while still holding his hand. Lena stumbled out a *"Nice to meet you"* as she returned his grip. He nodded, quickly dropped her hand,

and stepped back. Lena opened her mouth to fill the awkward silence that ensued, but he turned away from her toward the Conners. His withdrawal created a vacuum that nearly sucked her forward.

"Ben, can I talk to you a minute?" Stone asked, his voice rumbling deeper than Merle's D2 Caterpillar. "I'd like a little more information about the lake area." Ben nodded and gave Rayne's hand a squeeze before following Alex Stone out of the room.

Though Rayne, Quin, and Mrs. H remained, the room felt empty with Stone gone, as if the cosmos had swiped a gray watercolor brush across the scene, muting the colors.

What in the—?

"Well," Mrs. H chirped a little too brightly, "would you two ladies care to help an old woman with the green bean casserole and the vegetables for the grill?"

Teal waited until near dark before leaving the safety of the trees. Lights shone from the three cabins closest to the water. She'd come down from the falls about noon, and watched for the next couple of hours as three vehicles towing boats arrived. Men had helped each other guide their trailers down the concrete ramp and launch the boats, then they'd parked the cars in the space north of Cabin 1. The vehicles were all locked—she'd checked.

Finally, the blonde woman had driven away late in the day. She'd left her front porch light on, which meant she expected to be back after dark. Teal peered in each of the cabin's rear windows before trying the back door. Unlocked.

"Trusting," she said, as she slipped inside. "Lucky for me." All the cabins had pretty much the same layout. Living, dining, and kitchen in the front, bathroom and one or two bedrooms at the rear. This one had only the single bedroom, and Teal passed it in the short hall on her way to the food.

The three kitchen drawers contained dishtowels, silverware, plastic baggies, and utensils, and the first two cupboards Teal checked held a sparse assortment of glasses, dishes, and pots and pans. The usual eggs, milk, lettuce, condiments, and various other things did little to fill the refrigerator. The woman lived a simple life.

Then Teal found the pantry.

It was a tiny space, only about two feet wide and a foot deep, but it held the treasure chest she'd been searching for. Her stomach rumbled at the smells of food emanating from the packages. Saltines, cookies, peanut butter, dried soup mix, a bag of Fritos. Cans of tomatoes, beans, and other foods were scattered about the shelves. She helped herself to a handful of the crackers, carefully replacing the twisty on the paper tube, turning it exactly the same way it had been.

When the salty square touched her tongue, saliva flooded her mouth so fast, she had to stuff the rest of the cracker in to keep from drooling down her front. She kept the mealy softness in her mouth for as long as she could, then let it slide down her throat to her impatient stomach. Nothing had ever tasted so good...except for the handful of Fritos she ate next. Wow! Were those good, or what?

She pilfered one of four remaining granola bars from an open box and put it in her backpack, then filled one of the Ziploc bags with the crackers. Into another baggie went a handful of Special K cereal. Evidently, the woman balanced the Fritos with healthy cereal.

The Oreo cookie package had only three remaining. Much as she wanted one, she couldn't chance it. But she did break off the edge of one wafer before she re-rolled the package end and replaced the plastic clip. The chocolate was heaven, and God was smiling on her. She found a half-full pack of Mother's Taffy cookies and removed two—then took a third one.

Canned food did her no good since she didn't have an opener, and she certainly couldn't take the one she'd found in the drawer. Maybe she could pick one up in town—if there was a town, and if she had some money. "If we had some bacon we could make bacon and eggs...if we had some eggs." Her school friend's mom, Jonelle, used to say that.

Teal caressed a can of beans, and started to turn away when she had an idea. She searched for the utility drawer. Every kitchen had one, and she found it at the far end of the counter. The old drawer dropped down when she pulled it out, and she barely caught it before the whole thing crashed to the linoleum floor. She let out a breath and propped the drawer with her knee while sorting through the miscellaneous spatulas, slotted spoons, tongs, batteries, ice picks, etc. Finally, she located what she wanted: a paring knife with a short, sturdy blade. It was so beat up, no one would miss it, and she could use it to open the cans.

With her new tool, Teal loaded her backpack with a small can of corn with the jolly green guy on the label. It had been somewhat hidden at the rear of the shelf—less likely to be missed. Vegetable soup coated with a layer of dust on top followed. She adjusted the remaining cans, spacing them out. Pleased with her new supplies, she went to search the rest of the house.

Unfortunately, the linen closet didn't yield a pile of extra blankets like she'd hoped. There was a thin one, but the woman would notice if it disappeared. Other than the blanket, the shelves held only an extra set of sheets and a blue bath towel with a green washcloth.

"Man, she's almost as poor as I am," Teal whispered. She just had to talk sometimes, even if it was only Springsteen listening. After checking the tiny bathroom—where she scored a toothbrush and sample-sized tube of toothpaste along with a roll of toilet paper—she peeked into two closets. A few clothes, three zipped garment bags with fancy dresses in them, half a dozen cowboy and baseball hats, work boots and sneakers, a vacuum cleaner, and broom. Teal shook her head. This was pathetic.

Back in the living room, Teal almost shouted for joy. On a worn maple end table was a small music player, complete with an iPod plugged into a wall charger. She fished Springsteen out of her knapsack and swapped him onto the charger.

"Here you go, boy. Juice up, 'cuz we don't know where the next meal will come from." She watched the battery indicator charging and dropped onto the old sofa—or rather into it. She sank nearly to the floor before the broken down cushion finally stopped her descent. But it was the softest thing she'd sat on in several days, and she closed her eyes and reveled in the cushy feeling. And it was clean, not covered in dirt and leaves.

How long did she have before the woman returned? An hour? Three? If Teal knew, she could warm the soup in the small microwave and have a hot meal. Not that cold bothered her. She'd grown used to eating or drinking everything at the ambient temperature. Still…

She glanced at the darkened kitchen. It wouldn't take very long to heat soup. The woman had several coffee mugs. Teal could borrow one of the ones in the rear of the shelf, pour the soup in it…

Decision made, she sprang to action. In less than two minutes, she had the soup warming in the microwave. While it heated, she washed out the soup can and dried it before placing it in her backpack for disposal later.

Dinner was a lively affair at the Hamilton house. Although the early summer evening was cold, everyone voted to eat outside, so the men—Quin included —spent considerable time constructing an impressive firewood tepee in the round pit at the edge of the patio. Roarke took great fun in squirting what must have been half a can of charcoal lighter fluid over the wood, before Ben tossed in a match.

"What is it about men and fire?" Mandy snorted, as she shielded her face with a hand and slid back another foot. "Yikes." Everyone followed her retreat as the flames leapt skyward.

Rayne laughed. "I think it goes back to the Stone Age. Men returned from their hunt with a woolly mammoth and roasted it over an open pit." She indicated the raging fire with her wineglass. "Need big fire to cook elephant," she said with stern seriousness.

"Is that when the Neanderthals lived?" Mandy asked, and Rayne "clinked" her goblet against Mandy's soda can in acknowledgement of a good one.

Lena laughed with the two women. They obviously had a special rapport. Earlier, while helping Mrs. H and Rayne chop veggies in the kitchen, Lena learned Ben and Rayne had recently remarried after being divorced from each other for fifteen years while Rayne pursued a music career in Europe. That was a story Lena would like to hear sometime. When Rayne had returned to Storm Lake, she and Mandy became good friends first, aunt and niece later.

Lena envied their close friendship as she watched the two talking. She'd never had that with another woman. Always more tomboy than frilly girl, she'd spent her life bantering with—and competing against—men, rather than cultivating female friendships. Not that she hadn't tried. Meri Barker, a helper at the studio, had joined Lena for coffee a few times, and they seemed to hit it off—that is, until Lena found out Meri had been sleeping with the show's director and was vying for Lena's job. There was enough other cattiness and drama from women at Bobby's office to make her wary. Oh, well. Life was short, and you lived it as best you could. She'd learned that from Bobby too.

When the food was ready, they ate with steaming plates balanced on their knees, women on one side of the fire, men on the other—which was just fine with Lena. She had no desire to be anywhere near Alex Stone, though her eyes constantly betrayed her, seeking his face through the flickering orange light. How had he acquired the scar that trailed a white line from in front of his left ear to the side of his neck. It appeared well healed, but not an old wound. Had it been from some military firefight? Or a more mundane altercation in a bar?

As if he'd heard her, Alex Stone turned and looked straight at her.

Lena concentrated on her plate, hacking at a piece of steak and cutting straight through the bottom of the heavy-duty paper. Had he just scowled at her? She was glad the firelight masked any embarrassing blush from being caught staring, and tried to put it out of her mind as Mrs. H spoke to her.

"So, AJ, tell us how your cabin rentals are going?"

"My first renters came today." Lena couldn't help being a little proud of this milestone. "So far, so good."

"That's wonderful," Mrs. H enthused, patting Lena's hand. The old-fashioned gesture belonged in an episode of The Andy Griffith Show, but somehow it fit the setting here at the lake. Lena let her shoulders relax. She hadn't realized how tense she'd been. Maybe this tight community *did* resemble the fictional Mayberry. She glanced across the fire. Complete with lawman. Although Mrs. H might pass for Aunt Bee, Alex Stone was no Sheriff Andy Taylor.

She shook her head clear. "I do need some help, though," Lena said to Mrs. H, setting her plate aside before juice leaked onto her pants.

"Of course, dear. What is it?"

Lena explained about forgetting the barbecue grill. "I planned on buying a propane one, but then Colby stacked some wood where I want to place it and, after tonight"—she indicated the group across the fire—"I think men would prefer a charcoal or wood unit, don't you?"

Mrs. H laughed, and patted Lena's hand again. "You have that right, dear."

"Do you have any idea where I can get a barbecue on short notice?"

Mrs. H pressed a finger to her lips for a moment, then smiled at Lena. "I think I know just the thing you need."

"Oh, that's so helpful. I hear the bass are abundant this year, so the fishermen who arrived today might want to use it tomorrow if they catch anything. Is that too soon?" Lena said she had a small trailer she could hitch to the Jeep to pick up the unit.

"I think tomorrow would work out fine," Mrs. H said, "and I can arrange for free delivery."

"That would be great." Even though the first renters were here, Lena still had a long to-do list, and one less interruption was welcome. It seemed like all she did was go pick up materials.

"Now," Mrs. H said, "I wonder if you can help *me* out with a little need of my own?"

"No problem," Lena said, remembering the favor Roarke had mentioned. However, Lena was unsure what she could do for someone who knew everyone around the lake. It probably wasn't anything big. "What can I do?"

"Well, Alex Stone is on some kind of special assignment. It's all very secretive, I take it, from what Ben said—you know how these law enforcement types are," she said, patting Lena's hand again, as if Lena knew all about lawmen. "He asked Ben for suggestions, and Ben mentioned it to me."

"O-kay," Lena said cautiously, wondering how this involved her.

"He has a small camper, and I thought of you and the trailer sites on your property."

Well, that answered *that* question.

"...and he's got a budget to pay rent for the space. He gets a good place to stay, and you get ongoing income. Isn't that just a perfect match?" Mrs. H said, eyes gleaming.

Lena looked across the fire to where the men sat. Stone glanced her way, then went back to his conversation with Ben Conner.

Oh, yeah. Just perfect.

Teal closed the rear door of the empty cabin. The interior was warm from the day's sun, emitting woodsy smells of hot pine pitch and aged redwood. She hated feeling confined, but if anyone came in the front door she could be off the back porch in a flash and disappear into the nearby trees. After a second night at the falls, she was tired of sleeping on the ground with bugs, although this place didn't look much better in the insect department.

The living room and kitchen were already cooling, thanks to the broken window and the opening in the ceiling where the stovepipe should have gone. She retreated to the smaller bedroom at the back of the house. Its door and inside window were solid.

Teal used Springsteen's newly charged light to check the kitchen cupboards and the closets—all bare except for a tall cabinet at the end of the kitchen. It contained a broken broom, its shaft splintered about halfway down. She used it to sweep the bedroom, herding the dirt down the hall and out the back door. That bit of housekeeping accomplished, she spread out the blanket on her bedroom floor.

Her bedroom. While this wasn't hers anymore than the others had been over the years, it didn't hurt to pretend.

The square of cloth looked pitiful in Springsteen's bluish light, the fabric nearly the same color as the scarred floor. The blanket desperately needed washing. Everything she owned needed washing. In a real washing machine with detergent. Then dry the load with one of those fabric softener sheets that made things smell so good.

Teal sighed and sank down in a cross-legged position. Well, that wasn't going to happen anytime soon. Since the blonde woman had come and gone to the south, maybe tomorrow Teal could hike north along the lake shore and find a secluded spot to at least rinse things out. They'd dry pretty fast in the sun.

She curled sideways on the blanket, but soon the hard floor chaffed her hip, knee, and ankle bones. She rolled onto her back, but her pelvis and shoulder blades became four pain points. Finally, she turned onto her stomach, full from the can of soup, half of the saltines, and one Mother's Taffy cookie. She cradled her head on folded hands. Much better.

She drifted off with dreams of a fluffy mattress in her own cabin.

11

Lena stepped onto her porch in the early morning light and inhaled deeply. The air was crisp but already held the aroma of heat. According to the locals, summer warmed up fast, which was fine with her.

She settled carefully into the chair, which creaked ominously under her weight. Replacing it with something better was high on her list now that she had money coming in. Colby had mentioned a flea market the last Saturday of each month just down the road in Shelter Cove. Maybe she could score something inexpensive that at least had four sturdy legs.

Sunlight glinted off east-facing windows on the other side of the lake, sparkling across the placid morning water. Few boaters were out yet, and the fishermen kept to the rocky, undulating shoreline where the "big ones" took sanctuary. A string of ducks flew north, then circled low over the water, feet outstretched and wings backpedaling for a landing near her dock.

Two of her renters' boats were absent, so they were out early. She wondered if Brandon was one of them, or if he'd slept in. All of the guests were only staying through Memorial Day afternoon. Many California schools wouldn't begin summer break for another week or two. That's when the serious tourist season began, and people would stay for a week at a time.

Her cell phone rang. She pulled it from her pocket and read the display. *Unknown caller*. Who would be calling her at 6:10 in the morning? It could be about her mom.

She pressed the button. "Hello?"

"Lena," a husky voice announced. "It's Chet Marquette."

"Hi, Chet," Lena said, glad he'd called back. She'd heard from him four or five times in the first few months. And, while he'd always asked how she was doing and where she was, it had felt more like him keeping tabs on her than giving information about the case.

"I apologize for having to jump off yesterday. It's nuts around here. Well, you're a hard woman to track down."

"Oh, I'm sorry about that. I got a few strange calls, and changed my number. I should have called you with the new one."

He laughed. "No problem. I have friends in high places. But what kind of calls?" He turned all business, and she could picture him scratching on a legal pad. "Did you report them to Snyder? How come you didn't tell me about them?" Donald Snyder was the police detective officially in charge of the investigation.

"Yes, I contacted Snyder, then changed my number. I thought he'd tell you," she said. "You two are working together, right?"

Chet's noncommittal grunt might have been agreement. Or maybe not. As brash as he was sometimes, he was also an attorney used to keeping his cards close to the vest.

According to Snyder—who had interviewed Lena in the hospital, then initiated calls to her exactly twice—there were no leads, no tips, no witnesses, and no evidence except for dozens of spent shell casings on the street in front of their home. All the casings had been wiped clean, and the recovered bullets matched no known illegally used weapons. He'd let her know clearly that, unless they received a tip, they were at a dead end.

Over the phone line, a straw sucked air at the bottom of a cup—Bobby said Chet practically inhaled grape Big Gulps—then a voice sounded in the background. Chet's response was muffled, as if he'd covered the receiver. She hoped he wouldn't hang up again.

"Sorry, Lena," he said, back on the line. "It's a madhouse around here. Be glad you're out of the city. Anyway, I wanted you to know I haven't given up. I'm still convinced Bobby secreted some information somewhere that might give clues to what happened."

Lena had wondered this, too. But she'd told them her suspicions about him working on a big case, something secret. Chet had been the only one who seemed intensely interested in that, but investigators hadn't found anything on Bobby's computer, the file servers, or in the cases of paper files gathered from his briefcase, home office, and his drawers at work.

"You're sure he didn't have anything at home?" Chet asked. "Hidden somewhere?"

Lena had granted full access to the house after the shooting, and Snyder said they went through every paper, every file. Even their home laptop, CDs, and DVDs had been checked. Lena assured Chet that if Bobby had indeed hidden something, it would have been found.

Lena heard a female voice in the background, and Chet shouted, "*Okay, okay!*"

"Listen, Lena, I've got to get to court. But I'm coming up to see you—maybe this week or weekend if I can squeeze it in."

"You don't have—"

"Maybe I can take you to dinner? I know you're in Podunk, but surely they have someplace decent?"

Before she could reply, Chet yelled to someone in his office, told Lena he had to go, and admonished her to phone him if she received any more suspicious calls. The line went dead.

Lena looked at her phone's blank screen. Chet had always been sort of a whirlwind. She was grateful someone still cared about Bobby's murder and wanted answers. It had taken Detective Snyder four days to return her last call for an update, and he said nothing had changed. Maybe not in *his* world.

Lena went inside and gathered up her laptop. The blood smears were gone from its aluminum surface, cleaned by sympathetic lab techs, she supposed. She'd never asked. Probably some would think it macabre to keep the computer, but it was the last thing Bobby touched. She cradled it against her stomach and returned to the porch.

"Time to see what the future might look like," she said to the blue lake.

She spent the next twenty minutes projecting the costs for renovating cabins four and six. Even though six had been scheduled for demolition until she bought it, it was the newest structure and had solid bones. If she took that one for herself, she could utilize the small second bedroom as an office. It was farther up the hill, visually isolated from the other structures, which would give her a little privacy from her renters. Plus, it was near the old barn where she stored an ATV, tools, planting supplies, and all the various cabin refurbishing materials. Her current cabin, number 5, could easily be set up as another rental.

Lena detailed costs for siding, roof repair, electrical, plumbing, beds and other furniture, pots, silverware, and kitchen outfitting. The list scrolled down several computer screens as she included everything from screws, to light bulbs, to a refrigerator. She drew on her real-world experience from the first three cabins, and reused those actual costs. Then she compared the expense totals against her projected rent for both the booked dates and the occupancy she hoped to get as the summer went on.

Ouch. On the one hand, the more rent she brought in, the faster she'd get ahead and spread the monthly overhead costs for utilities, mortgage, and property taxes. On the other, she had to come up with a lot of cash to ready 4 and 6 simultaneously. But summer was the time to make hay.

She chewed her lip and carefully leaned back in the chair. A different option was to spend the minimal amount on her current cabin and make it rentable, then move into the bare Cabin 6 early while she continued work on 4. Requiring a smaller investment, she'd have the income of this cabin, though it meant practically camping out in 6.

But she could do that. All she really needed was a bed, a refrigerator, stove, and a coffeemaker. In a pinch, she could delay purchasing the bed and use her air mattress. But she'd still have to build out a whole new bathroom. It was possible, though.

With that new option firmly in mind, she spent another thirty minutes listing what her present cabin needed to make it ready for renters. This list was much shorter, and far less costly.

One thing she had hoped to do as summer occupancy improved was hiring someone to help clean, care for the grounds, and maintain the dock area. Lena sighed as she realized the money for help just wasn't there. And, except for a few jobs where she needed help from Colby, all the construction labor on the new cabins would fall to her. Good thing summer days were long.

Lena hadn't realized how much time had passed until she heard a car approaching. She saved her work, shut the laptop, then stood and rolled the kinks out of her neck and shoulders. An early sixties red Chevy pickup topped the hill from the crossing, pulling a vintage Airstream trailer. The truck rolled to a stop in front of her cabin.

Alex Stone stepped out of the truck and walked around its hood.

"Here we go," she muttered to herself.

"Morning," he said, standing at the foot of the cabin stairs, thumbs hooked in his jeans pockets, looking up at her expectantly. He didn't look half so scary with the morning light skimming his short brown hair. Another black T-shirt—or the same one, who could tell?—stretched tight across his broad chest. Being hugged by this man would be like being embraced by the Incredible Hulk.

As that thought zipped through her brain and toward her mouth, Lena fumbled and nearly dropped the laptop. She clinched her teeth, trapping the words in time. Barely.

"Coffee," she said. She needed more to make sure her brain controlled the rest of her body. She spun and started inside, then stopped at the doorway and turned back to where Stone waited. "I mean, um, would you like some coffee? I'm pouring another cup." She waggled her mug in question.

"No."

Lena waited, but he didn't elaborate. Not, *No thanks* or *But you go ahead and have some yourself.* Just *No.*

"Oh." Now she was really stuck, halfway through the door, juggling her laptop and mug. And if that wasn't enough, the man was frowning at her.

"Just tell me where to set up my trailer and I'll get to it."

She'd like to tell him just where to put things, recalling colorful phrases she'd learned from some of the rougher carpenters she'd worked with years ago. Lena felt her mouth clinch into a tight line.

"I'll be right back," she said with an effort toward civility. Inside she stored her laptop in its hiding place, an empty Cheerios box in the pantry, then took her time fixing another cup of coffee. Armed with the liquid fortification in a lidded travel mug, she pulled on one of her cowboy hats and went outside to face the enemy.

"Follow me," was all AJ Blaylock said as she walked down the road away from Alex. He wasn't sure if she meant on foot or to bring his truck. He chose his rig, and put the transmission in low gear as he crept at a snail's pace behind her.

She followed the road past a cabin marked #4, then turned off the road uphill past another unfinished cabin sitting on a concrete block foundation. Behind that last cabin, Alex made out the top of an old barn, its rough siding turned a dark silver-gray by decades of weather.

AJ stepped aside and waited until he pulled abreast.

"The trailer hookups are over there," she pointed to two sets of posts and four-inch drainpipes. The posts had gray electrical boxes mounted on them and a hose bib for water. "You can use the upper one. That'll make it a little easier in case I get another renter with a trailer."

Alex glanced in the direction she pointed, but watched her face and eyes as she explained the setup. Even this early in summer, her skin was tanned bronze. Fine lines radiated from the corners of her brown eyes. AJ Blaylock was far prettier up close and in person than on TV. The cameras hadn't zoomed in often enough. A natural beauty, used to working outside. She did appear to be a bit skinny, though.

"Did you have a question, Mr. Stone?"

She was glaring at him over the rim of her mug when his mind rushed back to focus. He gave himself a mental shake. It wasn't normal for him to zone out like that. Yeah, he hadn't gotten a lot of sleep last night, but that was no excuse. He was trained to function on almost no sleep. *Must be getting old.*

"No," he answered, and put the truck into gear.

In a couple of minutes, he'd swung around and positioned the trailer so its side door faced the lake view, glad the pads were staggered so his view wouldn't be blocked if another trailer or RV took the other space. He got out and checked the gravel pad under the trailer. Whoever graded it had done a good job. A few turns of his jacks would have the trailer sitting level and pretty in no time.

This was working out far better than he'd ever imagined. Unaware of the trailer sites on her property, he'd thought he would have to park somewhere else around the lake. That would have made contact with her much more difficult, and certainly less frequent.

Boots on gravel sounded behind him, and he turned to find AJ walking away.

"I'll be at my cabin," she called over her shoulder. "Once you get settled, come by and we'll talk."

Alex watched her retreat, admiring the view. Maybe she wasn't too skinny after all.

"Snap out of it, Stone," he said to himself, and turned to the task of unhitching the trailer from the truck. He set the jacks at the four corners of the trailer and used a laser level—one of the handiest inventions ever—to trim everything up. Then he attached the water, electrical, and waste connections.

At only sixteen feet long and seventeen-hundred pounds, the 1960 Airstream Pacer was a baby compared to many of the behemoths on the highways today, but he'd liked the looks of this vintage unit the first time he'd spotted it sitting in a driveway in Pomona. Its simplicity appealed to him. He didn't want one of the complicated coaches that needed a DVD to explain its operation. The trailer was older than he was, but then his truck was only two years newer than the camper. A good pair. There was enough complexity in his life and job. Some things he liked to keep uncomplicated.

He locked the trailer door, then jumped back in the truck. It felt light as a feather as he left the Airstream behind and rolled down the road, passing AJ's cabin on his way south. He had another errand to do before the day was his own.

Lena glanced out the window as Stone's red truck drove past without stopping. Hadn't she specifically told the man to come by so they could talk? She tossed the sponge she'd been using into the sink, splattering soap bubbles all over the glass.

"Great," she grumbled, and tore off a paper towel to wipe off the spots before they dried. The last thing she needed was Alex Stone camped out on her property. Yes, he was paying her, and she had a hundred uses for the money, but the man made her twitch, no matter how Mrs. H vouched for his character.

What had the old woman said? Something about Stone being on a special assignment and needed a place to set up at the lake. Secrets. Lena bit her lip as she tossed the wet towel into the trash. She hoped his "special assignment" didn't have anything to do with her.

Something about him irritated her. Maybe that he was in law enforcement like her… She blew out a breath. Like Simon McKinley, her father. The law made some people feel safe, but it hadn't done anything for Bobby except get him killed. And none of the dozens of detectives, uniforms, and DAs accomplished much after the dust settled and the days slipped by without a lead.

Except Chet. He was the only one who kept in touch. Still, she didn't want anything to do with that world, ever again.

Lena finished the dish she'd been washing, and set it in the drying rack. There was work to do, but for putting up with Stone she deserved a treat. The small pantry held the package of Mother's Taffy cookies. They'd always been her favorite, so she had to watch that she didn't wolf down the whole package in one sitting. Though she burned a lot of calories at this job, she didn't want to get fat, especially after her splurge on the Fritos this week. Her self-imposed ration was two cookies a day. She removed the clip and unrolled the end.

"Now that's weird." Not quite half the cookies remained. She could have sworn the package had been more than half-full. "Maybe I've been sleepwalking. Sleep-eating." She rubbed her stomach. Still flat. Not bad for thirty-four.

Before she could talk herself out of it, she grabbed one cookie and bit. The sweet flavors swept across her tongue, transporting her across time to her childhood when her grandfather on her mom's side would invite her to sit on the back stairs of their old home and open the cookie package for her. He'd been the first one to show her how to twist the halves apart and lick the white icing like a cat. Her mother had pretended to be appalled, but Lena could tell by her mom's expression that grandpa had taught her the same trick. Grandpa died when Lena was six, but she still thought of him often.

It was funny how the senses, the taste of a simple cookie, could evoke such vivid memories. Likewise, the smell of mowed, wet grass reminded her of high school football games and cold aluminum bleachers, and candle-seared pumpkin flesh recalled every Halloween costume she'd ever worn, no matter how tacky. Simmering spaghetti sauce transported her to the house in Pasadena where she'd lain stunned, unable to move, watching Bobby's empty eyes as sirens raced through the night, so close but miles too late.

Lena shrugged off the memories. She had to get to work. Activity was her way of coping with the loss. Not so much sorrow or mourning anymore, but simple loss, a yawning hole as big as the world. Instead of grabbing her to-do list, she sank onto one of the dining chairs and nibbled the remainder of the cookie.

It was a little after noon by the time Alex crossed the creek and drove to the cabins. Before the truck had rolled to a stop, AJ Blaylock hopped down her stairs and strutted to his driver window.

"I thought I said to stop by so we could work out your rent."

She was clearly fuming over something not his fault. So much for helping her out. He unlatched the truck door, forcing her back as he exited. He hooked his thumb toward the black steel unit tied down in the bed of the truck.

"Didn't you want me to deliver this barbecue today? Mrs. H said it was urgent."

Her eyes widened, recognizing what was in the truck bed. "Oh. I…"

"I'll take that as a *yes*," Alex said. "So, where do you want it?" She dropped her head, and he could have sworn her fists curled a little. His irritation at her vanished, and he fought the urge to grin. She reminded him of his sister, Kris: easy to tease. Except Kris wouldn't have hesitated to punch him. Being around AJ Blaylock might be more fun than he'd first thought.

"It goes down between Cabins 2 and 3," she said. "Follow me."

For the second time today, Alex drove the truck behind AJ Blaylock's swaying shapely rear end as she led the way down the path between the cabins. He parked beside a cleared area that already contained a rectangle of pavers and a small stack of firewood. He climbed out, and began untying the ropes.

"Look," AJ said, abruptly turning to him. "I'm sorry I snapped at you. The last few days—weeks, really—have been kind of stressful."

"Forget it." He meant it, and felt bad for pushing her buttons when fatigue pulled the corners of her eyes. He'd always been a sucker for anyone needing help. Especially someone with great eyes. He flipped the last rope over the bed and lowered the tailgate.

Alex pulled the grill to the edge. It was a simple welded frame of one-inch square tubing with a barrel split lengthwise and hinged. At Mrs. H's direction, he'd picked it up at a welding shop in Deer Cove that made and sold them all over the county.

"Wait," AJ said, "that looks pretty heavy. Maybe one of the men is around. I can check."

"Nah, we can get it. Just steady the end as I bring it down." Alex pulled the unit half off the tailgate and lowered that end to the ground while she braced the other end. The rest was a matter of swinging it off the truck. Together, they maneuvered the barbecue onto the pavers and positioned it where she wanted.

He climbed back into the bed and began tossing out pieces of split oak firewood and bark. There was already a stack of wood at the edge of the pad, but nothing flavored meat on the grill like moist oak bark—in his opinion, at least. By the time Alex jumped down, she had neatly stacked most of the wood by the grill. He helped finish the last pieces.

"Well, that's it," he said, dusting off his hands. "I'm starving. Ok if I fix some lunch first, and then come by in an hour?"

She nodded. "Thank you for going to get this. It's a big help."

Her contrition turned the tables, and he felt bad for earlier. A guy would have just slugged him, then helped him up. Women were really complicated.

Alex climbed into the truck and drove up to his camper, idly wondering what other buttons she had he could push.

12

The comfort of the cabin the last two nights had been nice, but after so many weeks in the open, Teal itched to get outside. However, sandwiched as her cabin was between the woman's cabin and now this man in his silver trailer, she had to be super careful. If anyone spotted her, she'd be toast.

Finally, in mid-afternoon, she heard the man's truck start up, and a minute later she peeked through the front window as he drove past, heading out on the main road. The woman's Jeep was parked by her cabin, but Teal hadn't seen her for over an hour.

Slipping out the back door, Teal looked and listened for any signs of life, then beelined for the back of the barn, keeping low. She carried her backpack and all her belongings with her, even the food. It was important to leave zero presence in case anyone decided to take a look inside Cabin 6.

She wanted to explore the old barn and see if it had any blankets or anything else she could use for padding. Two nights on the unforgiving floor were all her bones could take, and she dreaded the idea of another eight hours on it tonight. The soft beds of the three cabins by the water were in her mind again as she reached the back of the barn. A junk pile sat a few feet from the far corner, a twisted mass of pipes, shingles, wood scraps, vinyl flooring, a totally gross toilet, empty paint cans, and a bunch of other stuff. But the space near the wall was clear.

The structure had been built into the sloping hillside. There wasn't a door at the back, but there was what looked like a boarded-up window cut into the siding only a foot above the higher ground level. On closer inspection, she saw it was a simple wood panel made to slide sideways. She tried both directions, but it wouldn't budge.

"Must be locked on the inside."

Several of the old siding boards on the back of the barn were warped, and the cracks between them were wide enough for her fingers. She stuck her hands in the largest crack and wiggled. The board came away so easily that she landed on her rump in the dusty grass. She scrambled to the gaping hole. It was dark inside, but nothing blocked the opening, so she pushed her backpack through and lowered it to the floor, then climbed after it. She reached back and pulled the loose board against the outside to conceal her breaking and entering.

The interior air was warm, redolent with sweet hay. Why the woman needed hay when she didn't have any animals, Teal didn't know. Wide joints in the rough siding focused sunlit lines across the floor and, as her eyes adjusted, she made out several hay bales stacked along the front wall, and a few more halfway back. Beside them hunched a mud-caked ATV with big knobby tires, and a small trailer with sides about a foot tall. Three trash cans sat on the trailer. The woman probably used the ATV to pull the cans out where the garbage trucks could empty them. A larger, wood-sided utility trailer was parked right inside the front doors.

For such an old place, the building was surprisingly clean. The concrete floor showed broom strokes, and the corners were clear of trash. Even the thick overhead rafters were free of cobwebs. Rakes, shovels, axes and various tools hung on the wall opposite the hay bales, and hammers and wrenches were neatly mounted on a pegboard above a small workbench. A clamp-on work light was attached to one end. So the barn had electricity. Good to know.

Teal walked farther into the room and realized she'd been under an overhead loft that covered the back third of the barn. A sturdy ladder on one side led up through a wide hole in the loft floor.

Before venturing into the loft, she found and unhooked the simple latch on the sliding wood window on the rear wall. She slid it slowly a couple of inches, just enough to make sure it worked. With it unlocked, she could permanently replace the siding board, and gain access through the window anytime she wanted.

The heavy-timbered ladder didn't even creak as she ascended and poked her head up into the loft. Her intake of air was loud enough to be heard outside, but for once she didn't worry.

Thank you, God!

She wouldn't be going back to the hard floor in Cabin 6 tonight. Before her lay a haven.

Her perfect place.

Lena's three rentals were full for the weekend following Memorial Day, and one party of three guys had decided to stay all the next week. The barbecue had proved a hit. If the fish weren't biting, grocery store steaks filled in. By Saturday the firewood had run low, so Lena hitched her utility trailer to her Jeep and drove to Deer Cove where Merle Ferris sold cut wood. Since most of the lake homes and cabins had wood burning stoves, he did a good business, especially in the fall.

Merle's eyes cycled from happy to sad when he spotted her strolling toward him across his work yard—he was undoubtedly remembering their gruesome discovery—but then a grin spread across his face as he noticed the pan of gooey brownies she'd made for him. He'd devoured half the pan by the time they finished loading up the trailer.

It was past three o'clock when she returned home, urging her growling Jeep up the last hill into the yard. The tires on the trailer were nearly flattened by the two cords of dense oak. She parked at the barbecue area and began unloading the split logs.

On her fifth trip around the end of the mounded trailer, she smacked into a broad chest, and looked up into Alex Stone's warm, brown eyes. *Cop eyes,* she reminded herself.

"Need a hand?" he asked, smiling.

"No, I've got it." Lena sidestepped the man and dumped her armload, then turned back for more. Stone rested his hip against the trailer side.

"*Want* a hand?"

Lena stared at his bulging muscles. He could probably upend the trailer and dump the whole load in one swoop. She wiped her brow with the back of her leather glove, hoping she didn't leave a dirt streak on her face. Having help *would* be a lot faster.

"You're offering?"

He chuckled. "I *thought* that's what I said. And you make that sound like I've never done a good deed in my whole life."

"I didn't mean—"

"I'll have you know, I made Eagle Scout." Stone stacked a half-dozen chunks of wood in one arm. "Earned one of my merit badges helping old ladies."

Lena wasn't sure if that was an insult, but she mentally swore never to grow old around Alex Stone. He was the last person she'd trust to get her safely across a busy intersection. Probably push her under a bus. She gathered up three logs, irked they were as many as she could carry.

They worked side-by-side, and Lena matched him load for load in count, if not in size. In minutes the trailer was bare. She leaned against it, dripping wet and trying her best not to show how winded she was. Stone hadn't broken a sweat, the louse.

"Can you bake a cake?" Stone asked, his eyes searching hers like he was grilling a prisoner.

"What?" Lena sucked in a deeper breath. Had she heard him right? What did a cake have to do with unloading a trailer of wood?

"I'm partial to German chocolate," he said with a serious expression, "but any kind will do since I know you don't have time to go to the store." He pulled off the brown leather gloves he'd brought with him—twice the size of hers—and slapped them on his jeans, freeing a cloud of particles to dance in the sun.

Lena stripped off her own gloves and smacked them against the side of the trailer. "And just why would I bake a cake?"

"For the potluck."

"What potluck?"

"Seven-thirty. My place." He began walking up the hill. "Don't be late."

"Don't hold your breath, Stone. I'm tired. It's been a long day. I think I'll turn in early." This last she had to shout as he kept walking without looking back. "Ugh!"

Lena turned toward her Jeep and saw two of her renters standing near the dock, fishing poles and tackle boxes in hand. They were grinning at her. She climbed into the vehicle and slammed the door hard.

"Sorry, baby," she said, rubbing her hand over the dashboard while staring through the dirty windshield, "not your fault. Potluck. That man is irritating with a capital *I*."

Although she couldn't exactly figure out why.

13

By the next weekend, even the moldy hay smelled yummy to Teal. She'd actually chewed some of the cleaner pieces. Though not bad tasting, it was impossible to grind up the tough stalks. She gained a whole new appreciation for cows and their ability to digest the stuff.

The few cans of food and dry goods she'd pilfered from the woman hadn't lasted long, and now her stomach never quieted. In her weeks of travel she'd learned to tolerate hunger in order to stay safe. But safety without nourishment was no longer cutting it.

Teal settled onto the floor of the barn loft. She'd made a thick bed of straw from one of the broken bales, stuffing it under an old canvas tarp so it was like a real mattress—the most comfortable one she'd slept on in a long time. One of the wooden trunks had produced a horse blanket, scratchy, but it smelled reasonably clean. Counting the nights at the falls, this was the longest she'd stayed in one spot in…well, since she'd walked away from the school and foster care. Staying in one place felt wrong, dangerous.

And perfect.

A drawer beneath the workbench on the main floor had yielded some emergency candles and box matches. With a little work using a pair of tin snips off the tool board, she'd cut a scooped section out of the front of a large coffee can, leaving the back part high for a reflector. When lit, the candles sat tucked inside the can. Even if the burning candle fell over, it would remain inside the large container, an extremely important safety precaution in a barn full of dry hay. By rearranging the old chests, she'd created a walled nest of sorts that hid the candle from being visible from the outside.

In the last couple of days, she'd figured out the comings and goings of renters for the three cabins near the water, and she'd heard several of the men refer to the woman as "AJ." The man who'd parked his silver trailer a little north of Cabin 6, AJ called *Stone*.

One day mid-week when everyone was gone, Teal had walked around the grounds. The wine barrel planters had some pitiful looking flowers in them, wilting from lack of water. She found a blue plastic watering can, and filled and emptied it a dozen times, giving generous drinks to all. Then she'd explored inside the rental cabins, and found each stocked with a couple dozen secondhand paperback books, everything from Mark Twain to Clive Cussler and Elmore Leonard. Even Bibles.

Now, reading at night by her candlelight lantern, she was halfway through The Adventures of Tom Sawyer, and had fallen in love with the boy's mischievous ways. He was always getting into trouble, but somehow escaped the consequences—most of the time. Yet, even with a warm, safe place to lie and read, slow starvation put a severe damper on her ability to enjoy her bounty.

The main problem was that AJ shopped for one person, buying small quantities. Two bananas, two apples, one can of beans, a quarter pound of lunchmeat. Teal couldn't very well take any of those. The biggest item of quantity AJ purchased was a box of Raisin Bran or other cereal. On one foray, Teal had filled a sandwich Ziploc with the cereal and snacked on it for breakfast, lunch, and dinner—for three days.

She'd scored handfuls of tortilla chips and some cookies from one of the unlocked rentals, but what she craved more than anything was meat.

It didn't help when the fishermen grilled several trout or bass basted in lemon juice and butter. Even worse if their fishing luck ran out and they opted for juicy T-bone steaks over the oak fire. The breeze generally blew uphill, right toward the barn, and Teal could practically taste the garlic powder and spices. Her eyes teared at the mouth-watering aromas. After dark, when everyone had gone to bed, she'd been able to pick some charred bits of meat off the cooled grill.

Two days ago, she'd hiked down the road and found the tiny town of Gift. At least, that's what the sign said. But it was really no more than about twenty-five scattered cabins. Most showed signs of occupancy, though a few were still locked tight from the winter. Unfortunately, it seemed dogs were pet-of-the-year in Gift, and she'd had a hard time avoiding them. She used a rusty nail to push back the door latch of one small cabin that was somewhat isolated, but all the food was missing except for a can of tomato salsa. The lid had several spots of corrosion, and the bottom was stamped: Best if used by 8/16/1996. She'd only been a little tempted.

Teal rose from the mattress and slid open the loft window. The opening faced northeast, and the back of the barn was heavily shadowed now that the sun was low. The rental cabins were full today, but maybe she should snoop around. She couldn't stand the thought of trying to sleep when so hungry. Plus, she was bored.

She descended the ladder, slid the wooden window aside, and climbed through. Making her way through the brush and trees on the hill behind the barn, she soon reached the trail that led to the waterfall, but then she turned and followed the stream bank down to the lake. If someone spotted her, they'd assume she was just another day hiker returning from the falls.

The creek cascaded over a dozen feet of boulders before reaching the larger body of water. Teal found a large slab of rock sticking out from the bank ten feet higher than the water, but back too far to use it as a jumping spot. Even if she *could* jump in, she wasn't sure she'd have the energy to swim back to shore.

The sun hung just above the western hills, inching downward through wispy clouds. Two powerboats raced southward a hundred yards out, engines roaring against the quiet, and sending golden rays rippling across the lake surface.

"Probably going home with a cooler full of fish to fry," she mumbled, as she dangled her legs off the ledge. Her mom used to fix fish sticks from a box, usually burning them under the broiler. What she wouldn't do for one of those dried-out tiny bricks right now.

The rock surface was warm under her thighs, and she leaned back on her arms and stared across the water at the west side homes. The lake was beautiful with the boats zipping along. It reminded her that there were special places where people were nice. Maybe someday she could have her own house right here near the water. She could build a dock and sit out on the end with her fishing pole, pulling in fat trout for a sizzling frying pan. Truth was, she didn't even like fish that much, but she'd eat a dozen of them right now if—

Before she could react, an aluminum boat rounded the big boulder to her right. It was puttering along only a few feet from shore, its small motor's sound lost in the aftermath of the two big boats. Its lone occupant stared right at her—and waved.

It was too late to run away, but Teal's flight instinct still sent her heart racing. Dizziness swept over her and her arms wobbled. Her mind was a jumble, telling her to run, scream, wave back, find a weapon. The boat nosed onto the rocky strip of shore to her right.

"Hey," the silhouetted figure called. "You're all lit up."

Teal's stomach twisted in on itself and she fought down bile. She tried to control her breathing, but everything was coming apart.

"Like a golden angel." His voice held a laugh.

Squinting against the glare, Teal saw a young man. High school? He killed the motor, rose to a crouching position and stepped onto the shore rocks without getting wet. He looped the bow rope around a snag and climbed toward her rock. Toward *her.*

"I'm Quin Conner," the boy said, stepping nimbly up the stones until his head was even with her rock.

Teal's heart skipped a beat or two, and she couldn't get enough air to answer him. And what would she say? *Hi, I'm Teal Kinshaw, and I steal food to survive. What do you do?* Yeah, like that would work.

Her fingers twitched like a scared rabbit. If she ran fast enough up the path, she could cut behind the barn and disappear inside before he could follow. But one look at his long, tanned legs extending from khaki cargo shorts, and she knew he could outdistance her before she took ten steps.

The boy named Quin Conner leaned closer and rested his arms on the flat of the stone. She had to say something, otherwise he'd think her an idiot. Or mute.

Hey, now there was an idea. She could pretend she was deaf and couldn't speak. But what if he knew sign language and tried talking to her with that? Then what would she do?

"I'm...uh, I'm Teal," she managed, her voice cracking and squeaking like a third-grader in the principal's office.

"Good to meet you, Teal." He extended his hand toward her.

She stared at it, unused to shaking hands with anyone, let alone a boy. The last time had been with a social worker, and that hadn't turned out so great. Unable to think of an alternative, Teal gripped Quin's hand. Hers was warm from the rock, but his was hot, rough, and strong.

Safe.

Heat traveled up her arm, sending the hairs on the back of her neck standing straight up. When they separated, she wanted to grab his hand back and hold on. *Breathe.*

"I'd ask if you come here often, but that sounds like a bad pickup line."

He laughed, and she hoped her mouth formed a smile. She was out of practice.

Quin turned toward the lake, evidently not bothered by her lack of response. The sinking sun touched the treetops, and brushed the clouds gold-red. Now that the speeding boats were gone, the lake had flattened to a mirrored, muted version of the sky. Lights came on in some of the homes on the far shore, transforming the scene into something from a painting. For a few minutes, the birds and insects grew quiet, perhaps out of reverence for the beginning transition toward night.

"I never get tired of watching the sunset over the lake," Quin said, sighing deeply.

Somehow, it was his sigh that caused Teal to relax a little. "Tom Sawyer would like it here," she whispered in reverence to the beauty.

Quin turned back to her. "Tom Sawyer? You mean like in Mark Twain?" His brown eyes danced with curiosity.

Teal leaned forward to get off her trembling arms. "He liked the outdoors." Her stomach picked that moment to give a loud growl. She wrapped her arm around it and cut her eyes at Quin, but he wasn't laughing.

"I guess he did." Quin stood. "Well, I'd better get going. I was out fishing by the point and saw you sitting here all lit up by the glowing sky." He stepped back. "Do you live around here? Or are you here for the summer?"

"I, uh…" *Nope. Just hiding out from the authorities while I starve to death. You?*

"Sorry, I don't mean to pry." He stepped down two rocks, moving toward his boat.

Suddenly, Teal didn't want him to leave. "I can come back tomorrow—or the next day," she said. "Whatever works best for you. I mean, if you want to hang out…or something." If it sounded like she was desperate, well, she was. He was the first person close to her age she'd talked to in weeks, and the thought of not seeing him again twisted her stomach. To her relief, Quin turned. A breeze played with the ends of his brown hair, and its slight chill caused her to draw her thin hoodie tighter. She inhaled, seeking his scent on the air.

"Okay. Actually I'm pretty busy for the next day or so."

Teal's body sagged in on itself. Why would she think a boy would be interested in spending time with her? She'd cut her hair with dull scissors from the barn's workbench, and combed it with ten fingers. She probably looked like the *before* picture on a makeover show, when the stylists flinched in horror. "Oh, no problem." She hoped it was loud enough for him to hear.

"But I should be free after Tuesday morning. Say two-ish?"

Teal realized she had no clue which day was Tuesday. "Sure. Uh, Quin? With vacation and all, what day is today?"

"Today's Saturday." He laughed. "We can go for a boat ride if your parents won't mind."

"I don't...I mean, they'll be fine with it," Teal said. Her absent dad, whoever he was, wouldn't mind. And she was pretty sure her mother had more important things in her day, like how much soap to measure into washing machines at the prison laundry.

He looked up at the darkening sky. "I've gotta go while I can still see. Do you need a ride somewhere right now? I just have my boat, but—"

"No." It came out rushed, a little harsh, but he couldn't know about her. "I have a car. I mean, it's my parents' car. We're staying up the canyon." She gestured vaguely toward the hills behind her. She'd seen a road winding east out of Gift. It had signs warning *Road Ends 9 Miles Ahead*, and *Trailers Not Recommended Beyond This Point*. She hoped there were houses or cabins up there.

"Gift Creek Road."

She shrugged. "I guess that's it."

"Has to be," Quin said. "It's the only road out of Gift." He turned back toward the boat and had nearly reached the bowline when he stopped. "Hey, I just remembered. I have an extra bologna sandwich in my cooler I didn't eat. I'm having dinner at a friend's house tonight so it will just go to waste. Not trying to push it on you or anything, but if you're staying here at the shore a while…"

"Sure," she said, trying not to leap head first off the rock and scramble to the boat. "I mean, if you don't want it. I skipped lunch today." And yesterday, and the day before that.

Quin lifted a plastic ice chest from the bow of the boat and removed the lid. "Let's see. Sandwich, chips, a Coke." He sat the cooler down and cradled the items as he walked back to her rock. "Here you go."

Teal's hands trembled as she took the food, his fingers brushing hers with that startling heat. She hugged the packages and icy Coke to her, and her stomach roared loud enough to scare a flock of ducks.

"Wow, sounds like you're hungry," Quin laughed again.

"Yeah, some." Teal couldn't wait until he left so she could tear into the sandwich. Bologna. She hadn't had a bologna sandwich in maybe a year.

"Well, then, it's a good thing I didn't eat all the dessert." He dangled a plastic bag containing three giant cookies. "Chocolate chip. Made them myself."

Teal thought she'd pass out right then, and was thankful when Quin jumped down and put one foot into his boat. She watched while he pushed off, settled at the stern, then gave a sharp pull on the motor's starting cord. He spun the little boat around and waved at her as he opened the throttle. In seconds he was out of sight, the motor fading, and she'd taken her first bite.

"Thank you, God," she said around a big mouthful. Mustard and mayo—just as she liked—and three fat slices of meat. *Thank you, thank you, thank you.* It was absolutely the best sandwich she'd ever eaten.

But Quin Conner had gotten it wrong. She wasn't the angel. *He* was.

14

Lena still hadn't discovered Alex Stone's game. She'd thought about asking Chet if he knew anything, but he hadn't shown up last weekend like he'd said, or this one, either. And he hadn't returned her mid-week call. That irked Lena, but Chet was a busy man. If he had news, he wasn't in any hurry to share it.

The only other person she knew well enough to call was Eve Crescent, another assistant district attorney working her way up like Bobby. A member of the L.A. Four Ts set—Tall, Thin, Tanned, and Toned—Eve immobilized men with every swish of her ebony hair. She used her Monica Bellucciesque beauty to great effect in court, flirting with men when it benefited her case, yet at the same time managing not to alienate women jurors.

Eve had always been a little too chummy with Bobby for Lena's taste, but Bobby had dismissed Lena's concerns, saying that was just Eve, and that she behaved that way with everyone. Still, Lena hadn't missed the way the woman's hand found Bobby's arm or rested low on his back when she leaned close and whispered something that made him smile. Lena both hated and envied the woman for her easy sensuality—and for having spectacular acrylic nails.

Lena spread her right hand. Her thumb had a Band-Aid wrapped around it, and her nails could have been filed with a wood rasp. Beautiful hands weren't in her future, but she really should use more hand cream. With a sigh, she pressed her wounded thumb on her phone's call button and dialed Eve's work number.

"Eve Crescent. Please...leave a message." Eve sounded businesslike, but the slight pause after "please" was an imploring plea, seductive and intimate, as if she was expecting a close friend to call.

"Eve, this is Lena, Bobby's wife. I, uh, know we haven't talked since ..." She rubbed her forehead, wishing she'd thought out what to say. Eve hadn't been part of the investigation, so she probably didn't know anything. But she *had* sent a huge flower arrangement, and included a handwritten note that Lena read several times during Bobby's service while blocking out the official words spoken from the platform. What would Eve think when she got the message? "Could you call me when you get a chance?" Lena left her number and ended the call.

Finding out why Stone was here was the only reason she'd reluctantly agreed to his "potluck" tonight. Technically, she *hadn't* agreed. He'd assumed she'd come. But it was a chance to address the apprehension that had crept onto her property and home. First the dead man, then Stone showing up, then...

This.

She headed for Stone's trailer, but stopped when she reached the shadow of an oak tree. Stone was tending a small Weber barbecue that he'd set up on a cleared area in front of his Airstream. Two canvas folding chairs faced the lake, now aglow through the trees in the late sun. They were drawing closer to the longest days of the year, so it was a good hour before dark. Stone held the cooker's black dome as he stirred the glowing briquettes with a stick. He frowned at the fire and replaced the lid.

"Okay, then," he said and sat down, back to Lena. He rubbed his palms on his jeans, then picked his beer up from the wooden crate he used as a table.

Was Stone nervous? Lena shook her head. That wasn't a trait she attributed to him. Enigmatic, yes, and she'd get to the bottom of his mystery. But what could he be nervous about?

Lena stepped from under the tree and walked forward. Leaves crunched under her tennis shoes and Stone's head snapped around. He practically fell on his butt getting out of the low chair, and Lena covered her smile.

"Where'd you come from?" he looked around, as if searching for a hidden portal. It was a dumb question since she'd clearly been right there. "I mean...I didn't..." He closed his mouth and wiped his hands on his pants again.

Yep, definitely nervous. Lena nodded toward his beer. "Got one of those for me?" She walked past him toward the other chair, but not before she noticed his scent of soap, clean laundry, and wood smoke. Her nostrils flared involuntarily, and she fought the urge to lean toward him. Instead, she placed her Tupperware container between them on the table, sat down, and faced the lake.

Light danced on the sparkling surface. In the few months she'd lived here, she never tired of the unending panoply. Smooth as glass one hour, it could be churning the next, either from motorboats or storm. Its color ranged from sky blue to cobalt to gunmetal, as if reflecting some inner personality— melancholy or, perhaps, closeted secrets. Up until the last few days, she hadn't felt the unease that now niggled the fringes of her consciousness.

"Uh, AJ...you okay?"

Lena looked up. Evidently Stone had said something. "What?"

"I asked if you wanted something different to drink than beer, but you zoned out. Anything wrong? Or just tired?"

His gentle concern surprised Lena, and she wrestled with how much to tell him. It wasn't like she knew the man. Didn't even like him. Well, that might be too strong. Mrs. H and Ben Conner vouched for him, and sometimes living out here with no one to confide in wore on her. Especially after finding the body so close. She couldn't very well unburden to her renters, and Mrs. H had gone to visit friends in San Francisco. Lena didn't know anyone else well enough. Some days, that's what she missed most about Bobby and being married. He'd been her friend first, lover second.

She still didn't fully trust Stone and whatever enforcement background he came from. He had an agenda, and she was afraid it involved her.

"I went to check the barn and the new cabin," she began, then paused. His eyebrows lifted in question, and she realized her statement hadn't made sense to him. "That's why I came from the upper path and not up the one from below," she explained.

"Oh," he nodded, but made no move to get her anything to drink.

If she'd been standing, she'd be staring at her shoes, scuffing the ground. "Stone, have you... been in the barn or the new cabin?"

"You think someone is snooping?" He hadn't answered the question, but unless he was a pretty good actor, his surprise was genuine.

"I'm not sure." She stood now, feeling inferior with him looming over her. "I guess it could have been Colby. He did some work a couple of days ago."

"Anything missing? Tools or...?"

She shook her head. It was more feeling than substance. The flicker of light she'd seen in the barn last night could have been starlight lining up through the siding gaps from the other side. And she'd only noticed it that one time. Everything had seemed in place when she'd checked a few minutes ago, but then she hadn't thought to memorize where things were last week.

Organization wasn't her strong suit, except when it came to tools. At her old house with Bobby, her tool bench was always piled high with projects, plans, and items waiting repair. Yet she could find a drill bit where she'd put it a month before, even if it had rolled under the edge of a paper or was tucked behind the vise.

"It's probably nothing," she said, dismissing it with a wave.

"Tell me." He sat back down, no longer interested in his beer—or hers.

She sat, too, and angled her body toward his, suddenly anxious to have a confidante. "I hadn't been in the new cabin for a few days, so I took a yellow pad there yesterday to make a needs lists. You know, furniture, rugs, measure for curtains—things like that. I always outfit the cabins with brooms and dustpans. I guess I'm hoping one of the renters will actually use them."

Stone just nodded.

"Yeah, well. Anyway, that cabin was filthy inside from the move and placement on the foundation. I hadn't had a chance to clean it."

"So?"

"It was the weirdest thing. The small bedroom looked like it had been swept. There wasn't any dirt or dust in that room."

Stone didn't say anything for a minute, then, "You think someone's been in there?"

Lena shook her head. "I don't know. I mean, I doubt it. I didn't find anything that someone might leave behind. Besides, it's not that far from my cabin, or your trailer for that matter. We'd have noticed, wouldn't we?"

Stone held her gaze for several heartbeats. "I'll keep my eyes open. You keep your doors locked."

"Thanks." Nothing was resolved, but Lena felt better for having confided in someone. Or was it *having* someone to confide in?

Any nervousness had disappeared from Stone's manner. Even his eyes had changed, grown darker and focused. Just the talk of something unusual had put him in his comfort zone. "I've got beer, a crisp chardonnay from a local winery, and orange soda—regular, not diet."

"A man of discriminating tastes," Lena said.

"Better than *in*-criminating."

It wasn't exactly a smile, but Lena thought one side of his mouth quirked a little. Must be a cop joke. "I know it's cliché for women to drink white wine, especially me, but after this week it sounds good. If you don't mind."

Alex was squatting in front of the trailer's miniature refrigerator when he heard a noise behind him. AJ stood outside with her head poked into the trailer looking around.

"Nice place you have here. Very cozy." She stepped up and inside.

"All the comforts of home," he said, rising. He set the wine on the counter and searched through the drawer for an opener. After sifting through everything, he removed the entire drawer so he could see into the back. He gave her an apologetic smile. "Well, almost all the comforts. I swear I had a corkscrew."

"Never mind," AJ said. "I'll take a beer."

"You sure? I could probably get it out with a screw and pliers."

She laughed at that, deep and throaty. "Don't bother. If I wanted wine badly enough, I could go home and get *my* corkscrew. Beer's fine."

A few minutes later, they sat facing the lake as the steaks sizzled on the grill and sent fragrant streamers out the dome's vents. Foil packets containing potato slices, green onions, and red peppers were placed around the edges, as far away from the direct heat as his little grill allowed. A slight breeze blew upslope from the water, but the air was warm and carried summer dreams of boating and sunscreen, fishing and barbecues. Alex slouched in the chair and stretched his legs straight. Life could be a lot worse.

If alone, he'd close his eyes and snooze while the fire did its work, but he was hyper-aware of AJ sitting two feet away. She didn't seem to feel the need to talk, and he was okay with that. He'd invited her tonight to begin building some trust, something AJ Blaylock didn't do easily. After what she'd been through, he supposed that was expected.

"So, how are the rentals going?" He'd seen several different vehicles come and go, and AJ never seemed to stop running errands and cleaning. He wondered how she would handle the load when the fourth and fifth cabins were finished.

"The rentals are fine," AJ said, not elaborating. She sipped her beer, then regarded him over the neck of the bottle before continuing. "What are you really doing here, Stone?"

"Gotta check the steaks." Alex rose and pulled the cover off the grill. He'd just replaced the lid when a scuff of dirt sounded from the yard.

"Hey, you two." Mandy Conner marched up the path from AJ's cabin, a smile spreading across her face. Roarke Hamilton hovered on her heels.

Alex didn't like the look of the girl's grin. It could only mean trouble, the kind he didn't need.

"We thought we saw a light in your place when we drove up," Mandy said to AJ, "but of course no one answered the door. We didn't expect to find you up here. Together." She let the last word linger expectantly.

"It's not what it looks like—" AJ began.

"Oh, no need to explain," Mandy said, palms out. If anything, the girl's grin grew wider.

"Very cozy," Hamilton nodded with a smirk of his own. "We should have brought some steaks. Maybe some wine."

"Sorry. I only have two steaks. *Small* ones," Alex said, the words coming out with an edge. AJ gave him a glance with raised brow before turning back to the pair.

"And it seemed like a beer night," AJ said, indicating her bottle.

It was Alex's turn to raise his eyebrows at AJ's small defense. Maybe she wasn't too fond of Roarke Hamilton either. Alex hadn't liked the man from the minute they'd met at Mrs. H's house. His cockiness begged to be punched away. Alex certainly hoped Ben's niece had more sense than to get involved with the guy—not to mention Hamilton was more than twice her age. Still, stunted personality development didn't make the guy an enemy.

Most nights, Mandy was bunking at Ben and Rayne's while the couple toured in Europe. Quin Conner was old enough he didn't need a babysitter, but the two cousins got along famously. Mandy's own family was visiting friends in Missouri.

Mandy turned to AJ. "I wanted to ask if you'd like to come to lunch with me next week. I'm hungering for Wave Pizza in Perilous Cove." Mandy smacked her lips.

15

Lena's stomach growled as she made the turn at Flume and headed up East Lake Road toward Shelter Cove, Gift, and her cabins at Bass Point. She'd gotten an early start on her trip to Home Depot in Mission Peak, nearly an hour's drive due to the twisting roads. Trekking to the big box store only made sense for the more costly items, or for something that Brodie's Hardware in Perilous Cove didn't stock. Today's shopping quest was water heaters for cabins 4 and 6. She'd found forty-gallon units on sale, and they were securely tied in the trailer bumping along behind her Jeep.

The morning's warming air swirled through the open interior, carrying scents of fresh lake water, sage, and oak. She'd removed the Jeep's canvas top a few weeks ago and stored it in the barn. Now the only thing between her and the sun was the vehicle's bikini top, which she planned to leave in place until the last gasp of summer. The engine purred as much as it ever had, the six-cylinders not straining the least with its load.

Lena reviewed her to-do list as she drove. She'd noticed some litter around the cabins that needed cleaning up, and the two vacant units had to be scrubbed for the next renters arriving Friday. But now that she'd decided to fix up Cabin 6 for herself, her fingers itched to get going on the restoration. She only needed one water heater for that, but since they'd been on sale, she decided to get the basic infrastructure finished in Cabin 4. Once the water heater and the new kitchen faucet were installed, she'd have hot water for the rest of the refurbishing later on. Then, if she worked hard on Cabin 6, she could move in and convert her present cabin for renters by mid-July.

As she approached the spot where the body had been buried, she kept her eyes straight ahead, concentrating on the stream crossing. A tiny shiver ran up her spine at the unbidden image of the arm hanging from the tractor's bucket, and she held her breath as dust swirled into the Jeep's passenger compartment. The smell was probably gone, but the cleansing fall rains couldn't come soon enough for her. Most people went their whole lives without seeing a dead body except in a funeral home, and these days, even those were rare. Lena had seen two, and she hoped God counted that as enough.

The Jeep rolled to a halt behind Cabin 4, and Lena set the hand brake. Moving the water heater location out of the interior hallway had freed up the old inside space for a small closet. But now she had to build an enclosure on the back of the house for the new water heater. Sawhorses and lumber were already stacked beside the three-by-three concrete pad Colby had poured for her at the rear of the building.

Lena had just finished releasing the tie-down ropes when Alex Stone strolled up.

"Need a hand?" he asked, leaning a hip on the trailer.

Lena studied his casual pose. He appeared more coiled to strike than relaxed. It was as if the man prepared for the worst, every minute of the day. She shrugged, as much to accept his help as to dismiss his tension. She had enough worries of her own. "You don't have to."

"Ah, but I have to repay those exquisite Ho Hos you brought for dessert the other night," he said, and moved to the rear of the trailer. "Where'd you get those, anyway? I thought they stopped making them."

"Freezer." She grinned in spite of herself as they lifted one of the large, boxed units off the trailer, and set it upright on the waiting concrete. "I think they're still selling them, but I bought a bunch just in case. I was saving them for a special occasion, but those are kind of rare out here. And, when you said you were partial to chocolate cake…"

"I feel special." Stone helped her strip off the cardboard and jockey the round tank into position.

Lena and Colby had already run propane and water lines, so it was a simple matter to make the connections with the tools from her Jeep.

"How'd you learn all this?" Stone asked as he watched her wrap Teflon tape around the water connections at the unit's top, then thread the flex lines onto them.

"When I was little, the husband and wife next door used to buy old houses and fix them up.

"House flipping?"

"Well, they didn't call it that then. Sometimes they'd rent them out for a year or so, then sell them when something new and interesting came along. I used to go over to their house and watch home improvement shows with them." Lena unpacked an earthquake strap and attached it around the water heater.

"So you helped them out on jobs?"

She shook her head. "Only on projects they brought home, like furniture and cabinets. Mostly I just sat on a stool in the garage and watched." She hesitated, wondering how much to tell him. "I wasn't interested in college, so when I left home, I moved to Pleasanton and took a job at a construction site as a laborer." She'd picked Pleasanton, just north of San Jose, solely because it sounded like a nice place, somewhere she could escape her past.

"Tough work." Stone sounded impressed.

"The first few weeks nearly killed me," she laughed as they climbed into the Jeep and drove up to Cabin 6 to deliver the second water heater. "But the guys took pity on me and taught me framing and basic carpentry. Turned out I had a knack for it. Then a plumbing contractor offered me a job. I worked for him for a couple of years, then moved on to an electrical contractor. I got my general contractor's license."

They spent several minutes wrestling the boxed appliance onto a flat spot behind the cabin. Colby was coming back tomorrow to pour another concrete pad.

"Then I heard they were looking for a female carpenter for one of the remodeling shows on The Learning Channel. I decided to audition."

"And I bet it didn't hurt being a gorgeous blonde."

She studied Stone's face, wondering if he was kidding. These days, she looked nothing like a TV personality. Her hands were red and rough, and Band-Aids circled two fingers on her left hand where a burr on a piece of pipe had stuck her deep enough to bleed. She eschewed makeup for sunscreen, and in the dry summer air her hair needed constant conditioner. No one would call her for a hair product commercial, except if they needed a worst-case "before" photo.

But Stone didn't seem to be joking. Again she wondered what he was doing here. Mandy and Roarke had interrupted that part of their conversation at their dinner, and Stone had avoided the topic for the rest of the evening.

"Yeah, well it didn't turn out like I thought," she said. It turned out the producers of the L.A.-based show were looking for a token female face, but not smarts or ability. When the camera stopped rolling, they brought in male carpenters who built her projects, even though she had better ideas on how to do them. The excuse given was they didn't want to chance an injury. Eventually, she'd issued an ultimatum: let her do the work, or she'd walk. The next day, the male carpenters were gone. Except for one—who became her assistant.

The best part of being on the show had been meeting Bobby.

Stone left, and Lena went back to Cabin 4 to install the new kitchen faucet and frame the exterior water heater enclosure. If all went well, she'd have two coats of paint on it by four o'clock. She'd just picked up a two-by-four when her phone rang. She dug it out of her pocket and answered.

"Hello, Lena? Eve Crescent."

"Eve," Lena said. "Thanks for returning my call."

"Sorry it took so long. I was in court finishing up a rape trial. It's with the jury now." From the woman's upbeat attitude, Eve expected another win. "How can I help? Is it something to do with Bobby? Did you hear something?"

Lena's shoulders sagged. "I was going to ask you the same question. Chet called days ago and said he wanted to come up here, but he didn't show. I thought he knew something, but he hasn't returned the message I left, and I don't want to keep bugging him. I was hoping *you'd* heard something."

There was silence on the line, and for a moment Lena thought they'd been disconnected. Then she heard lacquered fingernails doing rolling taps, probably on the desktop. When Eve spoke, her voice was quiet and deep.

"I'll do some checking. Will you be home tonight?"

"Yes, I—"

"At this number?"

"Yes."

"Eight o'clock," Eve stated. "And where's 'here'?"

Few people knew where Lena was. Chet had found out somehow, but otherwise… "Storm Lake. It's—"

"I know it. Bass still biting there? Maybe I'll come up."

Before Lena could answer, Eve said, "Gotta go. Just got word the jury sent back a clarification question. Talk to you later," and the line went dead. Lena hit the End button unnecessarily. Eve Crescent was gone.

"Phew." Lena shook her head as she slid the phone into her pocket. The few times she'd been around Eve, she'd been fascinated at the speed at which the woman's mind switched gears. She could engage in three conversations at the same time, all the while checking her phone for messages. No matter how hard Lena tried, she couldn't picture the glamorous, professional Eve Crescent fishing from a boat on Storm Lake.

Alex rolled his truck down to the cabin where AJ was working. He was surprised to find her loading paint cans, scraps of lumber, and sawhorses into the Jeep's trailer. As he came to a stop, she approached his passenger window and laid her arms on the sill.

"You missed all the fun."

He looked beyond her to the water heater enclosure that was nothing but a pile of lumber a couple hours ago. It now had painted siding and a sloped, lean-to roof. The shingles matched the main house. A galvanized vent cap on the roof, and cross-braced door with hasp lock, finished the structure.

"Wow. You work fast. I'm impressed," he said. A grin spread on her face, her pride evident in the completed work. "I should get you to help me restore the inside of my trailer."

AJ rested her chin on her crossed arms. "I've never done a travel trailer. Might be fun." Brown paint stained her hands, and the sleeves of her blue work shirt sported smears of the siding color as well.

Alex hid a grin at the smudge on her freckled cheek. With her hair tied in its traditional high ponytail, she looked about seventeen. He could see why the television cameras loved her. He wished for his own camera right now, but knew she'd never agree to a photo session. Maybe a telephoto lens through the trees…

"Where you off to?" she asked.

"Mission Peak." He didn't elaborate and thought for a minute she might let it go, but curiosity got the better of her and she straightened.

"What are you doing here, Stone?" Where her eyes had been teasing before, they were now flint sharp and narrowed.

He gave her his biggest grin and eased his foot off the brake. The truck began to roll, and he lifted his hand in a wave as she stepped clear. "Don't want to be late. See you later, AJ." He started the engine, then stuck his head out the window as the truck continued forward. "Hey, need anything from town?" He was fifty yards away when he heard her shout.

"A half-inch by three inch galvanized pipe nipple. *And more Fritos!*"

He waved out the window, a smile covering his face as he accelerated over the hill.

Unable to sit a second longer, Lena rose from her lopsided chair and paced her front porch. Her phone was fully charged, and it had a steady two-bar signal, as good as it ever got. It was 9:15. Sunset had been nearly an hour ago, and the western horizon showed only the slightest remnant of blue. Overhead, stars twinkled merrily in the black canopy, unaware of Lena's anxiety.

A mosquito zinged around her left ear, and she swatted it away. Time to go in before she got eaten alive. It appeared Eve's promised eight o'clock call wasn't happening at all tonight.

Stone hadn't returned after he'd left, either, not with the Fritos or her pipe. She'd made do on the plumbing with a longer piece she'd found in a junk bin in the barn.

It wasn't like she could talk to Stone about Bobby, Chet, and Eve. One of the nice things about Stone was that he didn't know her history, and never gave her the pitying look she'd seen so much of in L.A. He was sort of nice to have around, even if she didn't know his agenda—and he was definitely hiding something.

As Lena pulled open the screen door, her phone dinged. Across the display read:

Can't call. Letter coming. – E

Weird. It looked like a text message, but there was no phone number for the sender. And there was no Reply button for Lena to respond. Obviously, it was from someone who knew her mobile number. The only person she was expecting to call was Eve, so the *E* made sense. But how could she send it so it didn't show up as a standard message? And why?

The phone shut off, and Lena clicked it on again. The message appeared briefly, but then vanished before her eyes. She checked her text message menu, but there was nothing there.

Another mosquito—or perhaps the same pesky one—whined around her ear. The sky was completely black now, and a shiver went up Lena's spine so hard her shoulders shook. The night was warm, so it wasn't that, but something was in the air. She hurried inside. Despite the overly warm interior of her cabin, she shut the front door and locked it.

16

By ten Tuesday morning, Lena had put in four sweaty hours on her new cabin, ripping up rotten floorboards on the front porch and replacing them with matching planks from the rear porch. Her plan was to smooth everything with her belt sander, then stain them a rich mahogany that would contrast with the white railing and spindles. Of course she'd have to paint the railings first since they were weathered gray right now. The back porch could be patched with new wood since she could use paint rather than stain so they looked uniform. The cabinet floor under the kitchen sink had been next, requiring replacement after years of leaks.

But the physical work wasn't enough to keep her mind off the cryptic phone message. If Eve was sending a letter, it would take at least a couple of days. Even if it went out in this morning's mail, it wouldn't get to Storm Lake until Thursday, or maybe Friday.

"I'll go nuts by then," she said, as she pounded the final nail into the new cabinet floor. After a vacuum and a quick coat of primer on the bare wood, she backed out from under the sink and leaned her aching back against the opposite wall. Between thinking about the message and getting up to check the barn through the kitchen window, she hadn't gotten a lot of sleep.

Lena rose with a groan. She had to keep moving or she'd freeze in one spot. Plus, anxious to tackle the new cabin, she'd skipped eating this morning, and the gnawing ache in her stomach couldn't be denied any longer.

Back at her cabin, Lena slapped together bread, mayo, mustard, and two pieces of American cheese. Her mouth was watering before the first big bite. Chewing, she thought of her lack of Fritos, which led to thoughts of Stone. Much as she tried to dislike him, it had been nice to trade jabs at their dinner. Oddly, she looked forward to his return.

Lena finished her sandwich and headed to the bathroom, nearly jumping at her reflection in the mirror. Sawdust sprinkled her hair, and the ponytail ends were frizzed like an abused paint brush. The dry mountain air had done a number, and it hadn't been professionally cut in at least three months. The scissors from the kitchen utility drawer didn't count.

"Too bad it's not Halloween." She thought of Stone seeing her like this. It was weird that he hadn't come back yet. Not that it mattered. She wasn't his keeper, and wasn't trying for the guy, but her hair needed some serious TLC. She didn't want to frighten any small children who happened to show up with her renters.

There wasn't time for a trip to Mission Peak, but Mrs. H had mentioned a place in Deer Cove. After a quick shower, Lena fired up the Jeep. Her plan was to be in and out of the salon, then on to other projects for the rest of the daylight hours.

Boaters were out in force, cutting swaths through the smooth waters on their way to favorite fishing spots, or just having fun. Warm days were here to stay, and most of the seasonal homes around the lake were opened and aired out. Brightly colored ice chests graced every porch, and towels and bathing suits hung on railings.

Vehicle traffic was noticeably heavier as Lena entered Deer Cove. With its permanent population of 1,256—hand-painted on the town sign—it was by far the largest community at the lake. But the summer swell that reportedly reached around four thousand had already begun, and it showed. The town sported the lake's largest marina, several restaurants, a pharmacy, gift stores, offices for a part-time doctor and his dentist counterpart, a grocery store with a regional bank branch inside and a decent hardware aisle, and the lake's only gas station. Deer Cove Auto had four cars scattered haphazardly in front of the double bays; two more were inside on raised lifts. Lena had brought her Jeep for a tune-up a couple of months ago, and the mechanic, Mark, had done a good job. Merle's firewood business was off a dirt road that ran west of town. Unfortunately, the lake's sole hardware store had folded a year ago and sat abandoned.

But her goal today wasn't any of those businesses. She drove through the village, taking in enticing aromas from DC Coffee and Peg's Waffle House.

As the stores fell behind, a large barn appeared on the left. Lena steered the Jeep into the parking lot and climbed out.

According to Mrs. H, Bibs' Beauty Barn had been an institution at the lake for years. The story was that Bibs' husband thought she couldn't make it in business. To prove him wrong, she'd opened up the beauty shop in the barn. The man was now long gone, but Bibs and her Beauty Barn lived on.

The mannequin at the sliding barn door gave her a moment's pause. Dressed in a sequined black frock with a pink boa looped around her neck, the skinny woman had one manicured finger pointed at all that entered, and the sign around her neck warned, *Don't mess with me*. Never one for traditional beauty shops, this looked like Lena's kind of place. She stepped inside.

Bare beam rafters faded into the high darkness, but the space below was brightly lit by suspended lights. A half wall separated the entry from the main salon area, but did nothing to hide the chemical odors of acetone, hair spray, and coloring products. A coughing jag hit as her throat threatened to seal shut. Although this barn had as many cracks between the boards as Lena's did, she'd bet there wasn't a non-asphyxiated spider or mouse in the place.

Along the front wall to the left sat a glass display case, and behind it was a raised dais holding a blue velour recliner straight out of someone's family room. Nearly obscuring the chair was a stout woman tapping her hands on the worn fabric. As soon as the woman spotted Lena, she gave the reclining lever a shove and catapulted upright.

"Hi there," the woman said, hopping off the dais with impressive agility for her size. She rounded the glass case and stopped so close that Lena took a small step back. The woman reminded Lena of a beach ball, except this ball had flaming red hair. If the deep lines in her puffy skin were to be believed, she had to be at least eighty. The woman squinted up through half-glasses strung on a gold chain, and circled Lena, lifting her hair. "Oh, honey, you need some serious help." A firm nod of her head sent the chain swinging.

Lena held up her hand. "Well, I just—"

The woman snatched Lena's hand in a steely grip. "Good heavens, your hands are a mess." She pulled the other one close and twisted it over. "You been chopping wood?"

"Well, I—"

"You need a proper manicure—after a thorough cleaning of course."

"I'm not looking—"

"I'm Bibs," the woman said, turning and waving a hand behind the counter. "And that's my sister, Irene."

Lena followed Bibs' gesture where another older woman Lena hadn't noticed rocked in a much more modest chair, this one not on a pedestal. Irene wore a blue dress with tiny white polka dots and a white headband à la Audrey Hepburn. Knitting needles flashed and clacked as a ball of multicolored yarn jerked and rotated in a stand-mounted knitting bowl.

Irene paused her knitting and said, "I'm going to die soon," a smile on her face, still rocking like nothing in the world was the matter.

"Oh, cut the dying bit, Irene," Bibs snapped, "you're going to scare her off." Bibs turned to Lena, still clutching her hand. "Don't pay no mind to that old lady. Doc Arnold says she's healthy as a horse."

Lena wasn't sure what she'd gotten herself into. Maybe she should have made the drive to Mission Peak and hung out at Home Depot. She could have dried her hair this morning with a leaf blower and no one there would care. She wasn't even sure why she was doing this. It wasn't to impress Stone.

"Yvonne!" Bibs called, and a young woman with purple spiked hair, matching lipstick, and at least ten silver rings in her right ear jumped from a chair where she'd been browsing a dog-eared People magazine. Bibs dragged Lena to the gum-chewing woman. "Yvonne, this is AJ Blaylock. She owns those rental cabins over north of Gift at Bass Point, you know?"

Lena wasn't sure how Bibs had known her name, but she supposed word got around quickly in such a small community. Perhaps Mrs. H had mentioned her to Bibs.

"Oh, yeah. Hey, AJ." Yvonne blew a tiny pink bubble. It popped as she gave Lena a calculated up and down assessment. Yvonne's eyes cut to Bibs, and her mouth formed a silent O.

Bibs addressed Lena. "I could have one of the older operators work on you, but I think Yvonne—being younger and all—is more your style."

Lena spared another glance at Yvonne's eyebrow piercing and nose ring, and tried to back away, but Bibs had a grip like a used car salesman.

"You go fix up her hair, Yvonne," Bibs ordered. "Make it look good, now, like a classy woman, not like you did with Mrs.... Well, never mind about that." Yvonne looked slightly offended, but Bibs didn't seem to notice. "I'll get Linda lined up for her manicure." Bibs steered Lena to a vacant hair washing station.

Before she could ask what it would all cost, Bibs had disappeared, and Lena's head was tilted into the shampoo sink with warm water flowing over her hair. A younger girl, whose name Lena hadn't caught, massaged coconut-scented shampoo into her hair, and prattled on about her weekend date with Rocky, her high school boyfriend. The girl's words blurred as her strong fingers kneaded the tension from Lena's scalp. She felt it circling down the drain with any missed sawdust, and her shoulders relaxed against the padded chair.

How long had it been since she'd pampered herself? The answer came, towing with it memories she'd buried: Bobby. He'd treated her to a spa package. She'd reclined against a porcelain bowl like this one, preparing for a cut and color. Life was good. She had a good job, and loving husband, and was thinking about what Bobby had said last night, about starting a family. She'd put up an argument, wanting to finish decorating their bedroom first. The master bedroom was always the last room done in a house. And, right after her haircut, she was heading to the store to hunt for the perfect window coverings.

Two days later, Bobby lay dead. Draperies no longer mattered.

As the nameless shampoo girl turned on the rinsing sprayer, Lena squeezed her eyes shut, not to keep the splashing water out, but to keep the salty tears in.

17

Teal arrived at "their" rock at 1:45 on Tuesday, and took up her familiar spot. At the sound of every outboard motor, she shielded her eyes and searched the water for Quin's small, silver boat.

She'd savored every morsel of the food he'd left her, stretching the surplus lunch across Saturday, Sunday, and Monday, then finished the last cookie for breakfast this morning. Food no longer fell into healthy groups, nor did she limit it to artificial designations such as breakfast, lunch, and dinner. It was *life*, plain and simple. Survival. And she'd take anything she could, any time she could.

The food Quin had left her was sparse when spread over three-plus days —not counting the previous days of next to nothing. Maybe he would bring something good today, but fear gnawed like the hunger at the realization that he might assume she'd already eaten lunch—with her parents.

Teal checked her watch again, a small Timex with a cracked crystal she'd begged off a thrift store employee. Although no longer waterproof, it kept good time. She adjusted the leather band to cover the scars on her right wrist.

Sweat trickled down her neck and she shifted a couple of feet into some shade. Shorts would have been cooler than her jeans and long-sleeved shirt, but they wouldn't hide her bony frame—or the marks. More than how thin she was, she didn't want Quin to see the flaws.

At least the shirt was clean. Or, rather, cleaner. She'd scored a towel left on a porch railing when one of the renters checked out, and they'd thrown out a partial bar of soap. After dark, she'd hiked up past the boat launch and washed in the lake: hair, body, and clothes. The lake water wasn't nearly as cold as the falls, and she'd done a little swimming.

She sighed as minutes passed and the sun shrunk her shade. By ten minutes after, she'd resigned herself to a no-show for the brown-haired boy.

More disappointed than she wanted to admit, she rose to leave when she spotted a boat cutting straight across the lake from the western shore, pointed right at her. When it grew closer, she recognized Quin, baseball cap reversed and hunched over in front of the motor, as if urging the craft to more speed. At the last second, he cut the throttle and let the keel groove gently into the gravel strip of beach. He walked forward, arms stretched for balance, then hopped out onto land, fists on his waist and one foot slightly forward like Captain Jack Sparrow. He grinned up at her.

Teal couldn't prevent the corners of her mouth from twitching. Showoff.

"Your craft awaits, milady," Quin intoned, sweeping the cap across his waist in a bow.

She sat and scooted off the rock, the shore gravel crunching under her tennis shoes. He held out his hand to help her aboard. Teal took it, flushing at the heat of his touch as she stepped into the wobbly boat.

"Aren't you hot in that?" he indicated her shirt. Covered head to toe as she was, she felt majorly overdressed compared to Quin's T-shirt, shorts, and sock-less deck shoes.

"I burn easily. Have to stay covered, you know?" He seemed satisfied with her response, so she changed the subject. "Where are we going?"

"Ah, if I told you, it wouldn't be a surprise."

Quin directed her to the bow seat, and in less than a minute he'd pushed off and had the motor humming. They turned south, and he opened the throttle full, slicing along the relatively smooth water and surging skyward at every lazy swell.

The air at water level was cool and fragrant, fresh with possibilities. Teal's hair wrapped around her face every time she glanced back at the grinning boy steering the boat. So much of the last three months had been only about staying alive. Here, she felt Quin's contagious joy at skimming the open water. He'd been lucky to grow up on this beautiful lake that was fed from a waterfall with butterflies.

She dipped her fingers in the rushing water, sending sprays rearward.

"Hey!"

Teal grinned as Quin brushed droplets from his face. Always content to be on the move before, she suddenly longed to settle, make friends.

Have a boyfriend. Her smile slipped a little.

Don't get your hopes up.

Teal tilted her face to the high, summer sun, wishing the day could go on forever. They could circle the lake until dusk, then stop at a gorgeous waterfront home and roast hotdogs over a crackling beach fire. She'd lean back and he'd wrap his tanned arms around her, keeping her safe.

The cabins of Gift slid past on their left. There were more cars parked around the cabins now than when she'd foraged there. The summer crowds were arriving, making it that much more difficult to sneak in to find food. Quin slowed and steered a wide crescent around a large outcropping he told her was Breakers Point. Several fishermen's boats bobbed in matching rhythm to the red and white floats at the ends of their lines.

"They wouldn't appreciate us scaring the fish."

After leaving the fishermen behind, Quin sped up again for a couple of minutes as they turned toward a beach. The nose of the boat fell as he cut the motor and let the aluminum keel shush into coarse pebbles. Teal climbed out of the boat and waited while Quin pulled the craft higher. She turned to examine their surroundings.

The shallow beach stretched along the base of jagged rock outcroppings about six feet high. Someone had hewn rough steps from above, taking advantage of the natural horizontal slabs. Horizontal uplift, one of her teachers had called it. Funny the random things her brain recalled.

At the far end from where they'd landed, half a dozen little kids splashed in a roped-off area of the water, while moms watched from canvas beach chairs sheltered under a royal blue popup canopy.

"This is a beautiful spot," Teal said as Quin turned to her.

"Welcome to my beach," he said, spreading his arms wide.

"*Your* beach?" Teal said, narrowing her eyes. In a whisper she said, "You must be very rich."

"Well," he said, that grin she liked so much tugging his mouth, "not really *mine*. I mean I don't own it or anything. But I grew up here. This is Shelter Cove. But you knew that, right? I mean, you'd have driven through here on the way to your house."

"Oh, yeah," Teal covered. "I just, uh, didn't recognize it from...from the water." A few rooftops poked above the ledge, and she wondered if any of them were empty so she could score some food. Shelter Cove. Good to know.

Did Quin live in one of them? As if reading her mind, he stepped behind her and extended his arm over her shoulder.

"See that house over there?"

Teal sighted along his finger toward the southern end of the cove, past the kids swimming and the end of the beach, to a house that sat alone on a sloping bank. The peaked A-frame facing the water was a wall of glass that overlooked a patio. Even from this angle, she could tell it had a magnificent view of the lake. At the water's edge, a wooden dock hung from thick posts that disappeared below the surface.

Quin swung his arm slightly left, brushing her cheek. "That's my room—the end one."

As amazing as the house was, Teal couldn't concentrate on the lodge-like timbers, the stone pillars, or the tall pines. Quin's breath tickled her neck, and her world became suntan lotion and the radiating heat of his tanned arm where it rested lightly on her shoulder. Her knees wobbled and her vision dimmed until nothing except his male presence remained. She could no more prevent leaning back than she could stop the sun's movement across the sky. His chest felt solid as stone, which was good because her world spun out of control.

Before she knew what happened, Quin's arms wrapped around her and lowered her to the hot gravel. Like a movie—if she could just stop her eyes from whirling.

"Hey, are you all right?" he asked, shading her face as he bent over her. Concern creased the space between his brows. His hair drifted in the warm breeze, backlit by the overhead sun like an angel's halo. "Do you need a doctor?"

It took her three tries to form a *No*. She licked her lips, focusing on her angel's brown eyes. So kind. Not like the others. She lifted a hand toward his face, wanting to smooth away the worry, but stopped short and let it fall to her stomach. "I think I just need something to drink."

Quin placed his palm across her forehead. Where his skin had been hot before, now it felt cool.

"Come on," he said, and scooped her up as if she weighed nothing. He carried her to the base of the rock where a towering pine cast a solid shadow pool, and lowered her to the sand. She leaned against the rocks, glad the motion had stopped.

"I could have walked, you know." She tried for a teasing tone, but he didn't smile.

"I'll be right back," he said all serious, and jogged toward the boat.

Teal closed her eyes against the glare off the lake and listened to the wavelets lapping the shore. Her eyeballs felt like they were swirling in their sockets and she willed them still. Or maybe they weren't moving at all. Deep breathing helped.

Quin returned with a cooler and a blanket that he spread out. She moved onto it, and he sat down and pulled the cooler between them. He unpacked peanut butter and jelly sandwiches, Doritos, chunks of cheddar cheese, and two bottles of water. He opened one of the bottles and passed it to her.

"Drink." He watched as she took a swig. "More."

Teal drained half the bottle, the cold liquid cutting a path down her throat to her stomach where it soaked the heat from her core. She capped the bottle and put it down.

"Are you hungry?"

"Starved," she managed with a straight face. He had no idea.

"If you're good and eat all your lunch, I brought dessert." Quin dangled a baggie bulging with Oreos. His joking words were colored with concern.

Teal bit into her sandwich, nearly fainting again as yummy peanut and grape jelly flavors hit her tongue. She washed it down with another long swig of water. Then the salty Doritos made her even thirstier, so she finished the bottle. Without waiting for her to ask, Quin pulled another one from the cooler and passed it to her. When was the last time someone noticed enough to take care of her?

She forced herself to slow down, knowing from experience her shrunken stomach would rebel and she'd lose it all on the sand. Everything tasted so good. She broke off a crumble of the cheese, popped it in her mouth, and closed her eyes. The tangy dryness melted into her taste buds.

"Cracker Barrel," Quin explained around a mouthful of sandwich. "Extra sharp. My dad used to buy it for special occasions—before he died."

Teal's eyes flew open, drawn to the beautiful home a few hundred yards south. "But I thought—"

"I have a new dad now. Ben Conner. He adopted me." He spoke matter-of-factly, but Teal detected something deeper, a sorrow carved in the soul.

"So Ben married your mom?"

Quin shook his head and looked across the lake. "My mom left when I was a baby. My dad and I never saw her again." He plucked a square of cheese from the bag. "It's kind of complicated. Rayne, my new mom, and Ben were married a long time ago. They got divorced for fifteen years. Ben adopted me, and now they're married again."

Nothing sounded unusual to Teal when it came to families. She'd seen several foster families in action. Talk about weird. Well, not all of them. Some were okay. She'd just never stayed in them long.

"Tell me about your mom and dad," Quin said. "Have they been married a long time?"

Teal choked on the chip she'd been chewing. Quin patted her on the back as she coughed and wheezed. Finally she took a few sips of water, using the recovery time to think of what she'd say.

No, they haven't been married long. In fact, they haven't been married at all.

It was well after 2:00 p.m. by the time Lena escaped Bibs' Beauty Barn and headed home. It felt like she'd blown half the day. After paying the tab, she'd definitely blown most of her budget. But her new haircut felt amazingly light, and her previously ruined nails were evenly filed and shone beneath a clear polish. Yvonne had even treated Lena to a facial mask during the haircut. Lena had brushed her fingers over her softened skin and promised Yvonne she'd regularly use moisturizer and hair conditioner.

As Lena passed Flume, she checked the intersection with the highway from the southwest, and noticed a small, black Honda merge behind her. At least she *thought* it was a Honda. Her brief glimpse was enough to see that the car had been de-badged of all emblems, and every previously chromed surface had been painted black. Even the windows had dark tint. Most of the vehicles around the lake were either pickups or SUVs, but she supposed it could be a high school kid from Mission Peak.

The car stayed fifty yards behind her the whole way up East Lake Road, and she thought of turning in at Shelter Cove Store, but couldn't decide in time. As she flew past, she saw the sedan brake and turn into the store parking lot.

Lena lifted her foot from the gas pedal and let the Jeep slow, and then stopped at the side of the road. She breathed a sigh of relief. Just a tourist. Her beauty shop calm had fled in the face of her paranoia. There was no getting it back, but she rolled the tightness out of her shoulders while massaging her temples. After a minute, she pulled onto the road and drove home.

She had just climbed out of the Jeep in front of her cabin when the black sedan roared over the hill and braked to a stop behind her. A hooded figure climbed out. Who wore a hoodie in ninety-five degrees? Lena backed around her Jeep as the man lifted his head.

"Lena Blaylock?"

Panic surged through her veins. If she confirmed her identity, would he pull out a gun and shoot her?

"What do you want?" She tried for authoritative, but it came out weak and squeaky when the man put his right hand into his parka pocket. Her breath caught as he withdrew… a folded manila envelope.

"I have a courier delivery," the man said, pushing back his hood with his other hand and pulling out white earbuds. He was Latino, young, perhaps twenty years old, with short-cropped hair, black mustache, and close-trimmed beard around his chin. A geometric tattoo covered the left side of his neck. He looked like a gang member who might show up on the nightly news.

"C-courier?" He kept advancing, and Lena kept retreating—until she reached the base of the porch stairs.

"Yes, ma'am. I'm with L.A. Metro Courier Service. We were hired to deliver these papers to you." He stopped three feet from her and extended the envelope.

"I saw you behind me," Lena said. "Why did you stop at the store?"

"Oh." He appeared genuinely surprised. "I didn't realize that was you ahead of me. The sender didn't give your exact address, so I just kept driving until I saw the store. Figured they'd know where you lived."

She relaxed a little. "What's with the hoodie? It's pretty hot today."

He laughed. "My car's got awesome AC, but the stereo blew. The hood hides my earbuds so cops don't hassle me. It's a pretty boring drive all the way from L.A. without my music."

Lena accepted the envelope and stared at her name printed neatly on the front. "You drove over two hundred miles to deliver a letter? Who hired you?"

He shook his head. "Don't know. Got a call from my boss this morning telling me to gas up. You can call him if you want." He dug in his jeans pocket. "Here's his number." He handed her a wrinkled business card.

L.A. Metro Courier Service, Manny Estefan, owner. We deliver!

"I'll need you to sign for it." He extracted a notebook from his other pocket, and Lena signed the offered page.

"I'm afraid I'm broke right now, but I can write you a check for the tip," Lena said, thinking of the giant hole in her wallet after her haircut.

Palms raised, the young man backed toward his car. "No need. Tip's already covered by the sender. Have a good day." He hopped back into the car, plugged in his earbuds, and pulled up his hood.

In seconds he was gone, leaving only swirling dust—and the envelope in Lena's hand.

18

Alex checked his watch as he turned off the headlights and cut the truck's engine. Past two o'clock—in the morning. A soft breeze brought the lake's soothing, wet scent through the driver window. He'd only been gone two days; hardly time to miss it. Yet he had.

Bones crunched as he rotated his shoulders and tilted his head side to side. It would take more than that to work out the kinks from the grueling drive from the Mexican border. His workday had begun with a drug raid before sunrise.

Technically, he hadn't had to be at the raid—he wasn't official DEA anymore, only a part-time information analyst. He'd just gone into Mission Peak to visit his dad, when his old boss called him and told him to get to the border. A tip had come in about a high-level cartel meeting. His boss thought they should crash the meeting and see what intel they could recover. He wanted Alex to have a firsthand look-see at anything they found.

Alex had started to decline—they could courier the information up to him after the raid—but then his boss mentioned a name: Bobby Blaylock.

Tired as he was now, he was glad his boss had allowed him to tag along. No one had gotten shot, not even the bad guys, though there were enough weapons inside the house to take the Alamo. It had been a total rush to storm the drug house with guns drawn and shouting—just like COPS on TV. As a private citizen, he'd been ordered to keep his head down and bring up the rear. Alex smiled as he slouched in the truck. He kind of missed the adrenaline-pumping action.

Unfortunately, only one of the six men at the meeting had proved to be of possible value, and except for some veiled references to strategic contacts in Los Angeles, the information they recovered hadn't revealed anything directly related to Blaylock. However, two names on a list were of known gang members with contract-for-hire history. This was the first solid link the DEA had between the cartel and an L.A. gang. His boss promised to sweat the detainees and let Alex know if they gave up anything more.

A snapping twig outside the driver window brought him to attention, his Glock's barrel positioned just out of sight below the windowsill.

"Don't shoot, Stone."

He relaxed, recognizing AJ's voice. What was she doing out in the middle of the night? He slipped the weapon under his seat as he opened the door. The dome light came on and spilled a wedge across the ground, illuminating AJ's flip flops and frayed jean cuffs as she stepped forward. She wore an untucked long sleeved shirt, but no jacket though the night was chilly. He swung sideways, his feet resting on the old truck's step.

"How'd you know I was armed?" he asked as her face came into the light.

She gave him a classic Lauren Bacall eyebrow raise that nearly had him laughing. But her lips were a straight line and clearly not amused.

Alex sighed and scrubbed his face with his hands. Nice welcome after a twenty-two hour day protecting the world from the forces of evil.

"So, what is it?" she snapped. "Sig, Glock, Barretta, H&K?"

AJ's eyes were hard, an impressive feat in the cab's mellow light, Alex thought. He retrieved the gun and laid it across his lap. "Glock. Nine millimeter."

She crossed her arms protectively and wouldn't spare the pistol but the briefest glance. "I don't like guns," she said, but didn't move away.

He picked up the weapon, dropped the magazine, confirmed the chamber was empty, and zipped everything into its travel bag. Clearly she knew guns, even if she didn't want them around. "They've been kind of necessary in my line of work."

AJ put a hand on the open door as if to steady herself. She nodded and let out a breath. "It's not the gun's fault."

Alex didn't comment, but appreciated her rational reasoning. Hard to do, especially considering her husband had prosecuted bad guys, and had carried a gun for protection after the inevitable threats started.

Like most law enforcement professionals, Alex had never shot anyone in the line of duty—or any other time for that matter. He'd been shot *at* twice in standoff situations and had returned fire in one of them, but in both cases others on the team ultimately talked the suspect down. As much as he trained, he prayed he would never find out what it was like to take another's life.

Bobby Blaylock never had a chance to use his gun the night of the attack. Not that it would have done him much good according to the report Alex had read. Over two hundred rounds had been fired into the Blaylock house. AJ's survival had been deemed a miracle, but was mostly due to the fact she'd fallen behind an old trunk stuffed with Bobby's college law books sitting in a corner of the dining room. In a way, the man had protected his wife. Bobby himself hadn't been so lucky.

"I'm sorry about your husband, AJ." Her head snapped up and he watched emotions ripple across her face for several seconds.

"Did you know him?" she asked, her eyes flicking between his like at a tennis match.

Alex shook his head. Of course he'd *heard* of Bobby Blaylock, up and coming assistant district attorney. Who hadn't? Alex had been in Los Angeles at the time, working out of the DEA office on Flower Street, but most of his assignments had been on field task force teams following leads toward the Mexican border. And, until reading the news reports of Bobby's death, Alex had never known the man was married. Completely by chance, Alex had also seen Lena McKinley on television, but he was gone on assignments so frequently he'd missed the entertainment news of their relationship.

AJ sagged a little and used the truck door as support. She'd moved within reach. In less than a second, he could draw her into his arms. Instead he asked, "Why are you out here in the middle of the night? Is something wrong?"

AJ regarded him as a mouse might watch a cat. "What are *you* doing here, Stone?" she asked with a shaky breath.

The turnabout caught him off guard. He studied her in the dim light. Something had upset her, forced her to come to him for help even though she knew he carried a gun—or maybe because of it. Yet she didn't know him, didn't trust him.

"You said you were going to Mission Peak. And you were going to bring back the pipe nipple and some Fritos."

Stone slapped his forehead. "I'm sorry, I forgot about—"

"Never mind," she waved him off. "You were gone two days."

Alex pinched the bridge of his nose. "I'm...uh. Well, it's kind of complicated."

"You don't seem like the complicated type," she said.

"Are you saying I'm all brawn and no brain?" He feigned offense, hoping for distraction.

"I'm *saying* I'd like to know why you're here."

AJ stepped closer, and he caught the scent of lavender shampoo as the breeze lifted the ends of her hair. She rested her palms on his knees, but kept her eyes locked on his.

"Why." It was no longer a question.

This wasn't the place to tell AJ that he'd followed her cable TV show—and not for the decorating tips. Probably like thousands of other guys, he watched the show to catch the occasional glimpse of the sexy blonde carpenter who stuck nails between lips that would make Jennifer Garner jealous, and who wiped smudges on her adorable face every time she worked. The director who kept cutting away from her should have been fired for incompetence.

He still didn't want to give the answer, but he could see in her eyes that more deflection would push her away. He didn't want that. He sighed. "I was asked to be here. In case there was any trouble."

Her gaze narrowed. "Are you talking about trouble for me? Like a body guard?"

He shrugged. "More like to be around...just in case."

"Who?"

It was half innocent question and half demand. Alex knew she wasn't asking from whom the danger might come. She meant who was footing the bill. Alex sighed, berating himself for not telling her sooner. Then she could have despised him from their first meeting.

"My boss—old boss. Bill Halwell."

AJ's brows knit together, as if trying to place the name.

"At the DEA."

AJ jerked as if she'd been slapped. She banged her elbow on the window frame and winced in pain. He reached out, but she warded him off with raised palms. Then she turned and fled.

Lena ran into the dark, ignoring Stone's shout. But with her blurred vision, she hadn't made it thirty feet before colliding with one of the trash bins and stumbling sideways into the only rose bush on the property the deer hadn't nibbled to oblivion. The long arms of the climbing vine tangled in her hair, shirtsleeves, and jeans. Mad as she was, she had to stop and fumble in the dark with the green branches and their shark's-teeth thorns. The more she twisted, the more entangled they got.

Steps sounded on the gravel behind her and a flashlight flicked on.

"Let me help you." Stone's voice was a breath in the dark, but she flinched anyway, driving several sharp points into her skin.

"Ouch." She tugged her arm again. She didn't want his help.

"Hold still." His hands settled lightly on her shoulders.

She didn't want him on her property with his guns and mysteries. Well, no longer mysteries. DEA. My God, could she never get away from it? Now she knew why he was here—to bring up past memories. The painful ones, not the good ones.

Lena remained rigid as Stone leaned close, his heat burning through the back of her thin shirt. Her hair lifted as he pulled the vine away. She followed the flashlight beam as it played along her right arm, then Stone reached around and began separating thorn from cloth.

"Hold the light." His breath tickled her ear, sending a shiver across her shoulders.

Lena accepted the flashlight and shone its beam across her trapped arms. His hard chest pressed against her, and she swayed under the sensation. Even that tiny movement caused a vine to tighten on her arm.

"You're moving." His voice rolled over her, deep, gentling, like he was working with a skittish filly.

"Sorry." She licked her lips. "I'm not used to—"

"Accepting a little help from anyone?" He sounded amused as he plucked the last barb away from her sleeve. He held the prickly stem away and encircled her waist with his other arm. He drew her backwards, leaving the bush free to trap another unwary woman running through the night.

Goose bumps rose in a protesting wave across her skin when he separated enough so she could turn. His arm still held her waist, and it took all her resolve to resist leaning into his strength. She flicked off the light, and they stood in the dark, letting their eyes adjust to the faint stars and the glow from the truck's dome light across the clearing.

Her eyes cleared as she processed what he'd said. DEA. Still, it didn't mean he knew—

"AJ, I didn't know about your father. I'd never met him until yesterday. He was there on—"

"I don't want to hear about it…about him." Lena tried not to think about Simon McKinley, ever. But the truth was, every time her mother's caregivers called, Lena couldn't help but remember the man who had walked out on their family.

Lena never thought of him as her father again, just the man who had ruined their lives.

Stone's hands moved in circles on her back. She was practically hyperventilating. After a final shuddering breath, she gave into the embrace. It wasn't *his* fault he'd chosen to work for the same organization as Simon McKinley.

Stone pulled her against his chest, and she turned her head sideways to lie against the warmth. She was grateful he couldn't see the flush running up her neck as her body betrayed her brain. Stupid hormones. Just because he was a hunk didn't mean she should throw herself at him in some primal response to preserve the species.

Hunk? *Alex Stone?*

Lena leaned back to meet his gaze, but a dark line running down his left cheek distracted her. "You're bleeding." She reached up, unable to stop her thumb from tracing the smear. Then her fingertips brushed his old scar where it began in front of his ear, and she yanked her hand away. "Oh. I'm sorry."

Stone's fingers replaced her own, smearing the streak of blood. "It's nothing," he said, but his eyes had gone flat. Not hard, but no longer friendly.

"Stone, I didn't mean…I mean—"

"Keep the light," he said, and turned back to the truck. The night chill that rushed in as he left caused an involuntary shiver.

She didn't know *what* she wanted to say. It was idiotic that touching the long-healed injury would feel intensely more intimate than running her thumb over the bloody thorn scrape, but it did.

She'd intended to tell him about Eve's letter, but the fact that danger was once again invading her safe haven had vexed her. Then he'd shown up in the middle of the night…with his gun. His presence—especially as DEA—was a reminder of a past she was trying to put behind her.

Now he was distancing himself from her, exactly what she'd first wanted when he'd shown up after Mrs. H's dinner. So why now did it feel like she'd lost something instead of getting her way? Lena opened her mouth to… What? Call him back? Apologize again? Caress his scar?

Stone locked the truck and went into his trailer. Lena waited by the rose bush until a light came on behind the curtains, then she turned toward her home.

He'd been nothing but nice, reliable, helpful, even fun. Now she'd rebuffed him with the touch of her fingers, and yearned for a do-over.

The thorn scratches stung as Lena shuffled back to her cabin, but she welcomed the discomfort. She deserved worse.

19

Alex was still bleary-eyed from the late night as he lifted the can of shaving cream and stared into the small mirror in his trailer. For the first time in months he closely examined the jagged scar on the left side of his face.

Cornell "T-Top" Lewis, a wannabe gangsta rapper—who had grown up in an upper class home in Brentwood instead of on the rough streets of South Central L.A. like his music PR sheet touted—had been higher than the roof of his Hollywood bungalow when Alex and the DEA team came through the front door. T-Top and his dozen druggie friends put up a scuffle, and the rapper broke free of the agent who had taken him to the floor. Alex lunged across a prostrate girl to assist just as T-Top snapped open a switchblade.

That had been two years ago.

He ran his index finger over the scar, tracing it from in front of his ear down the side of his neck where it ended an inch above his T-shirt collar. It was practically smooth now, at least compared to the puckered tissue after the stitches had been removed. The plastic surgeon had promised him it would continue to blend with his deeper skin tone, but it still stood out as a slightly raised white line. The doc had finally admitted with a shrug that some people were more prone to scarring.

His sister, Kris, said it lent him a dashing image—right after she blanched when they'd met for lunch six weeks after the attack.

He rubbed it again, pressing the ridge down as if he could flatten and mold it into the surrounding flesh. He hadn't paid the scar much attention, hadn't cared what people thought—until AJ last night.

But what could he do? The fact that T-Top still had over six years on his sentence was a bit of solace.

Still, AJ's reaction reminded him he wasn't some handsome, square-jawed lawman. More like Ron Pearlman after a really bad day on his Harley. Kris regularly, and unnecessarily, told him that she got all the good looks in the family, and that was *before* the scar.

Alex squirted out a blob of shaving cream, rubbed his palms together, then lathered his face. He scraped the razor down his right cheek. Maybe his baby sister had gotten the better half of the gene pool when it came to being pretty, but he could still outshoot her at the pistol range.

Most of the time.

Shortly before noon, Lena steered between sheer rock walls on the narrow, two-lane road that curved down into Perilous Cove. Town, if the tiny hodgepodge of businesses could be called that, faced the harbor, and masts by the hundreds poked the sky as Lena turned onto Harbor Street.

She spotted Mandy's distinctive Bronco on a side street, and parked in the adjacent spot. Her own red Jeep looked diminutive and dull compared to the raised Ford's shiny new fire-engine-red paint. Word was that Mandy had spent dozens of hours on the bodywork, having patch panels welded in where rust had eaten away the floor panels and door lower edges, and then sanding and smoothing before the body shop in Mission Peak did the final paint. Although she'd done much of the work herself, the girl's beauty had undoubtedly encouraged the guys at the shop to volunteer extra help.

Lena found Mandy window-shopping at a jewelry store two doors from The Wave Pizza.

"Find anything that catches your eye?" Lena asked, as she approached.

"Everything," Mandy sighed forlornly, not taking her eyes off a spread of turquoise and intricately wound silver. "I should get a job here to support my habit."

Lena laughed, not for the first time noticing Mandy's proclivity for the Native American style. With her raven hair and bronzed skin, the colors felt right, looked right. "Not a bad idea," Lena said, pointing to a flyer taped to the inside of the glass advertising a jewelry making class. "But why don't you learn how to create your own? Starts next Monday afternoon."

Mandy tore her gaze from the finished product and skimmed the announcement. "Ten bucks for three weeks. I can do that." She straightened and pulled out her wallet, looking at Lena for the first time. "Whoa, cute hair!"

Lena fingered the ends, not yet used to it being so short, but it was just long enough to put in a ponytail.

"And nice nails," Mandy said, grabbing and turning Lena's hand.

"Thanks. I just went in for a trim and…well, I guess I got carried away."

"Bibs?" At Lena's nod, Mandy's eyes narrowed. "I keep a distance. That woman is dangerous."

Lena laughed again, remembering how she'd staggered out of the barn with the works—and a rather hefty bill that would take at least three more weekends of rental profits to pay off. Still, when she'd looked in the mirror at home, she had to admit that the haircut *was* cute. Too bad Stone hadn't noticed last night, but since it was pretty dark she'd cut him some slack. She'd been ridiculous to get angry with him for working at the same law enforcement agency as Simon McKinley.

"Hey," Mandy snapped her fingers, bringing Lena's attention back to the present. "I've got an idea."

Ten minutes later, they exited the jewelry store and entered The Wave. Mandy had a receipt for the jewelry class in hand, and so did Lena. Somehow, Mandy had convinced Lena *she* needed to take the class too.

The girl was nothing if not decisive, Lena thought, silently observing as Mandy rattled off their food order, then led the way to the salad bar in The Wave.

"Well, this is great," Lena said, as they dug in. "I've heard about how good the pizza is here. Thanks for inviting me."

"Actually," Mandy said, spearing an olive, "I have something to ask you. I'm wondering if you could teach me how to use power tools?" She ate the impaled black oval.

"Why?" Lena asked, mentally calculating how much time such a task would take. She couldn't afford hours a week to teach a teenage fashionista about the subtleties of a circular saw.

Mandy shrugged. "Because I don't know what I want to do in life. I already know a little about cars, but I figure knowing about carpentry tools and building might come in handy—in case I want to build my own house or something."

Lena sat back against the booth and studied the girl. Envisioning Mandy Conner in a tool belt and eye-protection was like taking a Victoria Secret model and handing her a chainsaw. Of course, *some* guys would think that was smoking hot. Lena still had the photos Bobby had taken in their garage of her posing with her tools. No one would *ever* see those. She felt the corner of her mouth curl up as she recalled taking several of him too. Afterward, he'd held her down and tickled her until she signed a legal contract agreeing that she'd never show them to anyone.

She let the images fade, a little surprised they were *good* memories, and without a painful aftertaste. Perhaps time did help with healing.

Lena opened her mouth, intending to decline, but Mandy stopped her with a raised palm.

"Here's my proposal: teach me on the job. I know you're working on the other cabins. How about I work with you once or twice a week on whatever projects you have? I'm a fast learner, and I promise I'll be more of an asset than a liability."

"Shouldn't you be preparing for college in the fall?" Lena asked, still not convinced. Mandy waved away the question.

"I already took crossover classes at the junior college that doubled for high school. I'm over a semester into my freshman year already." She shrugged again. "College is easy."

Their pizza arrived, and the next five minutes were spent devouring the house specialty: Meaty Cheesy Ecstasy. Sometime before they each finished their second piece, it was agreed that Mandy would report for tool class and work on Fridays, starting in two weeks. Secretly, Lena wondered if she could keep up with the girl.

"So, Mandy, what do you think you *might* like to do for a career, other than working on cars or building houses?" The girl was undoubtedly multi-talented, but Lena could better picture Mandy working in something less blue collar.

Mandy lifted her third wedge and pinched off a dangling piece of melted cheese. "I don't know. Maybe the FBI. I'm really good with a gun."

Lena waited for the punch line. None came.

20

Teal shifted onto one side, then the other as her hips pressed against the rough planks underneath her makeshift mattress. According to Springsteen's bright display, it was 4:11 a.m. Although it was inky black both inside and outside the old barn, dawn was a little more than an hour away. With a groan, she rolled off and lifted the coarse covering. Using the iPod light, she surveyed the matted padding. Two weeks of sleeping had ground half the straw into powder that no longer provided the comfort she'd grown used to. If she wanted more sleep, she'd need to rebuild her bed.

The steps of the massive ladder didn't utter a squeak as she descended from the loft to the main floor. Springsteen lit the space as Teal skirted AJ's utility trailer to where the hay bales were stacked. The dried grass fragrance filled the still air as she quietly packed a five-gallon bucket with as much as it would hold. As she turned toward the ladder, a wave of nausea weaseled through her gut. She dropped the bucket and doubled over near the wall.

As her stomach surrendered its last spasm, Teal spit and wiped her mouth. There hadn't been much in her stomach. The leftover food from her picnic with Quin had run out and she'd had only some potato chips yesterday. Her body was punishing her for poor care.

She'd read a story once about a man who'd gotten lost while hiking in the hills of Arkansas in the fall of 1964. He had only some beef jerky and a canteen. He chronicled how his body began consuming itself. First to go was the spare tire he'd carried for several years despite occasional diets and regular trips to the gym. After days of endless wandering, his belly shrank enough to expose ribs he hadn't seen since high school. He found water, but nothing to eat under the canopy of brilliant leaves.

Each day began with hope, and ended with unassuaged hunger. His muscles shrank, until one day he could circle his bicep with the thumb and middle finger of his hand. His watch threatened to fall off his wrist, and his feet slipped in his now too big boots.

He tried eating some of the colorful leaves that rained down on him, but they made him sick, and a few remaining berries caused an even more violent reaction. He learned why the wild animals had left them be.

Four deer hunters found him by a trickling creek where he'd crawled to fill his canteen. He weighed far less than the buck they'd shot earlier that morning. Later, at the hospital, he told a doctor that the worst thing was he could feel his body eating itself from the inside.

That's what Teal felt like now as she lugged the bucket up the steep ladder. In reality, the plastic and straw weighed next to nothing, but every step drained her. Finally, she reached the top and shoved the bucket onto the loft floor. Only the promise of lying down gave her the strength to distribute the hay and drape the blanket over it. She balled her fists in her sweatshirt, shivering against the dawn. Soon the air in the barn would heat to ninety or more. It couldn't come fast enough.

First, though, she had to get some more sleep. Quin was picking her up at 6:45 down by the rock to take her to breakfast.

Teal closed her eyes and conjured up Quin, his hair ruffled by the wind. He'd carried her up the beach, fed her, and made sure she was feeling all right when he dropped her off back at the rock. Then he'd given her a bag of extra food and water leftovers from their lunch.

If she concentrated, she could catch Quin's scent of suntan lotion and hot skin. Her sweatshirt was stiff with dirt and sweat, but she couldn't bring herself to wash it while the barest scent of him remained. She squirmed into the new straw, and she dreamed of Quin. Together, they rode across the lake in his silver boat.

Lena kicked at the tangled sheet and blanket for the tenth time, trying to find a comfortable position before her mind fully woke. She lifted her head and blinked at the mocking red LED display: 4:02 a.m. Her head flopped back on the pillow.

"Oh, man."

Finally accepting defeat, she sat up and rubbed her face. The grueling work yesterday afternoon after lunch with Mandy should have put her out cold. What was supposed to be a simple job replacing the broken and rotted shingle siding of her new cabin had revealed some of the studs weakened by termites and dry rot, requiring she cut them out and replace them. She'd finished nailing on the last of the new shingles by flashlight. But it had to be done.

And there were at least another fifteen things on her to-do list for today.

"Okay, Blaylock, get your butt in gear." She swung her feet to the floor, found her slippers, and padded into the darkened kitchen to make coffee. Guided by only a nightlight, she filled the coffee maker's water reservoir. But as she closed the lid, a flicker of light gleamed through the small kitchen window. She nearly dropped the carafe.

She ran to the back porch, opened the screen door, and peered through the oaks toward the barn.

There! A faint light blinked on and off beyond the cracks of the structure's doors and split siding, passing one way, then the other. A few minutes later it flashed several feet higher and disappeared.

Lena backed into the house and closed the door. She turned the deadbolt.

Leaving the lights off, she dressed in jeans and a T-shirt topped by a chambray work shirt. Her tennis shoes felt too flimsy, so she pulled on her cowboy boots and stood until her feet dropped into place. Then she wrapped up in a Mexican blanket, perched on a dining room chair, and waited. A half hour. An hour. Praying for the morning sun. For Stone to be awake. Stone, with his gun.

She could have called the sheriff. Still could. But after his evident suspicions when the body was found, she didn't want to draw more attention to herself—or to her property. If word somehow got out to prospective renters about bodies and police visits... Well, she didn't want to think about her mortgage being in jeopardy right now. What she wanted was to know who was in her barn.

"Com'on, Stone, wake up," she implored the black window that faced his trailer. She'd be able to see if he turned on a light. Was he a morning person, tossing and turning for the last hour before rising like she did? Rubbing her brow, she tried to remember how early she'd seen him around. Maybe she should just go over and—

Her desk phone blared in the dark, startling her so she nearly fell off the chair. Annoying enough in the bright of day, the electronic chirping cut through the night for a second time.

Unbidden, her grandmother's words of many years ago came to her: *"Nothing good comes from a phone call in the middle of the night."*

21

Quin's boat cruised slowly along the north lakeshore where calmer water lay, but it was still too rough for Teal today. She'd asked Quin to slow down once, and she couldn't ask him again without him wondering what was wrong.

She'd been dizzy after rising this morning, and wobbled like a drunk while skirting AJ's cabin to meet Quin. The Jeep's engine had started while it was still dark, and it was gone when Teal left the barn. That was unusual for so early in the day, and Teal had been tempted to sneak in the back door and pilfer a little food. But Quin promised breakfast at a real restaurant, and she couldn't be late. Food was life, and she needed all she could get.

Water splashed from the low-riding bow, spraying her with a few drops, cooling her burning skin. She concentrated on the lake's tranquil beauty sliding along the side instead of her spinning head. Nourishment was what she needed.

It seemed like forever before they made it across the north shore and turned southward along the rocky outcroppings on the west side. Finally, they passed a large rock, and masts of sailboats in Deer Cove rose into view. Quin slowed more as they entered the harbor. The backsides of ancient buildings lined the docks, their jaunty primary colors masking sagging construction. The morning sun lit them like jewels, and their colors charged the air with expectation. A few people carried coolers, life preservers, and fishing gear to boats. One tow-headed boy of about seven waved to them from the end of a dock. Teal lifted her hand and returned his grin.

They putted by four or five rows before Quin turned in along a wooden dock with tie-downs for visitors. He cut the motor and drifted until the aluminum side bumped against the tire-padded structure. Then Teal watched as he reached out his golden arm and pulled their craft tight against the timbers.

She climbed out, glad to be on solid land. Well, sort of solid. The dock bobbed slightly on large barrels. She leaned against a piling, steadying herself. The nausea lingered like a persistent door-to-door salesman, and she wished she could send it away.

"Are you ready?" Quin asked, taking her hand. A lazy smile caressed his lips, and Teal swayed toward him. Concern replaced the smile. "Hey. Easy there."

"I'm okay," she managed, and stood taller. She didn't want whatever sickness plagued her to spoil their day. "Just hungry."

His smile returned. "Me, too. Peg's Waffle House has the best food ever. Wait until you taste their cream cheese-stuffed Belgian waffles." He pulled on her hand to get her moving.

Reluctantly, Teal released her grip on the piling and concentrated on putting one foot in front of the other. Quin talked about all the menu items, from homemade sausage to clover honey on buttermilk biscuits, but Teal barely listened. Normally, she'd hang on his every word, but the churning in her stomach wouldn't go away. What if she had cancer or some disease eating away at her innards? She might be dead before Quin ever kissed her.

That is, if he wanted to. And he'd sure never want to if she was infected with something nasty.

She studied his profile, memorizing the curve of his lips, shape of his ear, and the line of his nose as it left his brow and angled into his upper lip. She'd tried a few portraits, but hadn't been able to capture him exactly. It would be easier if she had a photo of him, or if he'd pose for her, but she was afraid he'd think that was a little creepy.

They left the rough boards of the dock behind and turned onto the sidewalk lining the street on the front side of the buildings. Soon, enticing odors filled the air, and Teal's mouth began serious watering. A half-dozen people crowded an open doorway to one of the wooden buildings. As they grew closer, glass panes revealed an interior crammed with tables and diners. Waitresses scurried, arms filled with overflowing plates of pancakes and waffles. To Teal's eye, it seemed each one had a bigger mound of whipped cream than the previous, like it was some sort of waitress contest of who could use up the most Reddi-wip cans.

"Wait here," Quin instructed and released her hand. "I'll get us a table."

Teal steadied herself against the wall as he shouldered his way through the waiting people. A little girl with pigtails stood pigeon-toed next to her mommy, sucking her thumb while staring at Teal. A ragged teddy bear poked its head out from the crook of her arm. Teal smiled, but the girl just stared. A loudspeaker called out, "Carroll, party of five," and the mother scooped up the toddler and joined a group heading inside.

A silver sedan pulled to the curb several parking spots down. Due to the morning glare, Teal couldn't see inside, but she heard the driver ask a man on the sidewalk how long the restaurant wait was. Teal's heart somersaulted. It was the same voice she'd heard a thousand times, both in the basement and in her nightmares. She hid her face and turned away from the restaurant, forcing herself not to bolt.

Don't draw his attention.

Blood swooshed in her ears, pumping faster and faster as her vision shrank to only her feet, her steps, cracked concrete. Her ragged wheezing provided scant oxygen as she scurried away. Where she could, she trailed her left hand along the shop windows, siding, and doors, bracing against her body's threatening collapse. The sidewalk joints went by too slowly, one–two–three–four, and she made it only half a block before a voice spoke.

"Where do you think you're going?"

She froze, hating how her knees shook, how her mouth, so recently watering at the glorious smells, had gone dry. Running was the only way. Her eyes burned at the thought of leaving Quin even as she took a preparatory breath.

A hand wrapped around her bicep.

Too late!

"The restaurant's packed, so I thought you might want one of these while we wait."

Quin's face swam into view. He held some kind of sticks before her, and gradually she focused on them. Churros—fried to a golden brown and dusted with powdered sugar.

She snapped her head toward the restaurant. The car was gone, the parking space empty. She peered past Quin's arm, seeking the missing vehicle and man.

"What's wrong?"

Teal willed her heartbeat down from terrified to only panicked, and worked to breathe. Was it him? It couldn't be. Not here. Not so far north. But that voice. Just when she'd—

"Teal?"

She sagged against the window of the storefront where they'd stopped. Skirts, belts, and shoes filled the display. A purple T-shirt with *Deer Cove, CA* embroidered below a sailboat hugged a mannequin's torso. Normal reality, so at contrast with that voice. Teal's knees wobbled and she fisted her hands in Quin's shirt to remain upright.

He put his hand on her forehead, cool and soothing. "Teal, you're burning up. I think you need to see a doctor."

"No," she said too quickly. She took several deep breaths.

"You're white as a sheet. Doc Arnold's office is on the next block. He lives in back and—"

"I'll be…all right. Just help me to that bench over there." She pointed to the crude wooden slats in front of the next store—farther from the restaurant.

The old boards were worn smooth by thousands of visitors, and she maneuvered Quin between her and the restaurant. He handed her one of the churros. Saliva flooded her dry mouth as she nibbled its end, the bread and sugar practically melting against her tongue.

"Sure you're all right?" he said, peering into her eyes for a moment.

She smiled at him and took another bite.

Quin draped an arm around her shoulders and she leaned into his protection. As much as she wanted to get away from the man, the voice, she couldn't go anywhere until the food restored some of her strength. Plus, fevered or not, she was loath to stir from Quin's firm side. In a few short days, this boy had become like that boulder in the storm the night she'd escaped—a wall of strength, solid. Hoping it wasn't too obvious, she slid closer, until they were connected thigh to shoulder. Even that wasn't close enough, but it would have to do…for now.

"I was just really hungry," she ventured after she'd finished half the treat, more dessert than breakfast. "I tend to be hypoglycemic if I don't eat." She thought she had that word right. She'd read about low blood sugar on a health poster at a library once.

"My sister is like that," Quin nodded, stuffing the last of his own churro into his mouth.

"You have a sister?" He'd never mentioned her, only his adoptive father and mother who lived in the house by Shelter Cove. She checked over his shoulder, but there was no sign of the silver car.

"Yeah," he said, wiping powdered sugar off his mouth with the back of his hand. "But she's a lot older and doesn't live around here anymore. She has two little girls—the demon twins."

A hot breeze swirled down the street, raising perspiration on her skin. Teal made an excuse about not wanting to be inside a stuffy restaurant, so Quin went back and ordered takeout while Teal "window shopped" a few blocks away. Before long, they were sitting at a picnic table on a grassy area overlooking the small harbor, forking down hot pancakes, sausage links, and perfectly runny fried eggs, all drenched in steaming maple syrup. If her blood sugar was low before, she'd probably lapse into a coma after this breakfast, but at least her wooziness had subsided. Maybe it was just hunger after all. Or starvation.

Teal laughed at his stories of how the demon twins tormented him when he'd stayed at their house before they moved away. He asked about her family once or twice, but she successfully redirected the conversation to music, what movies he'd seen—she hadn't seen any in a long time, but she faked it—and life at the lake.

All the while, Teal kept an eye out for the car. Was that really him? He'd always worn the ski mask. But the voice…

Dread settled like a brick on top of the food in her stomach. Nothing was worth the risk of being caught. The safe thing would be to pack her measly belongings and leave Storm Lake, the falls, her barn.

And Quin.

A new feeling clawed her stomach, and had nothing to do with being sick.

22

The scrambled eggs he'd had for breakfast had tasted good, but Alex was beginning to regret fixing them as he scrubbed at his frying pan. The skillet had an uncanny ability to fuse every food to its surface. He rinsed the soap from the dented metal, inspected the scarred surface for the third time, and set it in the drainer to dry. Maybe he'd use some of his consulting pay and pick up some better cookware in Mission Peak.

He opened the door and stepped down, feeling the twinge of pain in his lower back ever since the long drive north. Stretching had to be done outside. As much as he liked the trailer, it was meant to be lived *out* of, not *in*. Alex took a deep breath and leaned as far as he could from side-to-side, feeling the pull of the muscles as they gradually lengthened.

The cool morning air was retreating before an advancing warm breeze filled with summer's hot promise and the lake's fresh scent. Fish went deep during the heat of the day. But now, before the sun rose too high and warmed the lake's surface, trout begged for a baited hook. He'd caught a nice dinner a few days ago. He could get used to living here overlooking the water and its never-ending display.

Next to AJ. No matter what she hinted at or said, he wasn't leaving.

He really needed to talk to her, to explain his relationship with DEA, and with her father. But mostly to apologize for being so sensitive about his scar.

He turned to go back inside, determined to find AJ and work things out, but something fluttered at the bottom of the door. An envelope was wedged in the edge molding. His name was on the outside, and he tore it open as he walked to one of the lawn chairs. It was from AJ.

Stone. I got a phone call early this morning. Have to go to L.A. for an emergency. I know this is asking a lot, but could you possibly check in the guests arriving today? I'm leaving now—it's just past 4:30. There is a shoebox with the names, cabin numbers, and keys on my porch.

I know this is a huge imposition, and I owe you. Sorry about last night. Will call before 2:00 p.m. when I know more.

She went on to explain that the cabins were clean and ready, and that if he couldn't do it, could he just leave the keys in each cabin door with the guest's name taped to it. Then...

Also...saw a light moving in the barn this morning while still full dark.

He folded the note and sat gazing at the lake, but not really seeing it. The message contained no information about the nature of the emergency. He checked his watch: 8:10 a.m. He'd slept far later than usual. Depending on where she was going in the city, she might already have arrived. But he couldn't call now. She'd either be driving or in the middle of the situation there.

Rising from the chair, he gazed at the barn. He couldn't help whatever was in L.A., but there was something he could do for AJ on this end. But first, he had to get his gun.

After breakfast, Teal asked if she could stay at Deer Cove's library while Quin ran some quick ferrying jobs. He had half a dozen boxes of groceries and other supplies from the store to deliver to three homes around the lake, including a Mrs. H, who he wanted Teal to meet.

While he was gone, Teal perused the stacks, brushing her fingers along the spines. The pre-fab building, not much bigger than a double-wide trailer, soon filled with all sorts of people. Some lined up for the three public use computers, while several toddlers gathered on colorful rugs in a corner for story time. A white-haired grandmotherly type, so stereotypical that Teal covered her mouth to keep from laughing, read to them. The woman had rosy cheeks puffy like bread dough, and wore a dark blue dress with white polka dots, large white pearls, and a floppy wide-brim hat. Out of character were the orange and electric-green high top tennis shoes.

Two of the children sat so close to her legs they could touch her, and one little boy kept trying to climb onto her lap as she read from a large picture book. The woman was so animated in her storytelling about a vagabond squirrel, Teal was tempted to join the children. It would be nice to have a grandmother like this lady, someone to hang out with when parents got to be too much.

Teal had only met her mom's mother one time. A rail-thin, chain-smoking caricature of a failed fashion model, Fern Taylor had spared Teal a brief glance before launching into an argument with Teal's mother. Teal remembered how the woman's skin looked like sun-dried leather, and her streaked copper locks had been so burned with chemicals that Teal wondered why the coarse strands didn't break off when combed. After ten minutes of fighting, her mom dragged her out of the house while screaming she'd never be back. Teal had been seven or eight years old then, but she remembered clearly hoping she'd never grow up to be like her grandmother. Nor her mother, for that matter.

"Can I help you find something, dear?" a voice said, breaking the memory. A boxy blonde woman pushing a cart full of books had stopped by Teal's side.

"Oh, no, that's okay," Teal said, backing up a step. "I'm just waiting for my boyfr… a friend."

"Well, let me know if you need anything." She smiled and leaned into the cart to get it moving across the industrial carpeting.

"Uh, there is one thing," Teal ventured. The woman straightened. "Do you have a bathroom here?"

A minute later, Teal stood in the tiny restroom at the rear of the trailer. She locked the door and quickly doffed her sweatshirt and T-shirt. Using soap from the squirt dispenser and paper towels, she gave herself a sponge bath. This was the first mirror she'd had use of in a while, and she was more than a little shocked at how her collarbones and ribs protruded through her skin. She looked like those TV appeals for starving children. Somehow, she had to find a consistent food source.

Halfway through shampooing her hair, someone knocked on the door.

"I'll be right out," Teal called, and raced to rinse out all the soap. She slipped her clothes back on, ignoring their musty odor, and ran her fingers through her hair until it looked presentable. Finally, she used more towels to wipe the mirror and sink before plastering on a smile and opening the door.

A young mom uttered *"Thanks"* as she led a toddler into the room and closed the door.

Teal leaned against the wall to catch her breath. The hurried bath had tired her, and she looked for a place to sit down. Bodies brushed past in the narrow aisles as she searched for a chair or bench, but the packed building was obviously undersized for the community. A few people sat on the floor and leaned against the walls as they read.

Giving up, she exited through the front door. Hot air buffeted her face, and she was glad for her wet head. It was *way* too hot for a sweatshirt, and she remembered there were some benches nearer the water.

Wonderful smells escaped open shop doors. Tired as she was, a candle store drew her in, and she spent a few minutes sampling the endless fragrances. If she'd had any money, she would have bought a couple to use in her barn loft. Teal sighed as she closed the jar lid on a particularly yummy cinnamon candle. They would only make her hungry, and she certainly didn't need any help in that department.

"Hey!" a voice shouted as Teal left the store. Instinctively, she turned toward the source, but had sense enough to back away. She stumbled over a wine barrel planter and nearly landed on her rear. Her heart blasted to supersonic speed in the second before she recognized Quin jogging down the sidewalk. He skidded to a stop in front of her, his face covered in a goofy grin. It dissolved as he searched her features. "What's wrong?"

She forced her hand down from where it had been clutching her heart, but she could do nothing to slow the frantic, heaving breaths.

"Hey," he said softly. "It's okay. I'm here." He rubbed her arms with his strong hands.

"I thought...I thought...he..." She couldn't get enough air, and everything blurred. He gathered her into his arms and she buried her head in his chest. She felt his chin press her wet head as sobs wracked her body. The pent up emotion of the past weeks wouldn't calm down no matter what she wanted. Here was the only boy who ever liked her without wanting something, and she was falling apart in his arms.

She was dimly aware of passersby asking something, but she shut them out, concentrating on Quin's scent of cotton and sunscreen, the feel of his fingers combing the hair at the back of her neck. She breathed him in, replacing her panic with his strength. He was only a boy, but he was safety, the only safety she'd known in a long time, and she was so weary of facing everything alone.

He rocked her gently, like a slow dance, as her tears streamed, soaking his shirt. Finally, he turned her sideways and began walking. She kept her head tucked into his chest and her arms wrapped around his waist as they stumbled along, only loosening her grip as they reached a picnic table and he helped her sit down. It was the same table where they'd eaten breakfast. With a last shudder, she straightened and blew out a breath.

"Wow." Teal used her sweatshirt cuffs to wipe her eyes, and tried to cover her embarrassment with a laugh. "S-sorry about that." It sounded pathetic. Quin's arm rested across her back and she hoped he'd never take it away. But when she tentatively looked up at him, deep concern etched every part of his face.

"Want to talk about it?"

Teal waved her hand in dismissal. "It's nothing. I guess I just frighten easily." She gave him a little smile. A frown pulled down the corners of his mouth. He wasn't buying it. She wiped sweat off her brow. Their table was bathed in full sun.

"You're still burning up. Why don't you take off your sweatshirt before you get heatstroke?" Quin suggested. "You have a T-shirt on, don't you?"

"Yes," she answered too fast. "I mean no." She tried to think of an explanation, but her mind refused to function. "I'm okay."

"It's already in the low nineties," he said, as unrelenting as the day's growing heat.

"I run cold most of the time."

"You're sweating," he countered.

She sighed and laid her head down on her arms, facing away so she wouldn't have to see his disappointment. The table surface burned beneath the thick fabric sleeves.

"Teal…"

"I can't," she breathed, too weary to concoct another excuse.

His hand moved across her back in broad circles. "You can for me."

Could she? She lifted enough to swivel her head toward him. His longish hair shadowed his face, and his skin shone like a bronze statue, too perfect for words. There was no judgment in his brown eyes, only caring. But what would replace that once he saw how she looked? Saw the monster she was? He had no idea the ugliness that lay beneath his moving hand, shielded by two thin layers of cloth.

She sat up, and slowly gripped the end of one sleeve. Her eyes locked on his. Could she do this?

———

Alex had parked his truck down the road at a pullout in Gift, then he'd hiked back, keeping to the high ground that was out of sight of AJ's property. He'd come out above and behind his trailer where he'd previously stashed one of his camp chairs. With AJ's Jeep gone, it gave the impression the cabins were deserted. And they were—except for him. One set of guests had arrived at two o'clock and found the keys and note he'd left on AJ's porch, then they'd driven off again, probably to buy some supplies. Alex had resumed his post in his folding chair up on the hill behind his trailer.

Using his battered 10-power binoculars, he panned the property every few minutes, searching for any sign of movement. He sipped a soda from his cooler, frustrated that he still hadn't heard from AJ. She was in some kind of trouble, he was sure of it. He didn't want to push, but for heaven's sake—a dead body, strange lights in the barn, and now a mysterious emergency. The woman had more going on than an episode of *CSI*.

He was musing over what he had found in the barn when he heard the sound of an outboard approaching from the north. He swung the binoculars and spotted an aluminum motorboat. Because of the sun's glare, he couldn't see details other than there were two people in it. Although close to shore, it continued south past AJ's lakefront and dock. He'd lowered the glasses and reached for his soda when the engine cut out and glided out of view behind a rocky outcropping and trees. He trained the field glasses on the trees and waited.

The motor started again and revved up, but Alex kept the glasses trained where the engine had first quit. They could have just stopped for a second, maybe take a leak behind a bush. But his years in DEA had taught him patience. Never assume.

A few minutes later, a lone girl emerged from between two small pines and paused, turning her head left, then right. She skirted the far edge of the clearing, heading away from the lake along the creek. It was possible she was a regular hiker, but his cop radar went up when she stopped a few times behind trees and surveilled the area.

"What are you up to, little girl?" he whispered as she moved in his circular view of the world. He wished he had some of the professional binoculars DEA used. Those were 25-power or higher. But these were good enough to see she had short black hair, narrow hips, and wore jeans and tennis shoes. She looked young, even under the oversize sweatshirt, no more than thirteen in a stretch.

And why would anyone wear a sweatshirt in this heat? But he'd known a few bad guys who wore ski hats or hoodies all year long, even during L.A.'s hottest months. He'd never understood the need to fit in so badly. Then again, his parents had been pretty laid back, letting him do whatever he wanted, whenever he wanted. It was a testament to his good genes that he hadn't gotten in a lot of trouble—well, any more than he *did* get into. A smile tugged at his mouth. Good thing his parents never found out about some of those things.

Evidently satisfied with what she saw, the girl straightened and walked more boldly directly toward him and the compound of cabins. Expecting her to break into one of the structures, she surprised him by retrieving a leaf rake leaning against a tree and cleaning up a smattering of trash around one of the brown trash bins. Using her bare hands, she scooped the assembled debris into the can, smoothed out the dirt, and then moved on to the next area where she performed the same duties.

At the BBQ area, she restacked some of the logs that had tumbled off the firewood pile, vigorously scrubbed the grill with a wire brush AJ had provided but the renters rarely used, and raked careful lines around the area so it resembled a Zen garden.

Except for her furtiveness and the fact she kept checking over her shoulder, Alex had all but concluded AJ must have hired the girl without him knowing about it. But then the girl's head snapped toward the road, and Alex heard the crunch of tires on gravel seconds later. The girl shoved the rake against a tree and sprinted, arms pumping, towards the barn that lay uphill.

She reached the old structure and darted around its corner where she shrank back against the boards with arms splayed flat. He chuckled quietly. He had no idea who or what this girl was, but one thing was for sure, she wasn't a spy. No one could be that blatantly obvious. However, entertaining as she was, it didn't mean she was harmless.

The road noises grew louder and a white SUV lumbered over the hill and rolled to a stop in front of AJ's cabin. Alex watched the girl slide around the back of the barn out of view before he lowered the binoculars and rose. He'd have to deal with her later, but he knew where she was headed. He sighed, sorry his mini stakeout time had expired, and carried his chair down the slope.

"Might as well play hostess."

23

"A girl. You're sure?" Lena asked. She had no choice but to step aside as Alex Stone edged through her front door and into the living room. She hadn't exactly invited him in, but she couldn't very well toss him out, not after he'd checked in her guests. Even though it had been dark for hours, the air in the cabin hung heavy with the day's closed-up heat. She left the door open, hoping cooler air would filter in through the screen.

Stone made himself comfortable on her couch, stretching out his long legs, and draping his arms along the backrest as if he planned an extended visit. An infuriating smile played around his lips. He was enjoying this bit of news.

"What's a girl doing in my barn, Stone? Shouldn't we go confront her?"

"How'd it go in L.A.?" he said, apparently in no hurry to go anywhere.

She sighed. Finding the girl appealed to her slightly more than hashing out her personal issues. Still, after last night when she'd reacted to his scar... Maybe he deserved an explanation.

"Fine." It sounded snippy—a wrong approach with Stone. Sure enough, his eyebrows rose.

"Of course," he said, "it couldn't have been anything *too* much if you left in the middle of the night—"

"It wasn't the middle of the night; it was almost dawn."

"—drove for eight hours—"

"It was only seven."

"—and got home at midnight."

Lena opened her mouth to correct him that it wasn't *quite* midnight—not for another twenty-three minutes anyway—but he shot off the couch like a cat, forcing her back against the living room wall. Before she could say *personal space violation*, he was inches from her. But his eyes were tinged with a compassion that surprised her. She wanted to tell him, spill her guts. He must have been better at interrogation than Kyra Sedgwick on *The Closer*.

"Plus, you didn't call like you said you would."

The concern in his voice surprised her, asking rather than demanding. She lowered her eyes to his chest. "It was my mother. She..." Lena took a breath as Stone's hand settled on her upper arm, not moving, just lending support. It felt good. She was tired of carrying the burden alone. Talking about it couldn't hurt. "My mom's in a care facility in the San Fernando Valley. They specialize in patients with certain...mental issues."

That was the last thing Alex expected, but he tried not to let it show. He led AJ to the couch, taking a seat on the opposite end to give her the space he sensed she needed.

After a cleansing breath, she said, "What do you know about my father, Simon McKinley?"

"Like I said, I'd never met him until this trip. We—our DEA team—had a tip, and we raided a meeting house just north of the Mexican border where some high-level drug guys were supposed to be. It was a little too much coincidence when my boss, Bill Halwell, introduced us and I heard his last name. I asked Halwell later in private, and he told me he and Si worked together for years. Bill knew your mom. Even said he'd met you once or twice when you were little."

"I don't remember."

"At first, they were partners, then Bill got promoted and became the boss. Evidently that didn't go over well with Si."

AJ nodded, but gave away nothing. Then, "Why did you ask about his name? How did you know my maiden name was McKinley?"

"I, uh...I'd seen you on your TV show," he said. He'd searched the show's fast-rolling ending credits for three weeks before he'd discovered her name. He'd also seen it in the file Halwell had given him, but he wasn't telling AJ about that.

Her mouth quirked. "You watched me on *Nail It!*? I wasn't exactly top billing."

"I found it very entertaining." Especially when the camera focused on a certain beautiful blonde carpenter.

"Why would he want to be on the raid when he doesn't care anything about me?"

Alex touched her hand where it lay on the cushion. "Maybe he wants to reconnect with you?"

AJ's mouth grew hard.

"Tell me about your parents."

She rubbed her forehead, kneading the muscles. "Looking back, I can see their marriage wasn't a happy one. Of course, I didn't realize it then. Simon blew in and out from DEA assignments, gone for days or even weeks at a time. He never paid me much attention when I was little, and I learned to stay out of his way. Mom told me he always wanted a son. Obviously, I didn't quite fit the bill."

"He was an idiot," Alex said.

"Well, it wasn't like he was mean to me. Mostly, he ignored me. But when he was around, my parents argued constantly, and it always ended with Mom to blame and in tears. Hard as she tried, she couldn't do anything right. He'd been gone a week one time when a man arrived at the door one afternoon and served her with divorce papers. Simon never came back. It really knocked Mom for a loop."

"I can imagine." Alex rose and led her into the kitchen, where he began filling the coffee maker while she leaned against the counter.

"Mom was an emotional wreck from the loss of financial security, and she took an entry-level job to afford a lawyer and keep food on our table.

"We made it through the next few months, and Mom seemed to rally a little. Then, two weeks after the quick divorce was final, a friend came by and told us Simon had married a twenty-something coworker from the DEA named Jennifer. She was eight months pregnant, and she already had a three-year-old boy. I don't know for sure, but I'm guessing his 'assignments' weren't always out of town, if you know what I mean."

"Both kids were his?" Alex asked.

AJ shrugged. "As far as we knew."

"That must have been tough on your mom." His own home life had been so normal. He couldn't fathom what it was like to grow up with the anger, process servers, and lawyers.

"I came home from school the next day and found her standing at the kitchen sink, staring out the window. There was a paring knife in her hand, and the water was running. She'd been peeling potatoes, but there was nothing in the sink but skins and tiny slices of potato. She looked at me when I called her name, but her eyes were blank, as if she left the room but her body was still there. The doctors later diagnosed it as a mental break."

Alex pushed the start button on the coffee brewer, then took a spot beside her against the countertop. He wanted nothing more than to wrap his arms around her, but she'd already done that with her own arms. AJ was a strong, independent woman, and he sensed she needed to tell this story on her own. So he remained silent, and waited.

"For the next couple of weeks, I made simple meals from the canned food in the pantry, helped her dress, and did the laundry. I walked to the grocery store with some of the cash she kept and bought some fruit and vegetables. I thought if she ate better, she'd recover faster."

"Didn't you have any other family?" Alex asked. "Someone you could call?"

AJ shook her head. "Simon was a difficult man. He'd alienated everyone in *his* family and left them behind somewhere in Texas when he moved to California. That was years before I was born. I didn't know any of them. Still don't."

"Your mother's family?"

AJ tilted her head back and stared at the overhead light fixture. "My aunt, Mom's sister, evidently asked to borrow money from them one time. I was a baby, so I don't remember any of that; my aunt told me later. Simon got so furious, he dragged my aunt out of the house by the arm and threw her onto the lawn. Told her to never come back. Mom's parents were dead."

"So you were all alone. How old were you?"

"Fourteen. After about two weeks of caring for Mom, a district official came to the house to find out why I hadn't been in school."

"Did he call your dad?" It was slight, but Alex noticed the twinge that caused AJ's whole body to tense. She didn't answer his question. Maybe that was all the answer needed.

"He was a kind man, and helped track down my aunt. She took me in. Mom's been in one facility or another ever since."

"This trip...you went to L.A. to visit her?"

AJ nodded. "I saw her. But the emergency was that she fell and broke her hip. Mostly I met with her doctors. They operated early this morning, and they're optimistic that she'll be able to return to her long-term facility in a couple of days."

"Are you going back down? I can always look after things here for a while." His mind spun with the myriad of preparations AJ did between renters, but he could figure it out.

AJ smiled at him, then took his hand, lacing her fingers through his. "Thanks, but it's not necessary." She blew out a breath. "Mom doesn't know me. After I found her in the kitchen that day, I've never heard her speak a word. Even though I visited every week for years, she's never responded to me, not one time. And the caregivers at the facility are great. I don't see her as much anymore. She… she knows the staff better than she knows me—if she knows anyone, that is."

Unable to resist any longer, Alex drew her to him. She relaxed for a minute, and he marveled how they fit together. But then she straightened and pulled away. The coffee was done, and she went about fixing two cups.

"Why was Simon on your mission?"

"Bobby's name was mentioned in the tip about the drug meeting, but that wasn't the reason why Halwell called." Alex didn't want to scare her but, behind the surprise in her eyes, he could tell she wouldn't be satisfied without the whole story. He drew a breath. "Your name came up, too. Si knew about it, and asked to be on the team."

AJ's surprise changed to confusion. "Wait. You're telling me *my name* was mentioned by some tipster in conjunction with a drug meeting?" She turned away, rubbing the lines between her brows. "That doesn't make any sense. It's been over a year since Bobby's murder. Why would anyone mention *his* name, let alone mine?"

That's what Alex had asked when Halwell ordered him down to the border. Alex could understand Bobby's name coming up since he'd been an assistant district attorney. He'd lived—even specialized—in the world of prosecuting drug runners and top-level bosses. But AJ's name made no sense.

"All I know for sure is that both your names came up a month ago in another situation. Halwell didn't tell me everything he knew, but that's what sent me here."

"So Halwell thinks I might be in some kind of danger?"

"Well, he didn't say specifically that anyone was *after* you." Halwell was always cagey with information, never giving out more than necessary. "But he did say your husband was working with the DEA."

"Why?"

"Bobby suspected corruption high up in the L.A. justice system, perhaps in the DA's office. When Halwell met with Bobby, it was always somewhere secluded. Or they used phone lines they knew were secure."

She met his eyes, studying him intently. "So this is serious stuff."

"Very."

"So, you're hanging around waiting to rush to my rescue?"

Alex lifted his hands. "Boss's orders."

"Boss? Or Simon?" AJ shot back.

"Boss," Alex said firmly. But he, too, wondered how much influence Si McKinley had over Bill Halwell.

"I don't need a babysitter, Stone. I don't know anything about this investigation Bobby and your boss worked on."

"Understood."

AJ sighed, then nodded. "Okay. Now, how old is she?"

His brows creased momentarily before he realized she was referring to the girl he'd seen go into the barn. "Young."

"She *is* young," Lena whispered as quietly as possible into Stone's ear. They were kneeling at the top of the ladder's opening to the barn's loft. A dozen feet away, a candle flickered inside a tin can that had one side cut away. The soft light played across the girl's cute upturned nose and cupid-bow lips. Sinfully-long black lashes lay against porcelain skin. She slept on her back, arms at her sides, with palms up and fingers slightly curled as if, seconds before, they'd slipped from the paperback book open across her stomach. *The Adventures of Tom Sawyer* rose and fell with each breath. On the rough boards beside the candle were two other books, some folded clothes, and a backpack.

Lena had been fourteen years old when she'd moved into her aunt's house in Pomona. This girl looked no older. They should probably call the sheriff. Not that she wanted Sheriff Derrek Cabot involved again. Even more confusing was why this girl—as Stone had said—was doing yard maintenance around the cabins. Lena had noticed the trash cleaned up and the raking a couple of times, but she'd figured Stone was responsible.

"What do you want to do?" Stone asked, his heated breath tickling her ear like a lover's. When she turned to him, a small smile graced his lips. They looked full in the candlelight.

In fact, all of him looked good. Not for the first time, she wondered what it would be like to be held, really held, by such a man. By him.

Lena shook off the feeling. Obviously, she wasn't thinking clearly. He'd plied her with enough coffee to scramble her nerve endings *and* her reasoning as they had waited until past one o'clock in the morning.

"Let's go. We'll talk to her in the morning." Lena slid her leg toward the ladder hole, but as she looked down to make sure her foot was in the right place, the flashlight she'd stowed in her jacket pocket tumbled out and clattered to the floor.

The girl sat straight up, spotted them, and scrambled backward, eyes huge like a frightened animal.

"It's okay, calm down." Stone reached toward her.

But the girl kicked frantically at the old blanket and lurched sideways, away from Stone's outstretched hand. Before Lena could move or utter a word, the girl back-pedaled off the edge of the loft and disappeared into the dark.

A sickening crash came from below.

24

Lena and Stone reached the girl as a moan escaped the girl's lips.

"Just lie still," Lena said, putting a hand on her shoulder.

The girl's eyes popped open, and she jerked halfway to a sitting position. "Where…what are you…? Ouch!" Her hand touched a cut on her head.

"Easy," Lena said gently. Thank God she'd landed on some broken hay bales instead of the trailer or tool bench. "Stone, we've got to get her to the doctor."

"No!" The girl suddenly fought Lena like a tiger, and kicked Stone's arm as she wormed her legs to the floor. "No doctors!"

"Hey, calm down, young lady," Storm fired back. "We're just trying to help."

"Oh, my head. What did you hit me with?"

"Hit…? We didn't hit you," Stone said. "You fell off the loft."

Lena called Doc Arnold's emergency line, and three minutes later they were in Stone's truck and on the road to the doc's office in Deer Cove. The girl alternated an ice pack between her head and right wrist.

"Hurry, Stone," Lena said. In the truck's instrument lights, his jaw tightened. Pre-dawn ground fog blanketed the night so all they could see was the yellow haze of the headlights and the crooked arms of trees reaching toward them as the vehicle passed. The tires squealed as Stone swerved to avoid a large pothole.

"Hey, take it easy, big guy. I said I'm okay," the girl said, "but I'll be dead if you crash us."

Some of her earlier belligerence had subsided, but she still refused to tell them her name. Lena dabbed at the oozing cut on her head.

"I don't need to see a doctor," the girl insisted for at least the tenth time.

"Tough," Stone replied.

Lena and Stone hadn't given her a choice, and had her sandwiched between them in the cab. The girl's right wrist had swelled to twice its normal size.

The Chevy's wipers clattered across the windshield, clearing the constant mist. As defiant as the girl sounded, Lena witnessed an occasional grimace when the truck's tires hit a bump.

Stone spared Lena a glance over the girl's head, his expression firm, but otherwise unreadable. Lena wondered if he regretted their decision to go to the barn in the middle of the night as much as she did.

The truck swayed around a corner. Stone turned to the girl. "You're lucky you landed on those hay bales and not the floor."

"I'd've been a lot luckier if you hadn't pushed me off the loft," the girl shot back.

Lena saw the corner of Stone's mouth rise at that. He found this amusing?

Finally, they entered Deer Cove, and Stone slowed to a normal speed.

The girl looked between Stone and Lena, settling on Lena. "Please don't take me to the doctor. I'm fine. Really." Maybe she thought Lena was the softer touch.

Stone wheeled the truck into a dark parking lot. Doc Arnold stood in light spilling from an open doorway.

"Let's just get your arm and head checked out. It'll be okay. I promise," Lena said, as the truck stopped. Over the girl's head, Stone lifted a brow, but Lena just shrugged.

The next minutes were a blur as the three of them helped the girl into the clinic. As they traipsed to the exam room, Doc Arnold asked a few questions about the accident, then looked pointedly between the two adults when Stone explained how she'd fallen. No doubt the doc had seen his fair share of child abuse cases, but falling from a barn loft in the middle of the night was evidently bizarre enough to sound factual.

"Let's get you up here so I can take a look," the doctor said, pulling out a step at the base of the exam table.

But the girl froze, feet firmly planted as Lena and Stone held her arms. "No! Not on the table! *Not on the table!*"

"Okay, okay," Doc Arnold said, palms out toward the girl. "Just calm down. We're here to help." He pointed to one of the side chairs in the room. "How about if you sit over here?"

The doctor turned to Lena as he pulled over a rolling stool. "I forgot to ask you her name."

Lena opened her mouth, planning to say she had no idea who this girl was, this girl who had hidden on her property, then fallen and nearly killed herself. But over the doctor's shoulder, she saw the pleading look on the girl's face and the almost imperceptible shake of her head, so slight her black hair barely moved. Lena's mouth remained open, but no answer came out.

"My name is Teal," the girl said, and Doc Arnold turned to her. "Teal Kinshaw."

"Okay, Teal Kinshaw. Let's take a look."

Lena took the other guest chair as the doctor checked eyes, ears, nose, and throat. Then he pulled out his stethoscope. The teen again fought him about removing her sweatshirt so he could check her lungs and heart. Finally, after Lena scooted her chair closer, the girl consented.

Lena lifted the shirt's bottom hem, and carefully pulled it off the girl's injured wrist. For underclothes, she wore a dingy wifebeater T-shirt. Lena sucked in a breath at the sight of the girl's body. Her collarbones and shoulder blades poked through sunken skin, and Lena could count every rib against the shirt's cotton ribbing.

But her weight issue paled before the scars that covered both arms and up onto her shoulders. Some were scrolling lines, others were patterned like a maze. Purple, green, and red colored the designs, as if dye or ink had been rubbed into the wounds before they healed. Most looked months old, but a few were still swollen and ropy. An elaborately-colored tattoo on the top of the girl's left shoulder disappeared down her back under the T-shirt's neckline. Lena put her hand over her mouth. Teal noticed, and turned away.

Doc Arnold's mouth firmed into a straight line when he saw the scars. Lena couldn't see whatever look the girl gave him but, after a few seconds hesitation, he inserted the earpieces and instructed her to take deep breaths.

Had she done this to herself? Lena knew some teenagers were into cutting as a desperate form of self-control or cry for attention, but this was far beyond anything she'd heard about. And some of the scars were in impossible locations for a person to reach. If not self-inflicted, who could do such a thing?

The girl's eyes closed as Doc Arnold listened to her heart, and she swayed in the plastic chair.

"Okay, Teal," the doctor said, while his fingers explored around the head wound. "Can you tell me how old you are?

She cleared her throat. "I'm eighteen."

"Eighteen." Doc Arnold slowly confirmed, then made a note on a new chart. But his raised brows belied his acceptance of the statement.

"And you know these people?"

The girl's eyes flicked to Stone, back to Lena, then at the doctor. "Yes. That's Alex Stone. And this is AJ Blaylock," she said, sending another pleading look straight at Lena, "my Aunt Alena."

Stone chuckled intermittently as he drove them home at a much more sedate speed. The fog had thickened in the pre-dawn, cocooning the truck in a bubble of misty white. Lena stifled a yawn, concentrating instead on being mad for his good humor.

"I don't see anything funny about it, Stone," Lena hissed. "Why didn't you say something?" He could have explained to the doctor that they had no idea what the girl was talking about, but he'd remained mute as a turnip. Lot of help he'd been.

"Me?" He took his eyes off the road to look at her. "Why didn't *you* say something?" He turned back to the road, a grin covering his face. "After all…"

Lena cringed, realizing the setup she'd given him.

"…you *are* her *Aunt Alena*."

"Can it, Stone," but he put a finger to his lips and shushed her. She looked down at the girl nestled under her arm, sound asleep. Her hair smelled of soap, fresh air, and hay. After the doctor reported he'd found no evidence of a concussion and the x-ray showed her wrist only sprained, he'd given Teal a sample package of pain pills, and instructed Lena to take her "niece" home for some rest. He'd also reported the girl was very undernourished—no big news there—and suggested Lena buy some vitamins and feed her regularly.

He'd been concerned about the scars, but for some reason Lena had rattled off that those issues were already part of the girl's record, and were exactly why she was staying with Lena for a while. She hoped that wasn't *too* much of a lie.

Teal, if that was even her real name, took one of the pills before leaving the office, and fell asleep as soon as they began driving and the truck cab got warm, curled up against Lena like she belonged there.

Lena held tight when the truck took a sharp right turn, as if she could protect the young girl. But after seeing the terrible scars, Lena had a feeling nothing could protect Teal Kinshaw from the memories of her past, whatever it was.

By the time they rolled to a stop in front of Lena's cabin, the caffeine and evening's excitement had worn off, and Lena was half-asleep herself. She held the door while Stone carried Teal into the house. Since there was only one bed, Lena directed him to her room. The pain med had done a number on the girl, and her head lolled as he laid her on the bed.

"Looks like she'll be out for a while," he observed. The corner of his mouth twitched. "But you might want to lock up your jewels and silver before falling asleep."

"Get out, Stone." She shoved him out of the bedroom and into the hall. He bid her a chuckling goodnight, and Lena heard the cabin's front door open and close.

Lena removed the girl's shoes and socks, then she worked down the ragged jeans. In the light from the hallway fixture, Lena's eyes traced even more scars on Teal's legs. "Oh, honey. What happened to you?" Tears stung her eyes as she drew up the sheet and blanket.

She left the bedroom door open a crack and the hall light on, then she wrapped herself in the extra blanket she'd used earlier that evening and curled up on the small couch. Even with her eyes closed, she couldn't blot out the way the girl's skin had been carved.

Lena's hand rested on the spot where Stone had sat only a few hours ago. His warmth was gone, but she still felt his presence. She had come to Storm Lake seeking anonymity. Then she'd uncovered the body, Stone had shown up, and now this young girl. And she still hadn't had a chance to tell Stone about Eve's hand-delivered letter.

What had she gotten herself into?

25

Light streamed past the curtains into Lena's eyes, and she squinted against the brightness. Gradually, she realized she was in her living room, and memories of the previous night returned like the incoming tide at Perilous Cove.

But it wasn't the light that had woken her. She sniffed. Coffee. It pulled her off the couch like a fishing line, and dragged her to the kitchen where the coffeemaker waited with a full carafe. She poured herself a cup and took several sips, waiting for the caffeine to kick in. After a minute she recognized the background sound she'd been hearing. The washing machine.

In the short hallway on the way to the back porch, she glanced in the bedroom. The curtains were wide open, sunlight bathing the bare mattress. Lena continued toward the back porch where she'd plumbed in the laundry connections and hooked up a used washer and dryer. She silently opened the door and stepped onto the porch.

The washing machine churned and the dryer tumbled, and the smell of soap and hot linen filled the air. Lena stopped in the doorway. Teal, dressed in one of Lena's long-sleeved T-shirts that hung below her knees, used her left hand to fold one of Lena's shirts, then set it on a pile with others. The old washer growled into a spin cycle and began its routine rattle-dance across the floor. Teal used her hip to jockey it back into place as it came up to speed and settled down—exactly as Lena had learned to do.

Teal scooped up the small pile of folded shirts and tucked them under her chin, then turned toward the hall. Her mouth popped open when she spotted Lena sipping coffee, and she nearly dropped the load. Frozen in place, her eyes cut right and left as if looking for an escape route. Then she straightened and met Lena's gaze, mouth closing to a determined line. Or maybe it was resignation.

They stood contemplating each other until Lena took another sip and tilted her mug toward the girl. "Good coffee. You make it?"

The girl backed against the dryer, relief and hope rippling across her face. "It wasn't hard. I used to hang out at a Starbucks and became friends with one of the baristas. She showed me a lot."

Lena's stomach rumbled, and she checked her watch. It was nearly ten. She'd slept half the morning away. The girl had managed to make coffee without waking Lena only a dozen feet away on the couch. And strip the bed and do laundry. This girl was a ghost. "Did you eat anything?"

Teal didn't respond for a minute, then sighed. "I had a cracker. I'm sorry." She looked away.

A cracker? No wonder the girl resembled a concentration camp survivor. Tears threatened to spill down Lena's face. She'd never experienced hunger to speak of, certainly nothing like this poor girl. The bones of her shoulders poked upwards against the soft cotton shirt. What had happened to her?

"Do you like bacon and eggs?" The girl nodded without looking up. Lena stepped aside of the doorway and held out her arm in invitation. "Well, then, come on. If this coffee is any indication, you're probably a better cook than I am, but I'll do my best."

Teal brightened at that. "I can cook for you. And clean and do the laundry—"

"I can see that."

"—and I like yard work—"

"Teal," Lena interrupted the spiel as they reached the bedroom. Lena took the stack of laundry from the girl's arms, set it on the bed, and turned. Teal was shrunken back against the far hallway wall, eyes large. Lena sighed. "I'm a simple person. I *like* things simple. When we're hungry, we eat. That's rule one. Got it?"

Teal nodded once.

"Rule two is always coffee first thing. No," she said, shaking her head, "that's wrong. Coffee is *always* rule number one." She drained the remaining liquid from the mug, feeling the energy kick begin.

"What's rule number three?" the girl mumbled.

"Three?" Lena gently turned the girl toward the kitchen. "I just told you

I'm simple, and what?…you expect a whole list of things?" Teal grinned, and Lena was relieved she got the joke.

In the kitchen, Lena pulled her frying pan from the cupboard set it on the stove to heat.

Teal rose from behind the refrigerator door, the carton of eggs in her hand. "I don't see any bacon."

Lena rubbed her forehead. "Yeah, I forgot to buy it." She looked over the door into the white interior. One thing for sure, if she was going to fatten up this girl, she'd have to go shopping. She pointed to the deli drawer. "Grab that package of bologna."

Teal's eyebrows lifted. "We're having bologna and eggs?"

"Of course not," Lena said, taking the eggs from Teal and putting them by the stove. "We're having *fried* bologna and eggs."

Teal's mouth curved up as she handed Lena the package of meat. "Simple."

Lena pointed a spatula at her and winked. "You're on toast duty. I always burn it."

26

"I haven't promised her anything," Lena said in response to Stone's question two days later. "We're just taking it day by day." Truthfully, she'd never expected Teal to be around this long. The right thing would be to call the authorities and get professional help. Lena had planned to do that the first morning, but then she'd seen the girl's excitement over the fried bologna. And she remembered Teal's slight shake of the head in the doctor's office. The girl had secrets, and for some reason had chosen to trust Lena. Calling the sheriff in smacked of overwhelming betrayal.

Then, last night, while she and Teal were eating dinner, a second courier delivery had arrived. This one had a full letter from Eve. It's contents collaborated what Stone had told her. She wanted to run it by him. Compared to what was in the letter, Teal's situation would have to wait.

Lena had been on her way back from the market this morning when Chet called to say he couldn't make it up yet due to a big case. She'd started to ask him about some of the things in Eve's letter, but someone in the office had shouted his name, and he'd cut the call short to get to the courthouse.

Stone poured glasses of lemonade, and they sat down in his lawn chairs in front of the Airstream. They watched as Teal, broom handle tucked under one arm, swept the porch of one of the rental cabins where the guests had checked out on Sunday night. Her right wrist was wrapped in the ace bandage Doc Arnold had given her, and she had it cradled against her stomach as she worked.

"And you're sure you're not her Aunt Alena?" Stone smirked.

"No chance," Lena said. "She just said that so the doctor wouldn't question why two strangers brought her in. I think we're on Doc's short list for a call to social services."

"Don't worry about the doc. He seems like a good guy."

Maybe. But there was only so much leeway a doctor had before reporting it. Teal better not get so much as a hangnail in the next few weeks.

Weeks?

"*Alena*," Stone said, settling back in his chair and smiling. "Has a nice ring to it."

"That's AJ to you, Stone."

"She tell you how she knew our names?"

"She admitted she'd been in my house and saw some mail on my desk with my full name." And who knew what other information the girl had found or copied? For all Lena knew, Teal could have sold Lena's credit information to a crook. But as rough as the girl could be, Lena had pegged her as honest that first morning when Teal apologized for not asking first before eating a saltine. Who apologized for a cracker? "I don't know about your name, though. Maybe she overheard us talking? She's pretty observant."

"So, she's been around here a while. I'm surprised I didn't spot her before."

"Maybe your law enforcement skills are getting rusty."

Stone ignored her jab. "Hard worker, too," he said, indicating the girl's vigorous sweeping.

Lena sighed. "I tried getting her to rest. Didn't work."

"She takes after her aunt," Stone said, ducking when Lena swatted at him.

Lena took a long drink of lemonade. "I think she's trying to win me over so I'll let her stay." As if Lena could ever send the girl away. She was so skittish, sometimes flinching when Lena moved too fast. But she had a backbone, too, like when she insisted Lena take back her bedroom in the tiny house. Teal had even suggested she could go back to the barn loft, but Lena had shown her *own* backbone at that. They'd compromised with Teal sleeping on the couch for now. As soon as Lena could find a twin bed, they'd set it up on the back porch, opposite the wash area. The screened room would be too cold during the winter, but Lena didn't plan to be in the cabin much longer.

"Is it working?"

"What?" Lena rolled her head toward Stone.

"Has she won you over yet?"

She closed her eyes. No dishes in the sink, a dusted house, coffee brewing every morning. And who knew a dash of cinnamon, drops of vanilla, or a squirt of Hershey's chocolate could change plain coffee into something so delicious? Lena had always tolerated the bitterness, drinking it for the caffeine, not for taste. Now Teal was talking about getting flavorings and mocha powder, and offering ice-blended drinks for the cabin renters when they came back from a hot day on the lake—at a modest fee, of course. Starbucks, watch out.

"Yeah," Lena sighed. In only a couple of days, the girl had become part of Lena's life. An important part.

"Did she say anything about where she came from?" Stone asked as the sun continued to chase away the morning chill. "I mean, those scars…"

Teal had relaxed a little around Lena, sometimes wearing one of Lena's short-sleeved T-shirts while inside. But she still covered herself head to toe outside their house.

Their house. Lena almost laughed. She already thought of them as roomies.

"And really, how old is she?" Stone asked, and sipped from the blue Nalgene bottle he used for everything except wine or beer.

"Eighteen," Lena said, and laughed at Stone's raised brows. She held up one hand in defense. "Hey, you heard her with the doctor. That's what she said."

Stone mumbled something about a pig's eye. "Parents?"

"No idea."

"Where's she from?"

"Didn't ask."

"How did she get those scars?"

"Don't know."

Stone ran a hand through his hair. "Is there anything you *do* know about her?"

Lena nearly pulled a muscle holding in her grin. "Of course. I know she's eighteen."

Stone threw his head back and barked a laugh. Down at the cabin, Teal's head came up and she waved at them.

"Guess I had that one coming," Stone said more quietly as he returned the wave. "Be right back." He went into the trailer, returning a minute later with an open bag of Fritos he passed to Lena.

She crunched the first salty handful. She groaned around chews. "Ahh. The breakfast of champions. You know, these are my favorite." She plunged into the bag for another handful.

"Yep."

Lena squinted at him. He was serious. "Wait. How did you…"

Stone lifted his drink bottle toward Cabin 1. "Teal told me yesterday."

"How did she…" Lena began, then it dawned on her. The cookie package emptier than she remembered. The cereal boxes that ran out too soon. A missing can of soup Lena swore she hadn't used. And the Fritos disappearing at an alarming rate. Lena attributed it to the manufacture shrinking the packages while keeping the same price, and that she'd simply been mistaken about the soup. Little things, but now they made sense. Teal Kinshaw hadn't just been in the house, she was a food thief. Lena wondered what else she stole while hiding in the barn.

But that wasn't entirely fair. Lena didn't know what it was like to be on her own at Teal's young age—whatever that age was. Lena had at least had her aunt, a warm house, and plenty of food while growing up. Faced with hunger and no means of support, Lena suspected she'd do whatever it took to stay alive, even if it meant pilfering food from strangers. And looking at the state of Teal's near starvation, she hadn't taken enough.

"Well, hard labor counts for something," Stone said, ignoring the moral revelation. A small cloud of dust rose around Teal as she slapped a throw rug against the porch railing one handed.

"I don't ask her to do anything, but yeah, she works her tail off. She's still in pain from the fall, and…well—"

"You feel guilty for scaring her half to death the other night and causing her injuries?"

Stone wasn't laughing now, and his expression told Lena he felt just as responsible for the girl's tumble. If they'd only left her alone and confronted her in the daylight… Well, hindsight and all that.

"I just want to know how to help her," Lena said. "She's got to have family somewhere, someone who cares."

"Uh-huh. A family that nourished and protected her." He snagged a few of the corn chips. "Not all families know how to raise and take care of kids, you know."

Lena *did* know. She'd never experienced anything like the physical pain Teal had, but the world was full of good parents, bad parents, and everything in between. As a kid, you never got to pick. She stared across the oak studded land where Teal polished a porch window with a paper towel.

Except perhaps in this case. Had Teal picked Lena? The girl was certainly doing everything she could to curry favor. And, considering the life she'd had before arriving here, was that such a bad plan?

In many ways, Teal's actions were a lot like Lena's own journey. Leaving home and making her own way—although Lena had been older. Admittedly, Lena's life wasn't anywhere near the same survival threshold as the girl's. But before she'd gotten the TV job on *Nail it!*, there had been a few times between jobs when she'd slept in her pickup at campgrounds and truck stops. Even now, Lena was constantly aware she was only a few renters' checks away from serious trouble.

Speaking of trouble... Lena set the Fritos bag on the table and turned in her seat. "I need to talk to you."

He eyed the bag. "Must be serious if you're swearing off food."

"It is." His grin faded when he saw her expression. "I told you I hadn't gotten any info from Chet Marquette yet. He called again this morning, but we'd just started talking when he had to go. It's weird, Stone, but I just have this feeling that something's happened, or happening. So, a few days ago, I called a friend—well, not really a *friend*, per se—but someone I knew from the DA's office. She used to work with Bobby. I asked if she could check around."

Lena told him about receiving the strange message on her phone, not a standard text. "I don't know how she—my friend—did that, but now I know why."

Stone remained quiet, but he showed definite curiosity.

"The next day, a private courier company delivered a letter to me...all the way from L.A." Lena took a breath. "The other night, when you came back late and I...when I ran into that stupid rose bush...well, you said you'd been sent here to be around 'just in case,' right?"

Stone nodded. "Was there something in the letter that worries you?"

"Oh, yeah." Lena laughed, but it was all nerves. "The first one was short, telling me to buy a pay-as-you-go cell phone."

"First one? You mean you received more than one letter?"

She nodded. "Last night, a different courier company delivered another one. That letter has a lot more information. Let me go get it." She stood up and started for her cabin.

"I'll come with you," Stone said, matching her step.

AJ returned from her bedroom with two manila envelopes. Instead of handing them to Alex, she gripped them tight against her, studying his face. "You can't say anything to anybody, Stone."

"You can trust me, AJ," he said. "I'd never do anything to put you in danger."

Alex reached out. With obvious uncertainty, AJ passed him the envelopes, holding on for a second more before letting go. They sat at the little dinette table, and Alex slid the single sheet of paper from the thinner envelope onto the surface.

It was a typed letter, as in with a real typewriter. Every *o* was partially filled in with ink, and some letters were darker than others due to irregular strike pressure. All lowercase *f*'s were bent slightly to the right and set a little below other letters on the lines. Alex hadn't seen an original document composed on an actual typewriter in years.

L:

 It's best we keep things general, but I've got to go into some detail here. After your call, I asked two people in Chet's team--people I trust--if there had been any new developments in Bobby's murder or in any of the cases he'd been working on. They said they'd check. I also did some online searching of the files of his cases.

 A couple hours later, my cell phone rang, but there was no one there. I didn't think anything about it until my mother called later and I detected a couple of faint clicks when I accepted the call. Call me paranoid, but I immediately suspected the worst. Same reason I carry a 9mm in my purse.

 Long story short, I walked to a nearby convenience store and used the pay phone to call a techie friend who works at the phone company. Good guy. I close my eyes to his computer hacking activity info only, nothing malicious. Within a couple of hours, he confirmed my cell and home phones were tapped. I also had him check your cell number. Ditto. If you have a landline, assume that's tapped, too. My friend (I'll call him V) is the one who sent you the message on your phone. It's not a standard text message, and he did it somehow so it couldn't be detected.

 Buy a prepaid cell. I'll get you the number for the one I bought, then we can talk.

 Stay safe. – E.

Alex looked up. AJ watched him intently. Her regular cell phone lay on the table beside her, a potentially venomous snake poised to strike.

He replaced the letter, then emptied the second envelope onto the table.

Lena,

I took extra precautions getting this letter to you, sending it through two trusted friends before it routed to you, so I think we're safe on this front. One of my contacts got back to me; the other claimed nothing had changed. Don't know if it was one of the people I asked, or something from my computer searches but, needless to say, my inquiry triggered something. I did find a few things. Printouts enclosed.

Lena, I don't want to scare you unnecessarily, but Bobby was into some dangerous stuff I didn't know about. He'd been investigating the Lobos Negros cartel. They're relatively new, and cover much of Central America. It started with two brothers who made their first fortune developing product. Now they're expanding into the more lucrative distribution, so for the last four years they've been on a tear. Some cartels are cooperative, several rings coming together. Not these guys. Every expansion is a hostile takeover, eliminating the competitive leadership.

We know general info that they've already taken over at least three smaller cartels, and six months ago they assassinated the head of one large one. Executed his whole family: brothers & sisters, mother & father, cousins, plus his wife & 3 young kids.

Since Mexico is the gateway to the US drug market, it's their expansion target. Lobos Negros has a powerful and rapidly growing presence in L.A. They're always one step ahead of law enforcement in the southland. From the little I could find in the files, Bobby suspected internal corruption on our side--a link between the cartel and someone high up in the city government. I don't know if that's what got him killed (sorry, don't mean to be so direct, but I'm late with a brief I've got to get to).

I'll keep digging, but more carefully. I suggest you be careful as well. If you don't carry a gun, you might think about it. And watch for anything or anyone suspicious. I haven't talked to Chet directly yet, he's tied up in a big trial, but don't talk to anyone else on his team. If I were you, I'd only trust Chet-- and me, of course. If it didn't sound so corny, I'd shout, "TRUST NO ONE." Seriously.

Gotta go. Sorry to be paranoid and stress you. Never expected this, but now I'm determined to uncover what's going on.
Be careful. Will be in touch. – E.

The three other sheets were copies of Los Angeles Times articles about

Lobos Negros - the Black Wolves cartel. One had the date circled in red marker, and a scrawled note in the margin saying, *A month before Bobby Blaylock's murder.* The article cited an unnamed source in the DA's office. Alex had seen and read all the news stories before as part of DEA briefings, so there was nothing new there. He dropped the pages and sat back.

AJ stared at him beneath pinched brows, then went to the kitchen to make coffee. Her friend had said not to trust anyone, yet AJ had trusted him. And that was after she'd learned he was former DEA.

The question was, what would, or could, he do with this information? Bill Halwell was a possible contact. Alex couldn't imagine Bill being dirty, but the grapevine had Bill's wife presently undergoing chemo. That had to be expensive.

One thing was for sure, Lobos Negros was powerful and deadly. They were strongly suspected of the recent upsurge of drug-smuggling panga boats, high-speed open vessels that left from Mexico fully loaded, and traveled up the coast of California to isolated landing areas.

As shore authorities and the Coast Guard became more diligent patrolling known southern landing sites, the boats had begun bypassing those and heading farther north, some traveling over four hundred miles of ocean to the coast around Perilous Cove. There the crew would abandon the craft and transfer their cargo into waiting recreational vehicles used for distribution anywhere in the state. California's scenic Highway 1 carried a constant flow of RVs filled with retired couples and families. Except for a slightly sagging rear, there was little to give away the odd RV carrying a couple thousand pounds of marijuana with a street value of a million dollars. God help any innocent family that accidentally got in their way.

Both Ben Conner and his brother, Addison, had mentioned the uptick in local landings when Alex first asked about a place to park his trailer for his assignment to keep an eye on AJ.

Now it made sense why Bill Halwell had hired him. Halwell must know what Bobby Blaylock had been investigating and, for some reason, he was afraid the bad guys thought AJ knew something.

But it probably wouldn't be the cartel that was after AJ; it would be whomever Bobby had suspected of corruption, someone who knew the young district attorney was getting too close. It was likely that person who tried to eliminate the threat by killing him. AJ hadn't been the target that night, and Alex sincerely hoped Eve's inquiries hadn't done what she feared: put the focus directly on the woman fixing him coffee.

Lena worked all day on Cabin 6, planing sticky doors and windows, replacing broken hinges on cabinets, and wiring new light fixtures in all the rooms. She felt an even greater urgency to finish it now that Teal was here. Granted, the girl probably wouldn't be around much longer; they couldn't go forever without contacting the authorities. Surely people were searching for her. Lena didn't want to think about getting into legal trouble for harboring a runaway. But until then, she felt the need to give the girl a proper bedroom. Of course, there was always the chance Teal really *was* eighteen.

Right.

At four o'clock, she convinced Teal to quit working, take a shower, and relax before dinner. After drying off, Teal had promptly fallen asleep on Lena's bed, leaving Lena to figure out the meal.

She stood at the open kitchen pantry. Like the Old Mother Hubbard nursery rhyme, this cupboard was definitely bare. Weighed by guilt over the doctor's order to fatten Teal up, Lena was contemplating a quick run to the Shelter Cove Store when the afternoon light coming in the front door dimmed and she heard a knock. Beyond the screen, Alex Stone eclipsed the sun.

"Hey, AJ," Stone said through the screen, "I feel like pizza tonight. How about I pick you guys up in an hour or so and we'll head down to Wave Pizza in Perilous Cove? They have the best around."

Lena glared at him. The three of them in the truck again sounded a lot like Dad, Mom, and darling daughter out for family night. Stone was nice to have around and talk to, but she wasn't interested in a relationship with the man. Still, she was glad he hadn't taken her initial not-so-subtle hints she didn't want him here. Plus, he had Fritos, and her bag had run out yesterday. Points there.

Wave Pizza was indeed pretty spectacular, and Lena's mouth watered at Stone's invitation. Besides, she convinced herself, the extra calories in all that gooey cheese would do Teal good.

The sun disappeared behind the mountains while they rode in the old truck back toward Storm Lake. Teal sat in the middle, while AJ had shotgun. Alex drove with one hand, and fiddled with the radio with the other. He was partial to oldies, and Teal filed that away for future use.

Her eyes drooped after all the rich food and warmth of the truck. Her stomach felt stretched tight. Alex had ordered three different kinds of pizza, each with different and amazing toppings, everything from pineapple, to mushrooms, to spicy sausage. All her mom had ever bought was the cheapest cheese pizza from anyplace offering free delivery. And The Wave had a salad bar with so many choices she'd stood frozen in line until Alex helped her.

After eating, Alex had insisted they play all the games in the small arcade. He'd clobbered them in every shooter game, but Teal had bested him in classic pinball, even with her sore right hand. Unless, of course, he'd let her win. But he'd looked so crestfallen, she didn't think he had. He had a competitive side, for sure.

Then they moved on to Whack-a-Mole. Maybe it was AJ's carpentry background, but she outscored them both, pounding at the little creatures until Alex and Teal collapsed on the floor in laughter. The restaurant manager had come back and warned AJ to take it easy on his game.

Teal sank back into the soft truck seat. The cab smelled of Alex's cologne, onion from the leftover boxes at their feet, engine exhaust, and AJ's lavender shampoo. Teal thought it the best combination she'd ever experienced, and knew that every time she ate pizza she'd think of this moment.

The truck's engine throbbed as they climbed a hill. Alex told them over dinner that he'd restored the '62 Chevy himself. He was amazing, if a bit rough around the edges. She opened one eye and checked his profile. A small smile played on his lips as he sang along softly to the radio.

But he was still a cop—sort of—and she couldn't underestimate him. While she'd spent time the last few days making herself indispensable to AJ, Alex Stone was a lawman, and you could never fully trust the law. She had to make sure he wouldn't send her back into the foster care system in some misguided belief he was doing the best for her. No way she'd do that again. She'd discovered something special here, and didn't want anything to disturb the careful balance.

Teal covered her grin. These two were so totally right for each other. They just didn't know it yet. Maybe there was something she could do about that.

And Quin. He was coming tomorrow afternoon and they were going to hike to the falls. They'd set it up when they returned from breakfast at Deer Cove, so he hadn't heard she'd been caught, fallen in the barn, gone to the doctor. He still thought she was staying with her parents in a house up Gift Road. She sighed. She'd never even set foot on Gift Road, let alone driven the non-existent car she claimed her parents let her use. He still didn't know about her scars, either, not since she'd chickened out at Deer Cove and refused to remove her sweatshirt.

She'd let him believe so many lies. She blew out a breath. *Lucy, you got some 'splainin' to do.*

Boy, did she.

27

"Teal, are you in here?" Lena called into Cabin 2 as she climbed the front steps to the open door.

"Back here," came Teal's muffled response.

Lena made her way through the living room. It smelled of furniture polish, Pine-Sol, and Windex. The pillows on the small sofa were plumped, and the large throw rug showed vacuum marks. A sloshing sound led her to the small bathroom, where Teal knelt beside the toilet. Strands of her black hair had broken free from the rubber band and stuck to her face as she scrubbed the base and floor with a wet sponge.

Lena pursed her lips. She'd told the girl to relax while Lena drove to Brodie's Hardware, then stopped for groceries on the way home, but here Teal was, working her butt off. Her *skinny* butt.

Lena would have been back earlier if Stan Billows hadn't cornered her in the paint department while she was picking colors. He'd commented on how lonely she must be, living *"out there all by yourself,"* then crowded her personal space until she threatened to bean him with the gallon of low sheen latex she'd been holding. He'd checked her out, both literally and figuratively, while she wrote a check to pay for the new cabin's paint. The guy was harmless, but not easily dissuaded. Maybe next trip she should call ahead to see if Stan-the-Weasel was on duty.

"Teal, you're too weak to keep doing this," Lena said in her gentlest voice. "I don't want you working this hard."

"I'm done," Teal said, rinsing the sponge and squeezing it dry for a final swipe around the floor. She sat back on her legs and ran the back of her bad arm across her forehead. Her ghostly complexion contrasted with her dark hair, but her smiling face radiated pride in the completed job.

Lena shook her head, picked up the water pail, and extended her other hand. "It looks fantastic. But come on. I bought you a treat for lunch." Teal gripped her hand, failing to cover a groan as she got to her feet. She wobbled a little and Lena put an arm around her shoulders, again startled at the knobby bones. The girl still weighed next to nothing, even after several regular meals, and her stomach bothered her all the time.

Silently, she worried Teal had some internal injuries from the fall. She'd even called Doc Arnold this morning while Teal was showering. He'd assured her that, while the teenager was drastically undernourished, her body would eventually adjust to regular meals. He suggested a digestive enzyme, and to stick with bland foods. Good thing he didn't know about them pigging out on Wave Pizza.

Lena winced. Or today's lunch.

He'd also asked some pointed questions about the origin of Teal's scars and near starvation, more than hinting he was walking the fine line of legal obligation to report her condition to the authorities. But Lena had explained that was exactly why her "niece" was staying at the cabins, and that the authorities in Teal's hometown knew all about the scars. Surely that was true. Lena could tell he wasn't satisfied; he'd seen Lena's shock when Teal had proclaimed her as Aunt Alena.

Lena should have confessed the truth, but there'd been something in the girl's eyes that night at the doctor's office. Fear, longing, loneliness? Yes, all those. But what turned the corner for Lena was the resignation of betrayal. Lena knew that one personally—from her father. There was nothing worse.

Maybe Lena was reading her own experience into the girl's actions, but deep down, Lena was sure Teal expected those around her to give her up. It made Lena more determined to be someone the girl could trust, even if she had to pose as her aunt.

Doc Arnold—after failing to extract any more details about the girl's history—had explained Teal's stomach problems were probably that her body wasn't used to regular meals, and said things should settle down in a few days.

"So," Teal said, breaking into Lena's musings as Teal dragged slowly up the hill to their cabin, "what did you buy for lunch?"

"Just some SPAM."

"I *love* SPAM! Come on," Teal tugged Lena's hand, urging her faster. "SPAM's amazing. Did you know it's great in omelets, salads, and casseroles? You can barbecue it, too, that's the best."

"Better than bologna?" Lena laughed at the girl's enthusiasm over what Lena considered a slightly disgusting canned meat product. "How about we stick to fried SPAM and cheese sandwiches for today?"

"Okay." Teal practically skipped up the steps to their house and spun around to face Lena. "Then maybe we can get Alex to cook some on his grill tomorrow?"

"We'll see," Lena laughed, turned the girl's shoulders toward the door and marched her inside. "You're assuming we'll have leftovers."

After slicing the SPAM, Lena laid the pieces in a skillet. Some people ate the stuff right out of the can, simply scraping off the gooey gelatin—or not. She shivered at the thought, and turned up the heat. Although the can stated it was already cooked—like some giant, square hotdog—for Lena it was well-done or nothing.

To her surprise, the store had stocked Smoked SPAM, Jalapeño SPAM, Cheese SPAM, and a couple others she couldn't remember in addition to Lite SPAM. Who knew? She'd opted for the regular variety, figuring Teal could use the extra nutrients—if that word could even be mentioned in the same sentence as the canned product.

While the meat sizzled and filled the kitchen with a slightly revolting aroma, Lena assembled toasted whole wheat bread liberally coated with mustard, tomato slices, and lettuce. By the time Teal returned from washing up, the sandwiches were on the little dining table along with a jumbo bag of Fritos, a regular Pepsi for Teal, and a Diet Pepsi for Lena.

The girl took a bite and rolled her eyes. "This is *so good!*" She followed the bite with some corn chips and a swig of soda. She'd let slip at last night's dinner she'd been with one set of foster parents who'd moved to California from Hawaii, and they'd served SPAM at least twice a week. Evidently SPAM was legend in Hawaii.

Lena took a tentative bite of her own half sandwich and had to admit it wasn't too bad—providing one studiously avoided the Nutrition Facts label on the can. But who was she to talk when she consumed Fritos on a regular basis? Lena set her sandwich down. Now was as good a time as any to ask Teal about her past.

Before Lena could broach the subject, Teal stated, "I'm hiking up to the falls a little later."

"By yourself?" Lena was surprised. The hike wasn't strenuous, only a quarter mile or so, but given the girl had just tumbled at least fourteen feet onto hay bales on the barn floor...

Teal shook her head. "With a boy I met."

Lena sat back in her chair. A boy? When had Teal had time to get to know a boy? She'd admitted to being holed up in the barn for a couple of weeks before they discovered her, hiding from everyone. And all the while she'd carried on a *social life*? *Lena* didn't have a social life, and she wasn't even a fugitive. Dinner at Stone's or Wave Pizza didn't count.

"What boy?" she asked, trying not to sound like a mom. From the look on Teal's face, she failed. Well, too bad.

"I met him down at the water one day. He's really nice, and brought me food."

Sheesh. *Hey, little girl, want a piece of candy?* "This boy have a name?" Teal didn't seem like the gullible type, but how could Lena be sure? The teen might be a survivor, but that didn't mean she was capable of intelligent decisions, especially about boys who plied her with tasty treats.

Teal regarded Lena with hooded eyes for a minute before answering. "Quin." Her voice sounded a bit dreamy.

Lena raised an eyebrow. "The Conner boy?"

Teal's eyes widened. "You know him?"

Lena shrugged. How many Quins could there be at Storm Lake? "This isn't exactly L.A."

"He has this really great boat, and he took me to breakfast at Deer Cove." Teal's eyes brightened as she described eating pancakes, eggs, and sausage at a picnic table overlooking the harbor. It sounded better than bologna and eggs. Lena wished someone would take *her* to breakfast at Deer Cove.

As she listened to the girl expound about how "amazing" Quin was, Lena took another bite of sandwich. She had to admit, the crispy SPAM did make a pretty tasty wannabe BLT. An SLT. Maybe it *would* be good done up on Stone's barbecue. Wine paring might be a challenge. White or red? Maybe a light rosé?

Teal went on how Quin knew all about boats, and could cut the motor at just the right second to glide into a beach or dock, and how he seemed to know everyone around the lake. Obviously he'd made quite an impression on the girl.

"When did this breakfast happen?"

"Oh," Teal said, "it was the morning before..." she trailed off and dropped her eyes.

Guilt bubbled up in Lena. *The morning before you and Stone scared me into catapulting off the barn loft.*

Two vertical lines formed on Teal's brow. "Do you not want me to go? I'm sorry; I should have asked." A sigh escaped as she sagged in the chair, sandwich forgotten. "Is there something else you need me to do?"

There were so many things Lena wanted to say, she didn't know where to start. She wanted to scream, *No! Go have fun. Be a teenager.* She didn't want Teal to take on chores, hadn't asked her—the girl was still healing from near starvation and injuries. Lena hadn't even known Teal was cleaning the guest cabin today until she searched for her.

And Lena wasn't her mother. That was way too much responsibility, and she knew nothing about giving life direction to a teenager. Finally, she held her palms out and said the first thing that popped to mind.

"Hey, you can do anything you want. After all, you're eighteen. Right?"

Conflict rippled across the girl's face, and Lena nearly laughed. One thing she'd learned from her own teenage life was that forcing an issue was like poking an open wound with a stick—painful and unproductive. She kept quiet by stuffing the last bite of sandwich into her mouth and washing it down with Pepsi.

"Yeah…" Teal said in a small voice, "about that." She took a breath, visually weighing the options before continuing. "I'm, uh…not *quite* eighteen. Yet."

Lena raised a brow.

"She's hiding something, more than what she told me," AJ said, slamming a piece of firewood on the pile beside the barbecue.

"Ya think?" Alex had just arrived with another load from Merle Ferris' place five minutes ago, and AJ had spied him as he drove in. The dust hadn't settled around the truck where he'd parked at the barbecue area before she'd stalked up and began flinging pieces off the load.

"I mean, *sixteen*! What's a girl her age doing dropping out of foster care, hiking around the country fending for herself?" Another log slammed into the pile. "She said she doesn't even have a driver's license. She can't vote. Hasn't finished high school. Might not have a Social Security number for all I know."

"Worried about hiring illegal labor?" he said, then dodged as she flung another piece of wood toward the pile—or at him. He hid a grin. This woman was so much fun.

She threw both hands in the air. "She steals food and clothes, and probably money, although she didn't admit to that. And now she's off on dates. How does a thieving, starving teenager go on 'dates'?" AJ did air quotes, then tossed him another piece of firewood.

Alex stacked the piece and leaned against the truck. He'd been around enough women to know that the best strategy was to keep his mouth zipped and maintain a little distance when they were venting. Anything else was a good way to get your head bitten off—or whacked with a piece of firewood. But darn she was cute when fired up.

Proving his point, AJ poked a stick at his chest. "Do you know she's been in seven foster homes? Seven! How does that even happen?" She threw the stick at the pile, missed by a yard, and swore under her breath as she stomped to retrieve it. She came back to the truck and slumped next to him, spent from her mini tirade. She nodded over her shoulder at the half-full pickup bed. "Aren't you going to help me with this?"

"I thought you were doing a pretty good job *unloading* without me." He tried to keep his mouth from twitching—much—and was rewarded with a sigh and a sheepish grin.

"Guess I set myself up for that one." She tilted her head back and gazed up through the canopy of oak leaves.

He stared at her tanned face. Her eyebrows were sun-bleached, but dark lashes framed her expressive eyes. Or maybe she used mascara. That and lipstick were about the sum total of his knowledge of women's makeup. Whatever her beauty secrets, her full lips drew his attention. What would it be like to…? She turned her head and caught him.

Her eyes clouded for a second before she shook her head and pushed off the truck. "What am I going to do about her, Stone?"

"Well, she *is* a minor, not emancipated that we know of, and is a fugitive from the foster system. I'm no expert, but keeping her here must be breaking some state or county laws." He tried to remember what he was like at sixteen. Bursting out of his clothes from yet another growth spurt, begging to take the drivers test two minutes after his birthday party so he could charge another step toward independence. The worst thing that had happened to him was running his first car into a ditch out on Drake Road and bending a fender. He'd always had loving parents, who never missed one of his football games,

Teal had the independence thing down—except for running out of food. He had to admire the girl for her resourcefulness.

"We're not *keeping* her anywhere," AJ said, but sighed when she saw his raised brow. "Okay, okay, *I'm* not keeping her anywhere. But hey"—she poked a finger at his chest—"you're in on this too, mister take-us-all-out-for-pizza." She scrubbed her face with her hands, leaving a smudge of brown bark dust on her right cheek. His thumb twitched with wanting to brush it away. She needed to stop doing that or he couldn't be held responsible for his actions.

"Hey," he said, trying to focus on the problem at hand, "I was just trying to help you out. I know it's an extra expense to have her with you. Are you making enough money to support another mouth?"

"Are you kidding?" She laughed, then dismissed his question with a wave of her hand. "But that doesn't matter. I can't send her away." She turned to him again and her voice quieted and lowered in intensity. "I feel like she's starting to trust me, and I don't think there have been too many people in her life like that, you know?"

Alex admitted AJ was probably right about that. Teal had been as skittish as a barn cat for the first few days, jumping more than once when he came around a corner and surprised her. She hadn't revealed what had happened to her, but it must have been bad. He was somewhat surprised she hadn't already disappeared one night. Gradually, she'd relaxed around him—a little. But he'd caught her wary looks more than once, as if she expected him to slap on the cuffs and haul her off.

AJ turned toward him. "What do you think we—I—should do?"

"Well," he said, struggling to hold a straight face, "things aren't going too bad the way they are. You're getting pretty cheap labor." AJ glared at him. He continued in full seriousness, knowing he was pushing it and loving every minute of it. "I mean, in trade for room and board, that's a sweet deal."

She swatted his arm twice before he caught her wrists and pinned them against his chest. Those lips were inches away, but it was her sharp intake of breath and widening of her dark eyes that set his resolve. Slowly, he drew down. An instant before his lips touched hers, her eyes closed and he was lost.

AJ Blaylock tasted of sun and fresh air, softness and longing. Her hands snaked up his chest and around his neck. She pulled closer, heat radiated between them. Her breath came faster as he moved his mouth over hers.

"Ahem," a voice said, and AJ burst apart from him, ducking her head. A man and a boy stood several feet away, both with wide grins. "Sorry to interrupt." The man's eyes flicked to AJ, but he addressed Alex, "We were wondering if we could get the grill started?" He displayed a pan of several cleaned trout. The boy carried spice containers and a long handled spatula.

AJ turned and practically ran toward her cabin. Alex watched her for a second before turning to the pair. "Uh, sure. No problem. I'll help you get a fire going."

Alex grabbed a half-dozen pieces of kindling. He backed toward the barbecue, staring after AJ Blaylock's form escaping through the trees.

One thing he knew for sure: one taste hadn't abated his appetite.

28

Mist from the cascading water billowed across the pool, cooling the air where Teal sat next to Quin on a flat stone. It felt good after their hike, but she was still sweating in her sweatshirt. Duh. She cut her eyes toward Quin. What didn't feel good was waiting for Quin's reaction to her story.

She'd told him about the multiple foster homes, the unwanted advances by an older boy, and her ultimate kidnapping. She kept the more gruesome details about her basement imprisonment from him, choosing her words carefully as she alluded to torture and starvation. She'd even shared a little about her mom, whose addictions had terrorized Teal's early life. Quin had such a perfect family now with Ben and Rayne, how could he not think less of her after hearing that history?

Then she'd confessed about hiding in AJ's barn, stealing food, her fall, and that she was now living with AJ.

Letting down the protections she'd built up had been agonizing. She'd lapsed into long silences a few times, but Quin never interrupted. In fact, he hadn't uttered a word since she'd finished. If Quin couldn't accept the new her… Well, there wasn't any way she could ever be the girl she'd seemed to be before all this. She'd never be an innocent girl again.

Perspiration trickled down her back and between her breasts. She'd hated putting on the sweatshirt this afternoon after braving only a T-shirt around AJ and sometimes Alex, but she didn't think Quin was ready for the scars. The emotional ones she'd just shared were more than enough for now.

She waited, watching the sunlight spray its own waterfall onto the pond's surface, splashing color on the rocks and trees in ever changing patterns. The constant sound of the water substituted for Quin's silence for several minutes, so much so that she started at his throat clearing. Teal kept her eyes on the pool.

"I want to see," he said.

Teal pressed her eyes closed and shook her head. He didn't know what he was asking. Hearing was one thing, but seeing the damage done to her body… He wouldn't ever look at her the same way again. She remembered the way AJ and Alex had reacted in the doctor's office, the shock, not knowing what to say or where to look. They'd tried to cover their horror, but not fast enough. Teal couldn't stand that from Quin.

"Teal?"

Reluctantly, she brushed her hair back and turned. Quin's eyes were partially hidden beneath his brown hair. She reached up and pushed it back with a trembling hand. Only kindness remained. No judgment. She swallowed.

"I…" Her voice was a whisper, which only drew Quin closer.

"Trust me."

Could she? She'd only looked a few times herself, mostly in gas station mirrors. And they, thankfully, were usually scratched dull or broken into shards. In AJ's bathroom, Teal ignored the mirror, choosing to use it only for her face. The designs on her back remained a mystery, like the dark side of the moon, her surface blasted not by meteors, but by the hand of one man.

She pushed up the left sweatshirt sleeve a couple of inches and loosened the strap of her wristwatch. The leather band was nearly an inch wide, made for a man, but it had suited Teal's purpose perfectly. She let the tongue slip through the buckle, but held the watch in place, unwilling to open this first door. Where would it end?

Quin's deeply tanned hand covered hers, gently prying apart her fingers. Teal closed her eyes as the heavy timepiece fell away, unable to witness Quin's reaction. His fingers, calloused from years of ropes and oars, traced the scars. She didn't need eyes to see the marred flesh, cruel reminders of the handcuffs and bindings Fred had been so fond of. They'd cut deeper with every desperate pull, magnifying his pleasure—at least until she passed out. She'd faked pain early in hopes he'd relent. It had done no good. New wounds built on old, scar tissue upon scar tissue, until she'd finally escaped his knives.

Before she could stop him, Quin pushed up her right sleeve and, mindful of her strained wrist, tugged on the wristbands she wore. The yellow rubber one read LIVESTRONG, which she'd been told was from a bicycle racer. Quin stretched it and drew it down over her hand. He laid it on the rock.

Next, the braided band of teal-colored cloth that hid nearly an inch of skin. Black beads finished off the tied tails. Quin removed that one, too.

The final concealing accessory was one she'd found after leaving the foster home. She'd snuck into a YMCA to use the shower. When snagging some not-too-grungy towels from the laundry bin, the black band had fallen at her feet. The white letters, deeply carved into the silicone, shouted to her.

NO PAIN, NO GAIN.

It was a message just for her, both challenge and promise. The horror of her experience could become the focus of her life and destroy her, or she could *use* the pain, and grow stronger. At that moment in the Y, when her fingers circled the band like Quin's were doing now, she determined to do anything it took to survive. If it meant stealing, so be it. Sleeping in parks? She could do that. Staying off the authorities' radar? First priority.

But revealing the disfiguring scars to someone she cared about?

Quin dropped the confiscated band with the others and sat back, leaving her more naked than if he'd removed all her clothes. His eyes studied the grotesque gouges around her wrists, bands that couldn't be removed like the three on the rock between them. For what seemed like several minutes, he waited. He didn't seem repulsed. Then again, despite a couple of Oprah episodes, Teal was no expert on body language. Finally, she understood. The next step was her choice. Teal was used to people forcing her: her mother, social workers, foster parents, teachers. Fred.

Quin wouldn't press her on this. Somehow, that gave her strength.

NO PAIN, NO GAIN.

Teal gathered both courage and the bottom hem of the sweatshirt sleeve. It would have been nice to whip it over her head with flourish like a TV model, but her sprained wrist demanded some caution as she pulled her arms inside. Still, she was proud as she lifted the cotton neck over her head and shook out her hair. The sleeveless T-shirt AJ had given her left her arms and shoulders bare—the fleshscape where Fred had done *"some of my best work," chuckle, chuckle.*

With the sweatshirt gone, mist cooled her arms better than any air conditioner. Even the beauty around her seemed closer, like she was now part of it, not isolated and cocooned. She briefly closed her eyes and inhaled the airborne aromas. Free.

But it wasn't just freedom *from*; it was freedom *to*—to be looked upon by another.

Her stomach only quivered a little under Quin's scrutiny—then again, it could have been from too much dumpster-diving. She wondered if her digestive system would ever be the same again, even with the doctor's pills. Quin studied each mark, his eyes burning lasers, searing their own paths up and down each arm.

Fred had experimented with a few tattoos: a cross on her left thigh, a butterfly on the slope of her left breast that actually wasn't too bad, and entwined red and green serpents uncoiling at the base of her spine and rising up her back, their heads almost cresting her shoulders. Teal had never seen it, but the other girl at her last foster home said it was *"awesome."* All Teal remembered was the buzzing sting of Fred's needle gun as it pierced her skin day after day.

But Fred's "specialty," as he called it, his true art, was scarification. Cutting.

Using the tip of a razor blade or craft knife, he inscribed intricate, sometimes maze-like patterns on her arms and torso. He experimented with various irritants, like lemon juice, vinegar, and colored dyes to prevent the cuts from healing too quickly. This allowed raised keloids to develop and give more definition to his designs. Fortunately, he'd spared her face from his blades, saying he wanted her to appear unmarked when fully dressed. She was his secret work of art. However, he'd clearly never intended she escape.

Although still modestly covered, Teal quivered under Quin's gaze, and her skin twitched involuntarily when he brushed his hand along her right arm, sliding over a series of horizontal white lines. These were Fred's first slices and well healed. Quin's fingertips hovered above the red geometric maze that wrapped her shoulder. Fred had used tattoo ink in that one to give it color.

"Does it hurt?" Quin's voice was so soft, she strained to hear him over the soothing water.

How to answer that? Although it was one of Fred's newer undertakings, the dyed cuts were no longer tender, and would shrink more with time. The real pain went deeper. Her body shuddered, remembering the terror when the man had first dragged her from the cage and tied her to The Table, all the while showing her his knives, and explaining about cuts and art.

"Sorry," Quin said, dropping his hand.

Tears wetted her lashes, and she dislodged them with a violent shake of her head. "Not your fault. Bad memories." She drew a deep breath. "I'm the one who's sorry. I had no right to subject you to this. It was stupid." She gathered up the sweatshirt where it lay on the boulder behind her and twisted it around, trying to locate the neck. Her blurred vision didn't help.

Quin stopped her, pulling the shirt away and laying it behind him. Then he took her right arm in his hands and stretched it toward him. Her breath caught as he bent forward and lightly kissed those first scars encircling her wrist. He scooted closer and kissed a series of four stars below the bend of her elbow. Next came the horizontal lines.

Teal's tears flowed freely, but the painful memories retreated a little, forced away by Quin's intoxicating aroma of sunscreen and outdoors. He moved to her shoulder. With the lightest brush, his lips touched the red maze, beginning at the bottom and moving to the top where her skin slid under the shirt's strap. Quin straightened, and Teal swiped her eyes. She couldn't do anything about her quaking shoulders. Then he leaned in and, placing his hand behind her neck, pulled her forward until their foreheads touched.

"You are beautiful, Teal Kinshaw. Every part is uniquely you, both inside and outside." His eyes were wet, too, and she wanted to forget the past and sink into his comfort.

But Teal shook her head against his. "You haven't seen it all. There's… a lot more. And—"

"Doesn't matter." Quin's breath was soft on her cheeks. "No matter what he did, this…" he gave her head a squeeze, "…is still you. This is the only you I've ever known." He grinned. "I don't know if that even makes sense."

She smiled, too, not caring *what* he'd said, only *how* he'd said it. Fred had treated her like a piece of canvas, paying no attention to her screaming, crying, or fighting—unless her thrashing interfered with his fun. That would bring a fist to the head. She'd been property, something to be carved and discarded, like the others that had occupied The Table before her.

But Quin treated her like a precious jewel that he was lucky to hold. She loved him for it.

"I don't deserve you," she said, brushing his cheek with her fingers.

"You just like me for my boat."

She laughed, and he leaned in for another kiss, this one on her lips. She swayed forward and kissed him back. She could have stayed like this for an hour, but Quin gently broke away, got to his feet, and held out his hand.

"Come on, beautiful, we better get back before they send out Search and Rescue." As he bent to gather her sweatshirt, wristbands, and watch, Teal

185

noticed the sun had dipped beyond the western hills. Gloom shrouded the glen. Although the air still smelled like flowers and moss, the butterflies had disappeared, and a few crickets announced evening's imminent arrival.

But mostly she noticed he'd called her *beautiful*. She hadn't thought of herself that way since Fred. And, if she was honest, not for a long time before him. Yet here was a boy, a man, who thought she was. While she'd been afraid he'd reject her once he saw her ugliness, he proclaimed her beauty.

Quin held her hand as they picked their way across the boulder field to the path, then laced his fingers with hers. He carried her sweatshirt, so her arm was bare against his as they began the short hike home.

Home. It sounded so natural as they walked along swinging joined hands, yet also so completely odd. Home had been a place of frightening noises coming from her mom's room. It had been houses belonging to strangers, an underpass, someone's garden shack, a bus station, an abandoned car, or a blanket under the stars.

For the first time in a few years, a real home seemed possible, and Teal held tight to the brown-haired boy beside her.

Lena stood at the kitchen sink with her eyes closed, but that did nothing to blot out the embarrassment of the past hour.

Stupid. Stupid. Stupid!

What was she thinking, kissing Alex Stone like that? Kissing him at *all*? And in front of paying guests, no less.

Lena smacked herself on the forehead, too late realizing she still had a death-grip on a sopping sponge she'd been using to wear a hole in her kitchen countertop. Using her sleeve, she wiped water from her eyes and stalked to the front door. Before flinging it open, she pulled aside the curtain and peered out. Safe. No sign of Stone—or the guests, for that matter. The barbecue area was out of sight, behind one of the oaks. She sighed and stepped onto the porch.

The sun had just set, but the summer light would last almost an hour. An uncharacteristically cool breeze carried the lake smells she'd come to love: fresh water, fragrances from dozens of plants and trees—even the smoke from the barbecue. She frowned toward the spot. The father and son were probably still laughing over her embarrassment.

But it wasn't their fault. Sinking into the chair, she stretched her legs out, rolling her feet back and forth on the heels of her boots. She'd had no business kissing Stone. Or letting him kiss her. She scrunched her brows together, foggy on who had kissed whom. What she *did* remember was firm, strong lips moving across hers. Unwanted heat raced up her neck as she recalled putting her arms around him, pulling him closer. She smacked her forehead again.

"Morning-after regrets?"

The deep, male voice came from her right. Stone stood on the ground outside the porch railing, chin resting on arms crossed on the warped boards, watching. Lena's eyes almost slipped to his mouth before she caught herself and quickly stood.

"Not at all." When she couldn't figure out what to do with her hands, she shoved them in her front pockets. "And it hasn't even been two hours." Somehow, that admission only made the incident more real.

"Do you always pummel your forehead then?" A corner of his mouth lifted, and she would swear before a court of law that his eyes twinkled.

She supposed some would call his expression cute, but right now she wanted to smack it with the wet sponge. "Only when I'm trying to remember my shopping list," Lena said, with what she hoped communicated indifference. She yanked open the screen door and paused halfway through. "I have to go to Home Depot and buy some things for the new cabin."

"Now?" Stone glanced at his watch. "It's eight thirty." He stepped around to the front of the porch and paused with one foot on the bottom stair. "But I'm not busy if you need a hand."

"No! I...I have to...I mean..." She glanced up through the trees, wishing the sun would back up a couple of hours. Where had the day gone? And even though she needed a ton of things for the new cabin, she hadn't compiled a list yet. She couldn't afford to make the trip if she wasn't prepared, no matter how much she wanted to escape Stone.

He'd climbed the stairs while she'd been thinking, and now filled the small porch with his male bulk. A black T-shirt strained across his chest, outlining planes, ridges, and valleys. Her fingers twitched. She pressed back against the open screen door until it lay flat against the outside cabin wall.

This was ridiculous—she didn't even like the man. Plus, he was a lawman, and most of the ones she'd met tended to have over-active egos. Well, technically Stone said he was retired from DEA, but he still worked for them occasionally. Close enough. Lena realized he'd said something and was waiting for her reply.

"What?" She forced her eyes higher and met his.

"I'm wondering what's churning behind those pretty eyes of yours," he said, tilting his head and crowding closer.

Lena's mouth was hanging open and she closed it. *Pretty?* Just when she thought she'd figured the guy out, he threw her a curve. Maybe she *should* invite him to go to Home Depot. After all, how much trouble could she get into in the power tool aisle? But the thought of riding side by side in her Jeep or his truck sent her skin tingling. Distance was what she needed in this situation. They were from different worlds. No way could they be right for each other. And why was she even thinking about being *right*? There was no "each other."

"AJ."

She focused, aware he'd been talking again while she'd been lost in thought. Somehow he'd gotten even closer.

"I asked if you'd like to come to my place…"

His place? Her heart jumped to light speed, and she thumped against the screen door.

"…for dinner. If we're not going to Mission Peak, that is."

Lena expelled a breath. Her skin was on fire. She hoped it wasn't obvious how he affected her.

He tilted his head. "Thought you might be hungry. I made up some hamburger with chopped onions, diced red pepper, garlic powder, and Worcestershire sauce—all pressed into big… juicy… patties."

Lena's stomach picked that moment to agree rather loudly that dinner at Stone's sounded splendid. Was her whole body betraying her?

"And the grill is…" his face hovered inches above hers…"hot." His breath scorched her lips.

"Uh…I'd better not," she cast about for an excuse. "I have to fix dinner for Teal. She and Quin should be back soon. Any second, really." Lena bent around his wide shoulder and searched the yard for the girl and the Conner boy, but they were nowhere in sight. Probably just as well. If Teal caught Stone and Lena like this…well, the teenager would hoot and holler, then drag Lena all the way to the Airstream.

"Thought you said a few minutes ago you were going to Mission Peak?"

Stone leaned against the doorframe, the inch of space between them doing nothing to mask his clean scent. He'd showered before coming over. She wanted to sit down, but the screen was at her back. Inviting him inside wasn't an option. Her stomach sent out another noisy appeal for food.

A grin lit up Stone's face. "*Sounds* like you're hungry," he said, his breath tickling her skin. He leaned closer still, until only the material of their clothing separated them.

Lena placed both palms on Stone's warm chest, delaying just a second while her fingers molded to those hard planes. As his mouth descended toward hers, she pushed—hard. He barely moved. The guy lived up to his name.

His laugh rumbled against her fingers, but he straightened, giving her a few inches of space. "There's plenty for Teal. Quin, too. Leave them a note."

Silently, she cursed her food weakness, but she could no longer resist the temptation of juicy burgers. Lena wrote out a note and taped it on the door, then shoved him down the stairs and followed him toward the trailer. It seemed easier to go along than keep resisting. Besides, she was hungry. And how much trouble could she get into sitting outside an Airstream?

As they approached his clearing and the smoking Weber, it dawned on her this would be the third time in two weeks she'd had dinner with Alex Stone. She was so in trouble.

29

"Stupid computer!"

"What's wrong?" Teal asked, coming out of the bathroom.

"It won't print," AJ sighed, and reached for a legal pad. "I'll just copy everything onto paper like I had to last week."

"Want me to take a look?" Teal had itched to get her fingers on the Mac, but hadn't broached the subject.

AJ regarded her a minute, then pushed the laptop toward the other chair at the table. "Have at it. Just don't erase my list."

In five minutes, Teal had repaired the file permissions and deleted and re-added the printer. She hit Print, and the printer—on a stand in the corner of the tiny dining area—whirred to life.

"Wow," AJ said, retrieving the printout. "How did you learn to do that?"

"A girl at one of my foster homes taught me. We were in computer class together at school, and we built the school's website." Teal stood while AJ put the little computer in its hiding place—the empty cereal box in the pantry.

"Well, from now on, you're my tech support staff."

Teal grinned. "I could teach you," she said as they headed out to the Jeep and trailer, which were sitting in front of the cabin.

"I'll stick with power tools. *Those* I understand." AJ started the engine.

"I noticed you're running low on hard drive space. That can cause problems."

Lena glanced at her as she shifted into gear. "Maybe you can look at it when we get back. There's probably a lot of junk on there."

On the way down Highway 1, Teal spotted three dolphins body surfing the waves. Momentarily, she longed for their carefree lives, but great white sharks lurking in the depths were as scary as what she'd run from. Freedom was full of danger.

Teal had asked if she could accompany AJ on her shopping trip today. She desperately needed some new clothes, and AJ had insisted on paying her forty dollars for her work, though Teal argued she ate AJ's food and slept in her house. But, in addition to doing the laundry and cleaning the cabins, AJ had found out that Teal was the one responsible for watering the flowers in the wine barrels.

"You saved me at least this much for new plants," AJ had countered, forcing the twenties into Teal's hand.

Before they hit Home Depot, Teal spotted a Goodwill store. Twenty minutes later, they left with two shopping bags filled with long-sleeved shirts, two pairs of jeans, a like-new pair of Adidas, some flip-flops, and a cute pair of capris she wouldn't have picked, but AJ insisted on and paid for. Only a couple of her scars showed below the cuffs. Maybe on warm summer nights…

AJ drew the line at second hand underwear, and took Teal to a Kohl's store. AJ picked out a new blouse for herself, but Teal suspected it was so it wouldn't seem like she was buying everything for her. She felt guilty, though, as they carried clothing to the register, and resolved to work harder around the cabins to make up for AJ's generosity.

The checker greeted AJ, smiling. "It sure is a hot summer, isn't it? We have some cute bikini bathing suits on sale in the junior department that would look great on your daughter. Just got in some new leopard print ones. I bought one for my granddaughter," she said as she swiped a price tag under the scanner.

Teal tugged the cuffs of her shirt lower over her wrists and tried to step behind AJ, but AJ placed her hand on Teal's lower back, holding her in place beside her. "Thanks, but I think we're all set for swimsuits."

As they exited the store, AJ gave Teal's shoulder a squeeze, then let her go. They walked in silence to the outskirts of the parking lot where the Jeep and trailer spanned two spaces. A bathing suit, animal print or otherwise, wasn't in Teal's future, except maybe if she went somewhere with a private swimming pool. Or in the dark.

Nearly three hours later, the old Jeep rolled across the creek crossing onto

AJ's property, the loaded trailer clunking behind. They would have been home sooner, but Teal could barely drag AJ away from a new cordless power tool display at Home Depot. Teal shook her head and grinned. Most women could kill half a day in the shoe department in Macy's, but AJ had been practically drooling over a bright yellow, battery-operated reciprocating saw.

AJ drove past their cabin and on to number six where Teal had stayed that first night. She hadn't confessed to AJ about that. They stopped a few feet away from the back porch.

"Now we have some fun." AJ grinned at her and hopped out.

"I don't know how you learned all this stuff," Teal sighed, hefting a box of plumbing parts from the trailer bed. She'd rather mess around with the computer, but she owed AJ—big time.

AJ had identified each piece for Teal as they'd roamed the aisles: a new toilet with wax ring—*yippee*—and bolts, connector hoses for the water heater, P-trap, kitchen faucet, more connectors, a square of window glass and glazing compound, a roll of six-foot-wide vinyl flooring, and a bunch more stuff Teal had never heard of. She couldn't believe how much went into a simple cabin.

"The hard way," AJ smiled. "I learned on the job." She heaved a large box with a picture of the toilet onto the porch and scooted it aside. After most of the small items were unloaded, AJ set up a plastic folding table in the living room and laid out the wooden window frame and the newly cut glass.

"Since your wrist is still hurting, I'll give you an easy job," AJ told her. She centered the glass in the frame and tapped in small nails to hold it in place. Then she showed Teal how to use a putty knife to smear the gray glazing compound over the nails and seal the edge, molding it at a forty-five degree angle so rainwater would run off. AJ left to tackle the bathroom.

Teal had to admit, globbing on putty and smoothing it into place was kind of fun—like a second grade craft project. But each time Teal finished one project, AJ got her started with another, until Teal sank back in the folding chair and checked her watch. Almost three o'clock, and they hadn't stopped for lunch. She was hungry, but her stomach was still a little unsettled. She hoped she hadn't gotten worms or some other parasite eating some of the more creative fare she'd found behind restaurants.

"I'm going to make us lunch," Teal called toward the small bathroom, where AJ wrestled with their best find: a secondhand pine vanity Teal had spotted at a yard sale in Shelter Cove when she and Quin stopped there on his boat. He'd immediately motored her back to tell AJ, who drove down with the trailer and declared it "Perfect." It came complete with sink and a decent faucet. The porcelain had a couple of chips, but for fifteen dollars it wasn't bad, and you'd think by AJ's reaction she'd won the lottery. Teal had no idea how much a new one cost, but she felt she'd contributed a little toward the remodel.

Twenty minutes later, Teal found AJ stretched full out on the bathroom floor, head inside the small vanity doing something with the P-trap. The bathroom floor now sported a new sheet vinyl remnant. Teal still couldn't believe how quickly AJ worked. She'd cut and glued the flooring, shot in the molding around the edges with her nail gun, and painted the wall behind the toilet and vanity a soft yellow. The room would look great when done, but the rest of the house had a lot left to do.

Teal tugged on AJ's ankles until her head slid free.

"Sorry," AJ said a minute later around a huge bite of her sandwich of pimento cheese and mild green chilies. "I get a little focused on projects and forget all about eating." Her eyes grew wide as she chewed and held the sandwich out. "Hey, this is really good. Where'd you learn to cook?" She stuffed in a handful of Fritos, and took a swig of Coke.

Teal laughed. "Making sandwiches isn't cooking."

AJ shrugged. "Is in my book." She wolfed down another bite.

They were sitting on the living room floor, backs to the inside wall. Teal had a good view through the open front door to the blue of the lake. This cabin was higher up than the others. She leaned her head against the wall, enjoying the mild day. Boats skimmed along the bright surface, engines singing of freedom and fun.

"How'd you think to put green chilies on cheese sandwiches?" AJ asked, snagging another handful of chips. "It's genius."

"One of my foster mothers—one of the good ones—loved green chilies. She used them on everything from tuna to hamburgers to tacos—even in scrambled eggs. I figured you liked them since I saw the jar in your cupboard."

"I'm sorry, Teal," AJ said, as she finished her sandwich and reached for the baggie of apple slices, the only healthy items in the lunch, not counting the green chilies. "I should be the one fixing *you* lunch. You need to gain some weight."

"I'm a big girl, AJ." It came out a little harsher then she meant.

"Yeah, I know. Sixteen."

Teal ignored AJ's dig, and rose. She began gathering up the lunch debris. Time to get back to work and prove her worth.

"Teal?"

She stopped and met the woman's eyes.

"I'm sorry," AJ said, sagging back against the wall. "I'm awful with teenagers. Kids in general." She threw up her hands. "*Relationships* in general."

The afternoon light sketched a door-shaped rectangle on the wood floor, suffusing the room with golden light. A million dust motes spun in the mild breeze.

Teal walked to the doorway and stared across the sparkling water. "No, you're fine. It's not you that's..." she searched for the right word, but could only picture herself in a cute leopard bikini, slashes and tattoos covering her exposed flesh, "...damaged."

She heard AJ's footsteps, and arms wrapped Teal and pulled her back. AJ's voice was barely audible above the rustling leaves of the old oak out front.

"We're all broken, inside and out. Some of us just cover it up better than others."

AJ rocked her side to side as they stood framed in the warm sunlight. Teal wondered who AJ was talking about.

Maybe it didn't matter.

30

Lena turned from the window overlooking the tree swing outside the Shelter Cove General Store as Stone set down two cups of coffee, then slid into the chair across from her. It was the same table she'd occupied with the sheriff. The store's screen door slammed repeatedly as late morning customers streamed in and out.

Now at high season, Lena's cabins were full, and she recognized Art and Frank, two men who were staying in Cabin 2. They dumped armloads of Cheetos, wieners, buns, steaks, beer, sodas, corn chips, salsa, and a pre-made cheesecake on the checkout counter. Nothing green and leafy. Bobby used to say, *All the—*

"All the male basic food groups," Stone commented.

Lena flashed to his face. He was grinning at the men, but felt her shift and turned, a crease forming between his brows. "What's wrong?"

She shook her head to break the spell. "Nothing."

Weird. What was it about this guy? He looked nothing like Bobby's Rob-Lowe-meets-Owen-Wilson vibe that had set her heart racing the first time she saw him. And Bobby had lived life full speed, whether it was moving from case to case without skipping a beat, or whisking her off to Santa Barbara for a weekend at an indulgent Bed & Breakfast Inn. Lena had loved that about him.

But looking back, she wondered if Bobby had sensed his time on earth was short. Had he been determined to cram in as many experiences as possible? The many memories of their fleeting time together had been precious after his death.

Stone, on the other hand, never seemed in a hurry. His life consisted of an old truck, vintage trailer, barbecues under the stars and, from what she could see, few other possessions.

Stone looked skeptical at her lack of answer and took a sip of his drink.

"You own a house, Stone?"

He choked and wiped his chin. "Now *that* was totally random."

"Do you?" She wasn't letting him dodge.

He leaned back. "I did once. Little place in West Covina. Found I didn't like coming home after six weeks on a job and wrestling with a foot-high lawn and overgrown shrubs."

"That where you're from?" She made it sound as casual as she could, but for some reason it was important to know.

He shook his head. "I grew up right here. Well, almost. Mission Peak. I rent a house there, but I might buy one someday."

"Really? A hometown boy?" Lena couldn't suppress a smile as she rested her chin on her palm. "Are your folks still there?"

"Dad's an accountant. Mostly does individual taxes now, but used to have a firm with half a dozen staff. Mom worked at the Caltrans office for over twenty years. She passed five years ago."

"I'm sorry." The empty words escaped before she could think, and she looked away. Well-meaning friends had recited them to her hundreds of times after Bobby's death, until she vowed she'd never use them. And here they'd spurted out before she could think to say something significant.

"Hey."

Stone's voice was gentle, as the afternoon breeze ruffling the curtains near their table, but it was enough to break through her musing, especially when combined with his thumb rubbing the back of her hand.

"So, you've taken on Teal as a carpenter apprentice? Saw her stapling the new screen on the porch door. Pretty impressive. You gonna have her paint the whole outside soon as she heals up a little more?"

"I didn't come here to have you dis me, Stone," Lena said, withdrawing her hand, but thankful he'd changed the subject. He was good at that—at least when he wasn't avoiding her questions all together. She'd learned more about him in the last couple of minutes than she had in all the past weeks put together. "Besides, she's taking the day off from physical labor and working on my computer. Mandy Conner will be here at twelve thirty."

"Why's Mandy coming? And what's Teal doing on the computer?"

Lena smiled, recalling Teal's horrified expression when she found out Lena didn't have a website for her cabins. "Teal's taken over marketing. Evidently she's a whiz on computers. She's building a blog for the business, where we can post photos of the renters' catches, scenes from around the lake, and testimonials. And if people sign up to follow the blog, they get a discount on a future rental."

"Sounds like a good idea."

"It's brilliant. I didn't even really have a name for the cabins and business, other than the legal filing name, which is my own. Teal wants to call it, *Desperation Falls Camp*, and appeal to more than just fishermen. She has a whole list of things: game room in the barn, barbecue lessons and cooking camps, church groups and quilting retreats in the off-season. An online store, and a physical store in the barn where we'd sell local crafts as well as our own line of T-shirts, parkas, caps, mugs, etc. I already amended the DBA with the new name."

"I had no idea." Stone set down his coffee. "There may be a career in there somewhere."

"She's a smart girl. *I* certainly don't know how to do that techie stuff. And she said she could do the online mostly for free." Lean drained half her coffee.

"So what's Mandy doing?"

Lena grinned. "She's my *new* carpenter apprentice."

"Really? You're delegating."

"She wants to learn power tools. Now that's a girl after my own heart." She didn't tell him Mandy was also going to teach Lena how to shoot. She still had mixed feelings about it. She'd never been comfortable when Bobby carried a gun when they were out together. Sometimes he'd hug her close, and she would feel the unyielding lump of metal beneath his jacket—potential death a thickness of fabric away.

"How's the new cabin coming?" Stone asked, shaking her from her thoughts.

"Good. Even better if you hadn't dragged me away from finishing my project." He'd kidnapped her from Cabin 6 where she'd been installing a used potbellied woodstove she'd found at the secondhand store in Deer Cove. It had come with several sections of sooty triple-wall chimney pipe. Two more lengths assembled and she would have been up through the roof jack and ready for the cap. He'd interrupted the job and bodily carried her to his truck.

"And speaking of that, why do you want me?" she asked, then noticed his eyes hood, just like the hunks on any romance novel cover—not that she'd ever read any of those. Startled, she realized how her question had sounded. "I mean..." her body surged with heat. Stone's eyes never left her, no matter where she flicked her attention in the little store.

She wiped moisture from her brow. What was it about this guy? Then her stomach growled loud enough that a little girl at the next table giggled. "Why am I always hungry around you?" she hissed at him, then dropped her head in humiliation as he tilted his head back in laughter.

He muttered something about being irresistible, as he got up and disappeared down a food aisle. A couple of minutes later, he returned with a bag of Fritos and a foot long, plastic-wrapped sandwich. He peeled back the sandwich cover and handed her half. The remaining portion was dwarfed in his big hands.

Lena bit into the turkey, bacon, and cheese, and let out a small groan. She glanced at her watch. It was eleven thirty, and she couldn't remember if she ate breakfast. Mayo and pesto ran down the back of her hand and she licked it, stopping mid-stroke when she caught Stone watching the track of her tongue.

"So I'm starving," she said around the bite. "Deal with it." Lena tore open the Fritos, scattering several across the pine table. Their fingers touched when they went for the same piece, and she jumped.

Stone took the chip and, like a movie scene in slow motion, lifted it to her lips. She should have pushed him away, but instead, leaned forward and opened her mouth. As she closed over the Frito, moisture sprang from her taste buds at the salty flavor. But her attention was on his fingers brushing her chin. They were rough, warm, and not quick to retreat. Hands that held weapons, but also kindness.

The little girl giggled again. She'd turned around in her chair so she was leaning over the back, and was greatly amused by Lena's every action. Lena sat back, chewing. Stone concentrated on his own sandwich. By the way his lips curled, he clearly found this situation hilarious too. Fine.

After checking the proximity of his hands, she scooped up some more chips. She'd have to take up running if she kept shoveling in these little calorie curls, but they sure were good. She licked salt from her lips and Stone's eyes narrowed. Phew. The guy never missed a thing.

"Fritos always remind me of summer," Stone said, examining one of the chips before popping it in his mouth. "My grandmother used to fix us bologna sandwiches, pickles, and Fritos, then chase us out into the backyard with a bowl of sliced watermelon. We'd eat on the old swing set, then have a seed-spitting contest."

"Who's 'we'? I thought you didn't have brothers or sisters?"

He lifted a brow. "Did I say that?"

Irritated, Lena stuffed in the last of her sandwich. "Okay, Stone. Besides feeding me—which I appreciate by the way since I was really hungry—why did you drag me away from work. You know I have to get that cabin done and make the switch before we run out of summer renters."

Stone was silent a minute while he finished his sandwich, then he crushed the wrapper and slid it aside. From the way his brow creased, Lena suddenly wasn't sure she wanted to hear what he had to say, and wished he would have told her at home, in privacy. It was too late for that now.

"What is it, Stone?"

He drew a breath. "I have a friend named Clay in the sheriff's department here. We've been friends since grammar school days. I did some checking on what happened to Teal—the scarring and all."

Lena's heart nearly stopped. "Stone, you didn't tell him—"

He held up a palm. "Don't worry. I didn't let on I had anything but a passing interest. I let him think I'd heard of the story when I worked in L.A." He cleared his throat. "Of course, I wasn't even sure it had happened in this county."

"Tell me they caught the monster who did this," Lena demanded.

"Turns out," Stone continued, "it *didn't* happen here. After more checking with contacts, I discovered it happened in the L.A. area. Teal was kidnapped off a street in Pacoima, where she'd disappeared from a foster home. Near as they can figure, she was held for a couple of months, then somehow managed to escape one night. A guy who was camping in the woods above Altadena helped her. He gave his name to the sheriff's department as Del Force, but they found out later his contact info was bogus. In Teal's statement, she gave his name as Delta Force. They're still looking for him."

"What about the other guy, Stone? Tell me they got the son of a bitch who kidnapped Teal and cut her up like...like..." Tears stung her eyes.

He hesitated. Lena's shoulders slumped when he shook his head.

"My contact said there are tons of homes that back up to the mountains along that whole area. During her escape, Teal wandered around in the dark for a long time. She didn't know which direction she'd come from."

"But aren't those pretty exclusive homes? I mean, they have views over the city."

"Some areas are nice; others not so much. The informant found her over four miles into the hills down in some deep canyons. Plus, there was a cold, low-hanging storm that lasted several days. It swept down from the north and caught a lot of people unprepared, including several hikers in the L.A. mountains that had to be rescued. It dumped a lot of rain in those foothills, which made it impossible to trace her track. The storm must have prevented her from seeing the nighttime city lights."

Teal had been so close to safety. If she'd run the opposite direction, she might have been in a neighborhood. Lena brushed her eyes, then stilled, her mind spinning as she counted back the previous few months. "When was this, Stone? What was the date?"

Stone rubbed his forehead. "I think he said December 10th. Or maybe the 12th. Right around there. Why?"

A chill climbed Lena's spine. That was the same storm that had pummeled the central coast when she and realtor Roger Trollen had slogged through the mud to inspect the cabins at Storm Lake. The same time she'd signed the purchase agreement. According to reports, the storm had been a monster, covering three-quarters of the state and causing flood and wind damage. Lena had been curled up by the fireplace in her Perilous Cove Inn room the next morning, watching from warmth and safety as the ferocious gale beat at the glass. Teal had been out in the wilderness at that exact same time, hiding from a sick maniac.

Anger burned away Lena's chill. What she wouldn't give to have five minutes alone with that psycho. Just her and her framing hammer.

31

Lena pulled the trigger and fired the last finish nail into the baseboard molding. She rocked back on her heels as Teal elbowed open the screen door while balancing their lunch tray.

"Wow, you finished it already? I was only gone a half hour."

Lena stood and stripped off her kneepads. "What do you think?" The maple flooring covered the living and dining areas and continued down the hall to the back door. Lena and Mandy had done most of the work yesterday afternoon while Teal worked on the website. As Mandy had bragged, she was indeed a quick learner, and they'd fallen into a productive duo. It hadn't taken much to complete the remainder this morning.

"It looks so rich," Teal said, setting the tray on the kitchen counter. She knelt and ran her hand across the flooring. "And it's so smooth. Should we take off our shoes?"

Lena shook her head. "We'll do that once we get everything clean. I've got some carpet scraps I can put down temporarily at the doors to wipe our shoes on. But one good thing about laminate is that it's really durable."

She'd planned on the cheapest carpeting she could find, but had scored big on a trip to the flooring store in Mission Peak. A back room water pipe had sprung a pinhole leak overnight and sprayed a stack of the laminate flooring, soaking the end of every box and ruining part of every piece inside. Lena had offered to take it off their hands. Each plank had to be trimmed— some only an inch or two, some half their length—but that still left a lot of good wood for someone with a chop saw and a little patience, and she had more of that than money. The floor had turned out beautifully.

"I'm starved," Lena said, heading toward the food. "Let's sit out on the porch where it's not as dusty." She carried the tray out the front door, and they sat on the steps.

"So," Lena said around a bite of apple, "how's the web stuff coming?" Teal had been so heads-down on the project yesterday, she'd only given Mandy a quick hello.

"Good." Teal glanced sideways at her. "But there's something weird with your computer."

Lena stopped eating. "It's not broken, is it?" There was no money for a new laptop.

Teal shook her head. "Remember when I told you the hard drive was pretty full?"

Lena nodded, chewing an apple slice.

"Well, I needed room for some of the website art and docs, so I was going through, seeing if I could find big files that were eating up a lot of space, like old tutorial files that get installed. I found a folder called *Wisconsin Trip*."

"Really? Bobby and I never went to Wisconsin. And he never mentioned taking a trip there before we were married. I don't think he had any relatives there, either."

"There are hundreds of files in it. Almost all are photos, but all of those are touristy pics off the Internet, like from Flickr or Google, so not personal pictures. But here's the weird thing: scattered in between are a few files named things like *waterfall*, and *lighthouse*, but those are jpeg photos of documents—legal-looking documents. All the file creation dates are December 1st a year ago."

Lena's mouth went dry. That was when their house had been shot up. The night Bobby died.

"I only looked at a few. They're taking up a lot of space, but I thought I'd better ask you if we could delete them."

Lena rose, her remaining lunch drying in the hot sun. In spite of the heat, a chill slithered down her spine, raising the hair on her neck. She turned to Teal.

"Show me."

Hi Chet,

You asked if I had any of Bobby's files. Well, I found some files on my

laptop that Bobby evidently was working on. I'm attaching the smallest.
They are huge picture files, and I only have dial-up connectivity, so I can't
send the rest right now. I don't know if they're important, or just copies of
something you already have at the DA's office. In fact, I'm not sure if they are
even District Attorney files. Thought maybe you could take a look.

I'll read through the others, but the couple I looked at seem to be coded, so
I'm not sure I can figure them out.

Let me know what you think. I might be able to get to a Starbucks in the
next few days where they have a faster connection and send some more. Or I
can pick up a USB drive and mail it down to you.
Lena Blaylock

"There," Lena said, clicking *Send* on the email as Teal came through the front door. "Chet will let me know if we can delete the files and get you some more room, though we might not hear until tomorrow."

Lena had tried calling Eve on the new prepaid cell phone she'd purchased in Mission Peak, but the attorney hadn't answered. But Eve had said Lena should go directly to Chet.

"No problem," Teal said, waving a blue piece of plastic, "I asked Alex if he had a spare USB drive, and he did. It's big enough to transfer the files off your hard drive."

Lena changed chairs, and Teal plugged the device into the laptop. In a few seconds, she had a window open that showed the progress of the file transfer. As Lena watched the file names zip by, she couldn't help feeling a little sad that she was losing yet another part of Bobby. These were files he'd touched…at least electronically. They were important to some part of his work. To him.

She should show these to Alex, too. Maybe he could figure out their meaning.

When the transfer finished, Teal held up the drive. "Where should we put it so it won't get lost?"

They both looked around the space, and Lena's eyes came to rest on a Mason jar half full of odd-sized marbles where it sat on the dining room window sill. She'd discovered it at a garage sale in Perilous Cove one Saturday after shopping at Brodie's Hardware. At one dollar she hadn't thought twice, and had always enjoyed watching the sun filter through the colored orbs. She picked it up.

"Stick it in here. The blue plastic blends with the marbles."

Teal poked the stick into the center, burying it down. "Perfect. If we get robbed, no one will find it."

"Robbed?" Lena laughed. "Anyone who breaks in here will be hugely disappointed." Her laughter faded as she realized the girl in front of her had done just that. Teal slumped and turned away.

Lena put her hand on the girl's shoulder. "I'm sorry, Teal. I didn't mean—"

"No." Teal took a deep breath, but didn't turn around. "I stole your food and invaded your privacy. *I'm* the one who's sorry."

"You know I'd have given you the food, don't you?"

Teal didn't answer right away. Then she flitted a glance at Lena. "That's what makes us different."

Lena scooted closer and wrapped both arms around Teal from behind. She chose her words carefully.

"I haves no idea what I'd do if I were in your situation. You know what I see? I see a girl who saved my flowers and cleaned up the grounds. Why? Because she has a sense of responsibility and a good heart. I see a girl who works hard, who is smart, and talented in ways I'll never be."

Teal turned sideways in her chair, holding Lena's hands with her own. There was longing in the girl's eyes.

"You belong here, Teal. I don't know how we make that work legally, but like it or not, you're a part of this community, this house...and my... Life." Lena almost didn't get the last part out, and her vision blurred as tears overflowed and ran down her cheeks.

Teal came out of the chair and they hugged for several minutes. Finally, she whispered, "Thank you."

32

"I'll see you in ten minutes," Quin called. "Fifteen tops." He disappeared around the corner of the building with a grin and wave.

Although she still felt uneasy being back in Deer Cove, Teal couldn't help but grin as she nearly twirled down the sidewalk in front of Deer Cove Mercantile. She was acting like a love-struck teenager, something she never imagined for herself. It felt good. Normal. Was that even possible? How did anyone with carvings all over her body pass herself off as someone who belonged in polite society?

Quin hadn't had it easy, either. His mom had abandoned him and his father when Quin was only a baby—just walked out one day and never returned. Then his dad died in a car accident a few years ago. But from the way he talked about Ben and Rayne Conner, he'd lucked into a fairly routine household, even if Rayne was some kind of rock star in Europe. Teal made a mental note to look up some of her music on AJ's computer.

Teal plopped down on a sidewalk bench and watched a young mom unload three little kids from a minivan. Once the kids were safely holding hands and obediently lined up against the store wall, the mom unfolded an aluminum walker and helped an elderly woman out of the passenger seat. All together, they made their way down the sidewalk, away from Teal.

Maybe the most conventional *looking* families weren't truly that way at all, instead duct-taped together into something that worked. At least for a while. The high divorce rate could explain what happened when the tape frayed at the edges and broke.

Was the tape love? Something sticky that bound people together? And if Teal felt more whole than she had in months, was she experiencing love—from Quin, AJ, even Alex?

No, she couldn't take the analogy that far. She still didn't completely trust Alex. If the family services people came sniffing around, would he follow the law? Teal felt good about AJ, though. If it came down to a confrontation, AJ would fight. And, since Alex and AJ were so totally right for each other—even though they denied it, Teal could feel the attraction from fifty feet—AJ would pressure Alex. Yes, Teal could use that to her advantage.

She stood in front of the mercantile's display window, which was floor to ceiling with everything from colorful yard art to bathing suits. If she found something in here that AJ would like, Teal could suggest it to Alex for a gift. AJ's birthday was coming up in a little over four weeks. Did Alex even know the date? If she could find the perfect gift, he would owe her.

Bells announced her entry into the store. Perhaps Teal could never be normal in the traditional sense, but at least she could pretend for a few minutes.

The broad entryway was a two-story menagerie of desires and fulfillment. Multicolored candy dispensers lined the right-hand wall. A sign promised over one hundred flavors, and two girls were arguing with their dad about how many they could buy. The main floor contained circular clothing racks holding T-shirts and sweatshirts with Deer Cove and Storm Lake logos. Kites danced high overhead, buoyed by strategically placed fans, and darting dangerously close to a forest of tall fishing poles. Carved walking sticks stood next to cubbies of gloves and scarves. Surely she could find AJ a gift here.

Teal circled the large space, taking in a refrigerated section of gourmet cheeses and spreads, chilled wine, beer and soft drinks.

"Can I make you an ice cream cone?" a voice asked.

Teal turned. A girl stood behind a glass freezer case holding a dozen tubs of ice cream. She wore a sleeveless, white crop top that stopped a couple inches above navy shorts. Her sun-streaked blonde hair was pulled into a high ponytail that cascaded to her waist, and her flawless skin shone like golden suede. As if fitting her tan, her name badge read *Amber*. It might as well have read *Perfect*. Teal pegged her at fifteen or sixteen. Far younger than Teal, though they were the same age.

Teal shook her head and moved on. To be so innocent, so… unmarred. She tugged her long sleeves, making sure the scars stayed hidden.

She was crouched down, admiring a picnic basket display, complete with plaid blankets, corkscrews, champagne flutes, and plastic-handled silverware, when the doorbells tinkled.

"Welcome to Deer Cove Mercantile," Amber said from behind the ice cream counter. "Can I… make you an ice cream cone?"

Teal noticed the way the girl's voice quavered, almost faded out on her last words.

"That sounds really good," a man said.

The voice froze Teal for long seconds before she forced herself to scoot behind a rack of yard flags and streamers. Her lungs screamed for air, but she didn't dare breathe or make a sound. He might wake up, might see her snatch the hardened pizza crust from the floor.

Blue jean-clad legs loomed through the streamer gaps. She nearly whimpered when familiar boots stopped in the aisle.

Carefully, she retreated another inch.

"Where are you going, girl?"

Teal's heart stopped. Her life was over. He'd drag her back to the cellar. *"We're going to play a game on The Table today, little girl. Are you ready?"* The old question, but her answer never mattered. He'd strap her to The Table. Sweat, blood, and other odors stung her nostrils.

Then he'd connect the wires to each wrist strap. *"You see, you need a positive and a ground."* He'd reach for the switch. The current would sizzle in her brain, flow into her nervous system, and her body would convulse and bang on The Table—for the final time.

"D-did…did you want something?"

Teal cracked her eyes open enough to peer through the curtain. The blue jeans and boots were planted before the glass freezer case. She couldn't see above his waist, but through the frosty glass, Amber cowered against the wall, eyes wide as a large scoop.

Fred's voice went deep, more intense, like someone searching for the perfect cut of meat for dinner. "Yeah, cute thing." The words might sound innocent, but they weren't. Never that. "What time do you get off work?"

Amber's shoulders shuddered, and she inched sideways toward the swinging door at the end of the freezer—straight toward Teal's hiding place. Suddenly, Amber spotted Teal where she hunkered behind the display. Amber's mouth opened.

Teal stopped her with a fast shake of her head, pleading with her eyes.

"Anybody ever tell you, you have beautiful skin?" Fred's torso leaned half across the glass case, but Teal still couldn't see his face.

Squeaking shoes entered the room, and Khaki clad legs stopped in front of Teal's hiding place, blocking her view of Fred's jeans. "Is there a problem here?"

"Oh, no problem." Fred's voice had returned to good ole boy friendly. "I was just asking Amber here about some ice cream, trying to decide which flavor. Isn't that right, Amber?" A hardness crept in around the edges, jerking Amber's eyes to him, then down.

Submission was smart.

"I'll help you," the newcomer rounded the freezer and pushed through the swinging half door. Teal caught a glimpse of his profile. A good looking man about Alex's age, but he was no physical match for Fred. Nevertheless, his voice didn't shake as he said, "Amber, why don't you go help your older brothers in the other room. All *four* of them are here."

Amber's brow creased for a split second before she nodded and scurried through the door. Her eyes flicked over Teal as she ran for the exit.

"I don't think I care for any ice cream." Fred's voice was icy as the glass. His boots turned toward the door. The bells chimed.

Teal tucked her head, glad for her dark shirt. A few seconds later, squeaky-shoe man exited the freezer area, eyes trained on the front door as he hurried the direction Amber had gone. Teal's stomach churned as she rose and sprinted toward the back exit that overlooked Deer Cove harbor. She snatched a wide-brim sun hat from a rack as she went through the open door, cinched it low over her eyes, and escaped along the uneven wooden sidewalk cantilevered behind several buildings.

33

Lena placed the untouched chicken noodle soup in the sink, the congealed mass sticking to the bowl's sides. Only the crackers were gone, but four saltines were nowhere near enough for Teal's dinner. Lena leaned against the counter and stared at the wall, as if she could see through it to where the girl slept curled in a ball on Lena's bed.

She had been working on the roof of the new cabin, when she heard the boat and spotted Quin half lifting a stumbling Teal out of his boat. She passed out in his arms as he carried her up to the cabin. By the time Lena climbed down from the roof and raced to them, Quin had her to their porch. While he agreed with Lena that they should call Doc Arnold, he said Teal was frantic about getting away from Deer Cove and not going back. Ever.

"It was like she was terrified of something, something bad she saw there, but she wouldn't talk about it." Quin said. "As soon as she saw me, she ran straight to the boat and jumped in, begging me to start the motor and get out of there. I was afraid she'd leap out and swim if I didn't leave right then." He said the girl had remained tense as a board, but fainted when they were nearly home.

Lena checked her watch. Eight forty-five. Quin had left after Lena called the doctor, who promised to come by shortly after nine tonight. The boy had been torn between staying with Teal or finishing his scheduled delivery jobs, one of which was delivering an insulin prescription from the pharmacy. He vowed he'd be back as soon as he could, but night was falling now and he couldn't be on the lake after dark. She wouldn't be surprised if he showed up on a bicycle, though. Quin was clearly smitten by Teal, and worried.

Another check of her watch showed the second hand still moving—barely. She pushed open the screen door, stepped out onto the porch, and peered toward Stone's trailer. Still no lights shone through the dusk, but she already knew he wasn't home. His truck had been gone all day, and she'd hear him driving by when he came back. She really needed to talk to him.

That thought alone dug deep at her. When had she come to need Alex Stone? It wasn't like they were lifelong friends or lovers or... She squashed that line of thinking. What did he have that drew her to him? A couple of kisses didn't mean anything.

She paced the length of the porch, alternately listening for Teal or the sound of an approaching vehicle, until she forced herself down into one of the chairs. Her thoughts bounced between worry about Teal, and the enigmatic Alex Stone. He wasn't anything like Bobby, who'd been handsome, self-assured to the point of cockiness, and only an inch taller than Lena. True, Stone did have the self-assurance thing in spades, but he didn't flaunt it, sort of like no brag, just fact. And there was a warmth about him in spite of his law enforcement work.

Bobby tore through life like a road flare, burning bright but extinguished far too soon. Lena had been drawn into his light and loved him intensely, but to be honest, Bobby's life was about experience, goals, accomplishment. He loved putting bad guys away. When he focused on Lena, she glowed in response, and they were good together. Very good. But too often their busy schedules kept them apart. If only they had concentrated more on each other and less on work in their short time together.

Stone, on the other hand, radiated contentedness. Sure, he had a dedication to his career; every man worth his salt did. But it didn't define him, wasn't all he was. Figuring out what else made up the man was the appealing part of life with Stone.

What in the world was she thinking? Lena jumped up from the chair but only made one lap in the small space before headlights cut through the trees.

Lena rubbed the goose bumps on her bare arms. Unlike most summer nights, this one had turned cold, but she waited on the porch while the doctor examined Teal. Smoke from the crackling campfire ring at the water's edge drifted on the chilly breeze, and as the fire flared, she made out the silhouettes of four or five of her renters as they laughed and lied about past fishing trips.

Stone's truck came over the hill and she waved him down. He stopped behind the doctor's car, climbed out, and took the steps two at a time. She explained about Teal passing out.

"I'm really worried about her, Stone. She's still so weak sometimes, and she's not gaining weight like she should. Maybe we should take her to Mission Peak and get some tests done."

"That would raise a lot of questions, about her background and the scars. You could lose her."

"I know," she whispered as he drew her against his solid chest. His warmth flowed into her, bringing strength and safety. She barely knew the man, but she wanted to remain there forever.

Behind her, the screen door squeaked, and she pulled away to face Doc Arnold. Stone's arm remained locked around her waist, securing her to his side.

"What's wrong?" Stone asked, as Doc Arnold removed his glasses and dropped them into his shirt pocket.

"Well," the doctor began, rubbing the back of his neck, "I couldn't get her to tell me much of anything, but it seems like she had some kind of emotional shock when she and Quin were in Deer Cove this afternoon."

"You mean like she heard bad news or something?" Lena asked, thankful for Stone's heat spreading through her thin shirt.

"Whatever it was, it hit her hard. Sent her body into shock. I'm guessing, but it probably caused her blood pressure to drop—that's what caused the blackout. Her blood pressure is normal now, so I'm sure she'll be okay after a good night's sleep. At least her body will." He narrowed his gaze at Lena. "I have to say, Miss Blaylock, you may be her aunt, but I'm not too keen on treating her without her mother or father's written permission. Sorry to be so direct, but I don't believe for a minute that girl is eighteen."

The air hung heavy between them. He waited for an answer, and Lena desperately wished for one. "I'll do my best to get the proper paperwork for her. I promise."

Finally, the doctor's posture relaxed a little. "Thank you. Keep her well hydrated. Broth soups, Gatorade—that will keep her blood pressure up. Now, I'm no counselor, but I'd say she needs someone to talk with about whatever transpired today. Work through it. Maybe that could be you?"

"I've tried, but…" Lena trailed off.

"Well, try harder. Or find a professional. Your niece is too young and fragile to face whatever this is on her own, especially considering what she's undoubtedly been through before."

He referred to the scars and tattoos, of course. The story of those marks might help Teal cope, if Lena could persuade her to tell. And Lena didn't miss the doctor's skeptical reference to her supposed family relationship to the young girl.

"Are you feeding her anything at all?" Doc Arnold asked. "She's still much too thin."

"Of course." Lena bristled at his insinuation. "But she has trouble keeping food down."

"I see," he said, backing off a little. "There is another possibility, Miss Blaylock. Could your niece be pregnant?"

"*Pregnant?* No!" Lena pulled away from Stone, and turned away from the men, hands on her head, her mind spinning. She knew so little of Teal's recent history.

"Can't *you* tell?" Stone asked the doc. "I mean, you're a physician. Don't you know these things?"

The doctor cleared his throat. "I didn't test for it the first time when you brought her in after her fall. And this is the first I've heard about not being able to keep food down. If she's not far along, the undernourishment could be masking it. Although I did palpitate her stomach just now and everything felt normal. Honestly, I'm not the first doctor most women go to when they suspect they're pregnant, so I'm not an expert. But that could explain the upset stomach." He paused, glancing to the screen door and lighted interior. "After her trauma today, I don't want to go back in there now and bring it up. "

Lena turned to the doctor. "Should I take her to someone in Mission Peak?" Dread ate at her, twisting her own stomach to the point of nausea. Without verified parental permission, if Teal were pregnant—and once they saw those scars—Social Services would bring a SWAT team.

"I recommend getting a home pregnancy test first. If she *is* pregnant, we need to be more aggressive in treating this nourishment problem to protect the baby. She has to gain weight. And you should start her on prenatal vitamins immediately. Either way, they won't hurt."

Protect the baby. Oh, man. This just got a whole lot more complicated.

The roar of an engine drew their attention as headlights cut through the trees. Mandy's red Bronco skidded in a four-wheel slide, and the doors flew open. Quin and Mandy reached the steps at the same time.

"What's happening? Is Teal okay?" Quin asked, his brows creased with worry. Mandy put a supportive hand on her cousin's shoulder.

Lena took a hard assessment of the boy. He was strong, virile, and Teal worshiped him. Could they be intimate? Heaven knew, there were plenty of secluded places around the lake where the two... Now that she thought about it, Teal had seemed especially clingy with Quin when they'd come back from the falls and joined Alex and her for dinner.

Lena locked eyes with Stone. His mouth was a straight line. Slowly, he nodded his head, then looked at the boy.

Stone's sudden chuckling shook the whole couch.

"This isn't the least bit funny, Stone."

"I know. But I was just thinking of you being *Great Aunt Alena.*"

Lena had the overwhelming urge to smack him with something, but the only thing handy was a beige pillow, nowhere near up to the task. She needed an L.A. phonebook.

It was late. They sat side by side in her living room, not touching, but she was acutely aware of the intimacy of the shared sofa that, as if in perverted cahoots with the man, tended to roll her toward the middle. She couldn't figure out her strange and unwanted attraction to Stone. On one hand, she craved his presence as an ally in this twisted reality show, but on the other, she wanted her space. Except for her time with Bobby, she'd been on her own most of her life. Someone too close usually made her uncomfortable. Truth was, she didn't know *what* she wanted from him, but was glad she wasn't in this situation with Teal by herself.

The girl had fallen into a deep sleep as soon as the doctor left her room, and Lena persuaded a reluctant Quin to go home with Mandy and come by tomorrow.

Stone would be here to talk with the boy. Thank God for that. But Lena's duty was no less daunting. Somehow, she had to get Teal to open up to her. But how did she begin such a discussion?

So, how's the pregnancy going? And by the way, is the father a certain local boy?

She let out a sigh, and Stone, as if reading her mind, draped an arm around her shoulders. She gave up resisting as he gentled her against him. He was a rock of strength. Even if the man was a cretin, she loved his power.

She bent forward, covered her face with her hands, and shook her head. She should be worried about Teal, not analyzing her feelings about Stone.

He misread her turmoil. "Hey," he pulled her close again. "You'll be fine talking to her."

Would she? At thirty-four, she wasn't a mom, knew zip about having kids. Twenty feet away in the next room was a girl less than half Lena's age, perhaps carrying a baby. How was Lena supposed to play the wise counselor?

Well, that was tomorrow. She slid from under Stone's arm and got to her feet, aware for the first time that her shirt and jeans were smeared with black roofing tar. "I've got to shower and get some sleep." She probably stank from working on the hot roof, but Stone hadn't complained. He rose beside her.

"You going to be okay?" His hand was warm on her upper arm.

Only inches separated them, her body straining toward his like steel to a magnet. Was he going to kiss her again? Did she want him to? Tired of thinking anymore, she rose and pressed her lips to his in a hard, fast kiss, then squirmed away before he could hold her.

"Go home, Stone." *Before I do something incredibly stupid.*

He grinned. "Yes, ma'am." Halfway out the front door, he turned. "I can't remember the last time I was kissed by a great aunt." He ducked out the door a split second before the beige pillow bounced off the glass.

Lena turned toward the hall, her own lips curling upward. For one instant she'd felt a little in control of their...what? Sparring? Relationship? Maybe a little of both. His absence already made the room feel like something was missing.

She was too weary to ponder the mystery of it now. Whatever it was, his presence gave her strength to face the next day. And oh, what a day it would be. Who said life at Storm Lake was boring?

It had been an interesting day. Sure, it was a long drive back to Altadena, but he didn't regret the trip. He'd gotten an in-depth look at Storm Lake, up close and personal. Not like last time, when he'd come at night and been in a hurry to complete his task.

When he'd devised the plan to bury the body, he couldn't see how the location made sense. Bodies had to be buried somewhere, of course, but why there? Now it made perfect sense. It was all coming together, better than he'd ever imagined.

This time, he'd been able to observe his quarry's environment. Now he could begin the pursuit. The next trip would be even more interesting, but he had a lot of planning to do first to maximize his time. His day job was demanding, and there were only so many times he could call in sick. Work was interfering with his true calling.

His knuckles turned white on the leather-wrapped steering wheel as he thought of the ice cream girl, Amber, with skin so smooth, unblemished—a naked canvas, begging for his skill. She would be his, a prize for completing his primary mission. Whatever he did, the Mexican couldn't find out about this one. The Mexican had discovered his little hobby, and already had too much power over him.

He sighed. It was probably time to disappear. He'd been planning it for months. Perhaps there was a home for sale at Storm Lake? One that could be acquired under his alternative identity. He certainly had enough money; all of it in cash. At least the Mexican was good for something.

His one housing requirement was a soundproof basement—somewhere he and Amber could play games.

Before that, he had another matter to resolve in L.A. One option was to get the Mexican to take care of it, but he didn't want to owe him. In fact, he needed to distance himself from the Mexican, but without making it too obvious. The man was crazy…and dangerous.

No, he'd have to take care of things himself. Tonight.

He spotted a 7-Eleven and exited the freeway. The long drive had made him thirsty, so he grabbed his favorite drink, then returned to his car. He smiled as he sucked on the straw.

34

Teal pushed the covers back and stretched in the yellow sunbeams painting swaths of heat across the bed. The soft sheet soaked up the promise of the day and warmed her legs. Every muscle in her body ached as if she'd hiked up the mountain beyond the falls. For a moment, she wondered if her sore limbs would survive the cabin refurbishing projects set for today.

Then the sickening reality of yesterday slammed home.

Fred. Running. Passing out.

She'd stupidly assumed the cops had caught him after her escape. They'd assigned a sketch artist to work with her while she was in the hospital. Teal had taken the pad from the woman and drawn the man: close-set eyes, bushy brows, puffy lips that were always slightly purple, a small scar above his top lip. Everything else was always covered by his ski mask. She drew the mask, too—black and red, with coarse white stitches around the openings. It was a face that visited her nearly every night, and she'd never forget it.

But it was his voice she remembered the best, the same voice she'd heard so distinctly yesterday in the mercantile. Her shoulders shook with an involuntary shiver.

The police had never revisited her, not in the hospital, nor in the foster home that followed. As much as she dreaded it, she expected to testify at a trial. As time went on, hope grew that the cops had killed him.

A glass of apple juice sat on the nightstand. AJ must have put it there, part of the doctor's orders to drink a lot of fluids. Teal sat up and took a sip, thinking about the doctor.

He'd asked how she got the "marks" on her body.

They weren't marks. And they weren't blemishes or imperfections, either. They were scars, plain and simple. She hadn't answered his probing questions, only wanted to curl up under the covers and let the darkness take her away again.

She swung her legs over the side of the bed, expecting dizziness. Nothing happened. Actually, she felt a little better, stronger. Sunlight peeked past the curtain, a bird chirped a happy song outside, a dish clattered in the kitchen. AJ.

She had to tell her and Alex about Fred.

The cops would come and everything would change. There would be no more pizza nights, no more barbecues at Alex's trailer, no need to finish the second bedroom in the new cabin. It would never be hers.

Quin's parents would forbid him from seeing her again. AJ probably wouldn't want her here anymore. And even if she did, law enforcement and Social Services vehicles would scare off renters. AJ could lose the property.

Social Services would lock her away in a facility as a runaway risk, which she was.

That couldn't happen.

Teal glanced at the closet where her backpack was stored. It would hold most of her few clothes that were folded in the shared dresser. If she left now, she could always make an anonymous call to the cops and tell them about Fred.

Tears stung her eyes as she thought about giving up this haven. She'd found her perfect place, but Fred had ruined it all, just like he'd ruined her flesh. It would have been easier if he'd just stuck one of his knives in her heart and ended it back then. All this pain would never have existed.

Teal dressed quickly and quietly, filled her backpack, then tiptoed across the hall to retrieve her toothbrush from the bathroom on the way out the back porch. She'd be miles away before AJ came to check on her, but the thought of AJ finding the empty bedroom wrung Teal's heart. She swiped her eyes and edged through the back door, which made only the slightest squeak. She eased the door closed, her breathing labored with the need to say goodbye, yet knowing she never could.

When she turned, AJ was sitting on the rear steps, her back toward Teal, sipping a mug of coffee. AJ *never* sat back here. She preferred the front porch with the limited lake view.

"Morning, Teal," AJ said, not turning, but lifting a second mug from a foot wide tree round that functioned as a small table. "Thought you might need a cup of coffee before we get going this morning."

Teal slumped, whether in relief or resignation, she wasn't sure. She stood unmoving for thirty seconds, then lowered her pack to the wood planks and reached for the mug. No easy getaway this morning.

"Have a seat." AJ patted the wood, worn smooth by countless feet.

Teal stepped down one step and dropped beside AJ. The coffee wasn't so hot it burned her tongue, and had the right balance of sweetener and milk. She cut a glance at the woman next to her. The crow's feet were deeper today, as if she hadn't slept much. AJ smiled at Teal, then turned back to the yard. Teal took another sip. Who else in the world besides AJ knew how Teal liked her coffee fixed? No one.

She'd always thought that's what a home was about: simple things like knowing how another person liked her coffee, or when someone needed space or a hug.

Or when someone was about to run away.

The pressure on her lungs eased a little. Twenty feet away, a squirrel descended an oak trunk headfirst in fits and starts, its tail twitching at each pause. It hopped to the earth and regarded them with interest, tail snapping into a perfect question mark. Did they pose a threat or have a tasty morsel? After a minute's pondering, the animal dashed away and scampered up another oak. AJ cleared her throat.

"Coffee's probably not the best thing for you, but I figured one cup wouldn't hurt."

Teal nodded, wondering why AJ thought coffee was suddenly bad. She'd been drinking it every morning.

"Hungry? I've got scrambled eggs and bacon warming in the oven for us."

Teal nodded again, and AJ rose and went inside without commenting on the bulging backpack resting prominently beside the door.

For us. AJ expected Teal to eat breakfast with her. The elephant that had been sitting on her chest for the past several minutes eased its weight a little, allowing a deeper breath. Lake air, cool and dry, oak leaves, coffee, dusty wood—these were safety, friends, home. Maybe even love.

She could walk away right now while AJ was busy in the kitchen, grab her pack and flee, do what she wanted, go where she wanted. Get far away from Fred. AJ had to know that running away was Teal's intent. Yet AJ had left her alone, trusted her to do the right thing. She just wished she knew what that was.

She turned sideways and rested against the porch post. Why did life have to be so hard? Hadn't she been punished enough? Now she'd have to tell AJ the whole story. And Quin. He'd seen the scars, but he didn't know everything, not about the sickening way she got them.

And what about Alex? Teal looked to her left, through the trees to the sun reflecting off his Airstream. Would he decide this damaged, lying, stealing teenager was more trouble than she was worth?

AJ pushed through the back door, balancing two plates of food. She handed one to Teal.

"Quin came back last night," AJ said, again taking a seat on the steps. "Mandy, too. I told him you were sleeping, and to come back this morning."

Fear slid a dagger into her heart, its tip pricking the organ so it skipped a beat or two. But hope pushed back. She needed to see him at least one more time.

AJ indicated Teal's plate with a nod. "Eat." She waited until Teal mouthed a forkful of scrambled eggs. Butter, salt, pepper. Fluffy. AJ could never get eggs this way when Teal first arrived. Her cooking was basic at its best. It had taken extra effort to get them just right this morning.

Somewhere inside, AJ's cell phone rang, and she jumped up to answer it.

Teal leaned back as she chewed, and squeezed her eyes against the tears tracking down her cheeks. She didn't hide them. Deep inside she trusted AJ. She'd run from everyone for so long, and it didn't sound free or exciting anymore. Just lonely.

"Hi, Chet," Lena said as she recognized his number on her cell.

"Lena, I'm coming up."

Lena smiled at his lack of small talk. "Thanks for calling back." She glanced down the hall. Teal's head was visible through the back door window. Part of her was scared to death the girl would bolt the second Lena's back was turned.

"Got the file you sent," Chet said, slurping loudly.

"Is it helpful to the investigation?" Maybe something would give a clue as to who targeted Bobby.

"How many more are there?"

"Uh, I think thirty-five or so? They're just too big to—"

"Who else knows about them?" Chet interrupted. He sounded a little frazzled, but that was nothing new. Voices called in the background, and Chet swore at somebody to close his door.

Lena was frustrated he hadn't answered her question, but reasoned he'd know more after seeing the other files.

"Are you home today? Tomorrow? I've got to arrange—" papers shuffled, like he was looking for something on his desk. "Never mind." He swore several times.

The last part sounded like he was thinking out loud. It was like having a conversation with an oak tree.

"I'll be around both days, but it would help if I—"

"Good. See you soon." The line went dead.

She sat back in the dining chair, the cell phone warm in her hand from the call. Chet had sounded more stressed and scattered than usual. Of course, she didn't know him all that well. Maybe things were heating up in the investigation. She tried not to get her hopes up.

As she rose from the chair, the little corner table under the printer caught her eye. She opened the single drawer and picked up the prepaid phone Eve had suggested. The battery showed a full charge when she unlocked the screen. There were no waiting messages.

Hesitating only a second, she dialed the private number Eve had sent in a letter. There was no greeting, not even an anonymous announcement of the cell number reached. The call went straight to a message box.

"Eve, it's Lena." She quickly explained about finding the documents, sending one to Chet, and his promise to come up today or tomorrow. "I know there's nothing you can do, but just wanted you to know." She paused, not knowing what else to say to the woman she barely knew, then ended the call.

Instead of returning the phone to the drawer, she slipped it into her pocket. With her busy schedule, she typically forgot to check it more than once a day. But if Eve called back, she didn't want to miss her.

Lena stared out the dining room window. Blue water sparkled through the trees, the promise of another flawless summer day. She wished the hot sun could burn away the niggling feeling that something was building, and it wasn't just Teal's situation.

The jar of marbles on the windowsill was still in the shade, but when the sun hit it this afternoon, the refracted light would send colored splashes all over the walls and ceiling. Lena hoped the files on the USB drive buried inside the jar would send out some splashes of their own and shed light on the mystery of why Bobby died.

35

"Until I came here, my ninth birthday was my last best day," Teal began, her voice flat, emotionless.

Lena was standing on the back porch, and had just forked in the last of her cold eggs. Now they lay on her tongue like a lump of salted tree bark. If she'd been alone, she would have spit them out. Teal's statement was so terribly sad. Who had her life peak at nine years old? She tried to remember her own ninth birthday.

"It was a Saturday," Teal continued, eyes fixed on the trees, "and three girls from school came to my party. We played at a park by our house, then ate cake my mom bought at a grocery store. She wasn't much of a cook, and never baked anything, but she said she was proud of me and wanted to have something special, so she ordered a chocolate cake with raspberry filling. I still remember the taste of the tart filling and sweet cake. Mom was sober that day."

Lena tried to hide her shock at such a factual statement, as if it was an everyday determination by a birthday girl. Maybe for Teal it was. Right now, she appeared as fragile as a wounded bird, almost quivering. Lena didn't think it was from the memories themselves as much as telling Lena about it. She'd asked for the whole story, but was she ready to hear it?

"I went to bed that night with a new stuffed bear. He was really cute, with squishy white fur, black paws, and a red ribbon tied around his neck. I also got a manicure set, three blue hair clips, two books, and a sketchpad with a box of sixteen colored pencils. Before I got into bed, I arranged all the presents on my nightstand so I could see them as I fell asleep."

Teal sighed, and Lena held her breath, fearing what was to come.

"A loud crash woke me up. I don't know what time it was, but it was dark. Bright flashlight beams were flying all over in the hall, and there was a lot of shouting. A huge man banged my door wide open and shone a light right into my eyes. I remember screaming for momma as he grabbed me. He was hard and cold, all rough cloth as he carried me out of the house and into the front yard. Police cars were all over the street, red and blue lights flashing. The man put me in the back of one of the cars and shut the door, then he ran back into the house."

Lena brushed her eyes. Teal spoke as if reciting a television show plot, but this was reality TV at its worst. Lena couldn't imagine going though something like that at nine. Her own family tragedy had come later.

Teal took the last bite of sliced apple and chewed for a moment, still not meeting Lena's eyes. "They brought momma out a few minutes later. She had a robe all cockeyed around her shoulders, and her hands were behind her back. I guess they had her in handcuffs like you see on *COPS*. I pounded on the window until my hands bled." She opened her hands and examined them, first the backs, then the fronts, as if looking for telltale red smears. "I screamed for momma as they put her into another car, but no one paid any attention to me. Then I couldn't see her anymore.

"Next, they brought out Larry, Mom's current boyfriend." Teal paused, and looked up at Lena for the first time. "It's weird what I remember, you know? He had on a white T-shirt and plaid boxers. I could see his handcuffs. They dragged him down the front stairs because he kept trying to kick the policemen with his bare feet." She once again turned toward the trees. "I didn't see him again after that.

"A little while later, a lady opened the door and climbed in with me. She said she was with Social Services. I didn't know what that meant, not then. She took me to another car, drove me to a stranger's house, and left me there. That was my first foster home. I never saw my birthday toys again."

"Oh, Teal. I'm so sorry," Lena said, wishing there were magic words to erase all the pain for a little girl seeing the worst of an adult world. It was so unfair.

Teal shrugged. "It's okay. That was six years ago. I'm over it." She glanced up at Lena, then back down at the yard. "It's what came later that... that..."

Lena pulled Teal up into a hug. She laid her chin on the girl's hair. It smelled of lavender shampoo and summer.

Teal told how she'd bounced around the foster care system, staying at some homes for three months, six months, one for a year, but never long enough to feel at home. They *weren't* her home, and she always knew there was another move coming.

Some homes were good, but at others she felt like an imposition. At one place, they had five foster kids at the same time. Even though they were all supposed to have bedrooms, in this house Teal slept on a cot in the dining room, and stored her belongings in a corner hutch along with napkins, the good silverware the family never used, and extra serving bowls. There were too many kids in the system, with more coming in every day. As long as things ran relatively smoothly in the home, no one asked about sleeping arrangements.

For the first few months, she dreamed of her mother returning, sober, no longer frail, without a boyfriend. She would apologize for being away, then tell Teal about their new home. But her mother didn't come. Eventually, they said her mother was in prison. Teal learned it was best to stay quiet and keep to herself.

And she did—until a few years later when Carl, the oldest boy in the home she was in, came into her bedroom one night. She woke with him on top of her, his hand clamped over her mouth. She slugged and gouged his face until he backed away...but not before vowing to let a bunch of his friends at her after school. She'd seen the guys he hung around with—a group of lowlifes who smoked and drank behind the backyard garden shed at the house. Because Carl was a total suck-up, their foster parents thought he could do no wrong, and Teal knew they wouldn't listen to her if she claimed Carl tried to rape her.

Lena clung to Teal as much for her own comfort as trying to be comforting, but she didn't interrupt. The words were spilling out, gushing, as if a dam had breached. Lena was right in the floodwater's path.

"The next morning, I stuffed my backpack with clothes and supplies instead of my textbooks."

Just like she had this morning, Lena thought. What must life be like when the best option was running away?

"When the bus unloaded in the school parking lot and the kids headed into the building, I turned the other direction. I got lucky, and caught a ride with a girl heading back to college in Mission Peak." Teal let out a shuddering sigh—a cleansing.

Lena, on the other hand, felt anything *but* clean. There were good foster homes as well as some bad ones. Same as with biological parents. As a kid, you didn't get a choice—except to walk away if things were extremely bad. Her heart ached for this young girl and what she had experienced at the hands of others.

God, where were your guardian angels when Teal needed them?

"Can we go work on hanging the curtains in the new cabin now?" Teal asked abruptly, pulling back. Her body seemed drawn in on itself, as if the outpouring words of her story, the simple telling, had emptied her.

The doctor's admonition was still heavy on Lena's heart. Something had traumatized this girl yesterday, sent her body into shock and withdrawal. If Lena was going to help, she needed to find out what it was.

"Teal." Lena paused until she had the girl's full attention. "Will you tell me what happened yesterday? What upset you so much?"

Teal's brow tightened, and she turned toward the backyard. "I'd rather not talk about the rest of it right now." She exhaled a huge breath. "There's a… a lot more."

"Okay," Lena said. She, better than most, understood how much it took to tell a tragedy over and over, and she didn't want to push on this. Maybe after doing something positive, like hanging the new curtains, Teal would feel strong enough to finish her story. But there was one thing Lena had to know right now.

Lena cleared her throat. "Before we work on the cabin, there's one question I have to ask you. Is that okay?"

Teal nodded, but her body language shouted wariness. Lena pulled her down so they were again sitting on the steps. Lena would rather run away herself than have this talk. Just because she was the adult in the situation, didn't make her an expert.

"Teal, after the doctor left your room last night, he asked again for a parental permission slip."

The girl's eyes went wide. "You didn't—"

"No, no," Lena assured her. "I told him I'd try and get it. But he's concerned about your weight; even more so when I told him you had trouble keeping food down."

"I won't throw up anymore," Teal said, grabbing Lena's hands. "I promise!"

"Honey, it's not that." Lena held the girl's hands tight. "He asked…he asked if you could be pregnant." The *P* word hung there between them, and it seemed the rest of the world—the lake, birds, rustling leaves…everything —went still and silent.

Teal's mouth dropped open, transforming to an *O*. Then it closed to a flat line, and she slowly and vehemently shook her head.

"I mean, you and Quin have been spending a lot of time together, and—"

"Wait! You think Quin and I have been having sex? That he got me *pregnant?*" She jerked her hands from Lena's.

"Now calm down, Teal. I just—"

"You think we've been off in the bushes, *doing it?*" Teal jumped to her feet. "Maybe I should just leave. I'm already packed." She gestured to her backpack.

Lena stood. "No."

"Why not? I snuck into your house, stole your food. And now you think I'm corrupting the nice local boy and having his bastard kid." She stomped across the porch and shouldered her backpack. "I'm out of here."

Tears streamed down the girl's face, but there was a resolve and strength there as she shouldered the backpack. Lena's insides dropped out.

"No," Lena said again, blocking the exit from the porch and extending her hand. "Please don't go."

"Why?" Teal shouted through her tears. "It'll be easier for everyone when I'm gone. Quin won't have to worry about his reputation, and you won't have to babysit me anymore."

Lena's knees went weak when she thought of the rest of the day without Teal, let alone the rest of her life. Teal leaving now would be like losing Bobby all over again. Just when the gaping hole was beginning to heal over, this would tear it open again.

"Please, Teal. You can't go."

"Why do *you* care?" she yelled. "You don't trust me. And why do you think you get to say what I do?"

"Because…" Lena's eyes overflowed, and the girl became a blurry mass. Her legs wobbled as the truth slammed into her, and her throat constricted as she fought for the words. "Because I love you. And I need you…in my life. Please, Teal."

Teal remained a statue until Lena held open her arms, then the backpack crashed to the floor, and Teal flung herself into Lena's embrace. Skinny arms wrapped like steel bands around Lena's back, crushing them together, and Teal buried her head in Lena's chest and sobbed as they swayed on the porch.

"I'm sorry, Teal. So sorry," Lena whispered, her voice breaking as she stroked the girl's hair. There were a hundred things she wanted to say, but they were all jumbled in her head, scrambled by emotion and the realization that she'd nearly lost this precious girl.

They clung to each other, the raw need for love, *to* love, making them stronger together than they could ever be apart. Until today, Lena had thought she was there to help the girl, provide food, shelter, and be a parent figure, but it had turned 180 degrees. Lena now understood the depth of her *own* need, and she squeezed her eyes against its fierce insistence to keep this girl close and protect her from evil in the world.

She ran her hand lightly up and down Teal's back. With each pass, her fingertips bumped over raised patterns, cruel carvings that had stolen innocence. But those scored lines weren't all Teal was. Not even close.

Gradually, Lena became aware of sounds around them, as if they'd returned from a brief hiatus. A breeze set the trees in motion, squirrels chittered coded warnings, and the old boards beneath their shoes groaned and creaked with comforting familiarity as they rocked. This was home, and she and Teal were here together.

In the distance, a boat motor grew louder.

Teal immediately recognized the sound of Quin's boat motor, but after Lena told her Stone was going to have a similar talk with Quin, she agreed to wash up, unpack her clothes, and help clean up breakfast. Teal insisted over and over that she and Quin had never done anything except kiss a few times, and that he'd always been a perfect gentleman.

It took a while for Lena to convince Teal she believed her. After finishing in the bathroom and bedroom, Teal came into the kitchen with a shy grin. "I'd sure like to be a fly on the wall of Alex's trailer right now."

"Teal! How would you like it if he'd been listening in on *our* talk?" Lena said, pointing a washed spatula at the girl before she put it in the drawer.

"No way." Teal shook her head, then grinned wider. "But still…"

Lena laughed, relieved this young girl wouldn't have to go through yet another bodily trauma. Pregnancy might be natural and normal, but not at such a young age.

Even as she thought it, Lena wondered what having a baby of her own would be like. She and Bobby had always wanted kids, but now, without him, the thought of parenting felt way outside her capabilities. How would she be as a mom? Did she have the patience to raise a child through all the growing up stages? As her child grew, could she risk him or her to a world that held such evil as Teal had confronted? They were tough questions, but ones probably every mom faced.

Of course, first she'd have to find a man who could be a loving husband and a good father.

She blanched as a picture of Alex Stone filled her mind.

After "the talks," as Teal referred to them, the girl spent fifteen minutes with Quin at the shore where the creek emptied into the lake. Lena used the time to gather tools and supplies. A knot had formed at the base of her neck, catching each time she lifted anything. Sleeping on the sofa could be to blame, but she suspected it was tension from hearing Teal's story.

Quin left for his delivery jobs, and Teal met Lena at the new cabin. She watched the girl practically skip through the house to the Jeep out back where the new curtains and rods were waiting. Lena had to admit, Quin had a very positive effect on Teal. There were times she appeared not to have a care in the world. But at other moments, like yesterday, Teal succumbed to fear. Maybe keeping the upbeat outlook was partly show for Lena and Stone, not wanting to appear a burden. Heaven knew the girl was good at covering —probably necessary self-protection. And no wonder—what Lena had heard this morning was only the beginning of Teal's story, before the scars and whatever else she'd experienced.

Lena hefted her toolbox onto the worktable, and tightened a bit in the battery-powered drill she needed for mounting the curtain rods. They were really close to moving into the cabin, and Teal would have her own room— the first time, she'd told Lena, in the six years since she'd been pulled out of bed the night of her ninth birthday.

The power tool stilled in Lena's hands as realization dawned, and she sank slowly into the metal folding chair. Math, except for what she needed for carpentry, had never been her strongest subject, but she could calculate 9+6.

Fifteen.

"I've got the curtains," Teal called from the back porch.

"Oh, man," Lena groaned, but got to her feet. *Fifteen!* If Teal were her real daughter, she'd *never* let her date at fifteen. This situation was getting crazier every day, and she longed to talk with Stone. But there wasn't time right now.

Working together, they mounted the rods and strung the curtains in every room, while Lena stole glances at the girl. She *looked* older than fifteen.

Certainly not eighteen, but maybe late sixteen or early seventeen. The realities of life had caused her to grow up fast.

By the time Teal left to work on the website, Lena was moving room to room, efficiently attaching all the switch plates and receptacle covers, but all the while pondering the *very* young girl living under her roof. She'd been putting it off—probably in denial—but she had to work out a legal solution.

While finishing the garbage disposal outlet under the kitchen sink, Lena heard a *ding*. It took her a minute to realize it came from the prepaid phone she'd left in her tool belt on the worktable. *Eve.*

Lena unlocked the phone's display and found the same type of message she'd received days ago on her own phone, the one Eve's hacker friend had sent not using standard texting. Except this one was no brief message. Each screen she read grew more ominous than the previous. Lena had to find Stone. Fast.

36

Alex sat down at his table and opened his laptop. He'd finally got the Airstream's two-foot dish accurately aimed at a satellite that gave him online access—some of the time. Saul Pensky, a former DEA buddy, had switched careers a couple years ago and ventured into mobile Internet service for full time RVers. The system was still in beta, which meant it went down periodically, but Alex was more than happy to provide user feedback in trade for free access during the testing period. Plus, Saul owed him. Alex had dragged him out of a burning meth lab in National City seconds before it blew. If Alex squeezed a little, he could probably get Saul to cough up free service for life.

The laptop's software linked with the satellite, and Alex logged into his email. There were offers of free cash from Nigeria and the cliché promises to increase the size of certain body parts. Saul sure hadn't perfected the spam filtering yet. Alex selected the junk emails and forwarded them to the beta test reporting address. The only message remaining was from Kris Stone, his sister.

A former FBI field agent and hand-to-hand instructor, Kris split her time between private investigations, training mid-size company security departments and—her specialty and his least favorite—stepping into situations where women were threatened. He knew of at least four high-profile women who were alive because Kris had "persuaded" their abusive exes to back off. Kris's method usually involved baiting them until they did something illegal and wound up in prison. There were other cases she wouldn't tell him about, and he wasn't sure he wanted to know. He liked remembering his innocent little sister begging him to push her higher on their swing set.

He clicked the email.

> *Hey, big bro,*
>
> *Here's the info u wanted (attached). Wondering what you've gotten yourself into this time. Thot u were retired. No, don't tell me…there's a blonde involved. Am I right? Oh, yeah, I'm right. A model like the last one? I know u live in California, but puh-lease, not another vapid Holly Dolly actress! Bet she can't shoot.*
>
> *Seriously, watch your back, bro. These r some powerful bad guys. Do NOT ask me where I got the info. Burned several favors. Got more coming tomorrow, I hope.*
>
> *Call if u need backup. In Atlanta now, but got some time b4 heading 2 Colorado nxt. Flexible.*
>
> *Love, Kris (the better shot)*
>
> *Sent from my iPhone*

Alex laughed. Kris knew him well, but she'd be surprised if she ever met AJ. That would be a hoot. Did the *Nail It!* cable TV show put her in the category of actress? Maybe. And AJ might not be able to match Kris on the shooting range, but she handled a mean nail gun.

Still grinning, he downloaded the attached PDF and quickly scrolled the two pages of text. Then he started at the top and read everything twice. By the time he finished, his grin had long faded.

A sharp knock on the door startled him. "Stone?"

AJ stood in the sun, but her skin had lost its tan. Alex drew her into the trailer, closed the laptop, and made room for her at the small table.

"I got a message on my unlisted phone. It's from the same hacker guy Eve used before." AJ's fingers shook when she slid the phone across the dinette.

Alex began reading.

> *L.*
>
> *I'm the one who sent the message before. I thought I'd better tell you re: Eve. All over local news.*
>
> *Someone rigged her car to explode. I did a little digging and "found"*

initial report: a BBQ-size propane tank was in the trunk of her sedan. Valve jimmied so it leaked and filled the space with gas. Prelim investigation says electric door lock wiring was tampered with to generate a short, i.e. spark. Don't think any of that is public, so don't tell anyone.

Neighbor saw it. Said E always hit the remote unlock button when still good distance away, so E was partly shielded by cars in between. Thirty foot fireball took out four other cars and caught the building on fire.

In ICU. Critical. Burns, concussive injuries. Hit by debris. Coma. Docs very cautious.

Using network of "friends" to find info. Six similar MO bombs in Mexico in last 18 months. Targets were high-level drug ring leaders. LN cartel suspected or confirmed in all.

Totally weird: partially frozen human legs found in backseat of car. Badly charred. DNA testing at PD lab. Not LN MO.

Will keep digging. Not legal, so don't tell anyone. – V.

"Lobos Negros, again," Alex said.

"I assume 'MO' is modus operandi?"

Alex nodded.

"Stone," Lena said, rubbing her forehead, "the body we found before you came…"

"Ben Conner briefed me; told me about the missing legs." He set the cell phone aside and took her hand. "I'll contact Sheriff Cabot. He can follow up and see if there is a match. If it *is* the same person, I don't understand the connection. I mean, I can understand the bombing if Lobos Negros found out Eve was investigating them or something. But why the legs? And why take the chance of transporting the rest of the body clear up here? We're a long way from L.A."

"Not far enough."

Alex agreed. They couldn't be sure until they had confirmation, but it was highly improbable the legs belonged to a body other than the one AJ had dug up. Someone in L.A. had escalated things dramatically, and it just didn't fit that the cartel would play this kind of game, if that's what it was—and it certainly felt like one.

He needed help beyond the L.A. hacker who was tapping into government databases. He opened his computer and typed a short reply to Kris.

Come ASAP.

"Oh, one more thing," Lena said, rubbing her temples. "Our girl is fifteen."

Even with the tension of the situation, Alex couldn't help it. "Your niece is getting younger by the week."

AJ kicked him in the shin.

He fast-forwarded the DVR until it came to the next story. He'd recorded the news from several local stations so he could watch after work.

This reporter, an Asian woman with flawless skin and long black hair, stood on a hill a hundred yards behind Eve Cresent's condo complex. The reporter's cameraman slowly zoomed in on her, then slid over her left shoulder and continued the zoom on the still smoldering building in the background.

"Assistant District Attorney Eve Crescent narrowly escaped death this morning when her car exploded in the carport of her condominium. According to a police spokesperson, Ms. Crescent was walking toward her car just after seven a.m. this morning when it suddenly exploded, knocking her to the ground and doing extensive damage to other vehicles and the building itself."

The video switched to pans of emergency vehicles on the street in front of the building, then of smoke rising behind it.

"Ms. Crescent was rushed to the nearby Nethercutt Emergency Center at UCLA Medical Center Santa Monica, where she is listed in critical condition. A press briefing about an hour ago reported she is suffering from burns, as well as lacerations from flying debris. However, her most pressing problem is from what the doctors describe as concussive brain injury from the explosion and her resulting fall. This type of brain trauma is similar to what our soldiers experience from roadside bombs. It can result in bleeding and swelling of the brain. Doctors are guarded about her progress, but promise another briefing sometime tomorrow.

"No others were injured in the blast, but four families had to be evacuated from the other units in this particular building due to fire and structural damage. However, in a grisly twist to this horrific situation, we've learned that firefighters found two human legs in the remains of Ms. Crescent's vehicle."

The screen filled with aerial shots of the back of the building. A yellow tarp covered an object on the alleyway.

"At first, they assumed someone had been killed in the blast, and that Ms. Crescent was an injured bystander. But now, through witnesses, they know it was indeed her car, and that she had, thankfully, not yet reached it.

"Police are not speculating where the human legs might have come from, nor are they releasing any information about possible suspects at this time.

"Reporting live from Santa Monica, this is Lissan Wong."

He grew impatient when the same video loop repeated for the tenth time. The newsroom reporters speculated endlessly about the blast and who could have been behind it. But the big interest was the legs. One clueless reporter even wondered aloud who might be missing them, as if someone had misplaced them when sitting down at the dinner table.

The first four stations covered the same information, over and over, so he stopped the DVR and turned off the TV. A ding sounded in the kitchen, and he went to fetch his microwaved leftovers of takeout barbecue pork.

He'd never planned for Eve Crescent to survive. Depending on the outcome of her brain injury, she might be a serious problem. The legs, however, had been a streak of last-minute genius. On one hand, he'd divested himself of incriminating evidence. And on the other, he'd drawn more attention to Lena Blaylock, because it wouldn't be long before reporters discovered the Mission Peak story about a body without legs being found next to her property. Plus, dividing the body into parts made it far easier to handle. The media never seemed to realize how heavy a human body was, especially a grown man. And his freezer wasn't *that* big.

Switching on the TV again, he settled in his recliner and turned on the DVR. He had twenty-eight episodes of *Nail It!* saved, but only six had more extensive shots of Lena McKinley. Number twenty-three was his favorite. He chose it and hit Play, then fast-forwarded through the opening dross until her face filled the screen as she worked on a custom cabinet for a bathroom. The day had been warm when they'd filmed, and her flawless face and long neck shimmered with moisture and light.

For two years, he tried to resist her, letting younger subjects take her place. But none were a proper substitute. One girl had been exceptional, but she ruined it all by escaping. He got a lead on her weeks later with subtle inquires through Social Services, but she disappeared again before he got to her. As near as he could tell, she wasn't in any county services in California. Probably dead by now. It was a shame—he'd been so close to finishing her. A few strategic cuts; one more tattoo.

He ate with one hand while he nearly wore out the 30-second Rewind button on the DVR's remote control. Over and over, Lena cut out pieces on a table saw, aligned rectangles, glued and nailed. Her tanned arms were magnificently unmarred, waiting his skill. In another hot-weather episode, the cameraman had caught her in khaki shorts, exposing long, bronzed legs begging for his touch. A shudder of delight rocked him as he imagined the expanse of her bare back.

She had married Bobby Blaylock. But now, thanks to the man's meddling investigation, Bobby was permanently out of the picture. One good thing the Mexican did right. Lena McKinley—even though she now called herself Lena Blaylock—was free.

Suddenly, he realized this was the time he'd been waiting for, the moment of decision. He could stay with his career and all it brought, or he could pursue his "hobby." Many years ago, a guidance counselor had said he was smart enough to do many kinds of work to make money and have power, but that his *true* calling, his art, would eventually win out. It was his love, his passion, and it wouldn't be suppressed forever. Could he do it? Could he leave everything behind and pursue his art?

He turned off the TV, then dumped the remains of his meal into the kitchen garbage and leaned against the counter, pondering his next move. If Eve Crescent's recent inquiries about Lobos Negros became public, the Mexican would not be happy. He would come looking for answers. If Eve hadn't been digging where she shouldn't, she wouldn't be in the hospital. It was her own fault. And now it was his job to make the inquiries and evidence go away.

The need for the solitude of his workplace drew him to the basement stairs. Although it held no occupant at the moment, the smell of ink and blood always helped him think more clearly.

37

Two days later, Teal waited on the back porch holding a cardboard box packed with pantry food as AJ pulled the Jeep and trailer to a stop. When the dust settled, she walked down the steps and put the box in the trailer.

AJ had assigned her to kitchen packing, while Colby Hartgrave helped with the bigger furniture, both here and in the new cabin. He'd arrived in a U-Haul truck, loaded with beds, dressers, refrigerator, stove, dining table, sofa, and other items for both cabins. Then he and AJ sorted where the items would go.

Their old house no longer looked the same. A replacement sleeper sofa—still comfortably used—occupied the living room, and a different dining set, curtains, throw rug, and tables filled in the rest of the front space. These were in better shape than the ones AJ and Colby moved over to the new cabin. After all, these were for paying guests.

Teal didn't mind. Even AJ's meager belongings were luxurious compared to bus benches and straw. She really wanted to see how the new place was coming together, and had three of her best drawings of Desperation Falls ready to hang. AJ had insisted. Plus, Teal was anxious to try out the bed Colby brought.

But AJ had kept her busy packing, vacuuming cabinets, and cleaning the new used refrigerator. Renters were arriving around five o'clock, and they had a lot to do to get this place ready. Back in the kitchen, she reached for the last box.

"Here, let me get that," Colby stated, rounding the corner and snatching the box of canned food off the counter. He was down the hall before she could respond. She'd quickly learned Colby was more comfortable accepting a sandwich or cold drink than a direct compliment. Sometimes he talked a streak, then other times he worked silently. She liked him. He was a little strange, but then she'd met a lot people like that while out on her own, and some of them were the nicest.

"That it?" AJ asked, dusting her hands together as she entered the room.

Teal nodded. "Do you want me to start cleaning the bathroom?"

AJ shook her head, then grinned. "Colby's going to start cleaning here while we unpack at the new place. Then we'll come back later and give it some finishing touches."

Teal surveyed the small kitchen. Although it had a new coffee maker and toaster, an unstained dish rack, and new towels draped over the oven handle, it felt as if its personality had been stripped away, leaving only the skeleton of familiarity. These rooms were the first sanctuary she'd known in a long time. And it was here, on this back porch, that Lena said she loved her. Except for her mom a few times, no one had ever said that to Teal where she believed they really meant it. She'd never been that important to anyone.

"Hey," AJ slipped an arm around her shoulder. "It'll be okay."

"I know." Teal wiped her eyes. "Did I ever tell you that when I first came in here I found your iPod cradle over there on the end table and charged up Springsteen? He was almost dead." She sniffed and wiped again. AJ's grip tightened and Teal leaned into her strength.

"Shall we go top off The Boss in his new bedroom?" AJ raised an eyebrow.

Colby clomped into the kitchen with a bucket of sponges and squirt bottles, pointedly averting his gaze when he saw Teal's wet eyes. He sprayed the window over the sink and attacked it with paper towels. The oddness of Colby cleaning their old kitchen made it easier to view the cabin as a rental.

Teal linked arms with AJ and grinned. "We shall."

One minute later, AJ stopped the Jeep in back of the new cabin. All the cabins were on sloping ground, so it was easier to unload through the back door, but before Teal could grab the first box, AJ led her around to the front of the cabin.

"What are we doing?" Teal said, as they reached the porch stairs.

"Just want you to experience the grand entrance—at least once." AJ smiled and started up. "Come on."

Teal followed, but came to an abrupt halt soon as her foot hit the top step.

AJ stood beside the door, grinning ear to ear. The faded "Cabin 6" sign that had been mounted beside the doorframe was gone. In its place was a new lacquered redwood plank with white lettering:

AJ & Teal

She had trouble getting her breath, and her tears began again.

38

"Hey, neighbor."

Lena turned her head in her hands where she sat on the front steps of her new cabin. The sun had set thirty minutes ago, but there was light enough to see Stone as he came around the porch corner. She could only grunt a reply. Stone climbed a step and settled beside her.

"You look beat," he said.

"Moving's hard work," she mumbled, and closed her eyes.

"Not for me and my trailer," he said.

Lena heard the smirk. If she had an ounce of energy left she'd punch him, but she was saving it to crawl into the house on all fours later. She and Teal had lined the kitchen shelves, put everything away, made the beds, unpacked clothes, sorted towels, and a hundred other things. Lena couldn't imagine moving a standard, three-bedroom house. How did people do that? Then, after the new cabin was organized enough for the basics, she'd helped Colby spiff up the old cabin in time for the arriving guests.

"Where's Teal?"

"Shower. Or maybe bed by now. Where I'll be shortly."

"How'd she handle the move? Stomach okay?"

"The vitamins and digestive enzymes seem to be doing the trick." Teal's vomiting had ceased, and she was a little stronger, at least physically. But it was obvious to Lena the girl was troubled about something. She refused to go back to Deer Cove, even with Lena, and carefully checked the yard before venturing outside.

"Good." Stone lay back, supported on his elbows. He wore a long-sleeved flannel shirt the same shade as his worn jeans. His eyes were half-closed as he stared at the last light reflecting in the lake waters. A man relaxed.

"Where were you when the heavy lifting was happening, neighbor?"

He laughed, a deep rumble that vibrated the wood steps. "Mission Peak."

"Convenient."

"Mom always said I had impeccable timing."

"Umm."

"My sister will be here in a couple of days," Stone said, changing the subject. "Any word from Chet?"

"He's the most undependable man I've ever met." Chet hadn't shown up *"today or tomorrow"* like he last promised. Nor the next day, which was today. "But I did get a text from him. Said he'd be here 'soon,' whatever that means, and to protect the files." Lena was anxious to know what he had to tell her, but with Eve still in critical condition, Lena imagined the DA's office was chaos.

"Maybe I should take a look at those files. I could probably call on someone to help figure out their encryption or whatever it is."

Lena shook her head. "Eve was adamant I only deal with her or Chet. It's not that I don't trust your coworkers, but…"

"I understand," Stone said. "It's impossible to know who to trust. By the way, I haven't heard back from the sheriff, either," Stone said. "Maybe tomorrow."

They were silent while the sky finished its transformation from burnt orange to black dotted with stars. A cricket chorus serenaded them over the background swish of a cool breeze through the oaks. Lena caught the scent of aftershave. Nothing too strong, but solid as a mountain. She drifted, somewhere above sleep but below consciousness. The branches swayed and she rocked with them, like the old nursery rhyme.

Down will come baby…

When the air shifted, it brushed his gauze-like heat over her, tantalizing, so near, yet separated. He could move closer.

…cradle and all.

Her skin rippled in the sudden chill, and she tucked her arms against her sides. After a moment, warmth encompassed her and seduced her into its lair.

———

"Lena?"

The voice whispered her name, barely louder than rustling leaves in a night breeze.

"Sorry, hon, but I've got to move."

Stone's voice. Lena let her eyes drift open, but saw only darkness. She was somewhere warm. Her cheek snuggled against soft cotton, like flannel sheets on a winter night. She knotted her fingers in the material and shut her eyes. No way was she getting out of bed yet. It was still dark. Renters could wait.

But with her sleep disturbed, her mind began seeking answers. Where was she? She'd been sitting on the steps, then Stone had come over. Now she was… in bed?

"AJ?"

His voice vibrated against her cheek and her eyes popped open.

Oh!

Cold replaced warmth as she pushed away from his body, and she snatched at the blanket falling off her shoulder. But it wasn't bedding, she realized. It was Stone's jacket.

"Sorry," he said, shifting. "I have to move. The steps are cutting into my back."

Steps? Enough dim light spilled through the living room curtains and onto the porch that she could make out the stair treads, and his body—the very body she'd been practically laying on, and definitely snuggling against. She'd fallen dead asleep in Alex Stone's arms. Damn.

Lena sat up, shivering in the cool air. She licked her lips, hoping she hadn't left a drool patch on his shirt. Fortunately, it was too dark to tell.

"Man." She rubbed her eyes.

"That's me," Stone said, rising. "And I think you mumbled something about a 'down pillow.'"

Lena garnered enough energy to stagger to her feet, but her leg was still asleep and she nearly toppled into the yard. Stone wrapped his arms around her and pulled her close. Her palms were flat on his chest. His very *warm* and *firm* chest. Her fingers lingered half an inch from the top button.

Stone cleared his throat. "I'd, uh, better get back to my trailer and let you get some sleep. Real sleep, I mean."

His breath feathered her lips, and she licked them again, gratified when his gaze followed her tongue. His body heat warmed her, chest to knees, and she wondered what it would be like to stay like this, with this man. He wasn't what she'd, expected, or even desired—not when she was wide awake, anyway. But there was something…

"Want me to carry you to your bed?"

Lena's knees quivered, but she mustered courage. "No." *Yes.* That's exactly what she wanted. But Alex Stone? So bizarre.

It wasn't sex—well, not only that, although the attraction was building. Her real desire was for him to hold her, wrap her in his arms through the night. That's what she missed most about being married—the nights holding onto each other. Together, not alone.

Stone leaned down and she met him halfway. The kiss was light, then more intense, then light again before they separated. Reluctantly, she stepped back and let him steady her to the cabin door.

"Goodnight, Stone." Lena went inside, turning as he closed the screen door between them.

"Goodnight, AJ." He picked up his jacket where it lay on the steps.

Lena switched on the yellow porch light, and watched until it no longer reflected off his form and he disappeared into the night. Then she went into the dark kitchen and peered out the window in the direction of his Airstream. A moment later, through the trees and branches in between, the interior light in his trailer flicked on. She imagined him washing up in the minuscule bathroom and getting ready for bed.

Lena drew down the shade and leaned against the counter. Her lips curved into a smile.

39

Lena was drying her face in the bathroom when she heard car doors slamming and voices. Ladies' voices.

"They're here!"

Lena stuck her head into the hall in time to see Teal sprint out of her new bedroom and disappear out the front door.

"*Who's* here?" Lena padded out onto the porch in her bare feet. In the yard sat a green 70s Buick as big as Lena's boat dock. Mandy's red Bronco was parked behind it, taller on its raised suspension and oversize tires, but dwarfed by the gigantic green machine. Lena recognized Bibs and Irene from Bibs' Beauty Barn talking with Mandy and Teal.

"We've come to take a look at your old barn," Bibs said, breaking from the circle and striding to the bottom of the stairs. She wore a red, white, and blue vertical striped dress and, with hands on her hips, she looked like a beach ball ready to roll downhill to the water.

Lena suppressed a grin as Mandy climbed the stairs to Lena's level. "Teal said you guys have talked about creating a rec room, and I thought of Bibs and the Beauty Barn. They fixed up *their* old barn, and I figured they might have some ideas. I hope you don't mind."

Lena didn't mind at all, as long as they could do it on practically a zero budget. Teal was anxious to begin marketing for the off-season. For the types of groups they wanted to attract, a meeting room was a necessity.

"Teal, why don't you show them around the barn? I'll grab my shoes and meet you up there." The four women headed off, and Lena went inside to find her tennis shoes.

While sitting in the living room tying the laces, she heard another car drive up. This one had colored lights on top. Sheriff Cabot climbed out, adjusted his trooper hat, and climbed the stairs. He carried a large manila envelope.

"Good morning, Mrs. Blaylock." From the look on his face, it appeared that any *good* the morning brought had fled to the hills.

At her suggestion, they walked to Stone's trailer and gathered around his dinette table, the sheriff on one side, Lena crowded against Stone on the other. She wanted him in on this, and it didn't surprise her that the sheriff knew of Stone's assignment.

The small camper smelled like coffee and toast, but the carafe was upside down in the dish drainer, and Stone made no move to make more. Lena's stomach was too jumpy to tolerate it anyway.

"As I said, Mrs. Blaylock," the sheriff began, "we've learned the identity of the body found by the crossing." He lifted the envelope flap, and slid out an enlarged DMV photo of a young man with blond hair who looked to be no more than twenty. "This photo is from a few years ago. He would have been twenty-seven this year when he died. His name is Thomas Delbert Frost."

Stone glanced at Lena before asking, "You matched up his body with the legs?"

Lena stiffened, mentally picturing Eve, the explosion, and the gruesome discovery in the back seat of her car. Beneath the table, Stone's hand found hers and, as the sheriff nodded, Stone's fingers, warm and strong, entwined with her own.

"It took a little work. Once we knew to look farther south, we reviewed all the missing persons reports for each city and county. We found him— well, where he was from. San Bernardino. The missing persons report was filed by his employer, the manager of a sporting goods store."

"What about his parents, his family?" Lena asked. "Why his boss?"

"He grew up in the foster system. We checked, but the county lost touch with his biological parents years ago. No idea where they are now. They were into drugs. When Frost aged out at eighteen, he was on his own. Did okay, I guess, from what the store manager said. Quite the outdoorsman. Took time off a few summers and worked as a rafting guide in Montana and Wyoming. Also spent a lot of long weekends backpacking parts of the Pacific Crest Trail, often solo, according to other store employees. When he didn't show up for work after a trip, the manager filed the report. However, no one at the store knew where he'd gone, so the authorities didn't know where to look."

"So," Stone said, "the question remains: how did half of him show up here at the lake, while the rest of him wound up in L.A.?"

Cabot nodded. "Even stranger is the date of his disappearance. The store manager hadn't wanted him to go on that trip due to the heavy Christmas shopping season, but Frost had threatened to quit. He was supposed to return to work on December 15th, and when he didn't show, the manager figured he'd quit anyway. But they were friends, and he repeatedly went by Frost's house. He contacted the police on January 3rd. Frost's disappearance date was officially set as December 15th."

"But that was five months before we found the body here," Lena said. "Could he have been buried that long?" She hated to think about that shallow grave, the tractor, the arm, the decomposition. "Wouldn't he have been just a skeleton by then?"

"Our county coroner estimates he'd been buried four to six weeks," the sheriff said.

"So where was he for those months in between?" Stone asked.

"Excellent question," Cabot said. "The truth is, we don't know when he actually died. We only know when he went missing and then the individual dates when his body and then his legs were found. The L.A. coroner report says the legs were badly burned on the outside from the explosion and fire, but they were still frozen on the inside. Their theory is Frost was killed, dismembered, and put into a freezer. That makes determining the actual date of death impossible. Then his torso was taken out and buried here sometime mid-April, and his legs were kept frozen until placed in Ms. Crescent's automobile by whoever rigged it to explode."

Lena sank back against the dinette cushion, barely able to comprehend the horror of the simply-stated facts. The thought that someone could cut up a human body... She inwardly shuddered. Murder was bad enough.

How was this Frost connected to her, if at all? And that mid-December timeframe again. It was around the same days as when she bought the property and when Teal almost died in the woods, the days when the big storm had covered the state.

"What if the killer planned to bury Frost on your property," Stone said to Lena, "but he couldn't get through the creek crossing because of high water? You and Merle hadn't rebuilt it yet."

Lena looked first at Stone, then the sheriff. "That would mean he was directly targeting me."

"Umm." The sheriff rubbed his chin. "If that's true, Mrs. Blaylock, it might explain why the body was buried only a couple of inches below the surface. That area is old creek sediment, very soft. It would have been easy to dig a deep grave. Merle said he had that gravel for building the crossing dumped a couple of weeks earlier. If he hadn't, animals would have probably dug up the body. I wondered why they hadn't dug deeper. But if you're correct that someone was seeking you out specifically, it means they didn't care if it was found, or perhaps wanted it to be."

Lena's shudder was far more pronounced this time, and Stone's grip on her hand tightened, securing the length of her arm against his side. She breathed in his scent, and chased away the memory of decaying flesh.

The sheriff directed a raised brow at her. "It seems your plan to keep a low profile by moving up here wasn't working."

Sheriff Cabot had the ability to state the obvious.

Stone filled him in on what they'd learned about the Lobos Negros cartel's modus operandi of using propane tanks to blow up their competitors. The organization might be involved in the attack on Eve, or the explosion might be a copycat.

"There's one other thing I think you in particular, Mr. Stone, should know. The police searched Frost's apartment for clues. It wasn't their highest priority case at the time, but eventually they found a file on his computer. A log. Lots of dates and details about pot farms and drug houses in L.A. and the area mountains. There was one mention of DEA, so they sent it over to the local DEA office to take a look. He might have been feeding information to law enforcement, or he might have just been into some kind of geocaching reality game or something."

Lena glanced at Stone, but his only reaction was a slight narrowing of the eyes.

Sheriff Cabot gathered his hat, slid out of the dinette, and stood. "I have to say, I'm getting more confused by the minute. I don't like to think about this cartel moving into my county. But even if they are, I don't see how this Frost fellow ties into it all the way up here. From what his boss said, he was a health nut and runner. Doesn't fit the profile of someone involved in the drug world. And whether he was in the drug world or not, who buried half of him in your backyard, so to speak, Mrs. Blaylock?"

Cabot opened the door and stepped outside. He paused in the yard to adjust his hat squarely on his head while they joined him. "Please keep me informed if you think of anything that might help in finding this man's murderer. I'll stay in touch with my counterparts down south. I'm sure you'll be doing the same, Mr. Stone?"

Stone nodded.

They watched the sheriff drive away, and then she looked at the photo he'd left with her. The man had a slight smile on his young face, his blond hair was neatly trimmed, and he stared at Lena with blue eyes that seemed they could laugh on a moment's notice. Stone's hand rested on the small of her back as she wondered what Thomas Delbert Frost had done that was turning her world upside down.

40

Lena trudged back to her cabin, arriving in time to wave at Bibs and Irene as they drove away. Inside, Teal and Mandy were huddled over a sheet of Teal's sketchpad, drawing shapes and adding measurements.

"Look at this, AJ," Teal said. "Bibs thought that since the back of the barn is already covered by the loft, it would be the perfect place for the recreation room. Natural ceiling. That would make it easier to keep warm in cold weather." The paper showed a cutaway of the interior.

With a few quick strokes, Teal drew the barn from a front left corner perspective, then outlined a path leading up along the left side wall, stopping right as the hill began its upward slope.

"We can open up a new door here as an outside entry for the rec room," Mandy pointed to the spot where the path terminated. "Maybe I can try out your reciprocating saw?" The way the girl's eyes gleamed reminded Lena of her own love of power tools. Many carpenters placed the reciprocating saw in the top ten most useful tools, right behind a hammer, tape measure, and circular saw.

"There's not much stuff in the back area," Teal said. "We can move it into the front where the big doors are and keep that as a place for your trailers and tools."

"Well, we know the window in back works," Lena said, and was rewarded with an embarrassed grin from Teal. "How do you propose to separate the spaces?"

"This is the best part," Teal said. "Bibs has a smaller barn on the back of her property that's been falling down for years. She said we can salvage plenty of studs and siding to build the interior wall. And, since it's already weathered, it'll match. There's enough so we can replace any of our barn's siding that has big gaps so it will stay warm."

"And you already have electricity in the barn, so we can wire in outlets and lights," Mandy added, clearly onboard with the plan.

Lena had to admit, it was a pretty easy conversion. If they moved out the unneeded hay bales left by the previous owner, there would be more than enough room in the front area for the equipment. The overall structure was sturdily built with full dimension timbers and beams, and its roofline and wide doors gave it character not found on newer construction. Photos or drawings of it would look great on Teal's website. Even so, there was still the matter of cost.

"How much is Bibs charging for the salvaged barn wood?"

"We worked out a trade," Teal said. "Irene gets to use it for her monthly knitting group meetings. They meet on Wednesdays at ten for a couple of hours."

"And," Mandy chimed in with a mischievous grin, "Bibs gets to give Teal a new haircut!" Teal's own smile slipped at this, and Mandy was clearly enjoying this bit of the plan. "She couldn't keep her fingers off Teal's hair. She said she was 'horrified'"—Mandy did air quotes—"and it looked like it had been cut with a 'weed eater.'" More air quotes.

Lena couldn't help laughing out loud, and had to hug Teal's phony mad expression away until she, too, gave into the fun.

The girls were anxious to get started on the barn wall, but after Lena's meeting with Stone, she felt like crawling back into bed and calling it a day. The secret texts, body parts, cartels, and bombs weighed her down and sapped her strength. Teenagers, it seemed, had more resiliency.

She helped them hitch her utility trailer behind the Bronco, and Teal and Mandy headed off to Bibs', equipped with hammers, pry bars, and gloves. Lena was surprised Teal agreed to go to Deer Cove after her last meltdown with Quin, but Lena overheard Teal telling Mandy it was okay as long as they didn't stop in town.

They returned four hours later with enough timber and siding to build the wall. Lena had finished stacking the hay bales, rearranging the equipment, and moving the unwanted items from the rear of the barn. She was afraid if she didn't, Teal would tackle the job, and Lena didn't want the girl to strain her body. The digestive enzymes, vitamins, and better food were working, but she had a ways to go before anyone would pronounce her "filled-out."

After they all had a snack, Lena worked with them to construct the wall framing and tilt it up into place. Lena shot the base plate into the floor using a Ramset gun.

"Okay," Lena said, rising from the last shoot, "you're on your own, now." Nailing on the siding was the easy part—as long as they got it true up and down. They had decided an interior door into the back room was a good idea, so Lena went to work on that. If they ran out of daylight, the exterior door could be cut tomorrow.

Quin came by and helped for an hour between his jobs, but mostly he spent the time making mooneyes at Teal. The boy had it bad. After he left, Teal and Mandy finished the wall. Then they pounded large spikes into the side facing the tool area and hung up an old horse collar, a pitchfork, rake, other hand tools, coils of rope and wire, and other things that had piled up on the workbench. They lined two of the cross braces with paint cans. By the time they were done, the wall appeared as if it had been there since the barn's construction.

"Hey, looking good," Stone said from the barn's open bay doors. The setting sun behind him washed the entrance in a yellow haze.

Lena finished setting the last hinge screw on the door and tested the swing. Satisfied, she walked to meet him. "These girls are hard workers." She looked back where the two teens were sweeping out the newly completed rec room.

"Grilled chicken and corn on the cob sound good?" Stone asked.

Lena turned too fast and winced. "Ouch." She had strained her neck earlier, and the stiff area had grown to the size of a softball—at least that's what it felt like. She rubbed it, but couldn't get the right leverage. Maybe their next project should be a hot tub. There was a nice flat spot behind their new cabin, not far from the propane tank.

"Turn around," Stone said. Before Lena could protest, he maneuvered her onto a sawhorse, stood behind her, and began massaging her neck and shoulders.

She couldn't stop the groan as his thumbs dug into the cramped muscles, circling, spreading, kneading, and then doing it all again. In fifteen seconds her eyes were closed, and she floated away on an undulating sea of pleasure.

The dusty barn transformed into a spa of modern angles, glass, and white pine. Dozens of candles circled the floor. She lay on a massage table covered in crisp, white linens. A fireplace filled with glass beads hissed on one side, and floor to ceiling windows on the other overlooked an endless view of the deep blue Pacific Ocean.

Stone, clad in white drawstring pants and T-shirt, moved around her as he worked lotion into her skin. Coconut with a hint of vanilla. The tension between her shoulder blades melted away under his touch, the lotion a fragrant, restorative balm seeping deep into her pores. Far below, beyond the steep cliffs, the rhythmic ocean waves soothed her soul. She drifted, a boat lifting and dropping in the endless, marching swells.

Don't stop. Don't ever stop.

"What was that?" His words whispered against her neck, momentarily raising the fine hairs before his fingers smoothed them back into place.

Lena opened her eyes. Dust swirled before her in the last of the sun's rays. *Tell me I didn't say that out loud.* Stone's hands gave a final squeeze of her totally relaxed shoulders. She tilted her head back until she could see his upside-down smirk hovering above her.

"I may be wrong," his eyebrow rose, "but I thought you said, 'Don't stop.'"

"Cob," Lena said, her voice hoarse. "You must have heard me say 'Corn… on the cob.'" He came around the sawhorse and pulled her up. She couldn't help swaying against him.

"Uh-huh." He lingered above her, mere inches separating her from his smiling lips. Lena knew she should move, but couldn't remember why.

"Wow." Mandy's voice, though reverently quiet, echoed in the rafters.

Lena suddenly remembered "why." The girls stood in the new doorway, Mandy holding a broom with her mouth in an *O*, while dustpan-wielding Teal grinned ear to ear.

Two minutes later, as the girls followed Lena and Stone to his trailer with the smoking Weber, Lena heard Teal whisper to Mandy, "Told ya."

41

"I have something to tell you all," Teal said, putting down her plate and wiping her hands on a napkin.

Lena had noticed the girl was uncharacteristically quiet as they consumed the meal.

"It's not really the best dinner conversation, but it's important." The vertical lines in Teal's forehead were prominent in the waning light.

Stone had brought out two milk crates and turned them upside down for additional seating around the Weber, and they'd all been quiet as they munched on grilled lemon chicken and corn on the cob. After tearing apart the old barn, moving the wood, and building the wall, the two girls were winding down.

Lena, however, couldn't get her mind off Stone's hands working her sore muscles. Her skin had memorized his touch and kept reminding her brain how great it felt. They sat side by side in the canvas chairs, and she was acutely aware of his arm so near hers on the armrest. But now she turned her attention to Teal.

"Quin already knows... about me, what I went through." Her eyes glazed as she stared at the open Weber, as if the glowing briquettes held answers. She rubbed her forehead, breaking the momentary lapse.

"Teal," Lena said, "you don't have to." But the girl stubbornly shook her head.

For the next few minutes, she told Mandy and Stone what Lena had already heard: her ninth birthday, the police raid, her mom going to jail. She told them about the foster care homes, how some were good and some weren't, about Carl trying to force himself on her, how she'd run away.

"I was on the streets after that, hiding in laundromats, libraries, bus terminals, all-night service stations—just trying to get by." She shook her head. "I was stupid, but I was *so hungry*. He... he seemed nice, and offered to buy me a hamburger at the place next door to the laundromat. The smoke from the restaurant's grill kept seeping through the vents, and I was crying... Well, that's not important. It was late at night and...he took me. Knocked me out. I woke in a basement, locked in a cage."

Lena's breath caught, and Stone's hand wrapped hers.

Teal took her own deep breath. "I won't go into detail. Don't want you hurling this good dinner. Anyway, he basically used me as his personal art canvas." She turned to Mandy. "Alex, AJ, and Quin have seen my scars. You can see some of them later, if you want. I don't recommend it."

Mandy, to her credit, wasn't put off by that, and looped her arm around Teal's shoulders.

Quin had probably told her about the scars, and she'd certainly seen the ones on Teal's wrists while they were working.

"I don't even know how long he kept me there. Weeks. Months. There were no windows, it was always cold, and I was always hungry. I passed out a lot from the pain, and I knew if I didn't escape that he'd kill me. I sprinkled bits of dirt on the cage padlock for a couple of weeks, and one night when he'd had too many beers, the lock didn't fully close. He fell asleep, and I snuck past him and got out of the basement. But he heard me. I ran out the door and headed for the trees.

"It was almost dark, drizzling, cold. I didn't have any clothes or shoes, but I kept going for a long time—hours maybe—until I finally couldn't move. Even with cuts and bruises, it felt kind of good to be outside. The fresh air smelled wonderful, like sage and wet, dried grass. I was free.

"Then Fred came. I heard him stomping through the leaves and brush."

"Who's Fred," Mandy asked, mirroring Lena's question.

"It's what I called him. I didn't know his name, so I named him after Freddy Krueger from the *Nightmare on Elm Street* movies, you know?... because he used a knife on me."

Mandy shuddered, and tears wet her lashes. Teal said she was sorry for making her cry, but Mandy hugged tighter.

"Anyway, Fred almost caught me. But then this other guy came out of nowhere and grabbed me. At first, I thought he was Fred, but he held me tight and kept me quiet while Fred passed by really close. He would have caught me if it hadn't been for this other guy.

"When Fred was gone, we began hiking for what seemed like all night. When I couldn't walk anymore, the guy carried me. I woke the next morning in this cave where he was camping out. He was all dressed in camouflage, so I nicknamed him Camo Guy. He gave me food and some of his clothes, then he left to get shoes and clothing for me so I could walk out. Before he went, he said his name was Delta Force."

Mandy snickered at that, and Teal grinned. "I know, right?"

Teal told how Camo Guy didn't return, so after two days she began hiking out on her own. The storm raged, and she almost froze to death. But Camo Guy came back with help and found her. She described her next stint in foster care and how she'd been forced to shower in P.E. and all the kids at school knew her secret by the next day.

"That's when I hitchhiked north, found the beautiful falls, and ended up in AJ's barn. I found my perfect place, somewhere I belonged. Somewhere safe."

Lena couldn't stand it anymore. She got to her feet, pulled Teal up, and wrapped her arms around the girl. Mandy added hers, then Stone's long reach enclosed them all.

"I'm so sorry, Teal. You've been through so much. I'm just glad you found your way here." Lena's own tears burned at the injustice, the horror this girl had faced all alone, and for her bravery at escaping. She was incredibly strong.

As the huddle relaxed, Teal pulled back, blew out a breath, and faced them. "But that's not everything; and it's not why I had to tell you all this tonight."

Except for the trailer's small porch light, night had closed in. A balmy breeze carried sage, pungent tarweed, the scent of water. Regardless of the mild evening, a chill from Teal's story had wormed deep into Lena's soul. As had happened when she'd met with Stone at the Shelter Cove Store, she longed for a confrontation with the sick maniac who had defiled this young, precious girl.

"You see, the reason I..." She looked at the ground and shook her head. "This is gonna change everything." Her eyes caught Lena's. "I'm sorry. The reason I panicked and fainted the other day is...I saw Fred in Deer Cove."

"We need to call the sheriff," Stone said as he came out of the trailer with two mugs of coffee and handed one to Lena. Steam rose into the dark canopy.

Mandy had reluctantly left for home, and Teal was showering and going to bed. Feeling uncertain about what to do and not wanting to face it alone, Lena found her way back to Stone's.

She took a sip, inhaling chocolate and cinnamon. He'd learned that from Teal, and Lena's heart ached again at how much the teenager had changed their lives in the few short weeks she'd been here. Getting the authorities involved at this point was the right thing to do, Lena knew that. Yet even though it was what Teal expected, it still felt like betrayal.

"What will happen?" Lena asked into the dark. The grill no longer gave off heat, but the night was still mild, with only a hint of the chill to come before morning. Crickets surrounded them, a soothing chorus that made the blackness less threatening.

All wishful thinking. Nothing was safe now.

As if reading her mind, Stone reached for her across the tiny camp table between their chairs. His thumb rubbed circles on the back of her hand. "It's important the sheriff knows Teal's kidnapper is in this area, and only she can give him the details of her encounter with him. The L.A. investigation is at a dead-end, and they would never think to search up here."

"But she didn't see his face," Lena said. "How can she be sure it's the same man?" But Teal had never seen his face before, either, when she was a prisoner in that basement. He'd always worn a full-faced ski mask. It was his voice she'd recognized in Deer Cove, and of that she'd been absolutely certain.

"*Teal* didn't see his face, but the ice cream girl, Amber, did. And the male clerk, too. We need to get them with a sketch artist before more time passes."

Lena had been so focused on Teal's story and fear, she hadn't remembered the mercantile clerks. If they could identify this guy…

"We'll call him in the morning," Stone said. "After the work today and telling her story tonight, she's got to be exhausted."

Lena wanted nothing more than to crawl into her own bed and forget the last hour, but she feared sleep would be elusive at best. Stone turned her hand so his thumb now massaged her palm. It made her think again of the emptiness of her bed. Togetherness, holding, knowing she didn't face the world alone—that's what would bring sleep.

Knowing this maniac was prowling around Storm Lake—maybe right now somewhere in the dark shadows of the hills and trees—had every nerve firing. Or maybe it was the coffee. Or Stone's warm touch.

All of the above.

But it wasn't the time to dwell on a relationship. She had a young girl to protect. Mandy's offer to teach Lena how to shoot had sounded strange when she'd brought it up a few days ago, but Lena vowed to call her first thing tomorrow, right after they talked to the sheriff.

Lena disengaged her hand from Stone's and stood. Sleep or not, she needed a shower. Maybe that would be enough.

Stone rose and drew her gently until they touched. She closed her eyes as his mouth lowered to hers, gentle, and growing more familiar each day.

A scream cut through the night, silencing the crickets and raising the hair on Lena's neck.

"AJ!"

Teal.

Lena jerked from Stone's embrace and sprinted the short distance to her cabin. She took the stairs in two steps, and Stone was beside her as she threw open the screen door. He rushed past, fists clenched and ready for battle. Lena slammed into his back as he stopped just inside the entry.

Teal stood at the dining table. Her skin glistened white, and her breaths were ragged pants. On the table was the envelope from Sheriff Cabot. Teal's hands shook as she turned the eight-by-ten photograph so Lena could see it. But Lena didn't have to see it to know it was the blowup of the man's driver's license, the man whose arm Lena had torn off with the Caterpillar bucket, the man whose legs had been found in Eve Crescent's destroyed sedan.

Teal's eyes were wide, wet, questioning, and her voice cracked when she said, "Why do you have a picture of Camo Guy? How did you know he was the one who saved me from Fred?"

Alex called the sheriff's department from AJ's house phone. Sheriff Cabot was in Santa Barbara overnight for a meeting, but would return first thing in the morning. After doing the dance around if anyone else could help him, and no they couldn't, the dispatcher promised the sheriff would contact them tomorrow as soon as possible.

Alex scrounged in the pantry and came up with some saltines to settle Teal's stomach, and AJ got a small fire going in the stove. It wasn't cold, but

Teal was shaking like a leaf after they'd told her that the photograph was of Thomas Delbert Frost, a man who'd been buried nearby. Since Teal had hidden after arriving, she hadn't even known about the body.

It hit all three of them when all the facts came together. Thomas Delbert Frost, the outdoorsman missing from his job in San Bernardino, was known to Teal as Delta Force, aka Camo Guy, her Southern California savior.

Although rattled, Teal asked a lot of questions, so AJ sat with her and explained about the body, how the legs had been found in a woman's car in Santa Monica, how that woman worked in the District Attorney's office where AJ's husband had worked.

Alex listened intently as AJ told Teal about the attack that killed Bobby.

"Why didn't you tell me about Bobby before?" Teal asked. "I had no idea."

AJ sagged against the couch. But before Alex could go to her, Teal wrapped her arms around her, laying her head on AJ's shoulder.

He stood nearby, an observer of this instant when the younger comforted the older, where moments before it had been the other way around. But he didn't feel like an outsider. In the same way Teal had become an integral part of AJ's world, AJ had become part of his. Teal, too. Necessary parts he was not letting go.

The need to protect these two rose strong. Bringing in the authorities would change things, but he would do everything in his power to keep these two women safe and in his life.

From now on, he wasn't going anywhere without his gun.

42

Storm Lake didn't have an abundance of homes for sale, especially during the summer season. And buying would take time and leave a paperwork trail he couldn't have, false ID or not.

It wasn't hard for a man in his position to get a list of properties seized in drug raids, and he'd found one such place at Storm Lake, a single-story ranch east on Gift Road, near where it dead-ended. Close to Lena McKinley.

As he began driving out the winding lane, a sensation of rightness settled on his shoulders, and his spirits rose. Fifteen minutes later, he turned left into the nearly hidden driveway, a teetering mailbox the sole indication of his destination. Tall grass licked the sides and underbelly of his car as he bounced down two pocked ruts.

He reached a widened parking area and killed the engine. The only curb appeal was a few flowering weeds. The structure looked to have been built in the 1960s, utilizing plywood siding, now buckled from weather. The little remaining paint could be called dirty beige, and that would be a compliment. The house hadn't been occupied for over a year.

He exited the car and walked around the house, cataloging broken windows, warped doors, and...well, those were the *best* parts. But the house didn't matter; he had the money to refurbish it if he stayed that long. It was the outbuilding on the rear of the property that had caught his attention in the database description.

Approximately fifty yards across what might have once been a lawn, rose a much newer and far sturdier structure. A barn. He stomped a path through the grass, and pulled open one of the bay doors. Two high skylights bathed the interior in soft light, revealing large beams crisscrossing the upper area. Equally massive pillars ran to the finished concrete floor. At the back of the large space, sunlight illuminated descending stairs.

He took them down and passed through a wide doorway into a lower room that ran the length and width of the barn footprint above. There was just enough light coming from above to reveal this was no ordinary basement, but instead a massive space. Electrical cables ran across the twelve-foot-high ceiling, terminating in bare wires where lights had been removed. Inhaling, he detected the distinct reek of marijuana plants. This had been an underground greenhouse. He'd seen the pictures, but they hadn't done it justice.

It was perfect, and the impetus for his decision. It was time for change, a new direction. He knew a man who, for a reasonable fee, could alter this property's scheduled disposal date. He wouldn't need it for long. A dozen weeks, perhaps up to a year. It all depended how long his guest—or guests— lasted.

He'd found his perfect place. And he couldn't wait to fill it with his first occupant.

Walking back out into the sunlight, he was pleased to find he had a cellular signal. He made the call to make the property his.

43

It was after one o'clock, and Lena was in the barn rewiring a light fixture for the rec room when Stone stuck his head in the door and said, "Sheriff's here."

They gathered in the shade in front of Stone's Airstream. He moved the barbecue aside and arranged the chairs and milk crates in a circle. Teal sat between Lena and Stone, facing Sheriff Derrek Cabot for the first time. The girl was practically vibrating with nerves, and took Lena's hand in a vise-like grip.

"Well, young lady," the sheriff began, "I understand you have some information for me?" To the lawman's credit, he'd left his trooper hat in the car, making him a little less intimidating, an effort to put Teal at ease.

For the next ten minutes, Teal told her story: how she'd been abducted and caged in a basement by a man she named Fred; how he'd shocked, cut, and tattooed her; how she'd escaped into a stormy night; and how she'd been rescued by Camo Guy. And then, when she attempted to hike out on her own, how he saved her life a second time.

"I called him Camo Guy, but he told me his name was Delta Force. Sounded made up to me."

The sheriff suddenly sat forward on his chair, and his eyes narrowed.

Teal pulled out the sheriff's own photo of Delbert Thomas Frost. "This man is Camo Guy… Delta Force. He's the one who rescued me from Fred."

The sheriff nodded.

"Seems like you already knew some of that," Stone said, watching Cabot.

Nodding again, the sheriff said, "I got word back yesterday from the DEA on that log file from Frost's computer we sent over. All his entries matched tips given by an informant who called himself Delta Force. Evidently, he spent time scouring the hills for illegal drug activity. Pot farms, smuggling camps, and the like. His information resulted in some of the largest busts in the L.A. basin."

"So Frost wasn't hiking the Pacific Crest Trail on the weekends," Lena said.

"Evidently not," Cabot agreed. "So now that we've identified Frost as a DEA informant, it sorta makes sense that someone found him out. Although I'm still not sure why they buried half..." The sheriff stopped, looking from Lena to Stone, then to Teal.

"She knows," Stone stated, glancing at Teal.

"Well," Cabot said, "it is a mystery why half of him was found here, and the other half in L.A. If drug runners caught him, why would they go to all that trouble?"

That, indeed, was the question Lena had wrestled with all morning while they waited for the sheriff. Lena had been in L.A., and was now in Storm Lake. Same for Teal. Frost had been in both—sort of. And in a weird way, Frost/Force/Camo Guy was a link between Lena and Teal before the girl arrived at the lake. The whole thing made her brain hurt.

"I thought I found someplace safe," Teal said, and all eyes returned to her. "Here at Storm Lake, I mean. But a few days ago, I saw Fred in Deer Cove."

If Lena thought the sheriff was interested in Teal's revelation about Frost/Force, it was nothing compared to his reaction now.

"You mean you saw the man who abducted you? Here in Deer Cove?"

"Well, not exactly *saw*," Teal backpedaled. She explained about the ski mask in the basement, and how she only saw his shoes and heard his voice in Deer Cove."

"But you're sure it was the same man?"

Teal nodded.

"And where did you see, or rather *hear*, this man?"

"At the Deer Cove Mercantile.

Cabot's eyes widened and his fingers twitched.

"What?" Stone demanded.

Lena, too, expected Teal's story would come under serious scrutiny, if not downright disbelief since she only heard the man's voice. But the sheriff wasn't asking more questions.

Cabot's eyes flicked from Teal to Stone, back and forth, then he sat forward. Even without the flat-brimmed hat, he was every bit the lawman again.

"I intended to be here at your place earlier this morning—would have been if I hadn't received an emergency call." His eyes landed on Teal when he said, "The call was about a missing girl. She's sixteen years old, and she never came home after a party last night. She works at the Deer Cove Mercantile, and her name is Amber Michaels."

Stone said he would make some phone calls, so Lena sat beside Teal in their cabin at the dining room table as the teenager filled in the details of her story for the sheriff. Over and over he probed: What date had she been kidnapped? How long was she held? What was the restaurant name on the pizza box? Could she hear any background noises from the basement? What did the trees in the yard look like when she escaped?

Then he started on Fred: Was his voice high or low, soft or gruff; did he sound educated or lower class; did he have an accent or unusual word pronunciation; if she had to pick an actor who sounded like him, who would that be?

Teal told him the police in L.A. had the artist's sketch she'd done. He said he'd request it immediately, then asked her to draw another one.

When Lena's phone rang, she stepped out onto the porch to answer. It was an automated call from the county building department, confirming that the building inspector would be coming by tomorrow afternoon, sometime between 3:00 and 5:00. She'd only filed the building permit for the barn electrical through their online system this morning and requested an inspection appointment. Since tomorrow was Friday, she'd figured it would be next week before an inspector came out.

She didn't want to cancel it—some building inspectors were notoriously picky if they felt dissed—but the sheriff had been insistent she meet with Social Services tomorrow. Maybe Stone could be here for the inspection. He'd rebuilt his truck, so he had plenty of mechanical ability. If there were questions about the barn permit, she'd have to deal with them later, but if the inspector signed off on it, she could finish installing the lights and plugs.

Lena hoped the Girl Scouts and Sierra Club didn't have a say on wiring the barn.

———

While Teal drew her sketch, the sheriff joined Lena on the porch. Teal had told him Lena was not her aunt or any other relation. He was insistent Teal go into the county social services system.

"It's the law, Mrs. Blaylock. She's a minor."

Sound carried easily across the grounds, and Lena didn't want her renters hearing about her personal issues...especially with the sheriff. She led him down past the cabins toward the boat launch area where they could talk privately.

Derrek Cabot was a by-the-book man, tough as nails, black and white. She'd practically grown up around rough-talking men who swung hammers for a living, and the temptation was to face him head-on. But she feared that wouldn't work with his law and justice mindset.

"Sheriff, listen to me for a moment. Please."

They stopped in the shade of an ancient oak, and Cabot hooked his thumbs in his equipment belt, waiting.

"This girl never knew her father. She was traumatized at nine when her mother was arrested and put in prison, then she was tossed around an overcrowded foster care system that resulted in her nearly being raped. After running away from that and living on the streets, she was kidnapped by a sick maniac who tortured her for months, and who would have killed her if she hadn't escaped and nearly died of exposure. Then, after being dumped back into the foster care system again, she ran… again.

"By some miracle of God, she found her way here. You heard her: someplace safe. If you put her in another foster home, she'll run again, because she has no reason to trust the system. She picked *this* as her home, and she picked me. Now I'm picking her. And I'll do whatever it takes to keep her."

Lena waited for his response, determined in a way she'd never been. The letter of the law might motivate him, but she was driven by her heart. The sheriff stared back under thick brows, eyes narrowed, assessing. Then he turned his gaze across the lake.

"He could be watching right now. You realize that, don't you? All it takes is a pair of binoculars and he could be observing everything you and that young girl do."

"She saw *him*, Sheriff. *He* didn't see *her*. He doesn't know she's here." Even with that fact, the hairs of her neck stood on end at the thought of someone spying on them.

"She's a material witness, both to what happened to her as well as what might have happened to Amber Michaels."

The fact that he'd stopped insisting, and was now throwing out rational arguments didn't escape Lena.

"I want her here, Sheriff Cabot, with me. You know Alex Stone is a trained professional—"

"Who was assigned to protect you from a completely *different* threat, Mrs. Blaylock. Are you willing to expose this girl to danger from that front, too?"

It was risky to bring Stone's job into the argument, but it wasn't a secret. "I agree it's not ideal. But Stone knows the area, as well as every aspect of the situation. And he carries a gun. Who better to protect us?"

Cabot tapped his index finger on his lips for a long minute. Then he turned stiffly to her. "You'll need to come into the county offices and fill out an application as an emergency foster care provider. I'll add a letter stating this needs to go through posthaste." The slightest smile graced his mouth. "I carry a little weight with them."

Lena sighed. She would have collapsed onto a log if there'd been one handy. "Do I need to bake more brownies?" To her satisfaction, that produced a much larger smile as they began walking back.

"It's getting late today, but I'll call and tell them you're coming in tomorrow."

"Tomorrow? But—"

"*Tomorrow*, Mrs. Blaylock. You're harboring a runaway minor. And now that I know about it, that forces me to act. We need to get this all legal immediately. It's Friday, but I'll make sure they squeeze you in. My letter will be waiting. Don't say a word about the girl; I'd rather no one know of her presence. As far as they will know, you're doing the application for a future placement. Put a desired start date of a couple months out. We'll make it all official later."

Cabot called the county offices, talked for a minute, then turned to Lena. "Three o'clock. I trust that works for you?"

She'd make it work. All of it.

Her phone rang when they reached the cabin. The sheriff went inside to check on Teal's drawing while she took the call.

"Lena."

"Hi, Chet," she said, recognizing his voice.

"I'll be there tomorrow, sometime in the afternoon, probably."

He must have heard her sigh at that.

"I know I've said that before, but I promise. It's important I get those files."

But it wasn't that. It seemed everything was piling on Friday afternoon. She could have express mailed the files to him days ago if they were so crucial. "I have to be in Mission Peak tomorrow afternoon. Would it be easier if I met you there?"

"So you'll be home all morning?" Chet didn't wait for an answer. "No, my schedule is a little fluid. Not quite sure of the time. Maybe I can make it earlier. It would be better if I come to you. If you're not there, I'll wait. I'll be there. Don't worry."

"Can't you just tell me what's going on?" With all the other things happening, Chet might know something that could help.

"Well, I don't know about yours, but I know *my* cell phone isn't secure. I'd really rather meet in person."

Lena almost dropped her cell when she remembered it was being monitored—by someone. "Of course. Sorry. I wasn't thinking."

Chet ended the call, slightly less abruptly than the previous times. Maybe there was hope he'd actually show this time. She could use all the friends and help she could get.

44

"Now, if I'm not back before the building inspector gets here—"

"I've got it, AJ," Teal said. "Show him the barn wiring, and give him this inspection card to sign..." the girl waved the computer printout, "...*after* I've plied him with chocolate chip cookies." AJ's brows tightened, as if she thought Teal was serious. She laughed, and gently propelled AJ toward the front door. "Go."

"Oh, and if Chet Marquette happens to get here today, he already knows I'm in Mission Peak. Just have him wait for me." Lena crossed the porch and descended the stairs. "And be sure to let Stone know where you are at all times."

"Yes, Mother," Teal said, dropping into one of the porch chairs and picking up her sketching tools from the table. She flipped the pad open to a new page, but lowered it when she realized the Jeep hadn't started.

AJ was frozen at the front fender, arms limp at her sides, staring up at Teal. Teal stood, unsure what to do. But then AJ smiled beautifully and climbed into the Jeep. It disappeared over the hill fifteen seconds later.

Except for her own mother, Teal had never called anyone Mom before—never any of the foster moms, even though that's what they suggested whenever she arrived at a new home. And although she'd meant this one as a joke because of the way AJ was fussing over her, it clearly hadn't come across that way. It wasn't the first time Teal wondered what it would be like to have AJ as her mom.

In bold strokes, she began outlining a view of Desperation Falls from below the rock field looking up. Three people took shape: a woman, a man, and a teenage girl. The more distinct the details became, the more the woman resembled AJ, the man, Stone, and the girl, herself. Then she added in one final detail that changed the entire meaning of the picture.

Teal grinned, imagining AJ's reaction to this. After coloring in the cascading water, ferns, and butterflies, she took it into AJ's bedroom and thumbtacked it to the wall. It would be too embarrassing if Alex saw it.

Now it was time to get her chores done around the property before Quin came.

Lena's knee bounced against the bottom of the table, and the woman opposite, Tabitha Crane, stopped shuffling paperwork long enough to glare at her.

"Are you nervous about something, Mrs. Blaylock?" the woman asked. "Anything I should know about?"

Yeah...like how about getting this over with so I can get back to the kid I don't officially have living with me and make sure she's safe?

"Sorry," Lena said, and stilled her dancing knee. "Just anxious to get going on some... things." She wondered how owning a gun and going to shooting lessons might affect her chances at being accepted? Since she didn't yet own said gun, it wasn't on her application. However, everything she'd done in her entire life certainly was. She'd filled out paperwork for what seemed like hours, and that was after waiting for nearly an hour for Tabitha to return from an appointment that overlapped Lena's.

"Well," the woman said, clearly relishing every ounce of authority she thought her job imparted, "I wouldn't want to keep you from things that are more *important.*"

It was all Lena could do to keep from sighing. Teal would have rolled her eyes. That brought a smile, and she hoped the woman didn't take offense at that. Tabitha Crane seemed to take issue with every *N/A* on the pages of information, such as *Spouse's Name.* When Lena had explained that he'd died, Tabitha wanted to know how. And wouldn't you know being murdered raised even more questions?

"You do have Sheriff Cabot's letter there, don't you?" Lena asked for the third time in an hour.

Tabitha frowned more than the last time Lena mentioned it. "I'll remind you again, Mrs. Blaylock, it's *my* job to qualify applicants, not the sheriff's." She shuffled the dozens of forms again, searching for discrepancies. If none could be found, Lena wondered if the woman might draw in a few blanks of her own.

"I still have a few questions about your financial statements, your *many* former jobs in the construction industry, and your... television career," Tabitha said, pulling out a stapled sheaf and flipping it open. She'd already made it abundantly clear that acting of any kind was not on her approved list of vocations.

Lena checked her watch. It was already past three o'clock. The building inspector was probably there now, and Chet would be arriving shortly bringing some kind of news. Hopefully.

A *ding* sounded in her purse. Tabitha frowned, but Lena recognized the hacker's text tone and retrieved the cell anyway. Ever since leaving Teal this morning, she'd had an uneasy feeling things were coming to a head—more so than even the events of recent days. But Stone was with her, and Quin was coming by later. And if Chet actually showed this time, he'd be there, too.

L. – Eve slightly improved. Still unconscious. Found out more: State Attorney General investigating connections between Lobos Negros cartel and corrupt high level person(s) in L.A. govt. Don't know who yet. Found your husband's name in some AG docs—was he working with them? Latest status report yesterday said arrest imminent. Searching for the name now. Should be on a warrant somewhere. Be careful. – V

How could she be careful if she was stuck in bureaucratic quagmire when she should be home protecting Teal?

"Am I keeping you from something, Mrs. Blaylock?" Tabitha did nothing to disguise her patronizing tone.

Lena rose to her feet. "Actually, you are." She reached across the table and took the form Tabitha held. Then Lena swept all the paperwork into a pile and tucked it under her arm.

"Wait," Tabitha shoved her chair back and got up as Lena turned toward the office doorway, "you can't take those forms. They're county property."

"Well, perhaps I can fill in the gaps for you and bring them back another time?" Without waiting for a reply, Lena headed out the door and down the asphalt-tiled hall lined with hospital-green walls. As she skipped down the building's concrete steps, she crammed the papers into her undersized purse. "If I don't use them for kindling first."

Five minutes later, Lena passed the Mission Peak city limit sign and urged the Jeep faster toward home. Every nerve in her body screamed that something was about to happen. Maybe it was just that everything had piled onto today, but she needed to be there...with Teal.

As she approached the turnoff from Highway 1 to Storm Lake, the pre-paid phone *dinged* again. She pulled off at the junction and parked on the shoulder. A wall of thick fog was rolling in from the ocean, dark and menacing, blanketing the hills in the direction of the lake as she searched her purse for the phone. It was buried under the ream of county paperwork.

When she got it out, she saw another text message from the hacker.

L. – Found the warrant. It's for the arrest of Eve's boss, Chester A. Marquette. For taking bribes from the Lobos Negros cartel, for the murder of Bobby Blaylock, and attempted murder of Eve. They're serving it on him at his home in Altadena right now. I'll let you know when I hear they've got him in custody. Be safe! – V

Chet! It was Chet all along? *He'd* been the one who'd killed Bobby? Lena's head spun with understanding and the ramifications. He'd been the one Eve said Lena could trust. She'd sent him the file, one of the files Bobby had hidden. It must have contained information about the investigation with the attorney general's office...of Chet.

The cops, or whoever served the warrant, wouldn't find Chet in Altadena, because he was right here. He might already be at the cabins. Where Teal was.

Lena slammed the shifter into drive, screeched around the corner onto the road to the lake, and floored it. She tried to get her regular phone out to call Stone, but dropped it under the seat when she corrected a swerve over the centerline.

As she fished around for the phone, flashing lights filled her rearview mirror, and a second later she heard the siren. But instead of stopping, she mashed the accelerator into the carpet.

45

"Hey, Kris," Alex answered, recognizing his sister's mobile number. "Are you getting close?"

He'd been cleaning the ash buildup out of the Weber in anticipation of another meal together tonight, and used one hand to roll the grill back into its place by the trailer.

"Hi, bro," she sighed, her travel fatigue slipping through the phone connection. "I'm in Flume. Stupid rental car is spewing gallons of pretty green coolant all over the parking lot. And since when did the restaurant here turn into a biker bar?" He heard the distinctive sound of a Harley motorcycle firing up in the background.

"Been there about four years, I understand. Good chicken wings."

"Hmm. Tempting as that is, there are some creepy dudes milling around. Think you could come down and pick me up?"

"I'm sure one of the guys would be more than willing to give you a ride up here," Alex said. "When's the last time you straddled a Harley?"

"Never, and not going to happen."

Alex checked his watch. AJ should have been back two hours ago. How long did it take to fill out a couple of forms? And, before leaving, she'd insisted on his being here to keep an eye on Teal. He was in complete agreement with that; the girl should not be alone right now. Neither should AJ, for that matter, but she'd run off to Mission Peak by herself.

"Alex, you still there?"

"Yeah. Just thinking how I'm going to work this out."

"Well think faster. I swear Walter White just walked out of the restaurant."

He laughed. Kris loved *Breaking Bad*. "Isn't that show finished?" He was out of touch with television, but he remembered hearing something about a final episode.

"Yeah, but now I know where all the characters retired: Flume."

The sound of an outboard motor drew Alex's attention. Quin's boat slowed as it approached AJ's dock.

"Okay, Kris. Hang tight. I'll be down in a few." His sister mumbled something noncommittal.

Alex jumped into his truck, and intercepted Quin as the boy walked uphill. He explained his sister's car trouble and need for a ride. "I'll be back quick as I can," he said, wondering how much the boy knew. "And Quin, stay with Teal all the time, okay?"

"I understand—completely" Quin said, answering Stone's unspoken question. "I'm free for the rest of the day, so we'll hang out until you get back."

Alex gunned the engine all the way to Flume, glad it was only about fifteen minutes away. He kept an eye out for AJ's Jeep on the road, but didn't see her. As soon as he picked up Kris, he'd call AJ and find out where she was…and make sure *she* was safe.

It frustrated him he couldn't be with both women at the same time, but Kris would help solve that problem.

Flume was strategically situated at the only entrance road leading to Storm Lake. A century earlier, it had been the beginning point for a log-carrying water flume that ran thirty twisting miles down the hill and terminated in Perilous Cove. There, the raw timber from the lake's logging camps was processed at a sawmill before being loaded onto wagons or steamships to feed early California's insatiable growth.

In grammar school, Alex was fascinated by stories and pictures of the loggers riding flume boats down the trough as a fast way to get to Perilous Cove's many saloons. Sections of the old flume structure were still visible along the road between the lake and the cove, but most of it had been torn down after the trees ran out and the logging industry moved on.

For some reason, even though there was a boat launch at Flume, the settlement never grew beyond a few businesses and fifty or so homes, but it looked positively bustling today as Alex made the final turn on East Lake Road and descended toward town.

The parking lot of The Chain Gang was filled with dozens of motorcycles and pickups. That wasn't too unusual for a late Friday afternoon, but the sheriff's vehicle with all its lights flashing was. A Highway Patrol cruiser was parked nearby. Alex nosed the Chevy into the side of the road as close as he could, then sprinted past the front of the building.

A mob of leather-clad men and women were circled around the activity, quietly watching. Alex pushed his way through the bodies, some scowling at him, but moving aside when they saw his bulk and scarred face. Except for lack of leather, he fit right in. At the front of the group, he surveyed the scene...and grinned.

Kris Stone leaned casually against the deputy's SUV, chatting with the deputy and patrolman as if she had not a care in the world. The young lawmen—obviously somewhat in awe of the woman before them—paid sparse attention to the two handcuffed men stretched out at her feet like big game trophies. One of the men on the ground had a broken nose, and the lower half of his face was covered in crusted blood.

Dressed in green camouflage shorts and a snug white tee that did nothing to hide her toned body, Kris looked as if she was about to prop a shoe on one of the downed men and have a trophy picture taken. Her deep red hair with black highlights—or was it black with red highlights?—transformed her from innocent to dangerous. Evidently, the two guys on the ground hadn't noticed.

Alex strode toward Kris. The deputy put his hand on the butt of his gun, but Kris leaped forward and hugged Alex.

"'Bout time you got here. Thought I was going to have to take on the whole place by myself."

"Five minutes and you're already in trouble?"

The corner of her mouth lifted. "Like old times, huh?"

"You okay?" She was a grown woman, but he still worried about her, especially in her role at an elite security company. Keeping highly visible people safe wasn't easy when someone wanted them dead.

"Yeah, just getting a little exercise," she said, rubbing her reddened knuckles. "These guys wanted to give me a hand, if you know what I mean."

The men were glaring up at his sister when another car pulled up. Sheriff Derrek Cabot climbed out, eying the spectators while he fitted his trooper hat. After giving all parties the once-over, he approached Alex and Kris.

"Heard we had a little mishap here," Cabot said to Alex.

Alex introduced his sister, and she explained the altercation. The two men had been drinking—no surprise there—and had decided to assist the damsel in distress by offering a little *hands-on* help. Kris put them in their place… on the ground. The handcuffs belonged to the patrolman and deputy, but Alex knew Kris never traveled without her own.

The deputy wrestled the two men to their feet, and Kris dusted off their shirts. "No hard feelings, boys." She declined to press charges. The sheriff, however, was not so forgiving, and arrested the men for public intoxication.

"Ms. Stone, I apologize for—" but he was cut off by his radio with an emergency message. He moved several feet away to take the call, but Alex heard the name "Blaylock," and he walked closer as Cabot finished the call.

"What's going on, Sheriff?" Alex demanded.

"That was one of my deputies. He pulled Mrs. Blaylock over a few miles south of here for going almost ninety miles per hour. She convinced him it was a matter of life or death, so he's bringing her here. Should arrive in a couple of minutes."

Sure enough, Alex heard a siren's wail drawing closer as dark clouds obscured the sun and descended on the lake.

Teal had finished cleaning the one empty rental cabin, and now used a stiff rake to level the path alongside the barn to where the rec room door would be. Tomorrow, Colby was bringing pavers and pea gravel—whatever that was—to build the walkway, but Teal wanted to mark the area to make sure he left plenty of room between the path and barn wall for a flowerbed. That would really spruce up the old building.

Quin was in the new rec room, assembling a metal shelf unit AJ had found in a box when clearing stuff out.

She stopped and drained half her water bottle. Breaking the ground's hard surface was hot work, and she was thankful the dense clouds had come in to block the late afternoon sun. The temperature had dropped several degrees.

Popping gravel alerted her to a car, and she walked down to the front of the cabin to see who it was. A silver SUV stopped, and a man got out. He was wearing tan slacks, a light-green polo shirt, and sunglasses. He didn't look like a fisherman, so it was either the inspector or Lena's friend, Chet.

"Are you the building inspector?" Teal asked, smiling as she came around the front of the car. The man's eyes widened, and he backed up a step. It was such a strange reaction that she checked her clothes to make sure she hadn't accidentally worn a short-sleeved shirt exposing her scars.

Then the man recovered, nodded, and pointed to his throat and whispered, "Lost my voice."

Teal shuddered at the sound, but attributed it to the rapidly cooling air. Still, there was something about the way he tilted his head when he spoke.

"I'll... show you to the barn," she said, backing away so she could keep her eyes on him. He didn't look familiar, but he seemed a little off or something.

He held up one finger. "Let me get my stuff." From the backseat, he retrieved a black tool bag no bigger than a football.

46

He couldn't believe his luck! This was the one who'd gotten away, and she was walking not eight feet ahead of him, heading toward an old barn. He looked around the compound of cabins and single travel trailer, but didn't see any cars or trucks. If they were alone…

Lena was the one he'd come for—her and the files. But she could wait a day or two. Right in front of him was a loose end he couldn't afford not to tie up. He almost laughed aloud at that: tie up. Yes, this was too good!

The girl stopped at the entry to the barn's double doors, which were open wide and blocked with round stones. He stepped within a foot of her.

"The wiring to the barn was done a long time ago. We're just adding some lights and outlets on two new circuits." The interior was dark, but she pointed to a sub-panel box inside the right-hand door.

"You know a lot about electricity," he said in his normal voice. "I hope there's a good ground. It's important to have a good ground."

The girl's eyes nearly popped out of her head, and she turned and ran into the building's interior.

47

The hard plastic seat in the back of the deputy's car provided little comfort, and Lena banged against the door again as he made another high-speed corner. Thankfully, she wasn't in handcuffs and could brace herself. It had been a wild ride for the last ten minutes, but she wished he'd go even faster.

A second after she spotted the sign for East and West Lake roads ahead, the deputy braked hard and cranked the steering wheel left into a parking lot. More cars with flashing lights were there. Then she spotted Sheriff Cabot talking with a strikingly beautiful woman...and Stone. What was he doing here? He should be with Teal. The threesome turned toward the car, and she nearly pounded on the glass before the deputy got the rear door open and let her out.

"Stone!" Lena ran to him and grabbed his arms. "It's Chet!"

"What are you talking about?" Stone asked.

Lena whirled on the deputy who'd taken her into custody for speeding. "I need my purse. Now!"

"Better get it for her, Larry," Sheriff Cabot said, and the deputy hurried to the front seat of the patrol car and returned with her purse.

Lena didn't take time to dig for the phone; she just dumped the bag's contents on the blacktop and snatched the pre-paid cell from the pile. "Look at this," she said, turning it on. "It's another message from the hacker."

Stone read it, then held the mobile for the sheriff to see.

"Chet's the killer, Sheriff," Lena explained, "but he's not in L.A. where they're serving the warrant, he's right here. He could already be at the cabins. Stone, where's Teal?"

"She's at the cabins with Quin. Kris's car broke down. I told him I'd pick her up and be right back."

"We have to get there right now!"

It took a minute to sort everything. The woman, who Lena figured out was Stone's sister, Kris, popped the trunk of a car and pulled out a duffle bag, then she, Stone, and Lena piled into Sheriff Cabot's SUV and squealed out of the parking lot, pursued by the other sheriff's car and the Highway Patrol vehicle.

God, please let Teal be safe. Please.

She couldn't breathe. That voice. Promises of "games" not yet played. Instruction about electricity and the need for a good ground conductor. Her eyes shot to the man's upper lip. There, just above the left corner, the scar she'd come to know so well. How could she have missed it?

The memory of The Table's odor froze her for a split second, overriding her senses with its decay, fear, and death. Her skin twitched at the feel of his icy-hot craft blade as it cut curves and lines into her flesh, blood running onto the stained surface beneath her.

But she wasn't alone this time, and she wasn't letting him take her again. Teal turned and ran, weaving through the equipment on the barn's main floor. She crashed through the door to the rec room and slammed it behind her, twisting the cheap brass lock button. It felt flimsy, *was* flimsy, made to provide privacy in a bathroom, not protect from a psychotic maniac.

"What...?" Quin said, rising from a pile of half-built shelving and braces.

"It's him. Fred. We have to get away right now!" Her lungs hurt like she'd run a mile, and she couldn't get enough air.

The doorknob rattled, and the panel bowed inward under his weight.

"Go!" Quin said. He pushed the shelf unit in front of the door, then shoved her toward the open rear window...the same one she'd used dozens of times to get in and out of the barn.

Fred crashed into the door again, rattling the metal shelves, and then hit it again and again. It wouldn't hold. He'd hurt Quin. "Come with me," she pleaded.

He shook his head, spreading his legs and bracing his hands against the door. "Hide at the falls. I'll hold him. Trust me, Teal. Go now!"

With one last look at the boy she loved, Teal dove through the window and rolled onto the ground. In half a second she was on her feet running. She tried not to think about the huge crash that sounded through the window behind her.

48

The three vehicles slid to a stop beside a silver SUV that was parked in front of AJ's cabin. The deputy radioed in the license plate number as Alex and the sheriff mounted the stairs and quickly checked the house. Empty.

"The barn!" AJ shouted from the yard.

She was thirty yards ahead of them. Alex shouted for her to stop, but she disappeared into the black interior. Summer storm clouds had come in low and thick, casting everything into shadow. He pulled his gun as he stepped into the space, searching behind the ATV, trailers, workbench...anywhere a threat might hide. Cabot was right beside him. But where was AJ?

"Help!" Her voice came from the half-open doorway she'd installed as access to the recreation room.

Alex leaped over the ATV and elbowed the splintered door wider. Metal scraped on the concrete. In the waning light from the window, he found AJ bent over a body. *Teal!* The blood drained from Alex as he knelt. But it wasn't Teal. AJ pulled Quin onto her lap and stroked his hair. Alex checked the boy's neck and found a strong pulse.

"He's unconscious," AJ said. "And he's got a huge bump on his head."

In the background, Alex heard the sheriff radio for an ambulance, or have Doc Arnold paged if that would be faster. But even as the tiny speaker crackled a confirmation, Quin's eyes fluttered open.

AJ brushed long hair from the boy's forehead. "Sheriff, can you get the wire cutters from my toolbox? It's on the workbench in the main room."

Alex hadn't noticed that Quin's hands and feet were bound with wire ties, then linked hands to feet. If Chet had done this, he hadn't wanted Quin coming after him. Cabot returned with the cutters and quickly freed the boy.

"Quin? Can you hear me?" AJ said, brushing his forehead.

Quin stirred, then abruptly turned sideways and retched. Alex helped hold him until he fell back against AJ.

"A man," Quin mumbled, licking his lips. "Hit me with something."

"We know," Alex said. "Where's Teal?"

Kris brought a rolled up jacket and helped Alex position Quin's head on it. He winced as they moved him, but he mumbled something.

Alex leaned over AJ, but barely heard the boy's weak response. "He was after her."

"Why would Chet be after Teal?" AJ asked.

"Fred. She said he was Fred."

Lena fell back on her rear, blood roaring in her ears as her mind struggled to process Quin's statement. She turned to Stone. "My God! Chet is *Fred*? The one who cut Teal?" He'd fooled everyone at the DA's office about his connection to the cartel, but this… He'd been the one to kidnap Teal.

"Told her to run." Quin's eyes were closed, his words slurred.

"Where, Quin?" Stone said? "Where did she go?"

"Falls." His head lolled sideways.

"Desperation Falls?" the sheriff asked, but Quin was unconscious.

Lena got to her feet. "She loves that place. If she got a head start, she knows where to hide."

"His car is still here, so he's on foot." Stone said. "Sheriff, are you with me?"

"You'll have to lead the way," Cabot said. "Haven't been up to those falls in a lot of years."

"I haven't either," Stone admitted. "Not since I was a kid."

Lena headed toward the door. "I know the way."

"No, AJ, you're not going," Stone said. "It's too dangerous. He's probably armed."

"Then give me a gun," Lena demanded.

"No way. You don't know how to shoot."

"I'll learn," she growled, wishing she'd gotten together with Mandy when they'd had the chance.

Sheriff Cabot was as adamant as Stone about her not going, and they decided she should wait for the paramedics.

They decided.

Lena seethed with a combination of anger and fear. Teal was running from a madman, and Lena knew the territory around the falls, yet here she was, relegated to the sidelines.

Stone's sister came into the barn, strapping a belt and holstered gun around her hips as she walked. "Let's go."

Lena watched the three quick-walk across the yard, heading for the trail that led to Desperation Falls. She went back to the rec room. Quin was awake again and talking to the deputy. When Quin spotted Lena, he rose up on his elbows. The slight movement turned his face white.

"AJ, please make sure Teal is safe." He sank back against the makeshift pillow, panting.

Lena gave a noncommittal nod to the deputy, then strode out of the rec room, looking around the barn for a weapon. Her Paslode framing nailer lay on the workbench, Bobby's last gift to her before Chet had stolen him away. It had a full clip of nails, a new fuel cartridge, and a charged battery. She picked it up and hefted its weight. It wasn't a 9 millimeter like Stone's, but it was all she had.

49

Lena hurried along the shortcut that twisted up and over the scrub-brush-choked hill behind the barn. The stiff branches ripped her clothes and skin, but this route cut off almost two hundred yards when compared to the direction the others had taken. Finally, she reached the main trail, and began running along the ascending footpath that provided peekaboo views of the stream. The bleeding scrapes reminded her of what Fred—Chet—had done to Teal, and she used the minor pain to push faster.

She still couldn't believe Chet was also Teal's Fred, but she trusted the girl. If she said they were one man, then they were. But how could a respected district attorney, a man tasked by his career to prosecute criminals who preyed on the innocent, be guilty of far worse crimes than those he usually tried in court?

Her breaths came faster, and her thighs began burning as she ran. All those eighteen-hour days kept her in good shape, but running used a whole new set of muscles, which issued silent protests.

The others were ahead of her somewhere, as were Chet and Teal. The sheriff was older than Stone and his sister, plus the lawman had the disadvantage of carrying his heavy equipment belt. But Lena had the nailer, and even though the manual said the Paslode weighed less than eight pounds, it was beginning to feel like a twenty-pound sack of potatoes. The trail angled downward for a stretch and she almost sighed in relief.

The last time she'd been to Desperation Falls was two months after she'd moved in. It had been sunny, but not too hot, and she needed a break from the unending work. She'd packed a bologna sandwich, chips, cookies, and water into her daypack and set out. Intending to stay only long enough to eat, the falls proved so enchanting that she spent the whole afternoon exploring several trails that wound around each side of the cliffs, both above and below the cascading water. There were a few places where unofficial paths led to treacherous overlooks. Where would Teal hide?

They should have had a couple of hours of daylight left, but black clouds hugged the treetops, and moist appendages hung down and brushed her skin like wet ghost hands.

A wind suddenly picked up, scattering leaves down the path in front of her, as if pointing the way.

God, help us find her!

Teal talked so much about the falls and drew endless pictures, but Lena couldn't remember what she'd said about favorite spots. She should have listened more closely. *Please.*

About fifty yards below the main pool, where the path forked and led around either side of the falls, Lena caught the others. She stumbled to a stop, dropped the nail gun to the dirt, and joined the others in sucking lungfuls of misty air. Cabot was red in the face.

Kris raised a brow at Stone. He shook his head and faced Lena.

"You can't—"

"We'll pair up," Kris said, cutting off her brother. "Where do we go?" she asked Lena.

The water hitting the deep pool swallowed all other sound—except the wind. Its increasing power bent the oaks, and foggy tendrils snaked along the ground, sweeping up the rock-strewn narrow outlet and across the main pool. She could barely make out the spot where the falling water struck the surface. Teal always drew butterflies in her pictures, but there were no butterflies today.

"The path splits here," Lena said. "The left side is the main trail up to the brink overlook. The right side," she gestured across the stream with her arm, "winds around and is longer."

"Which is easier to climb?" Stone asked.

"Right side," Lena panted. "It has switchbacks."

"I don't think Teal would pick easy—not with Marquette chasing her."

Lena had to agree. She shuddered in the sudden chill. Or maybe it was the thought of Chet's hands, the things he'd done to her girl.

"I'll go left, up to the top," Stone said. "We're assuming she stayed here at the falls, but she may have continued up the mountain."

"I know the right side," Lena said, picking up the nail gun.

"Sheriff," Stone said, "why don't you check around the perimeter of the pool?"

"Be careful," Cabot said. "We don't know if he's armed."

"I hope he is," Kris said, unholstering her gun and working the slide. "Okay, AJ, lead the way."

Lena navigated across the stream on a dozen large boulders and hopped down onto the far bank with Kris right behind her. When she looked back, the sheriff was nearly lost in the mist, and Stone was already out of sight.

"Up here." Lena pointed up the bank that climbed out of the stream channel. The first switchback began shortly after they reached the top. This wasn't like a national park, where every drop-off has a steel handrail to protect people from their own foolishness. In some places the footpath was barely wider than Lena's shoe, and a wrong step would send them tumbling down a slope of sharp rocks.

Lena counted as they turned onto the fourth switchback. She couldn't remember how many there were. Desperation Falls was officially fifty-five feet high, but the terrain was rocky and undeveloped. The alternating lefts and rights blurred together and, although supposedly easier than going straight up, the surface of loose gravel negated any benefit. She and Kris landed on their knees more than once.

Tumbling fog obscured everything above the next corner. Chet could be anywhere, but she was more concerned about not missing Teal. The girl was here somewhere; Lena could feel it.

Halfway up, the trail split, and Lena pointed to the steep, left-hand path that was nearer the falls. The sixty-degree ravine had few handholds and was definitely challenging. She'd climbed it the last time she was here. "This leads up to a flat spot, then to the overlook on this side. The right-hand trail loops around and joins up just above the overlook."

Kris eyed the crumbling wall dotted with tenacious brush. A bed of sharp rocks lay at the base. "I'm not too keen on heights. Let's go around."

"That's okay," Lena said, facing the incline. "I'll take this side and meet you at the overlook." During her construction career, she'd spent a lot of time on ladders and walking along roof joists. She'd gotten over her own fear a long time ago.

"Wait for me," Kris admonished, then started on the longer path.

Lena worked her way up the channel, heaving the nail gun ahead of her and hooking it around rocks or the occasional bush as she felt for toeholds. She reached the top without incident and looked around. The offshoot that led out to the edge of the ravine overlooking the falls was straight ahead, and scuffed dry dirt advertised someone's recent passing. Teal could have come this way, hoping Chet wouldn't chance the steep climb. And, if he took the same route Kris had, he'd come out twenty feet above this spot and probably continue on up the trail. She had to check it out.

Somewhere the sun was shining, but not here. Unseen branches snatched at her arms as she pressed through the wall of vegetation, hoping the waterfall masked the sound of the rustling branches. After only a few feet, she reached a small clearing ten feet in diameter. Scrub oak and large coffeeberry shrubs circled most of the perimeter, providing plenty of hiding places. Straight ahead, though, the ground sloped downward toward an abrupt precipice. About ten feet above and forty feet out, water poured over the lip and hurled past on its plummet to the bottom.

Lena stepped cautiously from the path, pivoting slowly, searching the clearing's shadows.

Snap.

50

Teal figured she was about a hundred yards upstream from the falls before she found a place she could cross. She had come up the main, left-hand route, trying to strike a balance between going slow enough for Quin to catch up, and fast enough to outpace Fred. Being terrified didn't make that easy, but she'd scraped the ground, broken off branches, and made enough noise that anyone could determine her direction.

For the hundredth time, she searched the trail behind her, hoping to see Quin, but fearing it had been Fred she'd heard down at the beginning of the trail. The left-hand route around the falls was more open, but the thick fog made it difficult to see far.

Her plan as she ascended the trail was to have Fred follow her. Then she'd cross over and descend the other side, sprinting back to the barn. Every step pounded in the horror of what she might find there. Quin dead. Quin alive, but being cut up by Fred. In each scenario, there was nothing she could do to save him.

A giant sycamore had toppled across the stream, providing a partial bridge until she hopped off onto a boulder. Then she jumped rock to rock, and made it to the shore.

She thought she heard a noise behind her, and turned. It was far quieter here above the top of the falls, but the water still churned and gurgled as it rushed toward the brink. The light had grown too weak to see if anyone was out there. If it *was* Fred, she didn't want him getting too close. Continuing with her plan, she crashed through brush and kicked a few rocks to attract attention, then hurried as fast as she dared along the path on this side that led back to the brink of the falls.

She reached the overlook, but bypassed the clearing. This was no time to enjoy the view. Instead, she veered onto the descending trail. Plunging through the failing light constantly reminded her of her first escape from Fred, but that night she'd been more than half starved, naked, freezing, and she'd had no idea where she was going. This time she was stronger and knew the territory. But like last time, she wished for a weapon. One of Mandy's or Alex's guns.

As she descended, the top of the falls rose above on her right. The Y to the overlook on this side came up fast, visible through a break in the vegetation. Teal skidded to a stop. AJ stood in the middle of the clearing, but Fred was right behind her!

Teal was frozen for a second as AJ began turning.

"*No!*" Teal's scream was instinctive, but too late. His blow to AJ's head sent her careening toward the drop-off.

Fred glanced at Teal, grinned, then casually walked toward the fallen AJ.

Teal careened onto the path to the clearing and rushed at Fred's back as he bent over her fallen friend.

51

Alex was searching the second overlook on the left side of the falls. Since it was partially choked with a tangled mass of head-high thorny brush, he doubted Teal had come this way, but he had to check. He wrenched aside a stubborn bush, careful not to accidentally step off the edge.

A guttural cry brought his eyes up, and he spotted Teal two hundred feet across the canyon as she hurled herself onto a man's back. It had to be Chet Marquette. The man spun around, throwing Teal to the side, then he grabbed a form on the ground Alex hadn't noticed. Dread gripped him as, even in the gloom, he recognized Lena's blonde ponytail.

Lena's head rang from Chet's blow. Blood leaked into her left eye and down her face; she cleared it with her sleeve, spitting the iron taste from her mouth. Above her, Teal clung to Chet's back, her arms in a chokehold around his neck. But the slight girl was no match for a man his size. He spun around, breaking her hold. Lena tried to kick his feet out from under him as he threw Teal into a scrub oak. He laughed and grabbed Lena's shirt, yanking her half off the ground.

Teal came at him again, this time with a full body tackle. He staggered over Lena and the two sprawled on the wet earth with Teal screaming, *"Leave her alone!"*

Lena struggled up to her hands and knees, blood dripping from her chin onto the leaves skittering across the clearing. She shook her head, trying to clear her brain. Chet surged to his feet, dragging Teal up with him. She kicked and punched, but it did little good. Then she gouged his eye and it was his turn to scream.

Lena reached for her only weapon, the Paslode framing nailer. Needing two hands to hold back the safety and pull the trigger, she rolled onto her back.

Chet shook Teal off, but she came back at him like a tigress, screaming and clawing. Lena watched in horror as Chet wrestled Teal toward the falls overlook. She fought and clutched his shirt. But, with a maniacal shout, Chet broke her grip and threw her over the edge.

Chet turned to Lena, pulled a gun from his pocket, and pointed it at her face.

———

Alex aimed his gun, but Teal was tangled up with Marquette, blocking any clear shot. Combining mist, gloom, and distance, it was a risky shot anyway. His best hope was to drive the man off. Alex squeezed the trigger, adding slight pressure, but not too much. He waited for the best timing. But then Marquette and Teal were fighting at the edge of the clearing and, with a push, Marquette threw the girl over.

Alex watched with dread as Teal cartwheeled thirty or forty feet and smacked the water sideways in a terrific splash. She sank out of sight.

Across the open space, Marquette aimed a pistol at Lena. Alex brought his Glock up with both hands, sighted, and squeezed off three shots. Marquette jerked as two of the bullets struck home, knocking him to his knees. His pistol slid off the edge and dropped out of sight.

Then Alex tossed his gun on the ground and jumped feet-first after Teal.

52

Even with two bullets in him, Chet got to his feet and staggered two steps toward the path leading away from the clearing.

"Stop!" Lena ordered, cradling the nail gun. It was useless at this distance. Nail guns were never meant to be fired except when the safety tip was compressed against wood, and had surprisingly little penetrating power without the weight of the tool against the nail. She and her coworkers used to have contests to see who could get a nail to stick in a cardboard box at twenty feet. The tumbling projectiles rarely hit point first, and it proved a lot harder task than she'd thought.

To her surprise, Chet *did* stop and turn, swaying as he pressed his left hand against his side. Black blood seeped between his fingers. Devil's blood.

"It was you I wanted." His breath came out a wheezing hiss, and he bent forward slightly at the waist. "She was merely practice."

"Why?" He'd held a high-level job, worked side-by-side with Bobby. As much as she detested him, she had to know what drove him to his insanity.

His eyes danced back and forth. "You were to be my masterpiece. That's why Bobby had to go."

Lena's breath caught at the confession. The hacker had said Chet killed Bobby, but this was confession. This man was a monster. He'd blasted their home full of holes that could never be patched; ripped away a portion of her life, her heart. All because he wanted *her*?

"You sick—"

Chet took a step toward her, and she knew then he wouldn't stop unless she stopped him.

She lay on her back, waiting as he sank to his knees and straddled her legs. Vile, black blood dripped on her, and it was all she could do not to gag. But he was still too far away.

Sudden as a snake, his free hand struck at her neck, fingers tightening around her throat.

He bore down, and Lena's windpipe ground under his weight, cutting off her air. Even in the darkened forest, his eyes were lit with hate and fury, and it was all directed at her.

Lena brought the nail gun up, pressed it against his chest, and squeezed the trigger.

Thwack, thwack, thwack.

The three-inch, coated framing nails drove through his shirt and out of sight. His body sagged onto Lena, smashing the nail gun between them at an angle that prevented further firing, but his fingers still clinched her throat closed so she couldn't get any air.

Then, like a slow motion movie, his eyes glazed, and he rolled off to her side. Free, Lena sucked in the clean mountain air and rolled the other direction, keeping the Paslode at the ready.

Chet lay on his back a few feet away, face contorted in pain. His chest rose and fell, but he didn't move.

Lena's thoughts flew to Teal. Whoever shot Chet—Stone or the sheriff—must have seen her fall. Had she landed on rocks? It was a long way down.

She crawled to the edge of the clearing. Far below, only a few feet from where the falling water plunged into the deep pool, Stone had one arm around a limp Teal as he stroked for the shore. The sheriff was wading in to meet him.

Lena rolled away from the edge. Chet hadn't moved, but he was still breathing. Tears filled her eyes at the wreckage this man had wrought in so many lives. She had to get to Teal, but she couldn't leave him. He might still escape.

Lena clutched one of the scraggly oaks for support and pulled herself up. Near the bush lay a couple of six-foot tree limbs that had broken off one of the larger trees. She knew what she had to do.

53

Lena stumbled across the rocks below the pool, crossing to where the group sat on the ground. Water dripped from Stone's hair, and his clothes were stuck to his skin. The sheriff's pants were wet, but he'd stripped off his dry uniform shirt and wrapped it around Teal where she lay cradled against Stone. Lena dropped wearily to her knees beside the girl. Her eyes were open, and they were looking right at her. That had to be good, right?

"Hi, AJ," Teal said, her voice raspy. "Did you get the bad guy?"

Lena had trouble focusing as she pressed her forehead against the girl's. "Yeah, we got him. We *all* got him."

Stone's hand was warm on her back as she cried.

Kris splashed across the creek a minute later. "Lena! I heard shots! Where'd you go? That path split like two more times and led to dead ends. I got lost." She dropped to her knees beside them. "Oh, Teal."

"Can you go for help, Kris?" Stone asked.

Kris rose and sprinted down the trail, but returned a minute later, an EMT in tow. "He was on his way."

While the EMT began assessing Teal's injuries, Lena gave Kris careful directions about where the overlook was. Kris borrowed the sheriff's handcuffs and headed up the trail to secure Chet.

After a few minutes probing and listening, the EMT pronounced her amazingly unharmed by the plunge. Smacking the water that hard might leave bruises, but nothing lasting. She'd swallowed water but, according to Alex, had thrown up a lot of it.

The sheriff radioed for Search and Rescue assistance, a gurney for Teal and some blankets. Alex requested crutches. He'd sprained an ankle when he hit the bottom of the pool, but refused any plan to cart him out on a gurney. He whispered to Lena that Kris would never let him live it down.

54

Five long hours later, Lena slumped in a chair at the ER waiting room at Mountain View Hospital in Mission Peak, and massaged her pounding temples. The gash on the back of her scalp had required a few stitches, but the doctor said she had no sign of a concussion. The tender, egg-sized lump begged to differ.

Teal was been admitted for overnight observation due to the water she'd swallowed. Much to her delight, her boyfriend's room was four doors down the hall. Quin had a moderate concussion, and the doctors wanted to keep him for a day or two, but he was awake and joking with his aunt, uncle, and cousins Mandy and her little sister, Star.

Stone limped off, promising to return with truly horrible vending machine coffee. Anything sounded good to Lena at this point. The muscles in her legs were regularly cramping from the punishing run, and she shifted her weight with a groan.

The sheriff had left after promising there would be no hassle about Teal's medical care. He'd also given her the report from L.A. Chet's house had been searched, and they found the basement room Teal described. The scrolling news banner on the muted, wall-mounted television referred to the discovery as *"a modern day torture chamber."* They also found dozens of VCR tapes, many with Teal on the table, and some with Del Frost...Camo Guy. And there were others. Those tapes weren't to be released to the public, and Lena hoped they'd one day be burned.

The reporters had been speculating for hours how Chet Marquette had led an apparently normal life on the outside, while hiding the darkest of secrets below his house. And, of course, they found a few of his neighbors who testified: *"He seemed like such a nice man."*

She also learned that before Bobby had saved the encrypted files on their home computer, he sent them to the state attorney general. While authorities were searching Chet's house, simultaneous raids were conducted at locations throughout the southland, resulting in arrests of three high-level leaders of Lobos Negros, and seizures of weapons and money. Two other leaders had been detained trying to flee across the border. With much bigger problems to occupy them, Lena was no longer important to the cartel.

"Hey, girlfriend," Mandy said, approaching from the bank of elevators. She perched on the chair next to Lena. "I stopped by Teal's room on the way down. She's out cold. How are you feeling?"

"I can't say I've been worse, because I haven't," Lena admitted, but she offered a wan smile…about all she had in her. "How's Quin?"

"He's fine," she sighed.

Mandy was still pouting that she'd missed all the action and hadn't gotten to use her gun. Lena found that both deeply disturbing and oddly funny. Mostly funny, because Mandy was a bit of a drama queen, and Lena didn't think she *really* wanted to shoot anyone. Although, considering who Chet had turned out to be and the growing strength of Mandy and Teal's bond, Lena might be wrong.

Kris came in and asked, "Where's Alex?" She'd been delayed while guiding Search and Rescue to Chet's location at the falls. They'd had to airlift him out. According to Stone, Kris had spent most of the time chatting with one of the S&R guys—a particularly good-looking one.

The brother in question hobbled back with two steaming cups. He handed one to Lena, then sat heavily. "Just saw the sheriff on his way out. He got news they found Amber a little while ago."

Lena stopped breathing. She couldn't take any more bad news.

"Turns out, Amber got a little drunk at the party she went to, and was too scared to go home. Stayed at a friend's house."

Lena exhaled, her body molding to the chair like overcooked spaghetti.

Kris folded into a chair in the row opposite. "Well, big brother, I have to say, I was completely wrong about your choice of women this time."

Stone frowned. "How so?"

"You didn't hear?" Kris's eyes were wide and innocent.

"About what?"

"When I got up to Marquette, there was no need to use the handcuffs. He was spread-eagled and going nowhere. AJ used her nail gun to anchor his pants to some tree branches, and the S&R team had to cut the pants off to get him free." Kris's mouth twitched. "Some of the nails happened to be a little close to his skin. Like an *inch* too close."

There was nothing funny about Chet or what he'd done. He'd killed Bobby and Teal's rescuer, Del Frost, as well as others whose names weren't yet known. He'd meant to kill Teal and Eve. Given the chance, Lena knew Chet would have killed her, too—she'd seen it in his eyes. For all of them, for herself, she'd had to stop him. He didn't deserve to live, although he was upstairs in ICU and cautiously expected to recover. However, he *did* deserve every one of the Paslode's 48-nail magazine. She'd used them all. And if she'd missed and most of them caught some flesh, well…

"I still don't understand," Stone said. "What did you mean about my choice of women?"

Lena rolled her head sideways so she could see him. He really was handsome—in his own special way.

Kris laughed. "Remember I said in my email I bet she couldn't shoot? Boy, was I wrong!"

EPILOGUE

November

"I've been thinking," Stone said, nuzzling Lena's neck as she sat on his lap by the fire pit in front of his trailer. He'd covered the pit with a fine steel mesh to keep any sparks in, and the fragrant oak smoke drifted into the night sky.

"Dangerous activity for a copper." Lena squeaked when he tickled her ribs. She elbowed him. "Do that again, and no Ho Hos for you tonight." He'd told her to bring dessert.

"You're a hard woman, Alena Jewel Blaylock," he said, tightening his hold around her waist.

Lena snuggled against him, enjoying his warmth as the cool evening air swirled around them. Thanksgiving was in two days, and most mornings brought frost. It was really too cold to be outside, but these had been good days, and neither of them were anxious for them to end.

"So what's your big thought, Stone?"

"Well, I was looking at the back of your new cabin."

"My cabin? What's wrong with it?"

"It's fine. But it looks like—if you wanted to—you could move the unfinished cabin behind it, maybe spin it around so the two back porches match up, and join them together without too much work. The ground is already almost flat back there."

"And why would I want to do that?"

"Well, you'd have a much bigger place, and the addition would make a really nice master suite. The back cabin living room could become the main bedroom, and the kitchen could be reworked as a luxurious master bath."

Lena turned and looked at him. Flames reflected in his eyes, and she saw he was dead serious. Clearly he'd given this some thought. The idea ignited images in her own mind, and she wondered why she'd never thought of doing it. Actually, if she positioned the other building offset to the side instead of directly behind, the master suite would have a wonderful view of the lake. She could enclose the connected back porches and make a great laundry hallway. After moving the other cabin, she'd be left with an unused foundation. Maybe that's where they could build the game room/store that Teal wanted.

"You know, Stone, that's not a half-bad idea," Lena said. His eyes dropped to her mouth, and she chuckled, leaning into his kiss. "I think I'll keep you around…just to do the heavy lifting."

He raised his brows. "That's all I'm good for?"

"Well, you *do* grill a pretty mean steak."

Truthfully, ever since the "Chet Incident," as they all referred to it, Lena had been thinking about Stone in a whole new way. He was a protector. Shooting Chet and then jumping off that forty foot ledge to pull Teal from the water had been incredibly heroic. Very manly. Sexy. Lena hadn't seen him jump, and she'd begged him to do it again for her while the days were hot. He'd adamantly refused, insisting even the three-meter board in high school scared him. She knew better.

But mostly what she'd been thinking about was the picture Teal had tacked up in Lena's bedroom that fateful day, the drawing of three people at the base of the falls who bore resemblances to Lena, Alex, and Stone. Except the woman in the picture was quite pregnant.

"Hey, you guys." Teal came up the path holding Quin's hand, and grinning as always whenever she caught Lena and Stone kissing—which was often these days.

Now that the weather had turned cold, the girl was more relaxed in her long pants and hoodies. She was also meeting regularly with a counselor Stone found in Mission Peak, and the sessions seemed to be helping her deal with what she'd been through—and what she faced in the future. She'd even made some friends at her new school.

Quin Conner was constant in Teal's life, too, and that was fine with Lena. While she thought them too young for a serious commitment, she couldn't deny the deep bond they shared. Quin wasn't only protective of Teal, he was also proud of her strength and talents. She blossomed under his constant encouragement.

Teal correspondingly worshiped her young man. But the more difficult thing was giving her complete trust. Lena saw it in Teal's every glance at Quin, every touch. He'd stepped into the responsibility of Teal's scars. Lena had known thirty-year-olds without this couple's maturity, and she had a feeling they might just be together for the long haul.

Before Lena could acknowledge Teal's greeting, a noise behind the couple drew Lena's attention, and Mandy Conner emerged from the shadows, followed by Rayne and Ben Conner. Ben was helping Mrs. H over the path.

"Wow," Lena said, standing to take in the crowd. "Is there a party we didn't hear about?"

"Not 'we,'" said a voice from behind, and Lena turned to find a grinning Kris Stone rounding the back of the trailer, followed by her and Stone's father, Mark. They'd had dinner and visited with him several times. He loved woodworking, and Lena had liked him instantly.

"*You're* the only one who didn't know." Kris went right to her brother and slipped something into his hand before hugging him and giving him a kiss on the cheek.

Lena narrowed her gaze at the crowd. "What's going on?" If she'd had spidey sense like Peter Parker, it would have been tingling for sure as the group gathered around.

"Uh...Lena." Stone cleared his throat and faced her. He looked at the ground, then cut his eyes to his sister. "I have something I need to...well..."

"What are you talking about, Stone?" Lena asked. He looked nervous, and the big lug was *never* nervous.

Then he opened his hand.

A quivering awareness settled in the pit of her stomach, and she covered her mouth as Stone went down on one knee.

"Alena Jewel Blaylock," he took her free hand, "you make every day fun to live, and I love you more than I can express. But I promise to try. Will you please marry me?" He flipped the box open.

Lena's eyes filled so she couldn't make out the ring's detail, but she didn't care. She knelt too, facing him as he removed the ring. But she needed to know something first, and held back her left hand.

"And you're quitting the DEA? Permanently?" She'd been a wreck waiting for his return from the two consulting assignments since the Chet Incident. She needed time for the fear to heal.

"Already done. Starting next Monday, I'm going to work with Ben and Addison, splitting time between their security businesses," Stone said, again reaching for her left hand.

So that's why he'd spent so much time with the Conner brothers recently.

"And maybe I'll teach a course on nail gun self-defense. Does that meet with your approval?" He leaned forward, inches from her lips, waiting her reaction.

Lena linked her arms around his neck. "Close enough, copper." She pulled until their lips met.

Reluctantly retreating from the kiss, Lena held out her left hand and Stone slipped the ring over her finger. It was shiny and sparkly—not something she'd find at Home Depot. And it was a perfect fit.

"Phew! I guess that's a *yes*," Teal said, letting out a breath. "Good thing we brought extra Ho Hos!"

April

They were married in late spring at a tiny chapel in Deer Cove that Bibs and Irene had recently taken over to use for weddings. The pastor from Perilous Cove Community Church where the Conners attended performed the simple ceremony. Stone's father, Mark Stone, took dual roles, first walking Lena down the aisle, then stepping beside his son as Best Man. For Lena, Teal was the only choice for Maid of Honor. Kris, Quin, and Mandy covered ushering and guestbook duties.

Warm air swirled through the open windows, lifting Lena's hair as she pledged her love to Alex Stone. She never expected to be getting married a second time. And finding someone good, honest, and loving—not to mention fun—was a gift she would never take for granted. Life was too short.

After the ceremony, everyone trekked to Lena's. The barn doors were open wide when Lena and Stone arrived. It had been emptied and scrubbed, and the walls were artistically draped with white tulle. Small groupings of tables and chairs spilled out into the yard. Kris, Mandy, and Teal had crisscrossed the high rafters with colored lights, and the strands continued out the front doors to the oak trees, warming the dusk with a cheery glow.

Mrs. H had coordinated a lavish buffet prepared by friends all around the lake and in Perilous Cove. She and Lena laughed as Colby Hartgrave and

Merle Ferris—one toothpick skinny, the other with his shirt about to burst—heaped equal quantities onto their plates.

Just inside the barn, Rayne Conner played her keyboard, singing hauntingly beautiful music that somehow managed to mute the bad memories and recall the good ones.

Kris, dressed in a gorgeous sparkling midnight blue gown, approached Lena and Alex's table. "There are some people here to see you." She led them to one of the tables in the yard.

A woman stood beside a dark-haired man. Her black hair was short, but Lena recognized her immediately. One of the L.A. Four Ts set—Tall, Thin, Toned, and Tanned.

"Eve," Lena said, embracing the woman. "I'm so happy you came."

"Hello, Lena." Eve Crescent had spent weeks in the hospital, and had taken months to fully recover. But she was back in her post in the DA's office, and highly favored to win the top spot in the next election. "You look beautiful."

"I'm sorry I didn't visit during your recovery," Lena said. "Between my mother's health and things here…"

"Never mind," Eve waved her apology away. "I had great company." She extended her hand to the man, who stepped forward. "I'd like you to meet Vincent Falcone." Then she whispered. "Our hacker."

Lena and Stone spent the next several minutes making sure Vincent knew how critical a role he'd played in saving their family, and Lena didn't miss the way Eve's fingers entwined with Vincent's. This was clearly more than a business acquaintance.

The music changed, and Stone drew her away from the couple. "Time for our dance, Mrs. Stone."

Lena swayed against her new husband as the music played, taking in their guests and friends. Bibs and Irene were talking with Sheriff Cabot and his wife, a petite blonde with piercing eyes that equaled her husband's. The lawman wore casual clothes for once, and he looked younger without his trooper hat and equipment belt. Mark Stone chatted with Ben and Quin Conner, father and son who looked nothing alike, but *were* alike in every way that counted.

"Happy?" Stone whispered in her ear.

She tugged him closer. A year ago, she'd lived on this property barely three months, working eighteen-hour days in preparation for the summer season. It had been her therapy of sorts, part of the healing process, dealing with the past of losing Bobby.

There were still long days ahead this year—finishing the two cabins they had combined into their single home, building the camp game room and store, and having Merle grade two more pads for RVs—but these projects were future driven, focused on building their lives together.

And next week they would officially be three. Teal's mother, who was still in prison, had relinquished her parental rights, and Stone's attorney had immediately filed the petition for adoption. Teal would be theirs.

"Mom and Dad?"

Lena lifted her head from Stone's shoulder, and opened her eyes on her beautiful, smiling girl.

"Are you guys having fun?"

Lena drew their daughter into a three-way embrace.

THE STORY BEHIND THE STORY

I loved writing *Desperation Falls*. I won't lie, sometimes it was tough work, because even the author has to figure out the mystery, and my characters weren't sharing. But I couldn't stop. Lena's, Alex's, and Teal's stories are important; they live out hope, faith, risk, trust, renewed chances, family, and love. Our world has more than its share of bad and downright evil people, and we all need to hear stories of the good people out there.

The old saying shared among novelists is: Just because it's fiction, doesn't mean it isn't true!

Thanks for reading *Desperation Falls*. If you liked it and haven't read the previous books, *Perilous Cove* and *Storm Song*, I urge you to check them out. I know you'll have fun seeing some of the characters as they first appeared.

HOW YOU CAN HELP

First, please consider writing a review at your favorite retailer site. You can't imagine how much they help.

Second, I'd love to hear from you. Tell me what you liked or <gasp!> didn't like, and why. Your feedback will make me a better writer.

Finally, I have a great team of test readers and editors, and we work hard to catch every error. But if you find one that slipped through, please let me know! Just send a short phrase I can search for in the master document.

richbullockwriter@gmail.com

BOOKS BY RICH BULLOCK

<u>Perilous Safety Series</u>
Perilous Cove
Storm Song
Desperation Falls
<u>Glass & Stone Series</u>
Shattered Glass
Glass Revenge
Killing Callie
<u>Lake Effect Series</u>
Night Skyy

<u>Nonfiction</u>
Beyond Us: The Writings of V.M. Narrano
Wild Life: The Writings of V.M. Narrano

The Shortest Book On Marriage,
with Sheryl Bullock

ACKNOWLEDGMENTS

My great thanks to my excellent beta reading team: Sis Hammack, Carol Dickerson, Kerry Jepson, Matt Jensen, Patricia Bossman, Lee Starkey, and Jonelle Stevens. I couldn't have done this without you.

Rob Henslin at www.rhdcreative.com for working his magic on a fantastic cover.

Chuck Jennings provided numerous photos and educated me on the workings of Merle's old D2 Caterpillar tractor.

And thanks to my dad, who taught me how to fish and hunt, how to use power tools, string electrical wire, build walls, and plumb water heaters.

ABOUT THE AUTHOR

Rich Bullock writes stories of ordinary people put in perilous situations, where lives are changed forever. Desperation Falls is his third novel.

He is a member of American Christian Fiction Writers, and the Quills of Faith writing group in Redding, California.

His first writing experience was at ten years old on a well-used typewriter, where several keys added extra spaces after striking, and clearing tangled print arms was a continual chore. The old machine lasted through several high school all-nighters.

Fortunate to grow up in small-town San Luis Obispo, California, he developed an eye for settings that remind people of home. He now lives and writes in Redding, California where, on most days, he sees Mount Lassen, Mount Shasta, and the inside of a coffee shop.

Connect with Rich Bullock

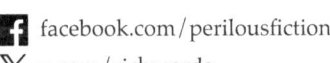
facebook.com/perilousfiction
x.com/richwords